LEGACY OF
STARS

J.N. CHANEY
TERRY MAGGERT

VARIANT
PUBLICATIONS

LAS VEGAS, NV • PORTLAND, TN

CONNECT WITH J.N. CHANEY

Don't miss out on these exclusive perks:

- Instant access to free short stories from series like *The Messenger*, *Starcaster*, and more.
- Receive email updates for new releases and other news.
- Get notified when we run special deals on books and audiobooks.

So, what are you waiting for? Enter your email address at the link below to stay in the loop.

https://www.jnchaney.com/backyard-starship-subscribe

CONNECT WITH TERRY MAGGERT

Check out his website

http://terrymaggert.com/

Connect on Facebook

https://www.facebook.com/terrymaggertbooks/

Follow him on Amazon

https://www.amazon.com/Terry-Maggert/e/B00EKN8RHG/

JOIN THE CONVERSATION

Join the conversation and get updates on new and upcoming releases in the awesomely active **Facebook group**, "JN Chaney's Renegade Readers."

This is a hotspot where readers come together and share their lives and interests, discuss the series, and speak directly to J.N. Chaney and his co-authors.

facebook.com/groups/jnchaneyreaders

CONTENTS

1

I EYED the massive hunk of rock as we swung past it, heading for the *Iowa*'s new home.

"So that's Orcus. It's dull, but at least it's featureless. Rock and ice, I assume?"

"Everything out here is some combination of rock and ice, Van, with maybe the odd bits of metallic iron and nickel thrown in for variety," Netty replied.

Netty was right. Out here, in the furthest reaches of the Solar System, countless hunks of rocky, icy debris—leftovers from the formation of the planets—plied their stately way around the distant Sun. There were literally hundreds of millions, and perhaps billions of bits and pieces of detritus.

Not that you'd ever know it. The bigger objects, the ones you really didn't want to slam into, averaged about a million klicks apart. So, even though we were in a *dense* part of the so-called Kuiper Belt, it was only *dense* in comparison to nothing at all.

Once again I was reminded of the sheer *scale* of space.

"Orcus. That name has a kind of ominous ring to it," Torina noted as the tiny planetoid fell away behind us, back into the endless night.

"Orcus was the punisher of those condemned to the underworld in Greek mythology. His boss, Pluto, the Greek god of the underworld, is about four and a half billion klicks that way," Perry replied, waving a wing vaguely toward the Sun.

"Charming. A god of the underworld, his chief hatchet man, and didn't you tell me that Pluto's moon was named after another jolly figure, someone who ferries the dead around on a boat? Karen, I think?"

I smirked. "Close. It's actually Charon, and yeah, he's another one from that cast of mythological Greek characters. While gloomy, he's not as frightening as an *actual* Karen in an HOA."

Torina lifted a brow. "What's an... HOA?"

"Homeowners Association. A lot like hell, but with cleaner streets."

Torina snorted, then her face fell. "Is everything out here named after something gloomy?"

"Now that you mention it... yes, at least from the perspective of Earth, anyway." As I said it, I glanced back at the Sun, a fierce point of light glaring against the void. I got Torina's point and even shivered a bit myself. I'd been much, *much* farther from the sun than this, but our position now felt heavy with an inarticulate lonesome quality that had a weight all its own. To the Earthbound, these distant reaches of the solar system were a dark, cold, and mysterious place. And as someone who'd recently been Earthbound, I still felt some of that. To see the sun, whose hard glare could make an Iowa summer day feel like an open furnace, reduced to a small, bright dot —it was a perspective that gave me pause.

I pulled my attention back into the *Fafnir*'s cockpit. Yes, we were sailing through the lonely fringe regions of the solar system. It was bleak and dark and coldly silent, but it was also the perfect place to park the *Iowa*. Lonely also meant *safe*.

We'd brought the old battlecruiser here from Starsmith, where she'd been cleaned, refurbished, and upgraded, simply because it was out of the way. The solar system didn't see a lot of interstellar traffic, at least not compared to other systems like Tau Ceti or Epsilon Eridani. And this far from the sun, with her drives shut down and no transponders or comms, the chances of anyone stumbling on her were remote.

As for her inadvertently being spotted from Earth—Netty summed it up nicely.

"Build a model of the Iowa the same size as your hand, Van, then put it roughly in the middle of Colorado and try to spot it from the farm in Iowa."

Enough said.

"Icky, how are you doing back there?" I asked over the comm.

Icrul, our engineer and general troubleshooter, was piloting the *Iowa* a few thousand klicks back from us as we settled her into what would, for now, be her home orbit. The fact that she was able to single-handedly fly a ship normally crewed by a couple of dozen was a testament to the automation she'd designed and installed. With Netty's help, she could helm the big ship from the bridge without anyone else aboard. That said, though, keeping the *Iowa* running required constant attention across dozens of critical systems. One person could move her from point A to point B, but if there was any fancy maneuvering to be done—or battles to be fought—that was a different matter.

"Everything's good here, boss," Icky replied. "Well, except for that portside plasma constrictor. Had to take it offline again, which leaves us without a redundant system. That's no problem once we've shut the drive down, but—"

"Add it to the list, Icky," I said with a resigned sigh, then turned back to the nav display. The *Iowa* had snuggled into the orbit we'd selected for her, one that would take her around the sun once about every three hundred years. I had Netty slow us, maneuvering so that the *Iowa* would overtake the *Fafnir*. Once she had, we nudged her against the battlecruiser's flank and thumped our docking adapter into place. When it locked and showed green, Torina and I unstrapped from our seats and clambered out of the cockpit to head for the airlock.

As we did, we passed through the new crew hab module now installed into the *Fafnir*, offering a lot more room than before. We'd bought the new module for one bond from its previous owner, the former Peacemaker Guild Master and now-mercenary Petyr Groshenko. His ship, the *Alexander Nevsky*, had been decommissioned upon his resignation, with most of its components being stripped off and taken away by lienholders. But he'd sold us the habitat module for a token sum, which was most welcome. Torina, Icky, and I were all sick of pushing past and stumbling over one another as we tried to maneuver in the tight confines of the *Fafnir*. It had been like sharing a one-bedroom apartment with two other people—and one of them, Icky, was the size of a gorilla.

But with two extra arms and occasional lapses in social graces.

It made the *Fafnir* just short of being reclassified from

"Upgraded Dragonet Class" to actual "Dragon" Class. The main difference now was the drive and powerplant. The *Fafnir*'s was pretty-much maxed out and couldn't support any further loads from weapons or new systems. Not surprisingly, this would also be the most expensive upgrade—currently out of my reach unless I wanted to cash in every asset and empty every account I could. The alternative would be finding someone willing to provide us with the upgrade in exchange for holding a lien on it, which I refused to do.

Besides, I thought as we strode into the vast emptiness of the Iowa, it wasn't really essential right now. We had a usable amount of space aboard the *Fafnir*, and more than we could possibly ever use aboard the battlecruiser. Which, in fact, presented us with our next problem—and there was *always* a new problem in space.

I stopped in the first corridor junction, now gleaming and sparkly clean—a massive contrast to the first time I'd seen it, when the ship appeared to be mostly made from rust and grime. Spreading my arms, I turned a circle.

"So much room. What are we going to do with it all?"

Torina just pushed past me, though. "I know what I'm going to do with some of it. Dibs on the Captain's cabin!"

After flashing me a wicked grin, she hurried off.

"Aren't you going to go after her?" Perry asked.

"Why?"

"Uh, the Captain's cabin? You know, the big one, right behind the bridge? Don't you want that for yourself?"

"Perry, I am not so small-minded and egotistical that I'll let myself get so worked up over a mere room."

"You've already had Netty lock it, haven't you?"

"One of the first things I did."

I'D TOURED the *Iowa* a couple of times since her refurbishment and refit, but those had both been more orientation sessions, just letting me get a feel for the layout of the ship. Now that we had her parked in a semi-permanent orbit, we had time to dig into some serious planning regarding how we were going to use all the internal space. Even though I'd snagged the Captain's quarters early, it didn't really matter, because both Torina and Icky had their choice of cabins. In fact, by taking over two of the larger cabins with an interconnecting door, Torina ended up with more space than I had. Icky, for her part, was happy to take one of the rearward cabins in the forward section of the ship to let her live as close to the engineering section as she could.

Staring at her new quarters, Icky put a hand up against the bulkhead and made a low noise of approval.

"What is it, Ick?" I asked, smiling at her obvious joy.

"I can feel the engines."

"They're not even running. Just subroutines," I said, but she held up a hand and tilted her head.

"Still can feel them. This is a good place to call home, Van. Very good indeed."

I put a hand on her shoulder and squeezed—it was a lot like touching a large ham—and then laughed, because it was apparent we'd all come a long way.

Of course, while the *Iowa* solved several problems—such as having a secure base of operations that we could move around as necessary rather than just work out of static locations—it raised several more.

Like furniture.

I stood in the middle of the Captain's cabin, looking around at the empty floor and blank walls. Linulla, the Starsmith who worked on my Moonsword, had provided the labor to get the *Iowa* cleaned up, and they'd done a terrific job. They'd even installed hygiene fixtures suited to human anatomy, since the previous owners, aliens, apparently had the same needs. And they'd painted and polished everything to an extent that would have made my father, a career sailor, proud. But they'd also removed all the old junk, essentially anything that wasn't nailed down, and that included all of the furnishings. Again, not only had they been designed to the ship's original alien owners, but they were also all in terrible shape. It left us with a clean, shiny, and almost entirely *empty* ship.

Torina appeared in the door. "At least you've got a bed," she said, nodding at the cot that had been bolted to the floor.

"Yeah, and it'd be great if I was, like, ten years old. Then I might fit in this thing." I sighed down at the tiny bed. "I wonder why the hell Linulla even had this in the first place. I mean, he's basically a giant crustacean. What would he need with an, um… minibed? Or whatever this thing is?"

"Well, the good news is that my parents agreed to buy us fixtures and fittings for the Iowa. It looks like the cost for the space hippies to clean up that cursed nanoplague back home is going to come in lower than they'd estimated. They asked what they could do to help out, so I suggested getting us the stuff we needed so we didn't have to sleep on the floor."

"So, what? We've got some interior designer coming to measure for carpets and curtains and stuff?"

"We do."

I blinked, taken aback. I'd been joking. "Really?"

"Well, unless you want us to go and pick out all the pieces ourselves and then haul everything back here and lug it all—"

"No, no, that's fine. It's just that I don't associate *battlecruiser* with *interior decorator* very often."

She shrugged. "Living in space doesn't have to be a chore."

"Yeah, I know, anyone can be uncomfortable—"

"Van, there's an incoming message from Anvil Dark," Netty cut in.

I looked around. There was a comm terminal built into the wall. I had Netty put the message through to it, and the screen lit up with the image of Lunzemor Nyatt, aka Lunzy, one of the Peacemaker Masters' chief liaison officers and emissaries.

"Hey, Lunzy. Are you a Master, yet?" I asked. I said it jokingly, but technically at least, her senior position put Lunzy in reach of one of the three vacant Masters positions if she wanted one.

She blew out a sigh chock full of exasperation. "Don't get me started. And, take my advice, don't come anywhere near Anvil Dark if you can avoid it. The politicking over those Master positions is so intense you almost taste it in the air."

"I'm curious—what would that taste like?"

"Equal parts narcissism, naked ambition, and ruthless opportunism, with spicy hints of treachery and sucking up. I hate it."

"Ouch."

"Indeed. Besides, what makes you think I even want to be a Master? So I can inherit Groshenko's big office and all the headaches and bullshit still piled on his desk along with it?"

Her flat dismissal of the idea made me think of my grandfather. He'd apparently had the opportunity to take on the mantle of Guild

Master of the Peacemakers, but had likewise turned it down. As a spec ops soldier back on Earth, he hated the necessity of spending time chained to a desk doing administrative stuff, important or not. He'd apparently felt the same as a Peacemaker.

"Anyway, I didn't call you up to discuss my career opportunities. I've got a job for you," Lunzy said.

I frowned. "Lunzy, I'm supposed to be on leave so I can sort out—"

"Your new ship, yes, I know. But I wouldn't be calling you if it wasn't important. Moreover, when I say I've got a job for you, I mean a job for *you*—as in you specifically."

That made me shift a little uncomfortably. "Dare I ask?"

"It's about your cousin, Carter Yost."

I swore, using a Wu'tzur curse I'd learned from Icky when she smashed her head on one of the drive mounts in the *Fafnir*'s engineering bay. I wasn't entirely sure of the meaning, only that it was apparently quite rude. And *quite rude* fit anything involving Carter Yost.

"Lunzy, why the hell do you keep coming to me to sort Carter out? A, he's a big boy and should be able to take care of himself, and B, there are hundreds of other Peacemakers—"

Lunzy cut in, raising a hand. "I know, and you're right. In fact, the only reason I'm after you about this is because your name specifically came up."

"That does *not* make me feel any better. Quite the opposite, in fact."

"Again, I get it. But just consider the situation before you write it off. Your cousin's ship is broadcasting a repeating, obviously automated message on one of the Guild's emergency comm channels. Have a listen."

She touched an off-screen control, and a message played, audio only.

"This is Carter Yost, aboard the *Dolores May*. I have an urgent message for Peacemaker Van Tudor. I need your help, Van. Please, come as soon as you can."

"And that's it. The message just repeats once every fifteen seconds," Lunzy said.

With a soft metallic whisper, Perry wheeled into the room in a glide and settled on the floor beside Torina and I. "What'd I miss?"

"Lunzy was just filling me in on my dear cousin, Carter Yost, and the message his ship is broadcasting—"

"It's a trap!"

I rolled my eyes. Torina, though, just looked mystified. "Why the strange accent, Perry?"

"It's a trap!" he repeated, then shrugged his wings. "No, huh? Well, it's an Earthly pop culture reference. Van gets it."

"You've been dying for a chance to say that, haven't you?"

"Since the first day we met. I've been saving it for an opportune moment, which is what we seem to have here."

Torina just shook her head. "Whatever. Anyway, I'm actually with Perry on this. It has to be some sort of trap."

Lunzy spoke up. "I have to admit to some serious misgivings about this myself, Van. Carter's managed to ingratiate himself to Master Yotov, and she and I don't get along. And that means Yost's actions and schemes are pretty opaque to me."

I sniffed and shook my head. "Yotov. Great. We lose Groshenko, but we get to keep her and her little empire of institutionalized corruption. It's no wonder Carter ended up with his nose buried in her—business."

"I don't disagree at all. But that's the reason other Peacemakers aren't rushing to Yost's aid. You're the one named in the broadcast, so everyone's content to leave this to you," Lunzy said.

"Fan-freakin'-tastic." I sighed. "Where's his ship?"

"On the edge of the Ross 154 system, to use its Earthly designation. Netty has already got the nav data calculated and ready to go," Perry put in.

"Ross 154. Okay. And what's there?"

"Nothing. It's literally a red dwarf star all alone in space. No companions, no planets, just a few rocks," Perry replied.

That made my senses go to a new level of high alert. "Why the hell would Carter go there?"

Netty spoke up. "Ships sometimes use Ross 154 as a waypoint during trips between Epsilon Indi and Tau Ceti. No one claims jurisdiction over it since there's nothing there of note."

"Why do I suspect it gets used for nefarious purposes, clandestine meetings, smuggling, that sort of thing?" Torina asked.

"Because you're not completely naive?" I offered, then turned back to Lunzy. "Do we have any idea what Carter was doing there?"

Lunzy shrugged. "I'd go with Torina's nefarious purposes. But you'll find out for sure when you go there."

"Um, one minor point. Has anyone tried just calling Carter Yost's ship to find out what's going on?" Torina asked.

"We have. Repeatedly, and across comm channels. We get nothing back but that automated message," Lunzy replied.

I sighed with genuine disgust. "So, let's see. Our choice is to stay here, fitting out our new ship with furniture and other goodies, or going to rescue Carter Yost—*again*, I might add. Hmm. That's a tough choice."

"Van, are you saying you'd value selecting wall coverings over possibly saving your cousin's life?" Lunzy asked.

"Let's put it this way. I'm not *not* saying that."

2

WE LEFT BETTY—THE instance of Netty that had been copied over to the *Iowa*, taking over its operations from the dumb-as-a-brick AI previously installed—to look after the battlecruiser. Technically, Betty and Netty were actually one, only operating as individuals when the Iowa and *Fafnir* were apart, then fully resynchronizing when they were together again. But we'd decided we needed a distinct designation for the version of Netty running aboard the battlecruiser, and Netty B had naturally just morphed into Betty. In all senses, they played well together, and the system worked.

"Okay, Betty, you know the drill. If you get detected and approached—"

"I'll twist to Anvil Dark and take company with the Nemesis. I've got this, Van. I'm not going to forget, because being a computer and all, I can't," she said.

"You tell 'em, Netty," Torina added.

"I'm feeling attacked, as the kids used to say," I told everyone.

"When? In 2014?" Torina asked, earning a high-five—okay, two high fives—from Icky, who wheezed with laughter while retracting two long arms from their mini-celebration..

"Good one, Ick. Cultural references are really shaping up," Perry said, turning traitor with the flick of a wing.

"Hey, I—" I began—

Icky pushed herself forward in the cockpit, interposing her head between Torina and me. "Is that a problem? Us girls sticking together?"

I glanced at Icky, who out-massed me by at least fifty percent, all of it muscle, and shook my head. "Not at all, ma'am. I think it's quite charming. Adorable, even."

Icky grinned and sat back at her engineering panel. We'd upgraded it to a more efficient design during the *Fafnir*'s refit but hadn't been able to free up any more room for her. The cockpit's rear bulkhead was a structural component, intended to be airtight and blast resistant. We'd have to replace the *Fafnir*'s entire command and piloting module, its front end, with a larger version if we wanted more room. And it was on the list—the long, long list. Or, as we'd taken to calling it, the *wishing well*. That came from a snippet of conversation Icky and I had during the refit on Anvil Dark.

She'd been glaring at various parts of the ship, muttering *I wish we could replace this*, or *I wish we could upgrade that*, and my answer, every time, had been the same.

"Well…"

The *Iowa* fell away behind us and abruptly vanished altogether when we twisted to Ross 154.

"You know, never thought I'd get tired of visiting new star systems, but here we are," I said.

Ross 154 was every bit as unremarkable as Netty had described. It was a dim, red dwarf. And that was it. Just this lonely, elderly little star, some dust, and a few rocks, the biggest of which was about the size of Mount Everest.

I stared at the emptiness outside. "This is the interstellar equivalent of driving through Iowa."

Torina gave me a quizzical glance. "Really?"

"Yeah. Think of driving through my farm, back on Earth. Now, think of doing that for seven or eight hours."

"Ah."

We were able to locate Carter's ship easily enough just by setting a course based on its monotonous repeating message. But I brought the *Fafnir* to a halt just outside of weapons range so we could study the situation.

Carter's ship hung alone in space, with nothing but wisps of dust and gas within nearly a million klicks. Among the closest objects on our scan, the biggest asteroid was a rock about three times as massive as the *Fafnir*.

"There's really nowhere anyone could hide out here," Icky said.

I nodded. "Netty, anything you can detect?"

"Nothing. Using active scanners at full power, I can say with confidence there are no other objects of consequence even remotely close to your cousin's ship."

I rubbed my chin and stared at the icon representing Carter's Dragonet. Torina narrowed her eyes at me.

"If this is a trap, Van, it's not a very good one."

"No. And that's what bothers me."

"That it's not obviously a trap?"

"No, that it's *so* not obviously a trap that it feels... off somehow. I mean, if he's having trouble, lost power or something—why is this message asking specifically for me and not a general distress call?"

"So what are you thinking, Van?" Perry asked.

"I... don't know. Netty, there's really nothing stopping a ship, or ships, from twisting in right on top of us, is there?"

"Not at all. There are no mass or gravitational influences strong enough to present a problem."

I jabbed a suspicious finger at the screen. "So that ship out there could be a honeypot," I said.

That had Torina and Icky both asking what I meant at the same time.

"Honey is a really sweet, syrupy thing made on Earth by bees—which are insects," I added, seeing both of them open their mouths again. "Anyway, they make the honey, and we eat it. But lots of other critters like honey, too, so you can use it to attract them. Hence, honeypot, something made to lure people in. We used the term when we wanted to draw the attention of bad guys on computer networks, too."

"Sounds like mrsch'ak'a," Icky said.

Now it was my turn to join Torina in a blank look.

"It's made from the concentrated sweat of a burrowing creature on the Wu'tzur homeworld. It's delicious."

"I'll... take your word for it," I said with a shrug, because honey was no less repulsive in concept, at least; then I turned back to the ship. "Anyway, if that's a honeypot, then it could react to us approaching, send a comm signal to ships somewhere else, and they could twist in all around us, right?"

"You're definitely starting to think like a bad guy, Van," Perry said.

"I'll take that as a compliment?"

"You should. Your grandfather often said that to be a good Peacemaker, you first had to figure out how to be a good criminal. Anyway, you're right. That could be the setup here. But we might have a solution. Netty, do you remember when we jammed the twist comms of that Lurxian ship Mark was trying to run down at Wolf 424?"

"Why are you asking her that? She just said a short while ago that she doesn't forget things—" Icky started, but Perry raised a wing at her.

"Yes. We ran the twist drive up to just short of activation, then kept it there. It created enough of a space-time distortion for a thousand or so klicks around us to prevent any other twist effects, including comms, from working," Netty replied. Notwithstanding Icky's comments, the whole exchange between the two AIs had obviously been for our benefit—but it also raised a compelling question.

"Wait. This is something we've been able to do all along? How come you guys haven't mentioned this before? I can think of a few times—"

Icky cut in. "I'll tell you why, Van. Because it's stupid. Not only will it burn antimatter fuel like crazy, but it will also force the drive to operate way beyond its specs. That drive core is meant to receive a brief burst of power to initiate the twist, not just keep receiving it without twisting anywhere."

"So we'll burn up our fuel and could damage our twist drive while we're here in the middle of nowhere," I replied, then waved grandly at our general surroundings. "The *undisputed* middle of nowhere."

"Damned right. If the twist drive goes offline, we won't even be able to call for help since we'll be stuck with subluminal comms only. We'd have to hope someone would come looking for us before we, you know, ran out of air or water, not to mention food."

"Your grandfather did use the technique to ambush and disable the Lurxian ship in one fell swoop, so there is that, yeah," Perry said.

I certainly wasn't willing to take the risk just to avoid some possible betrayal from Carter Yost. Frankly, the guy wasn't worth it.

Although...

"How long could we run the twist drive like that while ensuring we still have enough fuel to twist away?" I asked the cockpit at large.

"As far as fuel's concerned, no more than one minute," Netty replied.

Icky was consulting a data slate she'd grabbed. "The drive manufacturer's specs say it's designed to run at full power for up to ten seconds. That's their performance margin, but those are always really conservative, so you could double that to twenty seconds. Any more than that, and there are no guarantees."

"Twenty seconds? That's not much of a window to do anything useful," Torina said.

I nodded. "It's not. But it might be enough for what I have in mind. Netty, will Carter's ship have an instance of you, or an AI as capable as you operating it."

"I'm actually an upgrade to a Dragonet's standard AI, which lacks both my intellect and scintillating personality. According to Guild records, Carter Yost hasn't applied that upgrade to his ship."

"It just has the standard, smart-enough sort of AI running the show," I said.

"So it would appear."

I nodded. "Perfect."

"Everyone ready?" I asked.

I got affirmatives from the crew, including the AIs. Nonetheless, I gave my plan one last run through in my mind, making sure we hadn't missed anything.

We hadn't tried to contact Carter's ship, wanting to look the situation over first. I decided to keep it that way. From his ship's perspective, the *Fafnir* had arrived, and that was it. Anyone on board, or even the ship's AI, had no way of knowing if I was here with the *Fafnir*. Now, Carter Yost was a scumbag quite capable of plotting to murder me, but I didn't think he just wanted to kill people indiscriminately. It stood to reason, therefore, that if this was a trap, it would only be triggered when anyone or anything aboard his ship was sure I was actually here.

Thus, our plan. Icky, with Perry's help, rigged up a device that would simulate me trying to enter the other ship's airlock. It involved taking one of our standard crash suits, essentially unarmored space suits meant for emergency use, and me rubbing its exterior with my hands, paying particular attention to the gloves. This would leave traces of my DNA on the suit's exterior. I recorded a few sentences appropriate to entering an apparently derelict ship and loaded them into the suit's comm so they appeared to originate from it. All that remained was finding a way of getting it to the ship, which was Perry's job.

"Okay, I'm on my way," Perry said over the comm. We saw him sail past the cockpit with a puff of his built-in thrusters, pushing the empty suit toward Carter's ship. I watched intently, ready to intervene in case he ran into trouble. He made it without incident and nudged the suit against the Dragonet's airlock so that it contacted the access panel. Then he backed away and returned to the *Fafnir*.

"I guess this means there isn't anyone aboard that ship. I mean, it's not like our ruse here isn't obvious as hell," Icky said.

"You'd be surprised at how dumb Carter can be. But no, if there is anyone over there, they're either *really* not on the ball or not conscious," I replied, watching Perry cross the few hundred meters back to the *Fafnir*. The suit remained in place against the other ship, which just continued to broadcast its periodic message.

A few minutes later, Perry was back aboard. I backed the *Fafnir* off to about a hundred klicks, then we triggered the twist drive. A thin, shrill whine filled the cockpit, one that I could feel in my teeth. Everything got slightly out of focus, like I suddenly needed glasses. The distortion effect of a twist drive was normally almost instantaneous, there and gone. I'd never actually heard—or felt—the twist drive labor before.

But I didn't waste time dwelling on it. I triggered the suit's comms. My own voice hummed out of the speaker, the slight spatial distortion making it sound flat and clipped.

Okay, I've given things a good look. Don't see any damage or anything. I'm going inside—

A crash of static cut me off. At the same time, Carter's ship exploded with a dazzling flash.

Netty immediately cut the drive. The whine vanished, and the world refocused. But my head felt as though it was still being distorted.

"Ow. Anyone else have a headache?"

Torina nodded, once and curtly, then winced. Icky just groaned.

"Not me. I feel fine," Perry said, returning to the cockpit. "What'd I miss?"

"First, shut up. Second, Carter's ship just exploded," Icky snapped.

I took a deep breath. The pounding in my head had started to abate. I guess that having reality itself momentarily lose its shape wasn't good for organic brains *or* twist drives.

I looked at the expanding and cooling cloud of gas and debris that had been Carter's ship. "Well, I guess I shouldn't expect a Christmas card this year."

"Chris—er, what? What's that?" Icky asked.

"A major holiday where people celebrate many things. It's also an opportunity for shitty relatives to send out cards and emails blathering about how amazing they are."

"Oh, okay, like"—the translator choked on the next word—"ah... I guess it translates to something like *house visit*."

"Okay, right back at you. What's a house visit?"

"Your family sends images of their home and new things and kids, and it's almost *never* done in a spirit of love or anything like that. It's just to show off. We call them brag letters."

I laughed, most of the fuzzy pain in my head now gone. I saw Torina and Icky looking equally relieved.

"No shit. My relatives were really into that for some reason.

Gramps called them the same thing when he got them at Christmas. Good to know we have that in common, Icky."

"My family didn't bother with letters for our holidays. They did something even shittier," Torina put in.

"Oh, really."

"Yup. I remember my mother sending my aunt the name of a new hair stylist—you know, just to be helpful."

"Wow, what a bi—"

"Bit of a snarky insult? Yes, it was."

"No wonder your parents live in a compound."

LUNZY MET us when we docked at Anvil Dark and immediately led us to a conference room near the Keel, the section of the massive station reserved for use by the Guild's Masters. As we made our way through the concourses and corridors, I found myself increasingly on edge, as though anticipating something dramatic that was about to happen. It took me a few moments to figure out why.

The normally easygoing and generally collegial atmosphere of Anvil Dark had been replaced by something more... intense. Intense, and yet subtle. It was the way conversations stopped as we walked by, the small groups of Peacemakers and their retainers who seemed to be immersed in furtive discussion, and the overall subdued tone of the place, compared to its usually animated character.

It reminded me of a stopover on a flight from Jakarta where I'd been working a job. On my way back to the states, there'd been a layover in Riyadh. While I was standing there, groggy and travel-worn, some security issue came up. There were a few tense announcements about all flights being delayed, followed by the sudden presence of grim-faced paramilitary police armed with rifles and submachine guns. The atmosphere in the airport had immediately gone from its usual chattering chaos to a more orderly, strained quiet. People even started talking in hushed tones, their eyes darting like nervous prey. This was just the same.

I leaned toward Lunzy as we walked. "Is this tension in the air what you were talking about?"

"No. This is worse."

She didn't elaborate and brushed aside any more questions until we reached the conference room and the door sealed. It guaranteed us privacy, since the room was designed to prevent anyone outside from seeing or hearing the proceedings inside.

"We've got two major factions vying for the empty Master's slots. One of them has coalesced around Master Yotov. The other one consists mainly of Peacemakers who aren't part of Yotov's crowd, but it currently has no clear leader," Lunzy said, sinking into a chair. "Add to that all the people trying to position themselves to take over senior positions that might be left vacant if someone becomes a Master, along with the associated rumors, innuendo, and conspiracy theories—" She sighed again.

"What's the problem? Aren't there three positions open? Isn't that enough to go around?" Icky asked.

Lunzy gave her a tired smile. "You're adorable. We should make you a Master so you can bring some of that common sense thinking to their table."

Icky stared. "I don't get it."

I did, and I could tell Torina did, too. "This isn't about divvying up Master's positions fairly, Icky. Each faction wants *all three* of the positions," I said.

Lunzy nodded. "Especially Yotov's gang. If she can control three of the seven Masters, then along with herself she'd effectively control the Masters generally, and by extension, the entire Guild."

"Wow. Greedy, much?"

Lunzy smiled again. "You've got no idea. Anyway, she's essentially buried the replacement process in so much procedural bullshit that it might be weeks, or even months, before we have any new Masters appointed. Usually, it happens in a matter of days."

"Have I mentioned how much I hate scheming, greedy, manipulative people?" Torina asked.

"I'm right there with you, Torina. Believe me," Lunzy said.

Perry, though, just shrugged his wings. "Any time you get more than two people together, you get politics. That, and the speed of light, are the only universal constants."

Icky glanced at him. "There are a lot more universal constants than that—"

"Just turning a phrase, my dear Icky. Just turning a phrase."

I leaned forward. "This is all very interesting, but right now my main concern is Carter Yost—you know, the guy who set a honeypot to try and kill me?"

"It wasn't a very good trap, though, was it?" Lunzy said.

I cocked my head at her. "What do you mean?"

"Van, there are lots of ways to kill someone that are way more reliable than the convoluted mess you just dealt with. Like, oh, let's say a gun blowing your head apart."

"Thanks for the image, Lunzy. Where are you going with this?"

"I'm not sure that it was a trap, as much as it was a message."

I leaned back. "Okay. Well, let's go find Carter and ask him. He might be a little hard to understand, though, what with the fat lip and broken teeth I intend to give him."

"Sorry, Van, but you'll need to hold that thought. Your cousin is still missing."

"Well, he wasn't aboard his ship when it blew. We picked up some debris that we're giving to Steve down in Engineering and Science to examine, but we didn't detect any... er, organic remains. That is, unless he was completely vaporized?"

I said the last bit looking at Perry. He shrugged his wings again. "If he was in engineering when the reactor blew, maybe. But the engineering bay on a Dragonet is heavily shielded. Anyone outside it is likely to have been incinerated, and probably fragmented, but not entirely vaporized. There'd be some organic remains left, which is what we see in other reactor explosions."

I drummed my fingers on the table. "So he's probably still alive. The question is, where the hell is he?"

Lunzy shrugged. "No idea. But it is kind of strange for his ship to be rigged as a trap, probably as a message to you—and then for him to go missing completely."

Torina nodded. "There's definitely something going on here. Probably something nefarious. We just don't have enough information to know what."

I sighed. "Yeah, well, nefarious and Carter have each other on speed dial. And I agree. This all has a... sinister feeling to it."

We sat for a moment in silence, staring into the face of whatever this all represented. Unfortunately, that face was fuzzy and indistinct—menacing, but as Torina said, not yet recognizable.

"Van, it's probably going to take a couple of days for Steve and his people to get to that debris from your cousin's ship and examine it. This might be a good time to go to Starsmith."

Lunzy raised her eyebrows. "Another upgrade to your Moonsword?"

I shook my head. "No, this time it's armor. It turns out that when Icky hung around Starsmith overseeing the refit of the Iowa, her dad came to visit her. He and Linulla hit it off in a big way and decided to collaborate on a few projects. Their first involves incorporating a material he's been working on, a sort of buckminster-fullerene kind of stuff, into light, flexible armor that we can ideally wear over our b-suits."

Lunzy grinned. "Trialing armor, huh? That's pretty brave of you. Want to test out some experimental parachutes while you're at it?"

"Not really. Testing devices leaves me feeling flat, am I right?" I held up my hand for a high five but was greeted with groans and heads shaking in mournful disapproval. Even Icky covered her face with three hands, the other pointing toward a distant door.

"Take your dad jokes to… to another galaxy, Van. If I hear any more, I might *die*," Icky said with teenaged hyperbole.

Torina patted my shoulder like I'd just lost a friend, then sketched a grim salute. "The only thing that died here is comedy, dear."

3

WE ARRIVED at Starsmith to find that Linulla's children, all twenty-six of them, were now considered old enough to learn the family trade. Only one of them would eventually succeed Linulla himself and gain the coveted title of Starsmith, while the rest would go on to become engineers, designers, and material scientists. Oddly enough, there was apparently no sibling rivalry involved. In fact, the opposite was true. The children would, over time, willingly drop out of contention for Starsmith one by one as they decided their talents weren't equal to the position, until only one was left. They were a squabbling, clacking, boisterous team.

With about 156 arms, give or take a few.

"I can just imagine how that would go if it was twenty-six human brothers and sisters all after one hereditary title. Hell, we had whole wars of succession back on Earth between only two or three siblings who all wanted to inherit their parents' titles, treasuries, or lands," I said. I had to shake my head in wonder at such a collaborative, orderly approach to things.

But Linulla popped some of my balloon of wonder. "My race isn't really that altruistic. In our past, our young would kill and eat each other, until only the strongest remained. We made a collective decision over a thousand years ago that that was stupid. Just because one of my children might not be strong enough to prevent themselves from being killed and consumed didn't mean they weren't potentially valuable to our people. We decided to rise above our nature and stop wasting talent that would benefit us."

"It probably makes for more laid back family dinners, too—since, you know, members of the family *weren't* the dinner anymore," Torina said.

I shrugged. "I don't know. I think everyone back on Earth has at least one or two family members they'd be okay seeing served on a platter with an apple stuffed in their mouth."

"Well, there was also the issue of flavor," Linulla quipped, clacking along without breaking stride as we began to move away from the forge.

I stopped, turned, and lifted a finger. "Now hold. Right. Up. You cannot drop that kind of comment in our midst and just keep walking. *Flavor?* That's what stopped your kids from eating each other? Flavor? What exactly do your people taste like, Linulla?"

Linulla focused his eyes on me and was dead silent for a moment. "Like everything else in the galaxy. We taste like chicken."

Torina gigglesnorted, then executed a deep bow of respect.

Icky looked confused. "If they taste like chicken, why did you stop eating each other? I am told chicken is almost as good as crab."

"Excuse me?" Linulla huffed, his mouth parts moving in alarm.

Icky wheezed with laughter. "I too can make dad jokes."

Now Linulla bowed—or tried to, anyway. "Well done, friend." He eyed her with mild suspicion. "You don't own any giant kettles, do you?"

"None in which you would fit. Shall we go to engineering now?" Icky asked.

I pointed forward. "Let's. Less cannibalism over there, I think."

Linulla led me, Icky, and Torina to a small workroom apart from his forge. He had armor components for each of us—a set of shoulder pauldrons for me, forearm vambraces for Torina, and a helmet for Icky. They were trial pieces, all manufactured slightly differently and customized to each of us. They were intended mainly as proof of concept, to validate the materials and design before we had more pieces manufactured. We'd use them for a few weeks, and if they proved both practical and comfortable, while also adding significantly more protection, we'd start commissioning full sets from Linulla.

Which was going to be expensive since this represented an entirely new product for him. He'd given these first three pieces to us for free, but if we wanted more, we'd have to pay for them to be custom made.

I was impressed, though, from the moment I first picked up the set of pauldrons. They looked bulky and cumbersome but turned out to weigh almost nothing. Moreover, they didn't limit my freedom of movement at all. The material was somehow both rigid and supple at once, bending only where and when it needed to, but otherwise remaining as hard as steel.

Icky turned her head side to side, up and down. "This is amazing. I don't feel like I'm wearing anything on my head." She turned to Linulla. "Looks like you and my dad make a great team."

"That's because we both have children who inspire us."

Icky said nothing and just nodded, but with slow dignity.

I glanced at Torina and knew she was thinking the same thing.

Is Icky actually choked up?

We said our farewells to Linulla and told him we'd report back anytime we had something to tell him about the armor pieces. Our timing was impeccable. We'd barely gotten back aboard the *Fafnir* and started the preflight when a comm message came in from Lunzy.

The Peacemaker Guild had found Carter Yost.

KIND OF FOUND HIM, anyway.

We arrived back at Anvil Dark to find the air even thicker and danker with scheming, furtive whispers and sleazy politicking. I'd once attended the National Convention of a major political party to help a tech industry lobby group trying to influence the party's stance on potential legislation. The current atmosphere of Anvil Dark reminded me of that. Both still maintained a veneer of normalcy, of good humor and cheer and all that. Beneath the surface, though, every conversation in every out-of-the-way corner was an intensely earnest one, generally focused on one of two things: garnering support for your particular flavor of candidate, or undermining someone else's.

Oh, and money. Always, there was a palpable lust for money.

I couldn't get out of that damned convention center fast enough so I could finally breathe some fresh air, instead of the stale, cynical stuff hanging inside like a dusty shroud. I decided I hated politics pretty much then and there and sure wasn't happy to wallow my way back into it now.

"Unfortunately, Master Yotov is gaining more and more support," Lunzy said once we were sealed safely inside one of the Keel's briefing rooms.

"What does that even mean? This isn't a general election, right? Peacemakers don't vote for new Masters—" I paused, frowning. "Do they?"

"Not exactly. New Masters are selected by the existing ones—first by consensus, and then by majority vote. If they still can't resolve any choices, or if all the Masters have been wiped out or something like that, the Guild Charter *then* specifies that ninety-nine Peacemakers will be selected at random and will vote on whatever candidates put their names forward, using a ranked ballot system. If there are more than one Master to be chosen, a different ninety-nine are randomly selected each time."

"So if the four current Masters can't work out replacing the three missing ones, because politics, then the Guild just substitutes a different flavor of politics to get the job done," Torina said.

Lunzy nodded. "Ain't it great?"

I leaned back in my chair and blew a sigh at the overheads above me. "So, it's not just crime, corruption, and bureaucracy that links the stars, it's sleazy politics, too."

"Actually, Van, I think all of those things go together," Perry said.

"Yup. Just odious, repulsive peas in a pod." I sighed again and sat up.

"I'd love to be more into all this scheming, but I'm, you know, not. Like, not even the slightest—"

"You really do take after your grandfather, don't you?" Lunzy said, smiling despite the haggardness of her appearance. It struck me that it was people like her that were keeping the Guild running, actually doing its job, while the Masters engaged in their shitty little turf wars.

Torina leaned forward, eyeing me intently. "I'm curious, Van. If it ever came to it, would you—"

"Nope," I said, holding up a hand. "I know where you're going with that, and I'm not interested. I refuse to let this less-than-once-in-a-lifetime opportunity to actually travel amid the wonder and splendor of the stars become what amounts to a commute from Earth to here, to an office job. I could have done that on Earth, with much less risk of eating vacuum and exploding and stuff."

"Besides, aren't we here because of your cousin?" Icky put in. She'd been fidgeting and looking profoundly bored while we talked. It reminded me again that her upbringing, essentially alone with her father, hadn't really exposed her to things like politics. She was actually much like I was back in my teenage days, when it had mostly been Gramps and me on the farm. Politics was just one of those adult things that didn't really matter to me.

I kind of envied her, actually.

I turned to Lunzy. "I'm assuming that everyone here is aware that I detest my cousin."

"I've picked up hints of that, yes," Lunzy said.

"Yeah, but Icky's still got a point. What, exactly, is going on with Carter? You said you found him, but he's obviously not here."

"Is he alive? You never did specify that," Torina added.

Lunzy nodded. "Oh, he's alive alright."

I sneered. "Shit."

Torina turned to me. "Do you *really* wish that he was dead, Van?"

"No, of course not. He's an entitled, ambitious, narcissistic jerk. But if we started killing off all of those, we'd need to dig an awful lot of graves. And I hate digging."

I turned back to Lunzy. "So where is he?"

"He's being held captive."

"*Again?*"

"Again."

"Held captive by whom?"

Lunzy answered by activating a recorded comm message. The screen on the meeting room's wall lit up with the image of—

A platypus?

That had been my first impression, but I soon realized that this creature was really only vaguely platypus-like. It was probably the thick, coarse fur and the mouth and jaw that were drawn forward, extended, and flattened until they resembled a duck bill. It had short, stumpy arms ending in six stubby fingers each, all of them apparently opposable. It also had two sets of eyes, one set forward, like human eyes, and a second set on the sides of its head, more like an herbivore or prey animal.

And it was speaking. Or, at least, I assumed it was, because it was moving, gesticulating with its little arms, and its mouth moved in what I assumed was speech. The image was silent, though.

"Something wrong with the sound?" I asked.

Lunzy shook her head. "Oh, no. This goes on for some time,

actually. The real substance of the message doesn't start for another thirty seconds or so."

Torina scowled. "Fren."

"Fren-okun, actually, though it usually gets abbreviated to Fren. Unless, of course, you're saying it in front of them, in which case they'll pounce like a Cetian glow-bat and demand you correct it," Lunzy said.

"In fact, they'll insist on correcting you on a lot of things," Perry put in.

When I first became a Peacemaker, I had knowledge and memories literally injected into me, a sort of boot camp in a syringe. It gave me a huge leg up on my new and wonderfully bizarre situation at the time, but since then, my own experiences had made a lot of those implanted memories obsolete. They still came in handy from time to time, though, and this was one of those times.

"Fren-okun. A spacefaring race who's homeworld is—um... I've got this—one of two planets in the Gliese 876 system. They've colonized them both. They're renowned for twisting agreements in ways that were never intended. And—" I shrugged. "And that's all I've got."

"Oh, well, in that case, you're missing out on the true joy of dealing with the Fren. Here, let me introduce you to Unokte," Lunzy said, then touched a control, activating the audio.

"—now we've established who's boss, who's in charge, oh and it's me, not you! You will do what I say, Peacemakers, or terrible stuff will be visited on our prisoner!"

I glanced at Torina and mouthed *terrible stuff?* She just rolled her eyes.

The image slowly pulled back, revealing a second Fren who was

—eating something? It gave a deer-in-the-headlights look while Unokte jabbed a stubby finger toward the other side of the image.

"That—that way! Over there!" he hissed, apparently to whoever was recording this. The image suddenly slewed hard to one side, panning quickly past someone sitting in a chair that might have been Carter, before settling on a wall. It remained there a few seconds, then the whole image shuddered and bounced around.

And then panned again, straight up, and fast, until the image just showed a ceiling.

"They knocked the recorder over," Perry said.

Lunzy nodded. "Uh-huh."

Two Fren appeared in frame, staring directly down into the lens, then hissing and slobbering at one another. They vanished, and the recorder was righted, pointing at the bored-looking Fren who was still munching away listlessly.

"I thought you said this is the part of the recording with substance," I said to Lunzy.

She sighed. "Believe it or not, it is—here we go. There's Carter."

The image finally panned and settled on Carter Yost, sitting manacled to a chair. Unokte reappeared in the frame, which abruptly zoomed in until the image was filled with Carter's shoulder. Then it expanded outward again until both he and Unokte were in-frame.

"Miserable Peacemakers and your miserable Earth creatures! We have this one and won't give it back until you give us money, lots and lots of money!"

Lunzy froze the image, catching Unokte in mid-shout, a string of spittle from his mouth hanging suspended in the air. Carter, behind him, kept his head down but was watching Unokte under his brow. He hadn't apparently been injured or harmed and looked more humiliated than anything else. For some reason, he also looked —damp?

"We had to send a follow-up message to them, asking exactly how much money *lots and lots* is, because Unokte here never actually says. It turns out to be 3.38 million bonds," Lunzy said.

I blinked at that. "That's an awfully specific number."

"It is. It incidentally happens to be very close to what Carter owes to various creditors. Namely, 3.1 or so million bonds."

"So you think Carter set this up to try to wipe out his debts?" Perry asked.

"And it got away from him, since he looks genuinely unhappy in that chair," Torina noted.

Lunzy shrugged. "Maybe. I wouldn't put it past him. Oh, his creditors might be behind it. Former Masters Yewlo and Proloxus were both variations on that scheme, after all. They owed huge sums of money, and once their respective creditors knew they'd never make up those debts, they decided to try and extort it out of the Guild."

"Well, just to be clear, I am *not* coughing up three million plus bonds to bail Carter Yost out of trouble. If that's what it's going to take to save him, well, sucks to be him," I said.

Lunzy grinned. "Never expected you would, Van. No, I was thinking a fake ransom drop to get your foot in the door with the Fren, and then you could work from there at springing him."

I drummed my fingers on the table. "I thought these Fren had a reputation for being cunning—you know, manipulating the wording of agreements to their advantage, that sort of thing."

"They do."

"Then please tell me that Unokte and company aren't representative of their race."

Torina smiled. "No, they seem typical. My father had some dealings with the Fren a few years ago. I helped him handle the deal. That"—she waved a hand at the screen—"is not unusual."

"So, what? They're morons? How does that make them cunning? How does a race of dunderheads like that even manage something as complicated as spaceflight?"

"Their homeworld happens to host flora that are unusually rich in a complex organic compound known as KTT. By itself, KTT is no big deal. But when it's processed through the digestive tract of a Fren, KTT is altered to S-KTT, also known as skit," Perry said.

"Skit? That's—wait. Isn't that some psychoactive drug?"

"Very much so. It directly stimulates the pleasure centers in most organic brains, making it highly addictive. It's in *super* high demand across known space and, as a result, is worth a great deal of money."

"Apparently, it can make you feel like you're—you know, when you're making love, except instead of it being *there and done*, it just goes on and on," Torina said.

I stared at her. "You mean, it's like having an—"

"Yup, but continuously."

"I—oh." I shook my head. "Okay, then. So, let me guess—once this became known, all of known space beat a path to the Fren's door."

"Pretty much," Lunzy said.

"And the Fren were able to leverage this drug in exchange for things like spaceflight tech."

"They were. Their transition from pre-spaceflight to spacefaring race happened so fast it's a record that'll probably never be beaten," Perry replied. "They also earn a lot of bonds from tourism. Nearly a quarter million beings from near and far come for the yearly Ooont-zee Music Wave."

I stared. "Ooont-zee?"

Torina chimed in. "They stole it from your people, Van. You know, music that goes *oont-zee oont-zee oont-zee*, lots of sweaty beings dancing with colored lights and gas masks and—"

I covered my face with both hands and rubbed back and forth a few times before looking at Torina with naked disbelief. "You mean I came all the way into the stars to find platypus-shaped space ravers?"

"Rave! That's it. Not wave. Rave," Torina said brightly. "Um, yes. They have guest DJs from all over the galactic arm—"

"DJ Puffball is spinning this year," Perry added. "He's an actual mobile fungus, one of the only intelligent plant-based species around. When the bass drops during his set, he releases a cloud of spores into a sheet of laser light. Tickets are almost impossible to get, I'm told."

"I… I don't—why do people give a damn about a drug that's just glorified—" I said, then stopped. Dead in my tracks. The Fren hadn't developed spaceflight or advanced tech themselves. Instead, they'd just traded for it because of a drug that they—

My eyes widened.

Lunzy grinned. "I think it just sank in."

I looked from her to the others. Torina had a grin of her own. Perry couldn't grin, but I knew he would be if he could. Icky—was Icky. She was just reading something on a data pad, apparently oblivious to all of it.

"You said this plant has to go through their digestive tract," I said to Perry.

"Uh-huh."

"So that means it's basically—"

"Uh-huh."

Lunzy leaned on the table. "When people call skit *good shit*, they really mean it."

"That sound you hear right now? That's my skin crawling," I said, sinking back in my chair in horrified wonder. "Space raving platypuses with poop pills. If it's okay with you, I'll just go raise corn in Iowa now."

Lunzy chuckled. "Nice try, Tudor. Anyway, there it is. Carter Yost is being held by the Fren for a ransom of 3.38 million bonds. I can arrange for a rigged ransom payment. We have an agreement with the Quiet Room to use bonds they've specifically numbered and designated such that they can essentially declare them worthless forgeries at any time. It gives us ransom money that looks genuine—actually *is* genuine, at least until the hostage exchange is done."

I scowled. "I can't believe I'm going to stick my neck out for Carter *again*."

"Rescuing a Peacemaker carries a hefty payout from the Guild, so there is that," Lunzy said.

I sighed, a noise that sounded disgusted even to me. "It had better be an *awful* lot of money."

Lunzy responded with a thin smile. "Will this make you feel better about it?" She tapped a control, resuming the recording.

"And don't try to fool us, miserable creatures watching this! We will—"

"He must be kept moist!" a new voice, rasping and shrieky, cut in. At the same time, another Fren, smaller and stouter than Unokte, pushed into the frame—

And immediately vomited up a shocking volume of slimy goop like mucus, slathering Carter with the sparkling, resinous stuff.

Carter groaned and cursed.

I stared at the image for a moment.

"He must be kept moist!"

"I don't wanna be *moi*—!"

The image froze again. I lasted another few seconds, then collapsed into a laughing fit so hard I was afraid I might sprain something.

4

THE RANSOM DROP was a remote location on the edge of the system called LHS 288. This was an ancient red dwarf star about as bright as the glow from a stove element, with one companion—a brown dwarf about twice the size of Jupiter. The specific location was just a set of coordinates that, were this the Solar System, would correspond to a point somewhere in its Oort Cloud. The Fren's ransom instructions said there'd be a buoy waiting there for us that we could use to contact them and arrange the exchange.

"It's a trap!" Perry said, and I glowered at him.

"Would you stop that? First, I know it's a trap, and second, you don't do the voice quite right."

"Well, pardon me for being creative and putting my personal spin on it. But yeah, it's definitely a trap. A lousy one, but still a trap."

"I am aware, faithful companion. Now stop yelling and get ready for—"

"Moisture?" Perry asked helpfully.

"I guess. And very short punches, based on their little arms," I added.

We'd departed Anvil Dark, dividing ourselves between the *Fafnir*, piloted by Torina with Icky as her backup, and me aboard a standard class four workboat with Perry. The Fren had insisted we come in an unarmed vessel, so Torina would twist in to a point just close enough to realistically render us assistance if we needed it. Netty would power down the *Fafnir* and put the ship into silent running mode, and unless the Fren carefully scoured space around the buoy, it would escape detection.

As we prepared to twist, though, I couldn't help feeling something just wasn't right about any of this. I said as much to Perry.

"Well, would your cousin let himself be doused in mucus if it meant being able to pay off his debts?" Perry asked.

"Yeah, he probably would. But that's not it. I actually don't think Carter's behind this."

"So you think the Fren genuinely took him hostage? Why would they risk crossing the Peacemakers like that?"

"I don't know. Based on the crash course I took on the Fren before we left Anvil Dark, I doubt they would," I said.

"Okay, but?" Perry pressed.

"But, I can't help thinking they've been put up to it. It probably wouldn't be hard to manipulate the Fren, would it?"

"Harder than you might expect. They might be imbeciles in a lot of ways, but they do have that cunning streak to them," Perry answered.

I sniffed with suspicion. "I've run into lots of cunning people that have been manipulated. Usually, it's by giving them something they want, or at least promising to." And it was true. I'd caught more than a few supposedly savvy, clever people in cyberspace by appearing to offer them something too tempting to pass up.

"Let's say you're right. The Fren are just being used by somebody else. To what end?" Perry asked.

"Why did someone rig Carter's ship to blow up when I tried to board it, but did it in a way that immediately made us suspect a trap?"

"That would suggest that someone's playing a very patient, very subtle game."

"I know. And not to put too fine a point on it, I'm over it. I feel like I've been shadowboxing with someone or something that we can never quite see, except in glimpses here and there. We've got the stolen identities, the Sorcerers, Icky's mother, Hoffsinger and Ruiz-Rocher and that crowd, the Nesit and the missing artifacts—"

I released a frustrated sigh. "It's like the three blind men and the elephant."

"The who and the what now?"

The nav system chimed, telling us it had finished the requisite twist calculations and was ready to implement them. I glanced at Perry. "You haven't heard that one?"

"Apparently not."

"Three blind men run across an elephant—"

"If they're blind, how would they know that? How would they even know it's an elephant—?"

"Would you just shut up and listen? So they run across this elephant and try to figure out what it is from touch alone. One feels one of the elephant's legs and thinks it's a tree trunk, another feels its trunk and thinks it's a snake—"

"He'd have to be an idiot to think it's a snake, Van."

I sighed. "That swooshing sound you hear is the point going right over your hyper-literal little mechanical head."

"Then bring that point back around for a soft landing," Perry said.

"The point is that we can see bits and pieces of whatever this thing is, but not the whole elephant. And if you make a crack about our arch nemesis out there probably not being an elephant, I swear I'll make you fly to our next destination under your own power."

"I'll shut up now."

"Good idea. Anyway, what we need is to find the common thread, the thing, or things, that links all this together."

"If they, or it, exist. Your three blind men might have *actually* found a tree, a snake, and—something similar to whatever part of the elephant your third guy touched. In other words, Van, there might not *be* an elephant in the room."

"Maybe. I just can't help thinking there *are* elephant prints in the butter, though."

"Van, what the hell are you talking about? Do you need me to call someone?"

"What, you haven't heard that one? How can you tell there's been an elephant in your refrigerator? You can see his footprints in the butter? No?"

"No."

I reached for the nav computer to initiate our twist. "That joke was funny as hell when I was eight."

"So that's the bar you've set for what constitutes *funny as hell*, huh? The humor tastes of a prepubescent boy?"

I shrugged and grinned. "Remind me to let you hear my repertoire of fart jokes sometime. Those never get old."

"Well, this place is everything the tourist brochures said it would be," I muttered, eyeing the lonely red dwarf called LHS 288 and its companion brown dwarf. I was starting to realize that, despite the stunning number of habitable—not to mention inhabited—planets near Sol, far more were just like this, desolate stars devoid of—anything, really, but especially objects of interest.

Space was inconsistent like that. There were stunning vistas interspersed with vast stretches of nap-inducing empty.

I turned to what passed for the workboat's tactical overlay. It could reliably detect things only to about half the range of the *Fafnir*'s scanners, and even then had a much higher error margin. And speaking of the *Fafnir*, even though she hung about a million klicks away, she gave no return whatsoever. Which was good—that was the point of her sitting in silent-running mode, after all. But I had to remind myself part of it was just this workboat's shitty, off-the-shelf tech. The true test would be if she avoided the scrutiny of any other ships.

Of which there were, currently, none.

"We're only seeing the buoy. How about you guys?" I asked over the comm, which connected us to the *Fafnir* with a directional beam, another measure to help her avoid detection.

"Nothing. You, the buoy, and a few hunks of rock. That's it," Torina said.

"Okay, then, I'm heading for the buoy. If you guys notice anything untoward, make sure to sing out."

"Really? We figured we'd just keep quiet and surprise you," Torina replied.

"Funny. Or, wait—no. What's the opposite of that?"

We reached the buoy without incident. Like this workboat, it was just a generic hull, power supply, and positioning system that could be used for a variety of purposes. Navigation, marking out space-lanes and the like, was their most common use, but they could be employed for early warning, surveillance, studying various interesting phenomena, or even armed and used for security. This one had no weapons, though, and seemed to be just the basic design.

"It does have a comm array, though. My guess is that we're supposed to transmit a surety certificate for the ransom to it, and then it will shuffle it through a bazillion intermediate locations before sending the money where it's ultimately meant to go," Perry said.

I frowned at the buoy. "If the Fren are smart, the buoy will only contain the comm data for the next step in the chain. But, hey, who knows, maybe they were dumb and put complete routing information into the thing. Perry, once I establish comms with it, see what you can do about discretely hacking into it, and find out what you can."

"Will do, boss."

I turned back to the comm. Icky had constructed an AI-driven discriminator, a piece of hardware that sat between the comm processor and the rest of the *Fafnir*'s systems. It was essentially a sophisticated firewall, intended to block potentially malicious software or hacking attempts made over the comm. It was designed by her father to prevent snooping by the many enemies he'd believed he'd made in the wake of the bogus terraforming operation master-minded, at least in part, by his dead ex-wife. Even Perry had to admit it was about as cutting-edge as anything he'd ever seen. It just showed that there were many drivers of innovation, and one of the most powerful was good old paranoia.

"Okay, then. Let's open a comm channel to this thing and see what happens," I said. I tapped at the workboat's comm panel, queried the buoy, got a response, and established the link—

And that was it.

"Am I missing something?" I asked as time ticked by in silence.

"Maybe they're not home," Perry replied, then interfaced himself with the workboat's comm system. A few seconds later, he said, "Huh."

"Huh?"

"Yeah, huh. Huh, as in, there's no outgoing comm signal from this buoy, except for the local one it's using to talk to us."

"Meaning what, exactly? It's not transmitting beyond this system?"

"Nope. So either there's something wrong with it, the Fren are willing to wait about eighty-odd-thousand years to get your signal, or there's something else going on."

I turned my attention back to the workboat's scanner output, but nothing had changed.

"Torina, are you detecting anything at all?" I asked.

"No. At least, not using passive scanners."

"What the hell. You might as well power back up and go active."

A moment passed, then a new icon popped onto the workboat's rudimentary tactical overlay. Even its discount scanner suite could detect the *Fafnir* when she was pouring active scanner signals into space.

"Nothing," was Torina's verdict.

I let another minute pass, but nothing changed. We could talk to the buoy, but it didn't seem willing or able to transmit anything beyond this system.

"Okay, this is weird. I mean, if it's meant to trigger some sort of trap, it's doing a pretty shitty job of it," Icky said.

I grunted assent. "Maybe the buoy really is broken." The work-boat had a small maintenance remote, something similar to the *Fafnir*'s Waldo—or, more correctly, Waldo 2, since we'd been forced to leave our original Waldo on Venus. I deployed the remote but let Perry guide it to the buoy and investigate.

"Well, there's your problem," Perry said almost as soon as the remote reached the buoy. I peered at the image being sent back by the remote. It showed a neat, inward-dimpled hole about the size of a marble on one side of the buoy, and a bigger, more ragged wound on the opposite side. Something had clearly struck the buoy and completely penetrated it, probably knocking its twist comm unit offline.

I glared at the damage. "A rail gun?"

"Judging from the size of the impact hole, it was a *really* teeny one. If the buoy had any armor, it probably wouldn't have even penetrated. I'm thinking micrometeorite."

"Really? Isn't that, ah, wildly improbable?"

"Wildly improbable undersells it—a lot. But that doesn't mean the chances are zero, and, well"—he waved a wing at the display— "here we are."

I sat back. "Let me add—what now? Because I'm at the end of

my logic chain for this idiotic goose chase."

We ended up contacting Lunzy back at Anvil Dark. She smiled as soon as she answered the comm.

"Well, how about that, I was just going to contact you. I have a very agitated Unokte on the line who wants to know what's holding up the ransom payment. And, with that, over to you," she said, touched a control, and vanished. The screen filled with the image of Unokte, waving around his stumpy arms and fuming.

"—miserable Earth creatures, how dare you keep us waiting! Do you believe that we won't—?"

"Kill Carter Yost? Oh, please, don't tempt me," I cut in.

Unokte stopped mid-rant. "You want him back. He's a Peacemaker—"

"He's also a—what's your favorite line? Oh, right. A miserable Earth creature. A *very* miserable Earth creature, in fact."

"I—what? You're trying to trick me! You vile human-things are all alike, you don't respect the Fren—"

"Actually, I don't particularly respect you, no, but that's neither here nor there. See, I'm at your buoy at LHS 288, and I've tried to pay the ransom, but your buoy is broken."

"You're lying. You want to cheat us. You don't respect—"

"You, yeah, we've been through that. Doesn't change the fact that your buoy got whacked by a rock and is out of commission." As I spoke, I had Perry share the remote's imagery with Unokte.

"You—you did that, you unwashed beast!"

"It was like that when we found it, honest." I shrugged. "A *super* unlucky encounter with a speeding rock, I guess. So what's the plan now?"

"It's—you—I—the—" Unokte sputtered a bit more, then abruptly vanished as the signal terminated.

Lunzy came back on the comm. "So, Van, you having fun yet?"

"Yeah, this is a riot. What the hell are we supposed to do now?"

She shrugged. "Beats me. All we can do is wait for the Fren to get back—" She stopped as something caught her attention. "And that would be them now. Here you go."

The image flicked back to Unokte. "Fix the buoy," he snapped.

"Fix it? How? With what?"

"Just fix it, miserable—"

"Earth creature, yeah," I said. Then I muttered, "That's my new favorite thing. Right up there with papercuts and fat-free cookies."

"Abominable, and I can experience neither," Perry agreed.

"Thoughts on the damage?" I asked him, glancing over to see Perry shrug his wings.

"Maybe? If I had to guess, I'd say that rock ripped the guts out of the twist-comm system—which, incidentally, means there are probably a few grams of antimatter in its fuel cell that may or may not stay contained."

"Yeah, no. I'm not going to try and fix something that might blow up in our faces, even if we did have the parts. You need to come up with another solution."

"I—but—you—" Unokte balled his hands into adorable little fists and waved them wildly around. "Miserable Earth creature—"

"Look, Unokte, why don't I just come to you, bring you the ransom, you hand over Carter, and we go our separate ways. You know, how these hostage-taking things normally play out?"

"I—but—" He paused. "Oh."

"Is that a yes? Or do we keep the money, and you keep Carter?" I cut in.

"He's a miserable—!"

"Earth creature, yeah, I know. Get a new line, seriously. I also know that I'm a busy guy, with better things to be doing than this. So make up your mind, Unokte. Do you want me to come to you, or should we just forget the whole thing?"

"I—you—"

"Oh, for—Unokte, believe it or not, I've got absolutely zero interest in screwing you over. This ransom money isn't even mine. I'm just the courier here, the guy dropping off and picking up. I'll behave because I've frankly got no desire to do anything but. Besides, I'm just a miserable Earth creature. How dangerous could I possibly be?"

Unokte briefly carried on a wheezy, hissed conversation with someone off-camera, then turned back to me.

"Fine. I will send coordinates now."

The image flicked off.

"Rude," Perry said.

"Well, what did you expect? I'm just a miserable Earth creature."

OUR NEW DESTINATION was the EZ Aquarii system, a trio of red dwarf stars exactly three times as interesting as the solitary one we'd just left. Of course, three times zero is still zero.

We twisted to the coordinates Unokte had sent us, on the edge of the trinary system. A single ship awaited us, a chunky collection of spheres and cylinders stuck onto a torus, parts of which were apparently filled with water. The Fren were amphibious and required access to water to sustain themselves.

While the *Fafnir* hung back, Perry and I docked the workboat with the Fren ship, then moved to the airlock. I wore my b-suit and had The Drop and Moonsword both on prominent display, doing my best to look the part of bad-assed Peacemaker.

"When this airlock opens, we're not going to be deluged by water, are we?" I asked Perry as we waited for the other ship to open.

"They're amphibious, Van, not actually aquatic."

"They're also idiots."

Perry looked at me for a moment. "Good point. I'll stand ready to close the door in a hurry."

It finally slid open, and something poured through alright. It wasn't water, though. It was a musty, musky, acrid stink that somehow seemed vaguely familiar—

Right. As a teenager, I attended a weekend of science camp in Des Moines that had animals and the natural world as its focus. One of them was a porcupine, and it had been stinky in a way not too different from this. I remembered being surprised that an animal with a coat composed of dangerous spines could end up being any *less* appealing.

I gagged and swallowed. "That is *nasty.*"

"A significant component of that smell is a suite of pheromones. Would you like to know the details?" Perry asked.

"I'm good."

A Fren appeared in the airlock. I was pretty sure it wasn't Unokte, but I strode forward anyway and punched it right in its duck-billed face anyway. The Fren stumbled backward, shrieking and clutching at its nose.

"You lied! You said you'd behave! You are not honorable, you miserable—!"

"Hey! You're the ones who kidnapped Carter, so might I remind you that *you're* the villains here?"

A pair of Fren appeared. One of them was definitely Unokte. Both wielded big-bored weapons like shotguns.

"You lied, miserable Earth creature, and now you pay!" Unokte shrieked, then aimed and fired his weapon at me before I had a chance to react.

Something erupted from the gaping muzzle, zipped toward me with a loud hiss, and struck me in the chest, then caromed off and rattled to the floor. Still hissing, it skidded and bounced across the deck, finally going silent and coming to a stop beside my foot.

Immediately, I drew The Drop and jammed it in Unokte's face. "Before you squeeze that trigger, you might want to think about whether my death spasm will make me squeeze mine. Do we understand each other?"

"Uh, Van?" Perry said from behind me.

I kept my gaze locked on Unokte, who had gone cross-eyed looking at The Drop's muzzle just centimeters from his extruded nose. "What?"

"That projectile he fired—it's a cavitating round, meant for underwater use. And under water, it would be deadly. In air, it's got as much oomph as—well, you saw how much oomph it had."

Unokte gave a tentative shrug. "Oops?"

"You're just not very good at this whole being bad guys thing, are you?" I snapped. "Now, then, where is Carter Yost?"

"He's—"

"And if you lie to me, I swear I'm going to shoot and claim it was self-defense after the fact."

"—not here. He's aboard the *Prison Ship of Supreme Discomfort*, where all miser—er, all of our prisoners are kept."

"*The Prison Ship of Supreme Discomfort.*"

Unokte nodded.

"That's seriously what it's called."

He nodded again.

"Fine. You're going to take us there, and you're going to release Carter to me, and maybe I won't just summon a swarm of Peacemakers to come and seize you, your ship, your prison ship, and anything else not nailed down. We'll call it the proceeds of crime."

"No, no need!"

"I hope not. Oh, and Unokte, you're riding with Perry and me," I said, gesturing with The Drop toward the airlock. Unokte slumped in defeat, nodded forlornly, then surrendered his weapon and gave instructions to the crew of this Fren ship to twist back to their home system, and *The Prison Ship of Supreme Discomfort*.

As the airlock door sealed behind us, I hoped that Fren smell would diminish. It didn't. I glared at Unokte.

"Is there any way you can turn that off?"

"Turn what off?"

"That smell."

"What smell?"

I sighed, and immediately regretted it, because it tasted the way the air smelled, somewhere between *dirty litterbox* and *sweaty gym sock*.

"Never mind. I'll just wear my helmet."

5

WE WERE GOING to leave the workboat parked at EZ Aquarii. On reflection, though, I wasn't sure how much Unokte's involuntary reek might permeate my ship and didn't feel like investing a ton of bonds in air freshener. And after just a few minutes of flying with him, I wasn't sure there *was* enough air freshener. I did finally snap my helmet on, reasoning that while it might be rude, Unokte *had* tried to kill me. And, call me old fashioned, but I think a little rudeness in the immediate aftermath of attempted murder was perfectly justified.

This time, in company with the *Fafnir*, we arrived at Gliese 876, the Fren home system, and were immediately deluged with comms traffic. The comm lit up across the channels with incoming messages. I tensed up and pored over the workboat's paltry tactical display, expecting an incoming attack coordinated with what I assumed was a cyber assault. But, aside from a ship whose transponder actually identified it as *The Prison Ship of Supreme Discom-*

fort, there was no other traffic nearby. The next closest ship, in fact, was at least two hours away, inbound toward the Fren homeworld—or, more properly, Fren Homeworld. That was its actual name.

"Perry, what the hell is going on? What's all this comm traffic?"

"Do you really want to know?"

"I—what? Of course I want to know. Why wouldn't I?"

Perry answered by activating one of the channels. The comm screen lit up with a writhing, heaving mass of—tentacles, pseudopods, something, anyway. I sometimes ran across stuff like this in the darker, more pervy parts of the web back on Earth, although that was all animated. This was—

"What the hell is this?"

"Smut. Siliran smut, to be exact. That's all this particular channel carries."

"Why are you—?"

"Just wait for it."

A few more seconds passed as the—obscene, I guess—image continued flopping around on screen, then it vanished, replaced by a list of prices and payment methods to keep watching.

I turned to Perry. "Seriously?"

"That's just Siliran porn. The Fren broadcast spicy channels for pretty much every species. Several for humans, in fact. They also distribute high-stakes and probably rigged online gambling via comm, as well as a multitude of various 'natural' remedies for legions of ailments, on-the-spot, ridiculously high-interest loans—"

This time, I turned to Unokte, who'd been sitting in the workboat's jump seat being awfully quiet.

"Seriously?"

He shrugged. "It's a living."

Torina came on the comm. She was laughing. I could hear Icky laughing in the background. "Van, you should check out comm channel A-219. It's got a human, another human dressed up as a Yonnox for some reason, an *actual* Yonnox, and they're—"

"Do you mind? I'd rather not have, ah, *art* like that in the *Fafnir's* browser history, thanks."

Netty cut in. "I appreciate that, Van, since I effectively *am* the *Fafnir's* browser history."

I turned back to Unokte. "And just when I thought you couldn't get any less appealing."

Unokte's only response was another shrug. I was beginning to suspect that when they weren't getting their way, the Fren response to a lot of things was an insolent shrug.

We rendezvoused with *The Prison Ship of Supreme Discomfort*, an old class twelve cargo barge that had been repurposed and seemingly combined with pieces of other ships into an orbiting tribute to Rube Goldberg. It even took Unokte a few minutes to figure out where an open universal docking adapter might be. We finally boarded, to find ourselves confronted by four Fren, one of which brandished a blade at us.

"You are our prisoners now!"

Perry peeked around my leg. "We are? Sweet! I've never been held prisoner by the Fren before. Tell me, do you guys pipe all that stuff you transmit into the cells—?"

"Never mind the horndog bird," I said, drawing The Moonsword. Compared to its lethal shimmer and ethereally sharp edges, the Fren's blade looked like an iron bar. "And never mind the theatrics, either. You guys are lucky I don't just bring a swarm of Peacemakers here and take this clunky excuse for a ship apart, piece by piece, until we find Carter Yost."

I took a step toward the Fren. "Mind you, that option is definitely not off the table... yet. That will depend on whether you take me directly to him or not."

I stared at the Fren with the blade around the Moonsword. He wavered back. Unokte stepped forward and took charge.

"I have... come to an agreement with this Peacemaker. We will release the other Peacemaker to him."

I smiled. "And when, exactly, are we going to do this?"

Unokte glanced from the Moonsword to me. "Now. Immediately. Right away."

"Good answer."

I DECIDED to bring Icky and Torina aboard *The Prison Ship of Supreme Discomfort*, reasoning that we had no idea how many Fren were aboard, what their intentions were, or how much we could trust Unokte to not try something stupid. Icky, clad in her up-armored vac suit and wearing her helmet, presented a particularly menacing figure, especially since she was at least half again as tall as the Fren.

"Are you sure we need these helmets, Van?" Torina asked as she came aboard.

"No, not at all. Go ahead and take it off." I smiled sweetly at her.

She returned a narrow-eyed stare through her visor. "Think I'll keep it on."

We found Carter in much the same situation we'd last seen him, manacled to a chair and covered in a thin film of—something. Something slimy, with the sticky, resinous luster I automatically associated with the mysterious stains you often saw on subway platforms and alley walls. As soon as he saw us, he began to bellow and rant.

"Van, get me out of here! This is torture! You have no idea what they've—"

A door slid open, and Carter whimpered. "Not again—"

"Moist! It must be kept moist!"

"Van, please!"

Torina and Icky both stepped toward him. I held them back. "Let's just make sure we've got a clear understanding with Unokte and his colleagues here."

"Van!"

"Moist!"

"Working on getting you released right now, Carter. Just hang on a—oh. Ewww."

Torina, who'd turned to me, looked back at Carter. "Ewww? What do you—oh. Yeah. Ewww."

"Van!"

"Moist! It must be kept moist!"

Icky was grinning. "Who is that old… person, and why does she keep puking all over your cousin?"

"That… is my grandmother. She needs an operation but refuses to have it done, so I must keep her out here, where I can keep an eye on her," Unokte said.

I raised an eyebrow. "An operation?"

"Yes. Her brain needs to be fixed."

"No! Moist!"

Icky just stared in rapt and deeply amused fascination. "That's amazing. You wouldn't think someone that small could contain so much—whatever the hell that stuff is."

"Is she practicing some sort of ancient custom among your people? Something having to do with caring for your young, maybe?" Torina asked.

Unokte stared at her for a moment, then shook his head. "No."

"Oh."

"Okay, much as I'd like to pull up a chair and just watch this for a while, I have better things to do with my time. Not many, but a few. Let's get him out of there and… aboard the workboat, because there's no way I'm letting him aboard the *Fafnir* in that condition."

Carter shook his head, sending *moistness* flying in gooey droplets. "You know what, Van? Up yours, you preening asshole! When I get free, I'll—"

"Oh. Okay. Let's go, guys," I said and turned for the door. Icky, Torina, and Perry all moved to follow me without a backward glance.

"Van, wait! Dammit, you *prick*. Just—take me. I can't—I can't let them slime me anymore. The old bat won't listen to me when I say I'm not a frog or a salamander or whatever. She can't see, anyway, thanks to cataracts or something."

Grandma Fren blinked around the room with eyes that were, indeed, milky white. "Moist!"

I turned to Unokte. "Unshackle him, and we'll take him with us." I turned pointedly back to Carter. "And if he acts like an asshole, I'm going to flip a coin. Heads, he goes out the airlock. Tails, I'm going to bring him right back here and give him back to you."

As the Fren moved to comply, Torina gave a thoughtful frown.

"Something wrong?" I asked her.

"No, no. I was just wondering which of those two choices would be worse, and I realized that I'm not entirely sure."

As we departed *The Prison Ship of Supreme Discomfort*, bound for Anvil Dark, I decided to do a bit of interrogating—after Carter had cleaned himself up as much as the workboat's limited hygiene facilities allowed, anyway. Clad in a spare set of coveralls, I sat him in the jump seat, got the *Fafnir* on the line, and turned to him with a frank question.

"Carter, did you stage your own kidnapping?"

He looked aghast. "What?"

"Well, the ransom the Fren were supposedly demanding was a sum that almost exactly matched what you apparently owe to—I don't know, whoever you've dragged into your financial bed with you. That's a hell of a coincidence, and if space has taught me one thing, it's that coincidences almost never happen."

"We just saw a buoy that got hit by a micrometeorite, way the hell out in empty—" Perry began but stopped himself when he saw the look I gave him.

"I was just saying—okay, I'll shut up now," he said at my continued glare.

I looked back at Carter. "So, Carter, I'll ask you again. Did you stage all this? Were you trying a get-rich quick bit of nonsense to bail yourself out of hock?"

"I—no! Of course not! Do you think I would let those... those... *platypuses*—"

"Actually, I think the correct plural is platypusi," I said.

Perry interrupted. "Actually, Van, Carter is—incorrect, because of course he is. Platypusi it is, and on an entirely unrelated note, you aren't planning on running anything through the trash compactor anytime soon, are you?"

I glared at him. "We'll see, Perry. We'll see."

I spun back to Carter, who just looked indignant.

"Will you two stop debating some bullshit nuance of language? I was kidnapped! I didn't set any of this up. I was kidnapped and held against my will!" he bellowed.

I answered his bluster with a mild look, as though he'd just appeared and I'd just noticed him. "Oh. Right. You know, Carter, I'm inclined to believe you, that you weren't in on this. It would be a ballsy move, and you're anything but ballsy."

"You—!"

I just pressed on. "What you *are* is a giant asshole who has endangered my life, and those of my crew, at least *twice* now. Twice, as in we've saved your sorry butt two times. So, you're going to sit there and be quiet while we take you right back to Anvil Dark to explain yourself. Oh, and you'll do it with the knowledge that, some-day, I fully expect that I'm going to put a missile through your engines, and no one will care, least of all me."

Carter seethed at me. "We'll see about that—"

"Yes, we will, and I'm honestly looking forward to it. Oh, and before you ask—you're not getting any sort of payout from this job."

Carter was practically chewing his tongue in frustrated rage. "What about my pain and suffering? I should—"

"You should be tied to a chair getting slimed, but you aren't, and you're not getting a single bond."

"What, you're just going to keep the ransom for yourself?"

"Oh, for—there was no ransom, Carter. It was fake. Which means that, on the off chance you really *did* set all this up, you'd have gotten nothing anyway. I'm talking about *my* payout for this job, for rescuing you. Now, in case this part hasn't quite sunk into that mushy excuse of a brain, do *not* get in my way again. I will *not* be coming to rescue you a third time. Torina, you got all that in the minutes, right?"

"Uh—minutes? I—yes, sure. Minutes. It's been duly noted," she said, pretending to write something in midair.

Icky frowned. "What the hell are you talking about, minutes? How do you put something into a unit of time?"

Torina touched her finger to Icky's lips. "I'll explain later."

Perry tapped my arm with a wingtip. "You know what's interesting?"

"What?"

"Well, while all of the drama and moistness was happening back there, I just happened to find myself next to a data port on that Fren prison hulk. Now, being a curious bird, I wondered what sort of safeguards and encryption and stuff the Fren might use, and it turns out they're trash. Basic, off-the-shelf stuff."

"Where are you going with this, Perry?"

"Well, as I said, being a curious bird, I decided to see what I could find out about how that ransom payment was supposed to be routed from that wrecked buoy to wherever it was going to end up. It didn't go to Carter Yost. It went to the Quiet Room."

I raised an eyebrow at that. "Now that *is* interesting."

WE DUMPED Carter off at Anvil Dark, along with the workboat, which belonged to the Guild. The tech who checked it back into what amounts to the spaceborne version of a motor pool made a disgusted sound as he stepped aboard to inspect it.

"What were you guys *doing* in here?"

"Watching Fren porn," Perry said.

The tech shuddered. "Yeah, that'd do it. You're not getting your cleaning deposit back, you know."

I shrugged. "We all have to make sacrifices for the greater good."

We handed Carter over to Lunzy, who wanted to keep him out of the immediate grasp of Master Yotov. She was pretty sure Carter had ingratiated himself to Yotov, or was at least in the process of it, which meant he was also a weak link in a chain she wanted to know more about.

"Don't spare the rubber hoses," I said to her.

"Oh, I don't think that'll be necessary. I suspect Carter will give up information whether he wants to or not. He's not exactly a master of wordplay. . .or hiding his emotions, for that matter."

"Still, if you get the chance with the rubber hoses—"

"I'll keep them ready," Lunzy said, laughing.

We departed Anvil Dark, heading for Procyon, the location of The Quiet Room's largest public-facing branch. Torina had described The Quiet Room as something like an iceberg, outwardly appearing as just a retail banking and investment concern, but with the vast majority of what it did hidden away. The Quiet Room was apparently implicated in the financial and policy decisions of nearly every major player in known space, arguably making it the single most powerful entity around.

"They have a distinct Illuminati vibe to them, don't they?" I offered as Anvil Dark fell away behind us.

"Illumi-who?" Torina asked.

"Illuminati. A supposedly all-powerful Earthly conspiracy that runs everything behind the scenes."

"Is that real?"

I glanced at her sidelong. "Well, I could tell you, but then I'd have to kill you," I said, but something caught my eye. "Speaking of things being real, Netty, is that date and time correct?"

"It's based on the standard conversion of universal galactic time into a terrestrial date-time, so yes. Yes it is," she replied.

"Time sure flies when you're having fun, huh—?"

The comm chimed, announcing an incoming and urgent message from the Guild. It was a flash job, one that demanded an immediate response. I read the details.

"Ouch. A stolen warship—a heavy cruiser that someone apparently yoinked from the Seven Stars League. Netty, how would our firepower compare to something like that, he asked, expecting the answer to be *not well*."

"*Not well* is wildly optimistic. How about downright awful?"

Torina stared at me. "Yoinked? That doesn't translate."

"Netty, add *yoinked* to the translation database as a synonym for *stole*. I mean, it's a perfectly cromulent word."

"Cromulent?"

I grinned at Torina. "We've got to get you brought up to date on what the kids are saying these days back on Earth."

"I'm willing to bet that few Earthly 'kids' are using words like *cromulent*, Van," Perry said.

"Then they don't know what they're missing. Anyway, the

payout on this job is two hundred and fifty thousand bonds to return the cruiser intact, and four hundred thousand to do it undamaged." I turned to the others. "What do you guys think?"

"I think that very few Peacemakers are going to be interested in this job because, you know, it's a heavy-damned-cruiser. Even something like Groshenko's upgraded Dragon, the *Alexander Nevsky*, wouldn't really have been a match for it," Perry said.

Icky, though, leaned into the conversation from her jump seat. "You know, warships aren't all-powerful. My dad and I spent a lot of time trying to figure out where the weak spots on the Nemesis were. There are more than you might think."

Torina and Netty both offered what amounted to wary shrugs. I finally nodded.

"Okay, then. Let's go take a look, at least, and see if this is going to even be doable. We've got nothing to lose but time, right?"

"Well, that and our lives," Perry put in.

I tossed him a glare. "Always with the negative waves, Moriarty."

Perry sighed. "Van, you need to get out more."

6

"THAT IS ONE BIG-ASS SHIP," I said, watching as the tactical display filled with pertinent data.

She was class thirteen, a heavy cruiser of a design common across known space. The Seven Stars League had mothballed her and stuck her in a parking orbit on the edge of one of their member systems. It was similar to how the US military parked unneeded aircraft in the desert, awaiting either a future return to service or eventual scrapping.

"The good news is that she probably has no ordnance on board, so her missile racks and mass drivers will be empty," Netty said.

"And the bad news?" I asked.

"Her lasers. There are a lot of them, and since whoever stole this ship must have been able to breach its security lockouts, we have to assume that the lasers are live, too."

I opened my mouth to reply but noticed yet another ship pop into the system, which was becoming a monotonous string of red dwarf stars. The system was uninhabited, and probably just being used by the thieves as a navigation waypoint. The new arrival was another Peacemaker. That made four that had twisted into the system, besides us. Two had twisted away again, apparently just not interested in tangling with the big warship. The other two hung back, probably waiting to see what we, and each other, did next.

But we had an ace up our sleeve: Icky. She'd fallen into the role of expert when it came to fighting ships, and she'd been watching this one with a critical eye.

"They're having powerplant trouble," she finally announced.

"How do you know?" I asked.

"Well, aside from the fact that they haven't twisted away, despite all the interest they're attracting, take a look at their drive when they do a course correction burn."

We waited. Finally, a brief flare of fusion exhaust poured from her drive bells. Nothing jumped out at me, and I could tell Torina was blank, too. But Icky stabbed a finger at the image, and several graphs she'd had Netty display appeared beside it.

"See? Those fusion plumes are too cold, for a start, and look how their temperature spikes up and down. Plume temperature is a direct indicator of thrust output, and based on that, those are not healthy engines," she proclaimed.

"Well, she was sitting in a parking orbit for—what did the bulletin say? Sixty-two years?" Torina said, scrolling through the Guild alert on her data pad.

"Yeah, I'd think engines couldn't help being cranky after six decades of disuse. Hell, the tractor back in Iowa has to be started and run every week or so, especially during the winter, or it never will."

Icky gave me the side-eye. "This isn't a tractor, Van, and those aren't internal-combustion engines burning hydrocarbon compounds at a paltry twenty-five hundred degrees or so. A fusion drive is either running properly, or it's not. And those are not."

I nodded. "Okay. I believe you. How does that help us?"

"It means that if we're sharp enough, and quick enough, we can stay directly astern of her. That reduces her firepower by about, what, seventy percent?"

"Technically, sixty-seven and change, but close enough," Netty said.

"Okay, so now we're looking straight up her bum—sorry, that sounded bad. So now we're directly astern of her. Now what?"

"Now, Van, we put a missile or two right up those drive bells. Drives that wonky are going to pretty much immediately scram, and probably bring the powerplant down with them."

"So we can disable this thing?"

"Uh—define *disable*."

"As in, not destroy? Not render to a cloud of vapor? Have some-thing we can return to the Seven Stars League besides pictures and happy memories of their heavy cruiser?"

"Sure. Probably."

"Sure and probably are not the same thing, Icky. Pick one," I said.

"Okay, let me explain. I mean, there's a chance that a shock-wave from a missile detonation could propagate back up the drive plume if the conditions are right, and that might blow open the reactor, and then—well, when it comes to fusion reactors, blown open is usually only a problem for a fraction of a second."

"So we need to wrap our missiles in velvet," I said.

They all gave me a curious stare. Perry finally spoke up.

"You want our missiles to explode—gently?"

Torina smirked. "If you'd like, we could reconfigure the lasers to *gently* warm the target, too."

But Netty came to my rescue. "I know what you mean, Van."

"You do?"

"Sure. You're going to suggest firing reconfigured missiles with their warheads deactivated, at the shortest possible range and the highest possible acceleration curve. They'll strike the drive bells of that heavy cruiser hard enough to knock at least one of them out of alignment. If the drive is already running on the edge of scramming, that should finish the job." She paused. "That is what you were going to suggest, right?"

"It—oh, yeah, of course it was. Absolutely. In fact, I was just going to ask Icky to comment on exactly that idea. Icky?"

I turned in time to see her roll her eyes at me. But then she shrugged and nodded. "Netty *is* a fusion powerplant and drive, among other things. Who am I to question the expert?"

"OKAY, so I've finished the calculations, and checked them with Perry, and we both agree. For this to work, we need about 3.5 times ten to the twelfth—you don't really care about the numbers, do you?" Netty asked.

"Just how we make them work for us. I'm more of a big picture guy than a mathematician."

"Naturally. Configuring now," Netty said with what could pass for a digital eyeroll.

Netty and Icky had been chewing on the problem for the past fifteen minutes while we'd slowly closed to the very edge of laser range of the big ship. Whoever the thieves were, they'd managed to power up at least two batteries of the things, a pair of turrets each containing a trio of terrifyingly big weapons. From directly astern, they were the only two batteries that could fire at us, thankfully, but even a small amount of a crap ton of firepower was still a freakin' lot of firepower.

"They're shooting again," Torina put in, deftly nudging the *Fafnir* side to side and up and down. They'd lobbed potshots at us a half-dozen times now but hadn't managed to land any hits—yet.

"Well, the shooting's going to get worse before it gets better. We need to stay at least a thousand klicks back to give the disarmed missiles time to burn all their fuel as fast as they can, to give themselves maximum kinetic energy," Icky said.

I gave her a perplexed look. "So—we can do it from here."

"We can. And we'll probably miss. Oh, we might hit the thing, but not necessarily in the drive bells. And I'm assuming you don't want to go through all this hassle just to end up smashing a missile through their powerplant and—" She put all twenty of her fingers together, then flung them all apart while making an explosion sound.

"Great. And the next thing you're going to tell me is that we need to be within a thousand klicks to ensure that doesn't happen."

"Pretty much. For one, we need to give their point-defenses as little time to react as possible. For another, the missiles are going to have to be guided by something better than the stripped-down AIs that control them. They're only designed to get close enough to detonate, and then they've done their job. Still, this is going to come down to fractions of a second, way too fast for any of us to react. That means either Perry or Netty are going to have to control the missiles, feeding them data right up to impact if we want them properly targeted."

"And to do that, we have to be close enough that they can clearly see the target," Torina said.

"That, and to ensure there aren't any light-speed delays in comms, because the missiles don't have any sort of twist-comms. Even a teeny fraction of a second delay is the difference between hitting and missing at these sorts of velocities. I mean, if we had time to disassemble a missile and rebuild it—" Icky shrugged. "But we don't."

"Okay, then. Netty, Perry, which of you will do the honors?"

"I recommend Perry. He's specifically designed as a combat AI. I'm more about twisting and flying and keeping you guys alive," Netty said.

Perry made a sighing sound. "So, once again, it comes down to the bird to save the day."

I smiled. "Heavy is the head that wears the crown."

"That sounds like a quote," Torina said.

"It is. *Henry IV, Part 2*, by William Shakespeare. I had to study the hell out of it in high school. That line is literally the only thing I remember, but it seems fitting."

Netty spoke up. "Actually, Van, the quote is, *Uneasy is the head that wears the crown*, not *heavy*."

I stared at Torina. "I was just schooled in one of Shakespeare's quotes by an alien artificial intelligence."

"A *well-read* alien artificial intelligence, it seems," she replied.

"I can recite the whole play for you, if you'd like," Netty offered.

"No, I think we'll be good." I turned to Perry. "It looks, my friend, like this is your show."

Perry's eyes flashed. "Time to roll up the wings and get to work."

"Torina! Incoming!"

A laser shot from the cruiser had just scoured a deep furrow across two of the *Fafnir*'s applique armor plates and vaporized part of the auxiliary scanner array. It probably said something about my experiences in space to date that my first thought wasn't *we're going to die*, but *how much is that going to cost to fix?* Mind you, the *we're going to die* thing generally followed along shortly thereafter.

"Sorry, Van, but at only a couple of thousand klicks range, I'm surprised they're missing us at all," she replied through gritted teeth, her fingers dancing across the thruster and drive controls, making the *Fafnir* the most evasive target possible.

Netty cut in. "Actually, it would appear that they are firing—"

The *Fafnir* suddenly gyrated wildly, the star-scape outside the canopy slewing and spinning. The ship's inertial suppressors eliminated any feeling of motion, but the mismatch between what my body was telling me and what I was seeing still made me feel a little queasy. Alarms sounded, and red lights lit up the instrument panel in a crimson fury.

"—manually," Netty went on. "That didn't stop them from shooting off our upper point-defense battery and slagging pretty much an entire applique armor plate, mind you."

I cursed. *That* had been an expensive hit.

"Why would they be firing manually?" I asked, swallowing a sudden glimmer of nausea.

"Probably because they couldn't break into the fire-control AI. Warships have a whole AI dedicated to overseeing just the weapons, and if they're still locked out of it, they've got no choice, they have to shoot by eye," Icky said. As she spoke, her own hands were tapping controls, rerouting power around battle damage, and shoring up systems that were starting to falter.

"Perry, are *we* almost ready to shoot?"

"I've got hard data links to all three missiles, so I'm ready to shoot any time. But if you want this to work, we need to get a little closer," he replied.

I hissed in frustration. Even firing manually, it was getting hard for whoever was crewing the heavy cruiser to miss at what amounted to point-blank range. The worst part, though, was that everyone was busy doing something, except for me. I'd essentially become the classic supervisor, at risk of getting in the way more than helping.

But I had to do something. "How about using glitter? It could help protect us from laser hits, right?"

"Only if you're willing to fly in essentially a straight line, at a constant velocity," Netty said. "Anything but minimal maneuvering is just going to have us exit the glitter cloud."

"Yeah, understood, Netty. Is it better than trying to anticipate and dodge their shots, though?"

"For a short while, it probably is, yes, until incoming fire vaporizes enough of the glitter to strip away its protection."

I tried not to grind my teeth in frustration at Netty's measured reply. "How long?"

"One minute, give or take ten seconds."

"Perry, how long do you need?"

"As this rate of closure, about thirty seconds—"

"Firing glitter," I snapped, almost pounding the glitter-caster control. Four canisters erupted from the caster, flew about a klick to the left, right, above, and below the *Fafnir*, then detonated. In an instant, we were surrounded by a scintillating cloud of shimmering alloy foil.

"Ooh, pretty," Torina said, sinking back in her seat and taking a breath. Sweat gleamed on her face. The glitter had another benefit, giving her—hell, giving all of us—a moment to catch our breath.

"Almost there. When we fire, though, we have to emerge from this cloud or I won't be able to properly target the missiles," Perry said.

I glanced at Torina, who blew out a sigh, nodded, and sat up again, her fingers ready on the *Fafnir*'s maneuver controls.

Dazzling flashes lit up the glitter as powerful laser blasts ripped into it. A cloud several klicks across, it wasn't hard to hit, but the stuff was superb against virtually every frequency of laser energy, scattering much of it, and absorbing most of the rest. We registered several non-damaging hits, but the cloud was already starting to look thin.

"And… we're at optimum range. Torina-- when you're ready," Perry said.

She glanced at me, and I nodded, once. "Go for it."

Torina applied thrust, and we exited the cloud. An instant later, Perry fired all three of our reconfigured missiles. They leapt away, their drive plumes fierce points of white light. And an instant after that, a laser hit slammed into the *Fafnir* almost squarely head-on, and everything turned white.

I BLINKED AS FAST as I could, trying to clear away the massive, purple splotches that had replaced my vision. My first thought was, oh well, at least I'm alive... followed immediately by *I'm blind*. But things began to resolve again, including the *Fafnir*'s instrument panel, which seemed to be mostly colored red.

"Torina, break off!" I shouted, but Perry cut right in.

"Belay that, Torina. Impact—now."

I was stunned that Perry had been able to maintain control of the missiles despite the serious hit we'd taken. I could just make out the zoomed image of the heavy cruiser windowed into the tactical overlay, and I saw the missiles impact with searing flashes of light. I almost groaned, for a moment thinking that, after all this, we'd just ended up destroying the damned thing anyway.

But when the image cleared, I could see the cruiser rotating, showing us her port rear quarter, then her whole port flank. My toes instinctively cramped inside my boots as I expected a full broadside to follow. But it didn't, and the cruiser kept turning—port forward quarter, then bow-on, then starboard forward quarter, starboard flank, and eventually back to stern-on. And then she started all over again.

"She's tumbling out of control, and her drive has scrammed and shut down," Icky said.

I glanced back in her general direction, but the middle chunk of my field of vision was still splotchy. "You've confirmed that from the scans?"

"Oh, hell no. The scanners are offline, along with everything else but a few critical systems. But I… know. I just know. She's just a spinning derelict now."

I tapped Perry on the head. "That was damned fine shooting, my metallic-feathered friend."

"It's a living."

I knew Perry had no actual ego, but I heaped the praise on him anyway. He'd managed to simultaneously launch, track, and precisely target three missiles flying like proverbial bats out of hell, and do it in a real-time window of just a few seconds. The three missiles had slammed into the cruiser's drive bells, transferring their fearsome kinetic energy to the tough alloy constructs and not only knocking them out of alignment, but starting the other ship tumbling.

In other words, it had been perfect—which is why what Netty said next didn't surprise me one bit.

"Van, the Peacemakers who have been holding back are asking if we need help," she said.

I laughed. "Yeah—no. We did this much on our own, and to the victor go the spoils."

"Is that what you want to tell them?"

"Nah, just lie to them and say we appreciate their timely offer of assistance, but we have things under control. On second thought—tell them to enjoy their day elsewhere, too."

"Got it, boss. Maximum snark."

OKAY, *almost* under control.

The trouble we now faced was what to do with the big ship. It still had a crew of some unknown number of thieves onboard and was tumbling uncontrolled. We decided to deal with the first problem and abate her ponderous spin. It took an hour of carefully maneuvering the *Fafnir* into a stationary position relative to the cruiser—an expensive proposition in terms of fuel, and a demanding one in terms of flying the ship—then attaching a monofilament tow cable and expending yet more fuel in a series of careful bursts to reduce her spin. Ironically, our brief blasts of thrust, which had to be directed toward the cruiser to achieve the effect we wanted, probably did more damage to her than anything we'd done. Moreover, now we *could* have used the help of the other Peacemakers, but they'd all left after our chilly rebuff of their attempts to share in the glory.

And bonds.

Icky finally declared the cruiser as stationary as we were going to manage. She still spun, but we'd reduced the rate to a complete revolution every ten minutes or so.

Which meant that it was now time to board her and deal with whoever had stolen the thing in the first place.

We didn't dock the *Fafnir* but just parked her about fifty meters from the cruiser's airlock under Netty's control and crossed to the bigger ship. Perry hacked us in through the airlock, and we entered, armored and bombed up, weapons raised, ready for a fight.

Nothing.

I swung The Drop from side to side as we advanced into the main, central corridor of the cruiser. We had to move with care because the ship's internal gravity was wonky, as I proved to myself by slamming my helmet against an overhead fixture. The emergency lighting was on, and the ship was still pressurized, but we nonetheless moved as though we might run into hostiles any time. Torina and Icky turned and started sternward, heading for engineering, while Perry and I made our destination the bridge.

We encountered no one, and neither did Torina and Icky. When Perry and I reached a point just a few meters behind the bridge, we stopped and took cover.

I listened to the ship, which was eerily silent. Running on emergency power, her air recyclers only worked intermittently. When they weren't operating, there was literally no noise that we didn't make ourselves.

It was menacing, right down to the odd clicks of expanding joint plates, like an abandoned building cooling after sunset.

"Perry, is there any chance there's no one on board? That maybe this was all programmed into the ship's AI?"

"Including simulating shitty shooting over what amounts to open sights on the laser batteries? I'm thinking probably not."

I peered around the corner, at the door leading into the bridge. "Well then, let's see who's home. Can you do your dazzle thing?"

"Already warmed up," Perry replied and launched himself toward the door. I followed, ready to shoot The Drop at the first thing that presented even a hint of threat.

The blast door had been closed to seal off the bridge, but Perry pointed out that someone had cracked the panel and hotwired it to bypass the security lockouts and open it manually. So I took advantage of the thieves' work and opened the door. Perry flung himself into the bridge, flaring emissions across the spectrum and flooding the space with light and noise. As soon as he cut the effect, I leapt into the doorway, The Drop ready to fire.

"Found the crew," Perry said, alighting on what must have been the captain's station. Sure enough, figures were sprawled around the bridge. I counted four, all of them Nesit, all groaning and looking as though they'd been beaten up.

"What the hell happened to them?" I asked Perry.

"If I had to guess, I'd say that they were subjected to—let's see, considering how fast this thing was spinning, I'd say the bridge was probably subjected to about three g's of acceleration. And since the internal gravity is only offsetting about one half of a g of that, I'd further say that these clowns were squashed against anything to port of them by about two and a half times their own body weight, for over an hour."

"Ouch."

"Right? Imagine if you suddenly weighed, like, seven hundred pounds."

I narrowed my eyes at Perry. "You think I weigh almost three hundred pounds?"

"Sorry, Van, but my arithmetic processor must be on the fritz. I'm sure you weigh *much* less than that."

"Van, we found two Nesit back here. Both of them are looking a little bedraggled," Torina said over the comm.

"Yeah, four more up here in the same shape. Perry said it's because the ship was spinning like a big centrifuge," I replied.

"Looks good on 'em. What do you want us to do with them, boss?" Icky asked.

"Hold that thought." I turned to one of the Nesit, the one who'd apparently been in the captain's station. He had managed to get to his elbows, but only with a lot of wincing and hissing.

"Why, hello there. Tell me, where are you all going in such a hurry?" I asked him.

He gave me a defiant look, or as defiant a look as he could manage, anyway. "We're not… saying anything," he rasped.

I shrugged. "Suit yourself. Icky, do you think we can get this thing back to Anvil Dark?"

"The twist drive's working fine, and if we can hack the ship's nav AI, we can probably get her there. But she's got basically no normal space maneuver capability outside of thrusters, so she'd have to be towed from her twist point to the station."

"How long?"

"Um, couple of hours, maybe?"

"Please go ahead. Torina, you, Perry, and I will secure our prisoners."

The Nesit commander tried to intervene. "I demand that—"

I pointed The Drop at him and knelt beside him. "You, the one who stole this ship and tried to kill me and my crew, are demanding *what*, exactly? Please, I'm all ears."

The Nesit just groaned and sank back. "Never mind."

"Not very chatty, are they?" Perry said, hopping toward an open bridge terminal to start digging into the ship's computers.

"Nope, but I still like them better than the Fren."

"Because they're not quite so dumb?"

"No. They're not as *moist*."

7

SINCE IT WAS EVIDENCE, the heavy cruiser—which had no name, only a hull number—remained at dock at Anvil Dark, being scoured by the Guild's techs. It was partly to determine if there was anything else on board that might be illegal, but also because it never hurt to have detailed schematics of ships stored and ready to access in Guild databases. Unfortunately, since it was a warship, we couldn't actually claim salvage on it, because it remained the property of the Seven Stars League. On the bright side, though, the League agreed to pay the full four hundred thousand bond reward, since the damage to their cruiser had actually been minimal. It ended up costing us almost half of that to repair the damage done to the *Fafnir*, but at least we'd still come out well ahead.

Now, standing with Icky outside the *Fafnir* in a docking hangar, we could see the full extent of that damage. The laser blast that had temporarily blinded me had left the *Fafnir*'s nose scoured and pitted, almost penetrating the armor in a few places. The canopy, which prevented us from being permanently blinded or simply fried where we sat also needed to be replaced.

"We're actually lucky," Icky said.

I glanced at her. "Lucky?"

"Yeah. That blast caught her full on her prow, which is one of the toughest parts of the ship. Has to be, to resist micrometeorite impacts and dust abrasion and such. If the beam had hit a few meters higher or to one side, we'd probably have decompressed, and maybe even lost control of the *Fafnir* completely," she explained in a matter-of-fact tone.

She sounded far too blasé when discussing a near-death experience, but then I was coming to accept the fact that engineers see the world a bit differently at times.

Or all the time.

A dour maintenance support crew arrived soon after with our requested replacement parts loaded onto an AI-controlled sled. Given that we were receiving new armor plates, along with a Dragonet nose assembly and canopy, lugging everything by hand wasn't really an option. I let Icky do the actual receiving, giving her the chance to inspect the items before signing off. She pored over them with a handheld scanner, looking for defects.

And she found one—a microscopic crack about a quarter of the width of one of the applique plates. That led to an animated debate between her and the support crew foreman, a squat alien with dark, gnarled skin that looked like stone.

I just crossed my arms and watched, fascinated. Perry appeared, landing on the repair gantry we used to access the upper parts of the ship.

"What's up, Van?"

"I am watching a four-armed, anthropomorphic ape who happens to be a brilliant engineer arguing with a guy who looks like a boulder over defective spaceship armor. Gotta admit that I did *not* see this coming back when I was a kid."

"You were such a cute kid, too. Although, what the hell was up with those baggy jeans hanging halfway down your ass when you were fifteen? Those looked, uh——"

"Stupid?" Netty suggested.

I sighed. "*Et tu*, Netty? Not that you can understand the intricacies of youth fashion, you overly aggressive toaster. Anyway, I was being all cool and—well, trying to be cool, at least. Besides, there was a certain Kaitlyn Green at my school, thank you very much. I had to announce my coolness with authority. I chose denim as one such vector."

"The things that get your species' reproductive hormones secreting, I tell ya. And I have my doubts as to your success with the aforementioned Kaitlyn."

"Excuse me? I was——"

"Yeah, no. Anyone who uses the term *vector* in a stylized mating ritual is going to die alone, and no, don't shoot that look at me. You know I'm right. Anyway, the techs searching that battlecruiser found something interesting," Perry said.

I glanced at him. "Interesting, as in interesting to *us*?"

"Depends how you define *interesting* in relation to *us*——"

"If I wanted pedantry, bird, I'd go look up my eleventh grade English teacher," I said, grabbing my sidearm. "Especially after you slandered my appeal during what was admittedly my awkward years. Alright, Icky, I'm going to leave this in all four of your capable hands. Perry and I have something *interesting* to check out."

"More like *awkward decade*," Perry said. "I saw your yearbooks."

With great dignity, I waved Perry forward, saying nothing. Sometimes, being classy is hard.

"WELL, THAT IS INTERESTING—I GUESS," I said, slowly walking around the thing on the table. I made a complete circuit, then looked at Steve, the alien who ran Anvil Dark's engineering and tech shop. "What is it?"

I was studying a contraption composed of metallic rods and crystalline polyhedrons—mostly spheres, but also a few cubes and tetrahedrons—that made me think of models of molecules we used to assemble in science class. This one was obviously much more elaborate and—

I stopped, staring hard at the unknown object.

"I think he's seen it," Steve said.

I pointed at it. "Is that a figure? Something kind of humanoid?"

Perry nodded. "From that angle, yes. Come take a look at it again from directly opposite."

I did. Sure enough, I saw another figure outlined by the sticks and balls and things. It wasn't the same figure, though. Somehow, the first had radiated a sense of humility and supplication, while the second seemed to be all about power and control.

I walked back and forth, eyeing the two figures rendered in the arrangement of the pieces. "Okay, have to admit that that's pretty cool. Still doesn't answer the question, though. What is it?"

Torina, who'd been attending to some administrative matters

with the Anvil Dark bureaucracy, strolled into the room. "There you are—oh. Where did you get the Pathway Unburdened icon?"

I blinked at her. "You recognize this?"

"Actually, Van, we all do. I was just about to do the big reveal when Torina came in and spoiled it," Perry grouched.

"I recognize it because my aunt had something very much like it once when she joined the order. She eventually unburdened herself of it, too, when she decided to become an explorer."

"An explorer," I said.

Torina shrugged. "It was her dream, for some reason, or so she claimed. She jettisoned her life, bought a ship, and declared she was going to—let's see, how did she put it? Oh, right. *Expand the boundaries of known space, but more importantly, the boundaries of our knowledge.* She said it just that way, too, making it sound all significant and portentous."

"She sounds like a free spirit."

"Free spirit. Let's go with that. After all, crazy as hell has all sorts of negative connotations."

I smiled but turned back to Steve and Perry. "Pathway Unburdened sounds like some sort of religion, or cult, or something."

Steve raised an appendage. "We have a winner! Yes, it's a religious movement that started about a hundred years ago. It purports to show sentient beings a higher, more pure existence, unburdened of the troubles and cares of mundane life."

"I assume that includes unburdening their money, too," I replied.

"Gee, Van, it's almost like you know the good High Doctor Markov."

"Markov? So the grand high poohbah of this outfit is human? And from Russia?"

"Not exactly. You know how Retta is way into French culture? Well, the High Doctor is a big fan of Russian culture. From Earth. Specifically the time of the Czars," Perry said.

"You felt it necessary to specify Earth in case I confused it with Russian Culture from Antares?"

"Van, Antares is over five hundred light-years away, well outside the boundaries—"

"Didn't we *just* have a chat about being pedantic?"

"Yes we did, Mister Jumping On Me Casually Mentioning His Homeworld."

Torina frowned in thought. "Russian culture, under the Czars. Right…" She stopped and brightened. "Oh. They're the ones with those lovely, sparkly, ornate eggs, aren't they? The ones made of precious metals and stones?"

"They… are, yeah. Faberge Eggs. Very good. Someone's been doing their homework, I see."

She shrugged. "I became quite fond of Groshenko and his stories about Russia, so I figured I'd dig into them a bit."

I sniffed. "How does this keep happening? The whole aliens-adopting-earth-culture thing?"

Perry answered, "Earth has a lot of varied cultures—an unusually diverse number of them for a single species on a single planet, actually. More importantly, you humans broadcast into the void without any hint of information security or coding."

"I *have* heard humanity referred to as the biggest reality show in the galaxy," Steve put in.

"So you're saying there's a larping alien who thinks they're a Czar because we didn't scramble our radio broadcasts?"

Perry returned his avian shrug. "Pretty much."

"So what else is out there? A planet modeled after Chicago gangs of the thirties? One based on Rome? A world full of Nazis?"

"Don't be silly, Van. Individuals might style themselves after some Earthly culture, but whole planets? I mean, seriously," Perry said.

"Fine. In any case, is there a reward—"

Netty cut me off. "There isn't a single reward for breaking into the Pathway Unburdened and their scheme. There are actually three. I assumed this question would come up eventually."

"Okay. And these total how many bonds?"

"Almost two hundred thousand, in exchange for gaining entrance to their church, because of what they're doing—hacking financial networks as well as conning people out of their money."

I clapped my hands together. "Well then, once the *Fafnir* is flying again, our first stop will be the Quiet Room."

"Why there?" Torina asked.

"Because you mentioned hacking financial networks. Now, I've done jobs that involve hacking financial networks back on Earth, and it was banks that usually ended up on the losing end of those schemes. I suspect that The Quiet Room has lost more than a few bonds to our friendly Czarist cult leader. And, frankly? We could use the help."

HIGH DOCTOR MARKOV WAS A SYNIFEX, a reclusive race whose adult forms stood almost eight feet tall, had a long flat head ringed with eyes, eight limbs—four that functioned as arms, and four as legs—and was slightly translucent. It was the last I found especially off-putting. I'd been exposed to enough alien species now that I accepted the array of life.

But seeing a person's plumbing in action was… a bit much.

I grimaced at the image Netty windowed into the *Fafnir's* tactical display. It had taken her a few days scouring many different sources to find an image of the good High Doctor.

"You know, when I hear the word *Czar*, that is not the first thing that comes to mind. I mean, not only does he *not* wear pants, but I can see his guts." He didn't wear clothing, or anything else, for that matter, aside from some sparkling bracelets on all eight of his limbs, along with a headband. "And the headband and bracelets have ruined 80s culture for me. Forever."

Perry bobbed his head. "I'm an artificially intelligent machine, and even *I'm* kind of grossed out, yeah. What kind of high priest wears *rhinestones?*"

"Really? That's what offends you here, bird?"

Perry opened his beak in a laugh. "The visible guts aren't helping much, boss."

"Glad we're on the same page," I said, turning my head to regard the screens. Just then, Procyon system's traffic control cut in, confirming that they were clearing us to make planetfall at Outward, the outermost of the three habitable planets orbiting the big, pale blue-hued star and its almost invisible white dwarf companion. The Quiet Room's largest public-facing facility was located on a moon orbiting Outward, whose technical name was

Outward Alpha. Most people just called it The Quiet Room, since the bank, its staff, and their families were the only ones who lived there. And they did so in the lap of relative luxury, living in what amounted to a gated community that handled its own local security and traffic control.

Procyon traffic handed us over to their Quiet Room counterpart, which guided us the rest of the way to the surface. We settled the *Fafnir* down on an elevated landing pad, one of a dozen or so that radiated like spokes from the towering edifice at its hub, the Quiet Room facility itself. Meandering rivers wound among green fields and forests, throughout which were scattered the dwellings of The Quiet Room's staff. The first time I'd been here, I'd been so overwhelmed I hadn't really taken much of it in. This time, I was struck by the similarity between this pastoral landscape and Torina's homeworld, Helso. Most of the homes even resembled her family's ancestral estate.

As we walked toward the grav car that would whisk us to the central office, I waved an appreciative hand at the scene. "Reminds me of Helso. And Iowa."

She took my arm, smiling out over the landscape. "The Quiet Room used the Synergists to landscape their facilities. It was my father's connections to the bank that actually first put us onto them."

I stopped, breathed in air that tasted almost sweet, and sighed. "Oh, space hippies. Is there anything you *can't* do?"

We made our way to the main complex and were eventually ushered into the office of Dayna Jasskin, the same woman I'd met previously, shortly after my first trip off Earth. The striking picture that had grabbed me the first time I met her, one of

Zagreb, her hometown in Croatia, still emblazoned the wall behind her desk.

"Peacemaker Tudor, how are you?" she asked.

I flashed my most charming smile. "Great. Much more space worthy than the last time we met for sure."

She turned to Torina. "And Ms. Milon, nice to see you again as well. I understand that you finally seem to have things under control on your family's homeworld?"

"We do. I think. I still find myself waiting for yet another shoe to drop, though."

Dayna gave her a quizzical look. "I'm sorry, someone's going to drop a shoe? Why? What does that have to do with—?"

"Blame me for that. She's obviously picking up my little idioms. The shoe dropping is a metaphor for something bad happening," I said.

"Ah. Alright, shall we get to business," Dayna said, gesturing at a pair of chairs facing her expansive desk. They were profoundly comfortable, leading me to realize that even furniture technology was more advanced out here in space than it was on Earth.

"So I'll just park myself over here with the end table, shall I?" Perry said.

We all turned to him, and I frowned. "What?"

Torina gave me a stage whisper. "He didn't get introduced."

"But—you know Dayna already. You and Netty brought me here, remember?"

Perry shrugged. "It's just nice to be noticed."

Dayna drew herself up, gave a small bow, and smiled warmly. "You are, of course, correct, Perry. My apologies."

Perry dipped his beak in thanks, then turned to me. "Now *that* is what I call manners."

"I'll stock tea and crumpets forthwith," I said.

"Delighted, boss."

"May we continue?"

Perry extended a wing with some gallantry. "Please do."

Dayne took this all in stride, then asked me one question. "What can we do for each other, Peacemaker?"

"Do you know anything about a… being… named High Doctor Markov?"

Dayna actually twitched at that, then clasped her hands in a deliberate calming movement. "Ah. Yes. The Pathway Unburdened."

I smiled a little smugly. "Figured you'd know them. They've indirectly hustled you, haven't they? When you've had to cover clients' losses when your networks got hacked?"

"I can neither officially confirm nor deny any financial transactions conducted by the bank on behalf of its clients," Dayna recited, then leaned forward. "Off the record, though, yes—those sneaky, greedy assholes have cost us plenty."

"Why haven't you done something about them?" Torina asked. "Or, to be more specific, to them?"

"You have. You've reviewed your internal procedures and tightened network security. Am I right?" I asked.

Dayna's expression turned suspicious. "Have *you* been snooping around where you shouldn't, Peacemaker? Do we need to tighten up that security even more?"

I laughed and shook my head. "Nope. This isn't my first rodeo when it comes to banks getting scammed and how they respond to it. Keep everything close and quiet so you don't spook the customers."

Both Dayna and Torina opened their mouths to ask something. I headed them off with a sigh. "A rodeo is a form of entertainment involving horses and cowboys and clowns and things, and don't you people have access to a search engine to look this stuff up?"

Dayna smiled. "Why are you bringing this to our attention today, Peacemaker?"

"Because we want to try and bust into the Path Unburdened, partly for the rewards, but partly because we're trying to piece together a much bigger scheme." I went on to summarize the identity-theft ring and its tenuous connections to other bits and pieces of criminality, ticking off points about the sheer horror of sapient beings turned into chip-based slaves.

"They—they're stealing people?" Dayna asked, her face a mask of raw disgust.

"In numbers we can't imagine, and, yes—it's as grotesque as you imagine. The Path Unburdened does business on Halcyon, which is run by another cult, the Children of Resplendence. That particular den of scum is implicated in illegal trading of stolen artifacts, which might be connected to our identity thieves. In short, we have a lot of leads, some small victories, and I think this is worth investigating," I finished.

Dayna leaned on her desk. "You want to investigate something that may be connected to something that may itself be connected to something that's connected to something else."

"Something like that, yeah."

"Alright, that works for me. If a Peacemaker is interested in pursuing the Path Unburdened, that's all the justification I need to request a formal audit of them and their accounts."

I nodded. "That would be perfect. I'm hoping that The Quiet Room might actually be looking for a little help in doing that, as in, we'll turn over whatever information we can dig up."

Dayna gave a wicked grin, and for a moment, she looked impish and young. "That implies you have a scheme of your own in mind."

"I do. And I could use your help with it."

8

"Torina. Since I'm supposed to be filthy rich, I need to get into character. Do I need a pocket square and a contemptuous sneer?" I asked.

She raised an eyebrow. "Is that how you see me, Van? As someone who would sneer while using a—a pocket square? What is that, anyway?"

Perry chimed in, helpful as ever. "It's a piece of fabric that manages to be both haughty *and* free of function."

Torina tilted her head, then made a thoughtful noise. "Sounds fancy. But I don't sneer. Not often, anyway."

"When you do, I'm sure it's justified."

She reached out and pulled my lips down at the corner. "There. Now you look rich."

I let my lips rise to their normal position. "And sad. Not sure I can do both."

"Fair point. Let's just be… confident."

"I'm always confident," Perry added. "Part of my charm."

"Add charming to the list, and we're ready. Which reminds me, are we ready?" I asked Torina.

"We are. It's a good plan, if a touch obvious. But yes. We're ready," she said, fixing her features into something harder, with lifted brows and a subtle affectation of boredom.

Our plan came into being after a discussion with Dayna, as well as Lunzy, and the plan was simple—open subterfuge. Torina and I would travel to Halcyon, where the Pathway Unburdened maintained a small presence that was effectively a recruiting office. I wasn't sure why the Children of Resplendence were okay with having another cult—sorry, *unapproved faith system*—operating on their turf. I assumed it had something to do with money, because everything has something to do with money, and not some spiritual concordance between the two. For that matter, Halcyon might be cult central, a sort of clearinghouse peddling various types of salvation at market rates.

Which brought us back to money, or more correctly, *following* said money. Dayna was able to provide us with a loaned yacht and pilot, and a pile of bonds to throw around. I was surprised that The Quiet Room was willing to be so generous with its help, and said so.

Dayna had leaned on her desk. "Have you ever been involved in a forensic audit, Van?"

"Yes, actually. Well, peripherally, anyway. Back on Earth, I acquired the contents of a database or two and provided them to, ah, certain enforcement agencies so they could audit the crap out of them."

"Did you get paid well?"

"Well… yeah, I guess. It was one of the best paying gigs I'd done to that point. Why?"

She raised a finger. "And did you actually do the audit on the data you acquired? Did you—?" She paused and turned to her assistant, the androgynous and incredibly analytical Chensun, who'd taken up their discreetly accustomed place behind and to one side of Dayna's desk. "Chensun, you've done far more of these audits than I have. Assume this one is of, let's say, middling difficulty. What would be involved?"

Chensun's reply was immediate, delivered in their usual blandly pleasant tone. "A minimum of two thousand, one hundred and twenty person hours of work in immediate analysis, with overhead of five hundred and sixty-two person hours in ancillary support and overhead, associated salaries at a standard rate of seventy-five bonds per hour, plus twenty percent for benefits, for a ninety bonds per hour, plus associated—"

I held up a hand. "I get it. It's expensive."

"Chensun, what would be the expected bottom line?" Dayna asked.

Again, an immediate reply. "Between one hundred and seventy-five thousand and two hundred thousand bonds."

Dayna smiled. "And that assumes a forensic audit of average difficulty. If it gets particularly tricky, the cost can shoot straight up, like that ship of yours out there when it launches." Still smiling, she shrugged. "You see why providing you with a hundred thousand bonds and the cost of operating a yacht for a few days actually stands to save The Quiet Room money, if you manage to break open this… organization."

"Yes, but we might not succeed," Torina noted.

Dayna's smile didn't change. "Indeed. And then the next time you come to us looking for assistance, I'm afraid you'll have to stand in line at one of the teller's wickets."

I was surprised. "You actually have tellers?"

"No, we don't."

"Ah."

So here we were, preparing to travel to Halcyon in the lap of someone else's luxury, to throw around money that wasn't ours. The one consolation was that failure didn't carry what seemed to be its usual consequence of a miserable death in space. It simply meant The Quiet Room would write us off as a worthwhile investment. Conversely, though, if we pulled it off, we'd gain a very powerful ally.

At least until the next time we lost their money.

I looked in the mirror, a deck-to-overhead extravaganza surrounded by lights. Only a yacht would waste space and mass on something as ostentatious as an illuminated, full-length mirror. Considering the queen-sized bed, expansive stateroom with its own shower and lavatory, and general luxury, I could get used to being ostentatious.

But we weren't at Halcyon yet. We were still orbiting Outward in company with the *Fafnir*, and I didn't need to look uncomfortably wealthy. I unfastened my tight collar and rubbed my neck.

"What happened to everyone in the far future wearing the same thing, usually a pastel pant suit or something made of metallic fabric?" I asked my reflection.

Torina, who'd been adjusting her own outfit, shot me a look. "What the hell are you talking about?"

"I—never mind. Just another of those science fiction tropes."

"Are you still going on about those? Wasn't the fact that not every alien species is—what did you say? Like humans, but with different forehead bumps?"

"And noses," I said, peeling off the stiff tunic and flexing my arms through their new-found freedom.

"And noses, sure. Anyway, didn't that maybe convince you that your fictional worlds don't really live up to the reality?"

I shrugged and opened my mouth to say something clever right back, though I wasn't entirely sure what, but Netty cut me off.

"Van, Lunzy just transmitted something I think you're going to want to see."

I felt Torina tense. I know how she felt because I felt exactly the same thing—*now what?*

"Send it over, Netty," I said.

The stateroom terminal flicked to an image of—a bar?

"Is that your cousin?" Torina asked.

"It—is, yeah. It's Carter, and he seems to be in the Black Hole back on Anvil Dark." I frowned. "Why the hell would Lunzy think I'd have a hankering to see Carter drinking?"

Torina pointed. "That's why."

Carter had fished out a stack of bonds and ordered a round for the house. Given the cheers, and how packed the bar was, I didn't think it was the first round he'd bought, either. There was audio, Carter slurring something to the bartender with a boozy, shit-eating grin on his face.

"Netty, can you clean up that sound so I can hear Carter?" I asked.

The image froze, flicked back about fifteen seconds, then played again. This time, Carter's words were just intelligible over the background chatter.

"—amazing, am I right? Eh? It's just—just money. Hell, all this money from the empty space, I tell ya, it's—you know what? I'm making more money than a freakin'—um, god! A god! Gods are rich, right? And this god is gonna buy another round, another round for everybody—!"

The swell of cheers and table pounding drowned out the rest. I froze the image and turned to Torina.

"Do me a favor. Switch on your natural charm and let Dayna know that our Pathway Unburdened job has to wait." I turned back to Carter's stupid grin. "I feel like I need to know how my shitbag cousin is flashing stacks of bonds all of a sudden, considering how broke he was just a couple of weeks ago. He's never worked an honest day in his life, and out here, dishonesty usually means someone is suffering somehow."

Torina nodded. "I'd say to just ignore him, but yeah. I can't forget Lunzy mentioning him being in Master Yotov's camp—and how she seems connected, even distantly, to nearly everything we're trying to investigate here."

"So it's not just me being resentful of Carter."

"If it were, I'd say so. So, no, I don't think it is. Something is definitely going on."

I glared at the screen. "More money than a god. I mean, seriously. I just wish we had an idea of what he meant by that *empty space* crack. How do you get money from empty space? Is it maybe something about—I don't know, cargo capacity? A cargo that went missing or got stolen—?"

Netty cut in. "I think I may have an answer to that. A ship

recently departed Anvil Dark. Care to guess its name?"

"The… Empty Space?"

"Winner, winner turkey dinner."

I smiled. "I think it's chicken dinner, actually."

"I know, but your grandfather made his preference for turkey over chicken clear."

I just stared at that. Netty was right. Gramps would rant about chickens, calling them wannabe turkeys and eschewing chicken as a menu item, whether eating out or at home. I even remembered him bringing up Benjamin Franklin, who'd proposed the wild turkey as the official National Bird of the United States, not the bald eagle.

I'd forgotten all about Gramps' hard line on chickens. *Huh.* I made a mental note to talk to Perry and Netty when we had some downtime and see what else their flawless memories could fill in. I sensed that my own family history was at hand—in the memories of my new AI friends.

Right now, though, the important matter was finding out how Carter was suddenly flush with cash and what that had to do with the *Empty Space.* Maybe he just made a good deal on some cargo, earning a tidy profit from it.

Maybe. Except, where Carter was concerned, I'd long ago learned to kick the rock completely over and see what, exactly, *was* squirming beneath it.

———

"Netty, follow that car," I said as the *Fafnir* spun onto her new heading and accelerated.

"Car?"

"Car, ship, whatever."

Perry glanced at me. "Remind me to never go driving with you."

"Update from Lunzy, by the way. She said Carter's still staggering around the bars, pickled drunk," Netty reported. We were well away from Anvil Dark, having made a brief stop for fuel and tags. The tags were a nifty bit of tech that we could use to track enemies, and thanks to Icky leaning on the quartermaster, we now had four of them, free of charge.

Sometimes, being the size of two linebackers in a trench coat was a good thing.

"Is Lunzy still on the channel?" I asked.

"Sure. Put her on?" Netty replied.

"Please do." I heard the channel open with a click. "Lunzy, how drunk is he?"

"Hammered. Wearing-the same-clothes kind of drunk. You should see him. His hair is. . .quite something," Lunzy said. "And talk about throwing bonds around. Does the guy not realize the value of money?"

"Oh. No. No-no-no. Carter never wanted for a dime in his life. If he wanted money, he just asked mommy and daddy for it," I replied.

"Well, as a rough estimate, I'd say he's dropped nearly ten thousand bonds around Anvil Dark so far. Is he going to keep this up until he's broke?"

I returned a wry smile. "Is water wet?"

Lunzy procured the *Empty Space*'s flight plan for us, and assuming it wasn't bogus, the ship had transited to Crossroads, and then to Spindrift. We were able to confirm her arrival at and departure from the first, but she hadn't yet shown up at the second. That meant she was either taking her sweet time, was in trouble, or had no actual intention of going to Spindrift. I assumed the latter.

So did Lunzy. She alerted Gus, the Guild's Station Chief at Crossroads, and asked him to do some discreet investigating to see if he could determine where the *Empty Space* was actually headed. Fortunately, Gus was well-connected enough on Crossroads that he was able to tease out a probable destination, based on a surreptitious request for navigation data that turned out to be not quite surreptitious enough. The *Empty Space* had inquired about any traffic that might be heading to, or arriving from the poetically named WISE 1639−6847. I expected yet another of the monotonous succession of red dwarf stars, but this one turned out to be a lonely brown dwarf.

"There is absolutely nothing there. It doesn't even get used as a navigation waypoint because it's not near any well-traveled routes," Netty reported.

"That's not suspicious at all," I said, then told Netty to *follow that car.*

The trip to WISE 1639−6847 was an unremarkable one and, as expected, so was the almost-star itself. It was a barely visible purplish dot surrounded by virtually nothing closer in than the usual array of rocky debris forming its Kuiper Belt. We'd twisted in just outside it, counting on the distance and the debris to mask us while we looked the system over.

"There are four other ships present in this system. One of them matches the configuration of the Empty Space, a class twelve freighter. The other three are class fifteen bulk carriers. There appear to be robotic loaders moving cargo between them, but we're too far away to determine much more than that."

I studied the various icons painted onto the tactical overlay. "Three bulk carriers. That's an awful lot of carrying capacity for— what, exactly?"

Torina shrugged. "Good question."

Icky turned from her panel. "Boss, if you're willing to let some heat accumulate, I think we can do a hard burn now, then cut the drive and coast inward without presenting much of a signature."

"How much heat?"

"As much as you can stand, at least until I can't safely put any more heat into the *Fafnir*'s internal structure."

I glanced back at her. "We can do that?"

She grinned. "We can now. It's a little feature I added while we were doing repairs, using the internal structure as a heat sink. Surprise!"

I grinned back. "Alrighty then. Let's get a little closer and see if we can figure out what's going on."

ICKY'S SCHEME TO store heat in the *Fafnir*'s bones was a clever one, but far from perfect. Two hours after cutting the ship's drive, her internal temperature touched forty degrees Celsius. We all removed unnecessary clothing and sat in little more than our underwear, sheened in sweat.

"Oh, you wacky biological entities, you. What you need is a way to better manage your energy budget," Perry said.

I shot him a glare, which had an edge to it because of the stifling heat in the cockpit. "We're kind of stuck with what nature has given us, oh manufactured one."

"Too bad. See, if you did what I do and run your waste heat through a reclamator, then use the current to recharge your power-cells, you could go a lot longer without getting overheated, or having to eat, or… sweating. I mean, seriously, how much liquid do you plan to release from your skin? It's such an inefficient cooling system."

I hardened my glare. "You do realize that all this biological stuff just *happens*, right? That we can't just—"

"Van, the *Empty Space* is no longer present in this system," Netty cut in.

I turned to the overlay and snapped out a curse. The *Empty Space* indeed no longer registered on our scanners.

"Did they make us?" Torina asked.

Icky shook her head. "Not likely. We haven't been illuminated by active scanners, and our signature is so small on passives that they'd have to be scrutinizing this exact bit of space to even have a chance of detecting us."

"The better question is, where did they go, and how did they manage to leave without us noticing?" I asked at large but directed mostly at Netty, who was supposed to stay on top of things like this.

"I have no idea where they went. But as for how they left without us noticing, they were in close proximity to those three bulk carriers, and all four of them are far enough from the brown dwarf to safely twist."

"So the *Empty Space* just twisted away somewhere, right from where they were parked," Torina said.

"So it would appear."

"Van, we can have a warrant issued in every port and station across the known galaxy," Perry said.

"Do it. And let me know the second they're found. I was curious before. Now I'm pissed." I blew out a frustrated sigh. "Especially in this heat. Icky, how much longer can we safely do this?"

"As far as the *Fafnir*'s concerned, another four hours, maybe as much as six."

"I don't even want to think what the temperature will be here by then," Torina said, wiping sweat from her forehead.

"At the current rate of increase, sixty-eight degrees Celsius," Perry added helpfully.

"Guess that's too much for you guys, huh?" Icky asked.

Torina turned to her. "It wouldn't be for you?"

Icky shrugged. "The Wu'tzur homeworld can break seventy degrees near the equator on a summer day. That's definitely starting to get uncomfortable."

"Yeah, well, we left starting to get uncomfortable about a million klicks behind us. We'll give it another half hour, then the AC is coming back on," I said.

We actually managed another twenty minutes, and I'd had enough. I was about to say so when Perry spoke up.

"Van, we started intercepting broadcasts from those ships about fifteen minutes ago. I've been analyzing them and think that there's at least one, and probably several stolen identities out there."

I sat up, wincing as my sweaty skin stuck slightly to the seat. "First things first. Icky, let's start cooling things down."

I turned to Perry. "Can you tell anything about them? Who they are? Where they're from?"

"There's only one doing most of the broadcasting. It seems to be coming from one of the robotic loaders. The others are just sending out intermittent signals."

"Can we talk to the chatty one?"

"You can try. It's not making a lot of sense, though. In fact, they don't sound sane at all. They sound kind of… broken."

I nodded but paused to sigh as cool air began to waft around me. "Okay. Put them through if you can."

The comm came to life with—humming?

"Hello? This is Peacemaker Van Tudor—"

"Are you real?"

"I—um, yeah. Yeah, I'm real. And so are you. You're—"

"I'm not real. I miss the blue."

I glanced at Torina, who just stared and shrugged.

"You miss the blue? The blue what, exactly?"

"It fills the sky. It seals away the black. I don't like the black. I don't. It—it scares me, it's everywhere, always everywhere—"

I stared at the comm panel, as if it might offer some clue as to how to deal with this obviously damaged soul. As I did, Torina leaned forward.

"My name's Torina. Can you tell us—?"

"The blue, I miss the blue so much, it fills the sky, but it's so dark now, so dark away from the pits."

Torina leaned back, looking as helpless as I felt.

"What's your name?" I put in during a brief pause in their fever-dream rambling.

"I—name. I have no name. I lost it when I went below. But I couldn't see the big blue anymore, and I was lost, so lost—"

"The big blue. Tell us about the big blue," I said, trying to find traction anywhere among the stream of damaged consciousness.

"It's—it's everything. It's the sky."

"So the sky is blue where you're from?" Torina asked.

"No no no no no—not the sky. The sun. The sun is blue, and it fills the sky, but not in the pits, not in the stopes—I miss it, I can't take the blackness, the emptiness anymore, I just can't—"

Netty cut in. "Van, we're close enough for high-resolution scans of those ships. The cargo loader you're conversing with has just accelerated directly toward one of them."

I leaned forward, as though getting closer to the panel would make some sort of difference. "Listen to me. We'll take you back. We'll take you to see the big blue sun, nowhere near the pits—"

"You can't. I can't. We can't. No one can."

"Ten seconds until collision," Netty said.

"Please, listen to me! We can help you! We're here to help you!"

"I miss—blue. Just blue. I miss color. I miss blue—"

The signal cut off.

"I'm sorry, Van. The loader has just struck the port side of that bulk carrier. It's been destroyed."

I slumped back and slammed a fist down on the seat's armrest. "Shit!"

We coasted on in silence for a moment.

I wanted to hit someone. Hard. And repeatedly. Carter. Ruiz-Rocher. Master Yotov. Anyone who might be even remotely connected to the monsters that were doing this vile, obscene *shit* to other people. No one deserved that sort of horrible end.

Except for them.

I finally managed to shove words through the choking, incandescent cloud of rage and sorrow. "Netty. Broadcast mode on the comm. Flood every channel, highest possible gain."

"Done."

"This is Peacemaker Van Tudor. Pursuant to some law or other, and right now I don't really give a shit which, I'm seizing all vessels in this system immediately. You will all cut your drives, deactivate your scanners, and wait to be boarded. And if you refuse, I will blow you to pieces, and if you get away, I will *find* you and blow you to pieces."

Perry spoke up. "Van, you can't just—"

"See me doing it, Perry? That means I can."

"Van, you can't let your feelings—"

I spun on him. "What would you know about feelings, Perry? You're a machine, remember? You're already locked away inside a chip. All you can do is *simulate* feelings, *pretend* to have them—"

"Van, that's enough!" Torina snapped.

I swung my fury onto her, but she stood her ground and just stared right back. We stayed that way a moment, me practically hyperventilating with anger, her daring me to try and unleash it on her.

I blinked first and slumped back. It was like pulling the plug on a fast drain. My anger spiraled away, guilt and regret flooding in to replace it. I looked at Perry.

"Perry, I am—I am sorry. I should never have said those things because they aren't true."

"Well, technically, they are true. I really do only simulate things like emotions. They're just a complex series of electrical interactions in the hardware I use to process things like ego." He cocked his head at me but said nothing else.

He didn't need to. I just nodded. "Yeah, I get it. The same's true for all of us, isn't it?"

Icky, who'd pressed herself into the back of the cockpit and kept herself well below the radar the whole time, pointed ahead.

"Understand you being pissed off, Van. But I think the ones you should be pissed off at are that way."

"You're right. Absolutely. Icky, Torina, Netty, I'm sorry for all of that."

"Van, for the record, that outburst would barely break your grandfather's top ten angry rants in this cockpit. It might make number eight," Netty said.

"Pfft. I'd make it nine, at best," Perry said.

Torina smiled. "Sounds like you come by your temper naturally, Van."

I gave a tired smile back. "Yeah, now that I think back to some of his tirades—hell, especially the ones directed at me, and there were more than a few of those."

"We know. Like that time you went out with that girl, Nancy Dawson, and borrowed your grandfather's car. And when he opened it the next day, he found those—"

"That's... quite enough reminiscing, thank you," I said.

"He found those *what?*" Icky and Torina both asked simultaneously.

"Never you mind."

"I'll tell you guys later," Perry whispered.

I glared at him—fondly, this time. "No you won't, and that's an order, bird. Got it?"

He saluted me with a wing. "Got it, boss. I won't tell them anything."

"Ha ha, very funny. Netty, that order applies to you, too."

Perry sighed and shrugged at the others.

"Sorry, guys, I tried."

9

As we approached the bulk carriers, Perry was able to determine there were more stolen identities aboard them. Whether they were crewing them or serving other, no doubt unpleasant purposes, we weren't sure. Moreover, when we continued to broadcast orders to prepare to be boarded, all three of the big ships powered up their twist drives.

"Shit, they're going to get away," I said, but Torina abruptly flung her fingers across her weapons panel, selecting a firing mode then loosing a trio of missiles. My immediate reaction was stunned horror, until I noticed she'd fired the tags.

She shrugged. "We've got them. Might as well use them, right?"

"Look at you, being all quick-thinking."

Two of the tags landed and stuck and began broadcasting periodic bursts that would resemble a harmonic emission from a fusion reactor. For further security, they didn't contain any information, just a distinctive pulse pattern that we could detect and recognize.

The third tag missed and coasted on, dormant and silent, so we could retrieve it if we wanted.

The last of the three ships abruptly twisted away. And with that, we were alone, along with the lonely brown dwarf, and a few bits of debris from the wrecked loader that had contained a broken mind and our errant missile.

While Netty accelerated us after the tag to retrieve it, I played back the comm log of our interaction with the stolen identity. It wasn't any easier to listen to the second time around, but I gritted mental teeth and made myself stick it out, focusing on the words and not the lost and desolate misery.

"The sun is blue, and it fills the sky, he said. That sounds like a blue supergiant," Icky said.

"Well, the closest star of that type is Rigel, eight hundred and forty odd light-years away. Needless to say, that's well outside the boundaries of known space," Netty said.

"How long would it take to make that trip?" I asked.

"Time isn't a factor, Van. It would take no more 'time' to twist to Rigel than it would to twist to Anvil Dark or anywhere else. The issue is energy. Even if we burned all of our fuel in a single burst of power, we wouldn't be able to make that trip. The *Fafnir*'s twist-drive just isn't rated for that kind of distance."

"Are there any ships that could make the trip?"

"In theory? Yes, quite a few. Large ships with big twist drives and extensive fuel reserves could twist that far. They'd probably have to refuel at the other end, though," Netty replied.

I frowned at the star chart Netty had put on the central console. "Large ships like the three we just encountered?"

"Again, it depends on the specifics of their configuration, twist drive capability, and so on, but… yes, they'd likely be able to do it."

"Interesting."

"Uh-oh," Torina said, staring at me.

"What?"

"You're having another of those brilliant ideas, aren't you?"

"No."

She just gave me a look. "Van."

"Okay, maybe. But it's definitely at the half-baked stage." The *Fafnir* rotated again, burning to slow down and match the wandering tag's velocity so we could recover and refurbish it for reuse.

"What we need is an expert not just in stellar stuff, but also mining." I glanced at Perry. "Don't suppose you've got some mining expertise programmed into that nifty little brain of yours, do you?"

"A mine is a hole in the ground with a liar at the top," he replied.

"What?"

"Mark Twain. That was his definition of a mine. Other than that, I got nothing. I mean, next time we're at Anvil Dark I could download a mining module. It's going to cost a few bonds, but—"

"That's okay, Perry. I'm less interested in stats and mining tech and stuff, and more in the industry in general."

"Schegith," Torina said.

I looked at her. "What about them? Or her, since she and her race seem to be called the same thing?"

"The last time we were there, I had a really pleasant chat with her. It wandered into the realm of investment advice, and she gave me a few tips on mining ventures that I passed on to my father. She seemed to know the business pretty well."

"Well, I'm sold. Netty, can you link us to Schegith, please?"

While maneuvering to snag the tag and bring it back aboard, we got an automated reply from Schegith. She was apparently off-world and indisposed for the next few days. That left us with some time, and I knew exactly how to fill it.

I turned to the others and gave Perry a disapproving look.

"What?" he asked, looking behind him. "You're staring at me like I'm guilty of something."

"Not guilty. Just in need of… spiritual cleansing."

Perry cocked his head in suspicion. "You haven't bought into one of those online enlightenment scams, have you?"

I smiled broadly. "Absolutely not. To cleanse the years of snark and pithy remarks from you—"

"Pithy?"

"Yes, pithy. Now let me finish my plan, bird. You're going to love it."

Torina peered at me with suspicion. "Am I going to need nice clothes for this?"

I gave her a small salute, and she groaned. "Torina gets it. Good news, friends. We're all going to *church*."

"I COULD GET USED to traveling like that," I said, strolling with Torina away from the Halcyon airlock where our borrowed yacht, the *Aetherswift*, had docked. I'd spent the whole trip here lounging around her expansive suite of state and common rooms, putting my feet up on furniture polished to an insane shine, and enjoying the soft embrace of carpeted floors underfoot.

In general, I practiced being indolent. To no one's surprise, it came naturally.

Torina smiled. "All you need to do is buy yourself a yacht. My parents', which is about as basic as you can get, cost a little on the top side of two million bonds."

"Ouch."

We reached the main concourse of Halcyon, stopped, and gazed imperiously about. I'd been worried about being recognized—there *had* to be facial recognition tech and the like—but Torina and Perry had a solution to that, one that apparently wasn't uncommon among the wealthy. In order to remain discreet, rich people and celebrities often wore an impersonator, a small device mounted in a hat, headband, or similar article of clothing. It projected a distortion field that reshaped the face slightly, making bits appear different in small or large ways. Put together with more mundane disguising, it could easily make someone unrecognizable to people that didn't know them intimately well.

"You look good with a beard, by the way," Torina said, regally waving at a Yonnox uniformed in the garb of a major cargo carrier.

"Yeah, but then I have to trim it, and shape it, and—do you really think so?"

She smiled, but the Yonnox had approached us. I was curious where she was going with this.

"May I help you?"

"Yes. Our luggage is down that way, aboard our yacht. Have it retrieved and brought for us," she said, not bothering to even make eye contact.

The Yonnox stared at her, then me. I examined my fingernails and tried to look bored.

"Uh—I think you want a station—" the Yonnox began, but Torina cut him off.

"How tiresome. Darling, let's find someone who *can* attend to us," she said and sailed off without a backward glance.

"Yes, dove," I said, striding after her. I felt the Yonnox staring after us like—like *I'd* probably be staring at a couple of dismissive, rich assholes.

Torina glanced at me. "Dove?"

"Isn't that what rich people call one another? Cutesy little pet names?"

"Yes. Yes, they do. They also jump into their money off of diving boards and swim around in it, and they feast on poor people on holidays."

"Knew it. Tell Perry to wrangle a dump truck full of gold coins for our summer home."

Torina snickered.

We carried on, doing our best to look haughty—but with an air of natural disdain, topped off with a casual disregard for everyone except ourselves. We finally managed to track down the local representative of the Pathway Unburdened, a Vibariyun named Tosneek who kept a discreet office that opened onto an upper level of the station's main concourse. As we made our way there, I couldn't help noticing that the slightly tattered luxury of the place still held true. There were potted plants of many types and colors, but all of them appeared wilted and unhealthy. The bulkheads were clean scrubbed and freshly painted, but I could see the faint ghosts of streaks and stains just beneath the surface, echoes of a fading grandeur that felt sad and desperate.

Sometimes, history has a way of showing through, no matter how thick the paint.

"A Vibariyun, huh?" I said when we reached the office, which was a plain door. "Our dearly departed Master, Proloxus, was a Vibariyun, which doesn't exactly elevate my trust level."

"Yes, but the Vibariyun Invigilator we dealt with to get access to that sealed warren was up-front and honest," Torina reminded me. "I wouldn't paint them all with the same broom."

"Brush, but that's a fair point," I said, pressing a button to the left. Somewhere inside, a chime rang, muffled but still cheerily bright. A moment later, the door opened to reveal who I assumed was Tosneek.

"Can I help you?"

Torina brushed her gaze across the Vibariyun, barely bothering to make eye contact. "Perhaps. My husband and I are interested in —whatever it is you do. Something spiritual, I believe."

"I—"

"Well, do you do spiritual things, or don't you?"

"Well, yes—we are the Pathway Unburdened. I'm Tosneek—"

"Yes, yes, whatever. My husband and I have recently decided that one of the very, very few things missing in our lives is spiritual fulfillment. So, we shopped around, found your charming belief system, and sailed our yacht straight here. Isn't that right, dear?"

I shot her a look and got one in return that sparkled with mischief.

"Yes, dove," I admitted, my tone on the cusp of boredom. "Empty inside, except for the wine we had—that was superb, given we're in a backwater—but I digress. I am devoid of something and request that you give it to me. To us, rather." I gave Torina a fugitive look of apology, then patted her hand with all the warmth of a dead fish.

Torina turned back to Tosneek. "There you are. Anyway, we want spiritual fulfillment. Please provide it to us."

As we'd talked, Tosneek's eyes had gone wider and brighter. I didn't have to be psionic to know what he was thinking.

A couple of bored, rich, and somewhat dumb patsies. *Perfect.*

His eyes flicked to Torina, then me—and then he schooled his features into a beatific grin that was just short of patronizing. As a performance, it was perfect—after all, he'd gone from surprise to salesman in ten seconds or less. He was good.

"Won't you come in and take the first steps on the Pathway? That is what you seek, and here—and nowhere else, mind you— awaits the fulfillment you crave. You're obviously people of high character who have an intense need that the Pathway can, ah—"

"Like fill us up with wisdom and all that?" Torina interrupted.

Tosneek didn't even break stride. His smile widened as he opened the door and stepped aside. "*Exactly* like that, friends. Welcome. Let us begin healing your souls this moment."

Torina led the way, and I followed her along the Pathway, but not the one Tosneek was pitching. We were going to peel Tosneek and his crew like a rotten fruit, and they just gave us the one thing we needed—a way in.

TOSNEEK LED US TO A SMALL, luxurious sitting room, then turned to a device built into the wall.

"A variety of appetizers and delicacies appropriate for human physiology," he said to it, then he sat in one of the overstuffed chairs. Torina and I sat on a couch, slightly apart and turned away from each other. We'd agreed to try and convey the impression that, while married, we were bored with each other, moving past love to tolerance. That gave the Pathway Unburdened several alternative hooks to recruit us, either together or individually.

"It will take a few moments for the duplicator to assemble our refreshments," he said, every word oilier than the last.

I was a little surprised. Despite being a staple of science fiction on Earth, actual duplication systems were sophisticated molecular assemblers, slow, finicky and hideously expensive. They were rarely used outside of specific industrial processes. That the Pathway had one here, making snacks, spoke to their commitment to the long con.

Perry, monitoring from the *Fafnir*, which Icky had piloted here separately, piped up in my ear bug.

Don't be too impressed, Van. That duplicator of his is actually a couple of guys behind the wall slapping together finger food.

"That's quite alright. My wife and I filled up on *canapes* and— um, *hors d'oeuvres* on the way here," I said.

Torina sniffed, as though suppressing a sudden urge to laugh. "Yes, I'm just positively *stuffed* with *hors d'oeuvres*. It's practically all that I eat."

"Ah. I see," Tosneek said, although he clearly did not. Sitting across from us, he adopted the pose of a caring friend, then began his pitch. "Why don't you tell me what it is that's troubling you, my children?"

I did my best to look earnest, in a manner that told Tosneek it was an alien emotion for me. With a flash of hesitation, I looked to

Torina, who mirrored my uncertainty. I rubbed my hands together, nodding as I reached an internal decision. I'm no actor, but I thought my performance wasn't half bad. I pierced Tosneek with the look of a man who is asking for nothing less than his life and isn't used to seeking favors. "To be blunt, Tosneek?"

He waved airily. "We expect nothing less than utter honesty here. It is the surest path to spiritual growth."

I plunged ahead. "We seek to save our immortal souls from the fires of damnation, because—never mind why, just—that's what we seek. Oh, and we're willing to pay any price to do it."

"I LIKE how you opened with *pay any price*. That was music to our holy grifter's ears, *dahling*," Torina said, grinning.

I shrugged back as we rounded a kiosk peddling knock-off data pads, every one of them guaranteed to be preloaded with a *surprise*. Fake advertising, I thought. Malware wouldn't be a surprise at all.

"We were going to talk about money, eventually. I figured we'd get right to the point. Seemed in character for who we were channeling," I admitted.

Our conversation with Tosneek had gone much as I'd expected. We'd said those magic words, *pay any cost*, and everything after that had just been a forgone conclusion. We'd learned all about the *Pathway*, the spiritual course we each followed through life, and how we accumulated burdens upon our soul as we did. Tosneek assured us that the methods of meditation and cleansing pioneered by the elusive High Doctor Markov would divest us of those burdens. He committed to contacting the good High Doctor and submitting as candidates for initiation, whereupon we would enter the Pathway Unburdened as *Beginning Travelers*. That was where we had left it.

The bill so far? One thousand bonds, framed as a gift—apparently there were lots of gifts, for different things—and partly a contribution to help the Pathway offset the cost of maintaining their office on Halcyon. When we left, I asked Torina sidelong, "What, exactly, is the difference between a *gift* and a *hustle?*"

"The spelling, *dahling*. The spelling."

Now, as we made our way back to the waiting *Aetherswift*, I kept myself ready to answer the comm. I was sure that Tosneek would be calling us very soon to tell us that we'd been accepted as Beginning Travelers.

"There's no way he's going to let us leave Halcyon without getting a firm hook into us. You just watch," I said to Torina.

"I think he'll wait until we're off-station and on our way out of the system to call. It'll make it look more... measured. He doesn't want to look too anxious or desperate," Torina said.

"Ten bonds says I'm right."

"You're on."

Back on the main concourse, we steered our way toward our airlock. As arranged, Icky and Perry were hanging around a group of kiosks hawking yet more overpriced junk. Torina saw a piece of jewelry so gaudy it wouldn't have looked out of place in a toy store at the intersection of Yikes and Seriously?—and she went immediately to it, cooing.

"Darling, now this is a *statement*," she purred, leaning into what was an affront to my senses. It put us a couple of paces away from Icky and Perry.

Is the statement I am utterly devoid of good taste? Perry sent through our earpieces.

I fought not to laugh as Torina continued examining the necklace, which was composed of engineered diamonds that would have worked as drawer pulls in my Great Aunt Mildred's kitchen.

"How'd it go?" Icky asked quietly, eyes averted.

"On course. Greed is alive and well here in the cradle of spiritual rebirth. We've taken our first tentative steps on the path toward High Doctor Markov's bank account," I murmured.

"Well, ten seconds—and I mean ten seconds, as in 10.22 seconds—after you guys left, a terminal in that office connected to the comm system and began a series of transmissions and replies that lasted 1.32 minutes," Perry said, now speaking aloud since it was obvious we hadn't been tailed.

Torina glanced over. "I'm a little hurt that it would take that long for us to be accepted."

"Unless he made you," Icky said.

I nodded and glanced at Torina in time to see her *buying* that damned necklace, and for almost five hundred bonds.

"Isn't it exquisite? Clasp me, dahling," she declared, turning around.

I obliged her. "Aren't you overusing the whole *dahling* thing a little?"

"No more than your sudden fascination with *hors d'oeuvres*. As if I'd eat snails, you maniac," she chided, holding her hair up in a silken bundle.

"That's *escargot*, which I will never eat again because it reminds me of our friend Retta, and also because it's *escargot*. And—wait, would we really eat nothing but finger foods? If we were ridiculously rich?"

She turned around, a bemused look pulling at her lips. "Um—no? Having money doesn't mean you eat tiny, unpronounceable things at every meal. Just some meals. Anyway, how does my new necklace look?"

"Like you're wearing a string of ice cubes."

"Perfect. Well, except for the fact I can no longer look down—"

The comm chimed. I answered it.

"Excellent news, Mister Plantagenet. High Doctor Markov has been looking for new candidates to bring under his direct tutelage, and he believes you and your charming wife would be perfect companions on his own journey toward Fulfillment and Release."

I shot Torina a triumphant grin. "That is such wonderful news, Mister Tosneek. You caught us doing a little shopping here. Should we come back to your office?"

"Actually, High Doctor Markov isn't here. He's at the Waystop of Serenity, our order's sanctum."

I glanced at Perry, who shrugged. "Ah, I see. Of course. So, is he coming here soon? Should we plan to come back—?"

"Oh, no. You and your wife are invited to travel to The Waystop and meet with him there. I should point out that we do apply a tithe to all who visit there, regardless of reason, to help offset the considerable costs of our mission of salvation."

I made myself sound bored, letting the momentary excitement of good news drain away. "Yes, yes, of course. Is five thousand bonds enough to cover it?"

"It—" A pause, during which Torina smirked and Icky giggled. "Why, it—yes!" Tosneek paused again. When he resumed speaking, his voice had returned to its smooth, reassuring baritone. "Yes, that is more than generous, thank you. I'll send you the navigation data that you'll need."

"Oh, just send that to our yacht, the *Aetherswift*, to—" I stopped, drawing a complete blank on the name of the yacht's pilot who'd been ferrying us about. "To the, well, pilot. I don't recall his name, but when one has many servants, that's bound to happen, isn't it?"

"Yes, of course, Mister Plantagenet. And welcome to the Pathway Unburdened. May your journey be a fruitful one," Tosneek said, then signed off.

"Mister Plantagenet?" Perry said.

"Well, I didn't want to use Tudor, so I picked another of those British royal family names."

"So your quest for an alias took you back to the fifteenth century, instead of to, you know, maybe Windsor? The current Royal Family name?"

"I prefer the classy sound of polysyllabic words. I'm quite a dandy under all this manly exterior." I turned to Torina, who was gushing over a ring to match her necklace. Perry uttered something that sounded a lot like *bullshit*, and Icky wouldn't make eye contact at all. I gave them both my best glare and held out an arm to Torina.

"Let's go, my dear. We don't want to keep the High Doctor waiting."

She pouted, then tugged at her hideous necklace. "You never buy me anything nice."

10

I SHOOK MY HEAD. "Let me get this straight—the High Doctor is a squatter?"

"Pretty much. Ross 128-B, the former homeworld of a race known as the Shudduth, was evacuated owing to a botanical plague about ninety standard years ago. It was never ceded or surrendered by the Shudduth, though, so it's still their sovereign territory," Perry said over the comm.

He and Icky shadowed us in the *Fafnir*, which was once more stealthed and storing her waste heat. Without Torina and me on board, Icky, Perry, and the ship could handle much higher temperatures for longer, meaning we could have the *Fafnir* coast into the system in the wake of the *Aetherswift*, more or less invisibly.

The system being Ross 128, another of the ubiquitous red dwarf stars. Ross 128-B, the second planet, was a super-Earth orbiting insanely close to the star—so close that its year was about ten days long. But the close proximity meant the planet actually received a touch more heat energy from its dim star than the Earth did from Sol, so it was perfectly habitable. Or it had been, until a botanical plague had forced it to be abandoned.

"What the hell is a botanical plague, anyway? A virulent outbreak of flowers?" I asked.

"Think kudzu," Perry replied.

"Ah."

A short time later, the *Aetherswift's* pilot—whose name was Ran, which I was a little surprised I hadn't been able to remember because it was three whole letters—announced an incoming call from the planet apparently co-opted by the Pathway and named the Waystop of Serenity.

The voice that boomed over the speaker was rich, expansive, and embellished with a Russian accent so exaggerated I thought I smelled vodka. "My friends, my dear friends, welcome to the beginning of the rest of your lives. I am High Doctor Nikolay Alexandrovich Markov."

As though saying his name was some sort of unveiling, Markov's image appeared on the screen, translucent skin and all. I tried to keep my focus on his eyes, which were numerous but opaque, unlike his guts.

In my earpiece, Perry spoke up. *Nikolay Alexandrovich are the given and patrimonial names of Czar Nicholas II. Seriously, you'd have thought he'd have picked a Czar who wasn't executed by revolutionaries in a dingy basement. Why not Peter the Great, for crying out loud?*

"Yes, yes, thank you, High Doctor—"

"No, no, please, call me Nikolay. We are friends, *da?*"

"Um, yes—*da* for sure. My wife Torina and I are very pleased to meet you."

We exchanged a few more bland and empty pleasantries, then Markov handed us off to a rudimentary traffic-control system whose bored AI sent instructions that essentially said, come on in and land. When we'd signed off, I got on the beam comm to the *Fafnir*.

"Did you guys get that?"

"Yes we did, dahling," Icky said. I heard Perry laugh in the background.

I glared at Torina. "This is your fault."

She smiled sweetly back.

But Icky came back, her voice more serious. "Not sure how good the scanners are on that luxury bucket of yours, but we're picking up signals from several ships in orbit—Nesit, Yonnox, and one that Netty says matches a class 11 Salt Thieves' frigate we've encountered before."

"What a rogue's gallery that is. I assume none of them have detected you, or this would probably be a very different conversation."

"Nah. I've powered down everything except life support, and we're still storing heat—it's a balmy fifty-one Celsius in the *Fafnir*, by the way," Icky replied.

"Don't get my seat all sweaty."

"Don't worry, I'll wash it off for you, so any moisture you find on it is just cleanser, honest."

I turned to Torina. "Well, any sense that the Pathway Unchained—"

"Unburdened."

"Right. Unburdened. Anyway, the company they keep tells us everything we need to know."

While the *Fafnir* eased itself into a Lagrange Point orbit on the far side of Ross 128-B's single moon, we made planetfall and landed adjacent to the High Sanctum of the Pathway Unburdened, ready to be relieved of our spiritual burdens.

And, of course, our cash.

———

"MY FRIENDS, welcome to Pathway, your new spiritual home!"

High Doctor Markov greeted us personally, stepping out of a sleek limousine that wouldn't have looked out of place pulling up to the red carpet at the Oscars. He strolled toward us, the muscles and tendons in his four legs expanding and contracting in a display of anatomy in action that was almost hypnotic.

"Uh—oh, yes. Right. Our pleasure. This is my wife, Torina."

"Charmed," she said, holding out her hand. That surprised me, but not as much as Markov actually kissing it with his rubbery lips. I winced, not out of jealousy, but from being that close to a being's visible inner workings, which were busy digesting his lunch. Or something.

Torina just smoothly withdrew her hand, still smiling, but I saw her surreptitiously wipe it on her gown.

"Please, druz'ya, my friends, settle yourselves in," Marvok said, gesturing to his limo. "We will return to the Sanctum but take the long way around so you can see what we have built here."

Torina and I stepped into his limo. It was much easier than an Earthly car because the roof was at least twenty centimeters higher to accommodate Markov's height. It was also surprisingly comfortable. Markov sat facing our rearward-oriented seats. The limo sealed itself shut and began to move. There was no sense of acceleration or engine noise—it was as though the world outside had suddenly begun to slide past.

"Tosneek tells me that you are from Earth," Markov said to me, his voice measured and rich.

"Yes. Originally, anyway."

"Do I detect some Russian in you?"

"I—uh, no. I don't think so, anyway."

"Ah. It is simply that you have that discerning, subtle air of nobility I associate with the Russian people."

I thought about some Russian hackers I occasionally worked with. I got stupidly drunk with a pair of them in Prague and ended up arm wrestling them for rounds. They were… different.

I looked out the window at the—city? If it was, it was a strange city, consisting of scattered, large, and mostly isolated buildings, some of which resembled arenas or auditoriums. All of it was liberally festooned with olive drab leaves and fronds of what I assumed was the botanical plague, an invasive species that somehow made it here from its native world of Sunward in the Procyon system. I'd read the background on it—something about the combined effects of temperature, light quality and levels, and soil conditions being absolutely perfect for the stuff. The back-grounder said that you could actually see it growing if you watched closely enough—

"An amusement park," I blurted.

Torina and Markov both looked at me—Torina with confusion, Markov with a nod. "Yes, it is—or was. You are very perceptive, *moy drook*, my friend."

"Thank you, but that Ferris wheel over there is rather distinct," I replied, marveling a little at the presence of something I associate with the Iowa State Fair on an alien planet light-years from Earth. I guess the desire to go around in circles was a universal one.

Or they'd stolen the idea from us, which, considering the amount of culture we Terrestrials had inadvertently exported, wouldn't have surprised me at all.

We also saw some of Markov's followers. All were dressed in strangely iridescent robes, which made me feel a little vindicated. Finally, we'd found an alien planet where everyone dressed the same, in an outfit that looked both uncomfortable and impractical. There was a darker note to it, though. I noticed that many of these followers of the Path wore what looked like chainmail beneath their robes and carried swords on their hips. Torina and I were unarmed, and although I didn't think we were likely to end up in a fight here, it still made me uneasy.

The limo eventually pulled up in front of an enclosed amphitheater that seemed to be the focus of the amusement park. Like every other building, it was draped with olive drab foliage. Sections of it were cut away, though, to provide access to doors and windows. I saw several aliens, and one human, laboring away to prune the stuff back. It was probably a full-time job.

The limo drove into what seemed to be some sort of parking garage, a vast space beneath the amphitheater that was eerily empty of any other vehicles. We stopped at the base of a ramp and disembarked. Markov gestured for us to follow him and led us into an enormous, vaulted space as big as a cathedral.

"*Moi druz'ya*, my friends, welcome to the holiest of holies, our innermost sanctum, The Chamber of Revelatory Truth!"

Markov announced it like a proclamation, his voice ringing

against the rafters. It was actually well-timed and could have been pretty effective if it hadn't been for Perry snickering in my ear.

Chamber of Revelatory Truth, my alloy ass. According to the backgrounder, that building you're in was used for a Shudduth sport similar to Earthly soccer, with the main difference being that in the Shudduth version the winners eat the losers.

"Holy shit!"

Markov and Torina both looked at me.

"I mean—holy shit, this is, ah, truly wondrous. Impressive and all," I added with an apologetic grin.

Markov led us across a massive space that I assumed was the playing field. I found myself wondering how many Shudduth athletes had ended up on the wrong side of the menu in here—to my knowledge, even the Aztecs only killed the losing team in their version of this sport. As to the overall space, it was reasonably clean and well-maintained, and had been embellished with all sorts of fluted, rococo gewgaws and curlicues lifted straight from Saint Basil's Cathedral in Red Square. One end of the chamber was decorated to the point of parody, ornate panels the color and luster of honey framed and inlaid with intricate filigrees of gold—

Wait.

"High Doctor—"

"Please, it is Nikolay."

"Right. Nikolay, there's a—well, it's pretty much a legend, now, that there used to be a room in a palace in Saint Petersburg, in Russia, called the—"

"The Amber Room, yes. Isn't it beautiful?"

I stopped, taking in a dais, capped by a golden throne,

surrounded by luminous amber panels so intricately decorated with golden detail they almost made my eyes water.

"This is the Amber Room? That was sometimes called the Eighth Wonder of the World? Here?"

"Yes. I acquired it from a trader shortly after your race discovered nuclear power. Since everyone expected you to incinerate yourselves, it only seemed right to ensure that this priceless beauty was preserved."

"How beneficent of you."

"I consider it a service to sentient life," he said, folding himself onto his throne. Two of his armed minions moved in from the flanks to stand to either side of him, one Vibariyun and the other an insectoid alien that reminded me of Steve back on Anvil Dark. "Now then, I understand that you wish to unburden yourselves of the cares of the flesh. By coming here, you have taken the first step on that journey. I consider it an honor and a privilege to help guide you the rest of the way."

For the next ten or fifteen minutes, Markov spoke, dousing us with a torrent of New Age gobbledygook like the spray from a firehose. As he did, Perry made quips about which religion he'd stolen the various bits and pieces from. There were a lot of them—including, not surprisingly, Eastern Orthodoxy, the main religion of Russia.

As the religious screed dragged on, my attention wandered, and I took in the sheer, almost breathtaking beauty of the Amber Room. I was stunned to see it before me, as the whole thing had disappeared sometime during World War II—naturally, after being looted by the Nazis. The Amber Room was later replaced with a reconstructed version. The fact that the original was providing a backdrop to Czar Grifter I's sleazy religious show just pissed me off. This, the Vanguard satellites, the Venera probes—how much more of Earth's historical and cultural heritage had been looted away by aliens?

Said the guy who himself sold two of the original Vanguard satellites to an alien buyer. That had been for a good and selfless cause, though—restoring the damage done to the ecosystem of Torina's homeworld. It wasn't like I'd profited from it.

I was still trying to convince myself I really wasn't *anything* like this scumbag when he abruptly stopped talking, then looked expectantly at me for an answer.

Shit. I hadn't been paying attention at all.

Torina came to the rescue. "That's all fascinating," she oozed, and her tone informed the High Doctor it was anything *but* gripping information. With deliberate slowness, she continued. "What I want to know is how long will it take for us to achieve spiritual fulfillment, and how much will it cost?"

Even Markov seemed taken aback by such a blunt question. "It —er… well, it varies."

"If we pay more, can we be cleansed and purified and enlightened more quickly? I only ask because we're planning a getaway on our yacht—not the cramped little beggar we came here on, I mean the *big* yacht, of course—and I am simply *dying* to try my hand at the quangot tables on Reticulum. I'm feeling lucky, you see, but have *no* idea how long it will last. Lately, I've become much more in tune with my star positions—I'm a Capricorn, of course. We're all beautiful and humble—and my feeling is that it's time for me to absolutely take those tables for all I can—"

"I believe that we can make arrangements to ensure that… that you obtain what you are seeking more quickly than you might otherwise. Of course, as you allude to, the tithes—"

"Discussion of money bores me, *dah*ling. Just have your people call ours and work it out. My husband will provide the details. We've got tables to get to." Torina turned to me, her eyes sparkling. She was enjoying this.

"Dahling, I'm tired. I would like to return to the little yacht and lie down. In fact, I would like to return home—"

"Which home, love?"

"I don't care. Tell the pilot to choose one."

I turned to Markov. "We would like some time to think about the things you have told us. It is all very… moving."

"Of course, of course! In the meantime, as a token of our new relationship as brothers and sisters upon the Pathway, please, take your choice of one of the artifacts arrayed around you. They are all merely possessions, and if one of them can provide a focus for your spiritual concerns, it will be serving a noble purpose."

I blinked, then placed my hand over my heart. "You're so—so generous." I turned to Torina. "Dove, are you sure you don't want to join these people and put on one of those lovely sets of robes—"

"In time, love, in time. Right now, I feel one of my episodes coming on," Torina said and turned away.

"Oh, I—apologies. Her emotions can run amok, and it's not pretty. She's been medicated for years, but the doctors *insist* there's nothing wrong with her, the charlatans." I gave Markov a regretful shrug. "We really must get back then." I turned and scanned what I realized were a multitude of items, several dozen at least, sitting on pedestals all around us. I saw everything from framed paintings to statues, including a few that resembled the one we'd found aboard the stolen battlecruiser.

I finally settled on what looked like a four-legged duck carved of hardwood, smeared with dirt, and sporting crystalline eyes and a metal beak. "I will treasure it, Nikolay," I said, picking it up with trembling hands. "So close, and fast."

"What is?" Markov asked.

"Purity of our soul. And maybe some winnings at the—"

"I'm feeling unwell. I thought I told you that, like, twice?" Torina snapped.

"Duty calls," I said with a rueful shrug.

"Of course." Markov waved an arm in benediction, and we bustled away, Torina leaning against me, face covered with one hand. With her other, she held my shoulder, and we were at the limo in a moment. Our travel to the yacht was silent—by design, and we waited until the airlock sealed before uttering another sound.

That sound was fits of laughter.

"I can't believe he's got the Amber Room right there. That thing is *priceless*," I marveled as Perry and Icky settled themselves into the *Aetherswift's* central lounge. Since we had the yacht for the return trip, we decided we might as well indulge in its luxury.

Icky sprawled out, kicked off her boots, and propped enormous, hairy feet on a low table. She sighed in contentment. "Van, let's give The Quiet Room the *Fafnir* and keep this sweet ride. I could get used to this."

"Sure, until the first time we're in combat. Then I think you're going to want more than one point-defense battery," Perry said, then turned to me. "And Van, as for the Amber Room, I've seen at least three of them in different parts of known space. Someone is making knockoffs, probably with a molecular assembler, and selling them as the original."

"Well, much as I enjoy hearing that our scammer of a High Doctor himself got scammed, if they're exactly the same down to the molecular level, does it even matter which one's the original?"

"Ask Theseus."

I blinked. "What?"

"The Ship of Theseus? No? Theseus's ship is replaced, piece by piece, with new planks and stuff over the years. Eventually, every piece has been replaced. Is it still the same ship?"

I waited.

Perry sighed. "There's no punchline, Van. It's a thought experiment."

"Ah. Well, how about a real experiment instead." I gestured at the dirty, ugly little statue I'd claimed from Markov's collection.

"Oh, that's easy. I've already scanned it. It contains a data skimmer, memory, and a close-range encrypted burst transmitter to download whatever it's recorded when a receiver is within range. Well-concealed, too. Standard, off-the-shelf scanners wouldn't ping on it. Fortunately, my scanners are top-of-the-line—of course."

"So, wait—it's recording us now?"

"Probably. But since it's just us and the *Fafnir* out here, on the very edge of the system, there's no receiver in range."

"Huh. They give those things away, like that weird statuary we found on that battlecruiser, and use them to glean data from suckers all across known space?" Icky asked.

"Not sure of the details of the scam, but I'd assume that pretty much covers it," Perry answered.

Icky stood and padded over to the ugly statue. "No reason you couldn't put a person in here, right? Like, on a chip?"

Torina and I exchanged a look, then stood and joined Icky.

"No, I don't suppose there is. Perry, you didn't detect a stolen ID in this one, did you?"

"If I had, I would have said something. It doesn't mean there isn't one in there, dormant, though."

"It *would* be a good way of smuggling chips around. Or any sort of small contraband, for that matter," Torina said.

Since we didn't know what the stupid duck's data-skimming capabilities were, we didn't take it aboard the *Fafnir* for a more detailed scan. It could skim the yacht all it wanted, though, because The Quiet Room had given us a suite of fake comm logs and other data you'd expect to find aboard a luxury craft belonging to a couple of snotty, elitist tools. For now, we relied on Perry's scans, another of which he did to try getting a more detailed picture of the ugly little statue.

He finally shook his head. "Nothing, but there is a significant amount of empty interior volume that could be used to conceal all sorts of things."

I pulled at my chin, thinking. "Okay. Let's put the word out through the Guild to keep an eye out for these Pathway Unburdened artifacts. If any are found, they need to be seized and examined."

Torina frowned. "How is anyone going to know what's an actual Pathway Unburdened artifact, though? We saw a few dozen back in the High Doctor's Chamber of Revelations—"

"Chamber of Revelatory Truth," Perry corrected her.

"Whatever. Anyway, no two of them were alike."

"Simple. We just tell other Peacemakers to look for the tackiest, ugliest pieces of so-called artwork they come across and scan them per whatever parameters Perry's already established. If they get any hits, they take 'em in," I said, looking into the duck's beady little eyes. I wondered if they were getting my good side.

"Meantime, let's go meet up with Schegith. I have some questions," I went on.

"Such as?" Torina asked.

"Well, for a start, why we've got bumbling platypuses and huckster Czars all nibbling around the edges of things."

11

NULL WORLD WAS a contradiction to me. On one hand, it was a desolate Mars-like planet speckled with enigmatic ruins of a lost civilization. On the other, it was home to one of my favorite aliens, the massive, slug-like matriarch of the Schegith, who shared her name with her people. Moreover, deep beneath her subterranean digs was the Undersea, a vast underground lake Torina and I had adopted as our favorite getaway.

So, a contradiction, in the best way possible.

We found Schegith in her accustomed place, lounging on a massive palanquin. Every time I saw her, I was reminded of an illustrated copy of *Alice in Wonderland* I'd owned as a kid. One of the pictures depicted the Caterpillar sprawled on a palanquin-like thing, puffing away on whatever he burned in his hookah. Schegith was exactly that, minus the drugs. Instead, she had a pipe of condensed gases, which meant I'd traveled trillions of kilometers to meet a giant caterpillar who vaped.

Admittedly, she was funny and kind, despite her appearance. I called her friend, so when I stepped close, she gave me a languid wave, and I sat down without fanfare.

"Troubles?" she asked.

"Troubles."

"About?"

"That's the tricky part. More stolen persons, but this time, they were integrated into technology that has some unusual features. The person was altered in a way that left them with no real chance of survival because they were, ah, bound in a matrix and form that's different from anything we've seen before."

"This one is curious about the differences, and the rest of this story. Continue?" Schegith said, pulling at her pipe—okay, a bong nearly a meter in length and filled with bubbling silver like mercury. She exhaled mightily, then waved one of her arms. "This one would hear your details, please."

I brought her up to date on what had transpired since the last time we'd worked together. She listened closely, making *mmhmm* noises along the way, and I knew she would help. We'd gained a huge amount of goodwill with her by rescuing the last handful of members of her race from the digital servitude of the ID thieves, and I had no qualms about tapping into it. More to the point, she was now an implacably dedicated enemy of those same thieves, and while she might not be a warrior, exactly, she knew things. *Lots* of things. Maybe everything, for that matter, since her fields of knowledge and expertise seemed to have no bounds.

When I was done, I fell silent and waited. Schegith tended to be quite deliberate in her approach to conversing, meaning we had to sometimes wait through long pauses for her reply. Torina and I had left Icky aboard the *Fafnir* for that very reason. She wasn't the most patient of people and would probably find all of this boring. I was quickly learning, in fact, that when it came to Icky, she was happiest elbow deep in some sort of machinery, not sitting around and having thoughtful conversations.

Schegith finally spoke up. "This one agrees that the star you call Rigel is the most likely candidate for this poor, lost soul's origin. Spica is much closer, but is actually two stars, and he described only one to you, yes?"

"He did. He referred to *the blue sun*—singular—*covering the sky*."

"Yes. And no other candidates are close enough, in any practical sense."

"Still, over eight hundred light-years is a long way to travel. Why? What's so special about Rigel?" Torina asked.

"Ah, yes, well this one believes that now engages your second question, regarding mining. This one has considered what those involved in this vile trade would need to enable it. The chips containing those stolen personalities must be very sophisticated technology, yes?"

I looked at Perry, who bobbed his head in a nod. "Very sophisticated, yeah. They have to be, considering the amount of data represented by a sentient brain."

"They are of a unique type?"

"Well, yes and no. Yes, this particular type of chip is quite distinct, but no, their essential architecture is the same as a chip containing any other AI."

Torina snickered. "So, deep down inside, you're really just a chip?"

Perry glared back at her. "Deep down inside, aren't you really just a brain?"

I chuckled at Torina. "Score one for the bird."

Schegith went on. "To manufacture these sophisticated AI chips requires specific materials, does it not?"

Perry shrugged. "Sure. The tolerances are incredibly tight, so the materials used have to be——"

Perry stopped and went still.

I sat forward. "Perry?"

He didn't answer.

Now I stood. So did Torina. "Perry, are you alright——?"

"Yeah, I'm fine," he said, suddenly coming back to life. "Sorry, I wanted to do a database search about something, so I had to get Netty to connect me to Anvil Dark." He turned to Schegith. "You're right."

I blinked from him to Schegith and back. "She's right? About what?"

"About the usage of materials," Schegith said.

"I—don't get it."

Perry shook his head. "I need to run some diagnostics. I should have thought of this myself. We've been focused on the personalities and trying to track them, where and when they went missing, that sort of thing. We've paid no attention at all to the chips that contain them, because we've been assuming they're just standard tech."

Again, I looked from one to the other. "The chips. Okay. What about the chips?"

"Van, there are some specific elements that are needed to make high-end, AI-compatible chips. A few of them are really rare. One of them is osmium."

Okay, I've always been a bit of a science nerd, so I'd *heard* of osmium. Off the top of my head, I knew it was a metal, it was rare, and—and that was about it.

Torina was obviously in the same boat because she just stared. "Osmee-what?"

"Osmium. Element number seventy-six on the periodic table, the heaviest of the so-called rare-earth elements, the densest and one of the rarest natural elements known. It's fundamental to manufacturing the sorts of chips we're talking about here, which makes it beyond valuable. It also makes it a strategic commodity, controlled by the few operations that produce it—and tightly regulated," Perry said.

"Okay. You said something about usage," I said.

Perry turned to Schegith. "Ask her. She figured it out before I did, which brings me back to those diagnostics I need to do."

Schegith shook in what I'd come to know was her form of laughing. "Sometimes there are advantages to having nothing but time to think. This one simply wondered if there were new demands on the available supply of osmium in known space. You've found many of these chips, and have spoken of many more. That would require a considerable supply."

I turned to Perry, enthused at the prospect of a new angle on our biggest case. "And?"

"And, nothing. Based on the queries I just ran, there's no greater demand for osmium now than there usually is."

That deflated me. "Shit. So another dead end."

It was Torina that shook her head. "No, it's not. Van, if they're making these chips, but not getting their osmium on the regular market—"

"Ah. Shit, you're right. They must have their own supply."

"And the conditions of planet formation around large stars such as Rigel are ideal for concentrating osmium in the crust of rocky planets," Schegith finished.

"Then, they're mining osmium at Rigel and using that to manufacture their chips," I said. "It's horrific, but brilliant."

"We need proof, though," Torina said.

"Yeah. We do. We need to have an earnest discussion with Carter Yost. He made money off the *Empty Space*, which was implicated in whatever those bulk carriers we tagged were doing."

"Bulk carriers are definitely big enough ships to make the twist to Rigel and back, if they're carrying enough fuel," Perry said.

"Perhaps it's time to play—in your language, this one thinks it's *good cop, bad cop?*" Schegith said.

I turned to her with a grin. Where the hell had she heard that phrase?

But I just nodded. "Yes, I like that a lot. I just wish we had access to the *Empty Space* ourselves. Carter is one angle, but I've never had high expectations for him before, and he's rarely lived up to them, anyway. If we could get our hands on that damned ship, we might get exactly what we need from it."

"Since this one will accompany you in this one's ship, perhaps the search will be easier," Schegith put in.

But Perry spoke up, his voice almost triumphant. "And now, the bird redeems himself. When I queried the Anvil Dark datastores about osmium data, I happened to download the most recent intelligence reports. Remember how we put the *Empty Space* on the watchlist? Well, guess what ship just limped into dock at Spindrift, leaking atmosphere, and will be laid up for days doing repairs?"

"You're kidding. The *Empty Space?*"

"Bingo."

Schegith shook again with her laugh. "Ahh, Spindrift. The only place where this one feels more beautiful than the people all around them."

SCHEGITH'S SHIP docked at Spindrift first, sending back a message that the *Empty Space* was still there. She sent along an image that was taken as her ship approached the station, showing the *Empty Space* docked at a servicing lock and partly enclosed in a repair gantry. Her emissions were zero, her reactor cold. She wasn't going anywhere for a while.

We docked about an hour later. Torina and I donned our b-suits, strapped on our weapons, and went into full Peacemaker mode. Icky armored up and grabbed a *potent* hand cannon—which was literally what it was called, a stubby gun with a shotgun-sized bore that fired either rocket-assisted armor-piercing rounds or clouds of flechettes. The weapon could chew holes in a wall with one round, and when she hefted it, there was a playful cast to her features.

"Excited?" I asked her, looking to the hand cannon.

"Very. Maximum boom."

Icky rounded it out with her new favorite melee weapon: a sledgehammer. She'd actually added weights to it to better balance it, which allowed her to swing it in fearsome, appallingly rapid flurries of blows.

Perry brought himself.

We made our way into Spindrift's crowded morass of spacers—and the people who made their living, legal or otherwise, off of them. With our Peacemaker credentials on full display, no one gave us any trouble. The crowd just parted ahead of us and closed in behind, with some people simply making themselves scarce as we approached. I had no interest in the myriad of petty crimes being carried out around us. My destination was the *Empty Space*.

As a team, we strode through about half the length of Spindrift and met Schegith just outside the entrance to the repair docks. It was off-putting to see her here rather than reclining on her palanquin, as I'd never known her to travel.

Until now.

But with the few members of her race in attendance, I guess she had more scope to travel.

"Unfortunately, the repair docks are sealed against unauthorized visitors—and this one is apparently an unauthorized visitor," Schegith said.

I glanced around. If we'd been given a wide berth before, we were virtually alone now, aside from a few gawkers in the distance. Schegith had a reputation of being a voracious carnivore that devoured anyone and everyone that got close to her, including her own people. It was, of course, nonsense, but Schegith said that her fearsome reputation was useful to her. Considering she was the size of a car, and rippled with muscles, I understood.

I walked up to the panel beside the sealed blast door. "I'm Peacemaker Van Tudor. Here are my credentials," I said, holding them up. "I need access."

"I'm sorry, but you are not registered for entry to this facility. Please contact the facility overseer at—"

"Look, I'm going to give you five seconds to open this door, and then I'm going to declare your entire *facility* a crime scene. Then, I'll start tearing this shitshow apart, box by box, with your ass in cuffs and—"

The door rolled open.

"That's better," I snapped, leading the way into the repair docks. We found the airlock servicing the *Empty Space*, and it was wide open. We stepped into another rusty, creaky scow that looked one dent away from the scrapyard. I didn't get it. Engulfed in the airless chill of the void, you'd have to put a gun to my head to get me aboard that death trap, and yet, here it sat, obviously in service.

But for whom, I was uncertain.

As we cleared the airlock, I turned to see if Schegith could manage to enter. If she had a skeleton, it seemed able to crunch itself down to nearly nothing—she squeezed through without much difficulty at all. Of course, she also filled the corridor from bulkhead to bulkhead, so if we needed to beat a hasty retreat, I hoped she could back up as fast as she moved forward.

"This one wishes to apologize," Schegith said.

"For what?" I asked, confused.

"For having, in your terms, a *dump truck* of a behind."

It took a moment to regain my composure from laughter, and I liked Schegith a bit more. She was funny *and* lethal.

After several minutes of searching, we found no one aboard. The bridge was empty, as was engineering. Her expansive cargo holds were likewise barren. The only section of the ship we couldn't check were the gangways above the cargo holds, because they were sealed with blinking red pressure alarms. That meant on the other side of them was vacuum, or close to it, which probably explained her atmospheric leakage.

I scowled all around me. "What the hell? Is it another automated ship? Do we have more trapped identities crewing it?"

Torina shrugged. Schegith had no idea, either. Icky was doubtful, though.

"I don't see enough automation, unless it's all behind the bulkheads and overheads." She gestured to a nearby control. "This panel operates the outer doors of this hold. Buttons, see? Meant to be pushed? As for whether it's automated—"

She extracted a tool from her belt, jammed it under the faceplate of the panel and pried it open, then grabbed it and yanked it free. I guess I should have been concerned about what amounted to petty vandalism, but frankly, I didn't care. As far as I was concerned, this ship was now officially impounded anyway.

Icky held a flashlight in her mouth and poked around inside the panel, then pulled back and shook her head.

"Oh ine uh—"

She pulled the flashlight out of her mouth.

"Sorry. No sign of any automation at all. Someone has to manually work this panel."

"So there's a crew? Where the hell are they?" Torina asked.

I opened my mouth, but Icky cut me off. "Perry, what is that?"

Perry had just arrived, carrying a piece of dingy fabric in his beak, which he dropped. "This, my good Icky, is a sock, an article of clothing used by several species to cover their feet—"

"Oh, for—I know what a sock is. Why do *you* have it?"

"Because, based on the chemicals outgassing from it, it was worn by a human. And given the excess moisture trapped in the fabric, it was worn recently. And *that* would suggest this ship had a crew aboard it not that long ago, that included at least one human."

Torina wrinkled her nose. "Drawing conclusions from a sweaty sock. Eww."

"Whatever works. Although, yeah, better you than me, Perry." I sighed. "So where the hell are they, then?"

"Aren't we missing an obvious answer here? That they've all scurried off into Spindrift to get drunk or laid or whatever?" Icky asked. "Probably both."

But Schegith disavowed us of that idea. "This one checked to determine if anyone debarked this vessel upon its arrival. No one did."

"Okay, I'll say it again. Where the hell are they?" I asked.

"That's a very good question," a new voice said.

We all turned, tensing and reaching for weapons as we did. But the speaker was a S'rall, of all things, wearing a set of coveralls and a tool harness, and carting an oversized data pad called a slate.

I kept my hand resting on the Moonsword's pommel anyway. "Who are you?"

"N'rika Second-Born of House C'mir."

"I—um, okay. Let's try this. Why are you here?"

"I work here. I'm a heavy systems engineer, and this ship"—he consulted the data pad—"has an outstanding repair order for compromised atmospheric integrity in sections One-Alpha through One-Delta. Now, what are *you* doing here?"

I held up my Peacemaker credentials. "Investigating a crime—or, actually, a series of crimes."

"If you've got a repair order, it must have come from someone. Who would that be?" Torina asked.

N'rika shrugged and held up the slate. "Says here *owner*, along with a confirmation of payment of all fees and a deposit on the work order."

I narrowed my eyes at him. "Humor me for a moment. This ship arrived without a crew and docked itself—"

"Nope. It arrived without a crew, stopped a hundred klicks out, and then began to broadcast a request for aid. We towed it here."

"All without a crew."

"That's right."

"Okay, and then you get a cryptic work order from an unspecified owner, with everything fully paid—and you just say okay, fine, and get to work?"

"This is Spindrift," Schegith said.

N'rika nodded. "Give the—er, lady, I guess, a prize. I mean, look. I get the work order, I organize the job. That's it. There just aren't a lot of questions asked around here if the right amount of money shows up to cover the bills."

"Not to mention the money that flows behind the scenes, into the right pockets," Perry said.

N'rika shrugged again. "If there is, none of it's coming to me. Now, if you'll excuse me, I have a broken ship to fix."

I decided not to get in the engineer's way. For one, I didn't think he was a villain here, just a guy doing his job. For another, I didn't want to piss him off because we might yet need his help.

"I've never seen a S'rall off your homeworld before," I noted as he walked past.

"That would be because my people are almost universally assholes. Who needs that in their life?"

I sighed, waving my hands in disgust. "Well, at least *you're* honest."

I ASKED Schegith if she could stay and do her best to debrief the engineer—by chatting, of course, not interrogation—and see if he knew anything useful. I'd been kind of leaning on her terrifying reputation to encourage him to open up, but Schegith had a different approach.

"This one can be quite winsome, if the occasion demands," she purred.

I grinned. "You do you, my friend."

"What about us? Where are we going?" Torina asked me.

"We're going hunting. I'm thinking that the crew of this old heap wasn't likely to have abandoned her before they twisted here, right?"

"No, probably not. You think they're still somewhere in this system."

"That would be my guess, although—" I thought for a moment as we started back to the *Fafnir*. "Just to make sure, Perry, can you and Netty determine if any ships that have entered or departed this system since the Empty Space arrived behaved strangely? Like they maybe rendezvoused with something on their way to or from this station?"

After a few paces, Perry replied, "All done. Eight ships fit the criteria. None of them did anything but the most fuel-efficient runs in or out of the system—no strange maneuvering. Unless there's an escape pod or something out there that just happens to be traveling exactly on the course of one of those ships, and at just the right velocity, the answer would be no."

"Alright. Netty, do the preflight, please. We'll be departing as soon as we get back to the ship."

Our trek back through Spindrift involved just as much sliding out of our way as the trip to the repair docks had, but with fewer people running for cover. Icky suggested they'd stashed all their illegal stuff, knowing a Peacemaker was on the warpath. That suited me just fine.

We had a mission, and I wanted a clear path.

———

"VAN, I've detected a small object about two light-minutes to our ten o'clock, fifteen degrees elevation," Netty announced. As she did, she painted an icon onto the tactical overlay.

"Well well, who'd have thought. Kind of has the signature of an escape pod, doesn't it?" I said.

We changed course to intercept and went to active scanners. They showed us a pod of non-standard design, which meant it wasn't just off-the-shelf tech. But Netty saw no evidence of a twist capability, which wasn't surprising. It also meant that the pod couldn't just twist away from us—which meant that we had them pretty much squarely in our sights.

"You know, I'm *really* looking forward to talking to these guys," I said, watching as the range ticked down.

"Even the guy with sweaty feet?" Icky asked.

"I won't be interrogating his feet, so I don't care." We were close enough now to light the pod up with our fire-control scanners, so I did. I wanted whoever was aboard to know we weren't going to put up with any bullshit.

"One hundred klicks," Netty said, cutting the drive and flipping the *Fafnir* around. We'd been decelerating to match velocity and course with the pod, and now coasted the rest of the way.

"Anything from that pod? Transmissions, emissions, anything at all?"

"Nothing," Netty replied.

"Huh."

Torina, who'd been bringing the weapons online, glanced at me. "Huh?"

"Yeah. Huh."

"Can you be more specific with your *huh*?

I shook my head. "Nope. There's just something about this whole situation that makes me go *huh*. Netty, are we able to determine if anyone over there is alive?"

"We could ask."

"Um—yeah, sure. I'm looking for something a little more objective. After all, they might be either unwilling or unable to answer us."

"If there ever was anyone alive aboard that thing," Perry put in.

I shot him a glance. "You think it's not an escape pod?"

"It's not a standard design for an escape pod. On its own, that doesn't mean much, but some things are just better being completely off the shelf, you know? Standard escape pods are reliable as hell, easy to install complete with their ejection system, not that expensive, and— they're standardized. You don't have to figure out what they are, like we're doing right now."

I glanced at the range. Twenty klicks.

On impulse, I took the controls, activated the port bow thrusters, and began to yaw the *Fafnir* away from the other craft. "Thank you, Perry. You just made my *huh* a lot more—"

—was all I managed to say before the world ended.

12

I WAS CONFUSED.

Why was it so windy? And also foggy? I'd spent a day in Brighton, in the UK, once, on a day that had weirdly combined a stiff breeze with a thick sea fog. But this wasn't Brighton—was it?

Shrill, piercing tones cut through the blustery fog, which was quickly fading. For some reason, I seemed to be lying on my side. My eyes stung, so I blinked. They just kept stinging. And now the wind subsided, a gale to a breeze, a breeze to barely a whisper. I struggled to breathe.

Silence.

Something abruptly covered my face. I tried to struggle, but something strong pressed me down. I felt a snap, then a stabbing jab of pain in my ears.

"Van!"

I blinked. I recognized that voice. It was Icky. But she hadn't been in Brighton with me, had she?

"Van!"

"Icky?"

"Shit, Van, you're alive. We've been hit!"

"Hit? What?"

"Oh, for—Van, snap out of it! We're in trouble!" Icky boomed.

Trouble. I grabbed the word and used it to drag my lethargic thoughts back to the present. This wasn't Brighton. This was the *Fafnir*, and we were—

I shoved myself upright, and the *Fafnir's* cockpit resolved around me. Half of the instruments were dark. The rest were variations of lurid red.

"Shit—Icky, what happened?"

"Bastards got us."

"Thank you for the illuminating commentary, Ick."

"Sorry, busy."

I swept my gaze back and forth, trying to find something that was working. Everything seemed to be offline, though. Main power, auxiliary generator, scanners, nav, helm, comms, fire control, even life support, all offline.

The critical urgency of our dire situation slammed into me like an adrenaline tsunami. It swept away the last dregs of shock, and I looked around the cockpit, trying to make sense of what had happened.

Icky sat in her jumpseat, punching commands into a data pad she'd jacked into her panel. Perry reappeared in a puff of thrust that nudged him back into the cockpit from wherever he'd gone. One of his wings hung limp. Torina—

Oh, no.

There was blood.

So much of it, slicked across her neck and face and floating in wobbly little globules—and she wasn't wearing her helmet.

I snatched it from the rack on the back of her seat and moved to shove it over her head. Before I could, though, I saw where the blood was coming from. Something had neatly sliced her neck, maybe deep enough to cut something serious, like an artery. She was bleeding out. But she was also exposed to near vacuum. If I jammed her helmet on and sealed it, she'd die from blood loss. If I didn't, she'd asphyxiate.

None of this felt real. Things like this didn't happen. I hung suspended in time, like a fly in a spider's web, thrashing around uselessly while death came inexorably closer—

"Van, put her helmet on," Perry snapped.

"But she'll—"

"Van, listen to me. Put her helmet on and seal it. Then use The Drop to shoot her in the neck."

"What?"

"Van, we've got seconds here. Trust me. Shoot her, and the suit will release sealing foam, which will plug any damage and also seal up her wound."

"Perry, I can't—!"

"Van, trust me."

What the hell? I couldn't shoot Torina, shoot her—

Except my body decided to ditch my brain and just start moving on its own, and I slammed her helmet in place, latched it, and reached for The Drop.

This was insane—!

Trust me.

It took every particle of willpower I had, but I drew The Drop, aimed it at the side of Torina's neck, flicked off the safety, and pulled the trigger.

As THE GUN bucked in my hand, I realized I'd just fired whatever was loaded in the chamber. If it had been an armor-piercing round, it would have simply blown her head off. Fortunately, when we anticipated a possible boarding action, I chambered a flechette round so I didn't blast holes through what might be critical space-ship components. The flechettes, still in a compact bundle, slammed into her b-suit at the join of collar and helmet. Several stuck there, protruding like porcupine quills, while the rest rebounded and whirled off in all directions. We now had a dozen or so tungsten-carbide needles floating around us to add to the fun, but my only concern was Torina.

I saw sealing foam burble up inside her visor and coat the side of her jaw. More oozed out around the embedded flechettes. The stuff went from foamy liquid to rubbery semi-solid in seconds, closing off the damage to her suit. It was also sterile, having both antiseptic and anesthetic properties, acting as a sort of immediate, automatic first aid. I could only hope it sealed her wound.

But I couldn't dwell on it. Torina may or may not be safe, but the *Fafnir* was clearly in serious trouble. That had to be my next focus, or saving Torina might not matter because we could all be dead in a moment.

"Netty!" I called.

No reply.

"She's gone into safe mode, in protected memory. All that's left is an emergency kernel module designed to handle critical functions," Perry said.

Okay, if Netty was out, my next stop was—

"Icky! Talk to me!"

"You want the good news or the bad news?"

"Icky, just tell me—"

"The good news is we're having this conversation. The bad news is I'm not sure for how long."

"Damn it, Icky—"

"Just hang onto your shit, okay? I'm working here. Gimme a second or two."

I bit back any further reply and turned to Perry.

"What the hell happened?"

"We got hit."

"Perry, I do not need your shit right now—"

"Understood. We got hit. That's all I know. I'm artificially intelligent, not omniscient."

"So—extrapolate, or something."

"Okay. It would appear that we were hit by a mass driver shot at point-blank range. The projectile seems to have passed completely through the ship just behind the cockpit. It caused an explosive decompression and threw shrapnel around, which is probably what injured Torina."

When he said her name, I looked at her. All I could see was her lifeless pallor behind her visor. The rest was just helmet and b-suit.

"Those *bastards*. Are they still out there? Lining up another shot? Icky, we need some control—"

"What did I just say about letting me work?" she snapped, still hammering away at the data pad. "I'm using what amounts to a glorified clipboard to try and get some control over a wounded spaceship—oh, wait."

She tapped one more time, and a suite of instruments came back online. One of them was the tactical overlay. That was my eyes' first stop, locating the enemy vessel.

It was over a hundred klicks away, accelerating away from us. Seeing that ripped a sound from me that was half gasping sigh of relief and half frustrated rage. If I'd had any control over the *Fafnir* at all, I'd have charged off after them, guns blazing.

But I didn't, so I didn't. I just gnashed my teeth and made myself be thankful they hadn't finished us off.

I spun to Torina. No change.

"Icky, we need to get some atmosphere in here! And get back to Spindrift as soon as we can!"

"The first ain't happening until I plug the holes in the ship. And the second—"

"What? What about—?"

"Hold that thought," she said before unsnapping her harness and pulling herself out of the cockpit. I turned back to the tactical display, then to the comm panel. The latter was still dark.

"Perry, we need to call for help. Have we got anything we can use that isn't the *Fafnir*'s comm system?"

"Emergency beacon, which is showing activated, and your personal comms. And those don't have nearly enough power to reach Spindrift, or any other ship in the system, for that matter."

"Can we route the suit comms through the beacon? Boost their signal?"

"We... could, yes. Try plugging the patch cord from your b-suit into the alpha jack on the panel to your left."

The patch cord was a thin data cable spooled up in a pouch on the b-suit's belt, offering hardwired access to external systems. It was mainly meant as a backup to the suit's regular wireless function.

While I did that, Perry jacked himself in to the center console. "Okay, this is going to take a minute, Van. I have to find some way of patching together two systems not meant to work together," Perry said.

Icky reappeared. "Do you want the—"

"If you say bad news, I'm going to lose it," I growled.

"Okay, well the good news is that the powerplant and the drives seem to all be in one piece," Icky answered with remarkable serenity.

"So we can maneuver?"

"That would bring us to the bad news. That shot punched clean through the ventral longitudinal main spar, passed through the cabin just behind us, and nicked the dorsal spar on its way out. That means two of the four spars that give the *Fafnir* her internal structural integrity are compromised. If we bring the drive online and apply anything more than a nudge or two of thrust, we'll break the ship in half."

I slumped back. "So we're dead in space."

"For the time being, yes."

I turned back to Torina, uttering a silent plea to things I'd neglected for a long time, desperately asking them to help her.

"There is one bright spot. The only reason that slug didn't pass through the cockpit is because you went *huh* and started to turn the *Fafnir* away from them. We didn't get lit up by fire control, so my guess is that they were aiming by eye, and you threw them off just as they fired," Icky said.

By instinct alone, I may have saved us. I would have felt a lot better about it if I'd listened to my instincts when they first piped up. If I had, we might not be here right now, crippled, dead in space, with Torina—

I blinked fast, clearing away the residue of an incandescent fury I was fighting to hold back.

Perry spoke up. "Well, how about that? Believe it or not, Van, you've got a comm connection through the emergency beacon. I used the nav system as a bridge, since we apparently won't be going anywhere for a while—"

"Awesome, Perry. Thanks." I glanced at Torina, then made eye contact with him. "For everything."

"Don't mention it. It's what I do," he said. "Oh, and Van? Thank you for trusting me. It means a lot."

I tapped his head, then turned my attention to the comm.

"Any ship, any ship, this is the *Fafnir*. Mayday, mayday, mayday, we need assistance—"

WITH THE TWIST drive still offline, our comms were limited to the speed of light. It made for a delay of almost two and a half minutes each way for messages, which meant we could only sit and wait. Icky set about patching the two circular holes that had been drilled through the *Fafnir* so we could repressurize the ship from her emergency air supply. I kept a close eye on the tactical overlay. The lasers were offline. So was the rail gun, but Icky made it clear firing it would be as potentially bad as lighting up the drive.

That left us with the missiles. With Perry's help, I was able to bring them back online. They soft launched, so they posed little risk to the ship when we fired them. At least we could defend ourselves.

A scratchy, static-filled voice sounded in my helmet set. "*Fafnir,* this is the freighter *Third Star.* We received your request for assistance and are inbound. What's your status?"

I opened my mouth to say some variation of awful but closed it again. I didn't want to broadcast to the universe just how badly damaged we were in case *would-be rescuers* decided to become *opportunistic assholes.*

"Thank you, *Third Star.* We're holding our own for now but do still need assistance. It would be particularly helpful if you could relay a message to—"

I was going to say Spindrift but changed my mind.

"If you could relay a message to a particular ship docked at Spindrift. It belongs to Schegith."

SCHEGITH MADE a high-energy run to reach us, burning a lot of fuel but arriving only a couple of hours after the Third Star had relayed our call. During that time, Icky bustled tirelessly about, getting more systems back online, the hull patched, and the ship repressurized. Perry assisted her where he could, despite his damaged wing. I split my attention between Torina and the tactical overlay, worrying frantically about the first, and almost daring something threatening to appear on the second so I could turn them to scrap.

As soon as we had atmosphere again, Icky and I pulled off Torina's helmet. Her face was pale and waxy in a way that made my gut clench. She was alive, though, the sealing foam having indeed slathered itself over her wound, closing it tightly. Despite being alive, she was unnaturally still, a comatose state rendering her limp and pliant, her limbs moving only when the ship rotated.

When Schegith was a half hour away, Perry was able to get Netty back online.

"Did I miss anything?" she asked.

"Not the time, Netty."

"Sorry, trying to ease the tension and all that. Anyway, *wow*—we were hit hard. I'm surprised we even lived through it."

"It was Van's last minute course change," Icky said. I could tell she was trying to be encouraging, which I appreciated, even if I still felt responsible. I had a sense of danger and ignored it.

I made a note to never do that again.

With Netty back up, we were able to restore essentially all of the *Fafnir*'s critical systems. We just couldn't go anywhere, at least not fast. Icky and Netty calculated that with one main spar damaged and a second completely severed, we could only safely apply low-power, half-second bursts of thrust from the drive.

"How long would it take us to get back to Spindrift?" I asked.

"Two weeks, four days, and about fourteen hours, assuming the best possible aggregate acceleration the ship can handle," Netty replied.

I looked at Torina, who was still alive, but just hanging on.

"I think we'll wait for Schegith."

I was never so glad to see another ship pull up alongside the *Fafnir*. Schegith's pilot, one of her people that we rescued from digital bondage, deftly maneuvered her ship to within a hundred meters of ours. At the same time, he ramped their fire control scanners to full power, switched all weapons—and she had a lot of them, for the size of her ship—to semi-autonomous mode, and made it clear that no one and nothing was coming close without her say-so.

More importantly, we were able to transfer Torina to her ship. She had already arranged for a salvage tug from Spindrift to come retrieve us, so she could take Torina back immediately.

"Salvage tug? They do realize we're not salvage, right?"

"This one has already paid all fees, and has agreed to pay a reasonable equivalent to a standard salvage value upon safe return of your ship to the specified location," she said while I maneuvered Torina onto the floor of one of the cabins. There were no furnishings or fixtures suited for humans aboard, so we used the *Fafnir*'s stretcher as a bed for her. Schegith assured us that she had sufficient knowledge of human anatomy to care for her during the brief trip back to Spindrift, though—

Wait.

I looked up at Schegith. "To the specified location? Don't you mean Spindrift?"

"No. Spindrift is assumed to be unsafe, perhaps even collaborators in what has happened here. We are going to meet a friend instead."

"Who? And where?"

"*Who* is my cousin. *Where* is nowhere at all."

I paused in confusion, but before I could ask her what she meant, Icky, still on the *Fafnir*, called over the comm. "Van, why don't you go with Torina? Perry, Netty, and I can take care of the *Fafnir*."

I looked at Torina. She still had that same grey, lifeless pallor. It looked so—so *wrong* on her normally lively face.

I finally shook my head. "Nope. I'm coming back right now. Torina's in good hands here, and the ship and you guys are my priority now."

"Van, seriously—"

"On my way back now," I said emphatically and turned for Schegith's airlock.

———

"Okay, that is one hell of a ship. Class fourteen, heavy cruiser type," Perry said.

"But with the weaponry of a battleship," Icky said, eyeing the *Fafnir's* tactical display.

Schegith's ship was already docked with the massive vessel. The salvage tug eased us to within two hundred meters of it, as instructed, then backed off. Almost immediately, a small swarm of drones erupted from a hatch that opened in the cruiser's flank and began swirling around the *Fafnir*, scanners illuminating us like searchlights.

"Looks like you don't need us anymore," the master of the tug said.

"It appears not. Thanks for your help," I replied.

"Thank your friend over there. We made salvage without having to actually salvage anything. I'll take that any day."

I had to smile. "Yeah, she's getting a big hug and maybe a sloppy wet kiss from me for that."

"Better you than me. Safe flight to you, captain."

The tug accelerated away. By then, the maintenance drones had already done their work and prepared to gently pull the *Fafnir* within reach of several manipulator arms that unfolded from the bottom of the cruiser's hull. A few minutes, and a few bumps and clunks later, our ship was firmly cradled in the arms, an airlock was connected, and we were asked to disembark while repairs were made.

"Netty, you keep an eye on things, okay? Call if you need us," I said on the way out.

"I will. But I've already opened comms to the cruiser's AI, and he seems right on top of things."

"Well, you kids have fun now." I clambered through the airlock, into the cruiser that apparently belonged to Schegith's cousin, bracing myself for another wonder of the stars.

———

SCHEGITH'S COUSIN looked exactly like another Schegith. I'd understood that she'd been the only surviving member of her race before we'd rescued the other Schegith, but that wasn't *quite* true. There were a few others, such as this cousin of hers, who roamed around known space. Since they'd left Null World, though, they didn't count—at least not to the official story.

I spent some time working on the details of the repairs to the *Fafnir* with Icky and Schegith's cousin, essentially a smaller, more compact version of her also named Schegith. It seemed that all of her species used the name, although it was only truly hers. Cousin Schegith's "use name" was Kischkek. When we'd finalized the list of things to be done, I braced myself and turned to him.

"So, what's the damage?"

Kischkek stared, then gestured at the list of repairs on the terminal. "It is all enumerated right there."

"No—sorry, I mean, what's the final cost?"

"For?"

It was my turn to gesture at the list. "For all of that."

"There is none."

"There's—what? No charge?"

"That's correct."

"But there must be tens of thousands of bonds worth of work there—"

"One hundred and seventy thousand, two hundred and sixteen, at current market rates," Kischkek replied.

"Ouch. Well, okay, then that's what we owe—"

"This one will not take your money. You saved this one's people from extinction. If anything, this one still feels a debt to you for that."

I sagged in relief. We could have afforded the price, but it would have left us tapped out for funds without busting our annuities held in trust by the Peacemaker Guild.

"Thank you. How about we call it square?"

"Call what square?"

I smiled. "We're even. Our *quid pro quo* is complete."

"With this one's thanks, it is agreed."

"Van?"

The voice that wafted from the comm was as forceful as crumpling paper, but I recognized it instantly. It was Torina.

"Holy shit—Torina, you're awake."

"I'll take your word for it."

I was already heading for the cruiser's medical bay, where she'd been taken. Icky was right behind me, carrying Perry, whose wing was still out of service. I was intrigued to note that he wasn't complaining about Icky handling him this time.

Well, they *did* say that trying times were one of the best ways to bring people—or, in this case, a four-armed alien and a smart-assed AI bird—together.

13

"Two hundred and eighty thousand bonds? Ouch!"

Icky had just handed me the repair quote from Anvil Dark. Unlike Schegith's cousin, they weren't willing to waive the fees out of sheer love and admiration for us. Still, while it was a huge bite out of our finances, we maintained a reasonably comfortable margin.

Even so—almost three hundred thousand bonds. If Schegith's cousin *had* billed us for his services, then we would be skirting the edge of being able to afford fuel. Or food. Definitely not both.

But the Schegith repairs had only been temporary. They'd bonded the broken spar and reinforced the damaged one, but we were still limited to a pokey three g's of acceleration. I was glad we'd met Schegith's cousin far enough outside any gravity wells that we could just twist directly away. But the run in to Anvil Dark, instead of taking us a few hours from twisting in, was going to take nearly four days.

It gave Torina time to recover, at least. Once her wound had been melded shut and she'd received a top-up of prosthetic blood—two medical technologies that, by themselves, would be worth a fortune on Earth—she was good for light duties. I avoided hanging around her or coddling her, because she'd made it abundantly clear the first time I tried that it wasn't welcome.

"I didn't let my mother mop my fevered brow when I was little, and I sure as hell don't need you doing it to me now," she groused.

I smiled, though. If she was feeling well enough to be snarky, then she must be on the mend.

Our pursuit of the *Empty Space* hadn't been a complete write-off, either, thanks to Schegith herself. While aboard her cousin's ship, waiting with Torina for temporary repairs to the *Fafnir* to be completed, I'd bemoaned the fact that the Empty Space would likely leave Spindrift before we could get back to her. We couldn't find any Peacemakers available to keep an eye on her, and would end up being pushed back to *start* as far as tracking her down went. But Schegith had given me one of her—smiles, I guess, although her mouth wasn't really meant for the task, at least not in any human sense.

"Where is your duck?"

I stared blankly. My duck—?

"Oh. You mean that ugly little tracking device-slash-holy relic? Um—on the *Fafnir* somewhere, I guess, sealed away?"

"It is not. This one contrived to retrieve it, repurpose it for our own surveillance purposes, then hide it aboard the *Empty Space.*"

My blank stare grew into an appreciative grin. "Well done, ma'am. How'd you slip it past that Spindrift engineer?"

"He was definitely wary of this one, apparently concerned that he may be eaten. It is an irrational fear, of course. This one never eats other beings," Schegith said, turning to leave Torina and me alone. Partway out of the room where Torina was recuperating, she stopped and turned her head back as far as her anatomy allowed.

"At least, not *living* beings."

She moved another meter or so, then stopped and again turned back.

"Anymore."

We were now at Anvil Dark, the *Fafnir* laid up in a repair hangar to have two of her main structural spars replaced—a big, laborious job requiring a full repair crew. Aside from the effects of the explosive decompression, and some inexpensive modules, conduits, and other control components, that had been the only serious damage. But it had very nearly been fatal, both to us and the ship.

Icky heaved the remnants of one smashed control module into a recycling bin. "There's your problem. That's the main signal router. It gathers systems data from all over the ship and determines the most efficient way to route the commands we send from the cockpit. That railgun shot went clean through it. One-in-a-billion shot that managed to temporarily take out all of our critical systems at the worst possible time."

I grimaced at the shattered component in the bin. "There's a backup, though. A redundancy for such a critical component. Isn't there?"

"Two of them, in fact. But shrapnel damaged the first backup, and guess what, the second backup's defective. I checked the logs and it passed its diagnostic tests every time. When the time came for it to do its job, though, it decided not to. I got it back online, which is why we regained control of the ship, but yeah—I'd say that's a warranty repair."

"I'll leave you, your enormous size, and your many arms to work that out with the manufacturer's customer service department."

I sighed at the *Fafnir*. Her hull plating removed to expose interior structure, she looked like a cutaway diagram. And that was only the start. In fact, we had to clear out of the bay before the *Fafnir* was declared off limits. A big chunk of her repair cost was removing her fusion reactor to allow the severed spar to be replaced. It was modular and meant to be relatively easy to switch out, but it was also a serious radiation hazard—the reactor's shielding underwent constant neutron bombardment when the thing was operating, and that, in turn, *activated* elements in the shielding and made them radioactive. The power plant bay's own internal shielding blocked the effect when the reactor was installed, but unless we wanted to hang out in rad suits, we had to leave.

I was still brooding over her when Torina and Perry appeared, coming back to the repair bay from a trip into Anvil Dark itself to pick up any scuttlebutt. I gave Torina a once-over.

"How are you feeling?" I asked.

"For the eleventh time—and yes, I've been counting since we left Schegith's cousin—I'm fine. It would be unusual if I wasn't, Van. It wasn't *that* serious a wound."

"Yes, I frequently gush blood from my neck. It's a real inconvenience."

She tapped the side of my face. "I appreciate the concern. I really do. But it's also starting to wear a little thin."

"Fine. I hope you feel like wet laundry in a cold rain."

"That's better."

I turned back to the *Fafnir*. "Icky, is there any way we can prevent an, ah, *mishap* like this from happening again? I mean, Torina's recovered, but the *Fafnir* hasn't." *And we all came within centimeters of dying*, I added in my own thoughts, though not out loud.

"Sure. We could install REAB armor on her midships, the least armored section."

"REAB?"

"Reactive-ablative armor. It's designed to defeat lasers and kinetic energy thingies. But are you sure you want to? Most ships don't bother with the extra mass and just leave non-critical sections, like crew habs and such, pretty much unarmored."

I gestured at the stricken ship. "That's what getting hit in a *non-critical* area looks like?"

Icky looked at the ship, then back. "Okay, *theoretically* non-critical. That really was a fluke shot, Van."

"Getting this REAB stuff would make the ship a lot tougher overall, though, right?"

"Yup. And more massive. That'll affect our performance, acceleration, that sort of thing.'

"The drive is running, what, ninety percent efficiently?"

"It's 91.3, give or take, but who's counting?"

I reached up and clapped her on the shoulder. "I have every confidence you can get it to ninety-two or ninety-three or whatever and make up for it."

Icky scowled, a genuinely unnerving sight. "I'm glad you have every confidence in that."

"That's the trouble with being a miracle worker. People expect you to work miracles."

We left the bay, leaving Icky with the repair crew, who were suiting up in preparation for removing the ship's reactor, and headed back into Anvil Dark. As we walked, Torina and Perry brought me up to date on the rumors and innuendo they'd gleaned.

"So the feeling generally is that Master Yotov's going to get her way and get her people installed as Masters," Torina said.

"Most people seem to think it's inevitable and are lining up to be on the winning side," Perry added.

I glared at the deck ahead of me. I knew Yotov's type. A control freak, she would seize every opportunity to put her fingerprints on any successes and thoroughly distance herself from any failures. The people arranging themselves on their knees before her were going to be sadly disappointed when they screwed up and she suddenly wasn't around to protect them. If they were smart, they'd get dirt on her, some sort of leverage to ensure they weren't suddenly kicked into the cold. Most of them wouldn't, though. I'd seen it happen in the army, I'd seen it happen in any number of tech companies, and I'd seen it happen very publicly in government—so, pretty much everywhere you had people in a hierarchy.

But that explained why Carter Yost had hooked his suckers into Yotov's camp. He smelled someone being successful and wanted a piece of it. And I wanted a piece of Carter, to find out what he knew about the *Empty Space*. It made our next stop easy—the Black Hole, the place he'd been tossing around money like confetti at a wedding. We expected to find Carter, or at least information about where he was.

We discussed the case on our way there. I stopped us before we entered the bar. "So let's find another relic from the church. If they're listening, then the circuit can be reversed, right?"

"With Icky's help, shouldn't be a problem," Perry said.

"Oooh, clever. I like it. Where would we find a new convert to the church, though? I think if we put our rich-idiot personas on and go back for a second one, High Doctor Markov might get suspicious."

"That's easy. Look for someone who's broke."

———————

CARTER WASN'T in the Black Hole. He hadn't been in a couple of days, according to the bartender. We checked and found that he'd sunk to a new low—*leasing* a Dragonet from a dodgy Yonnox frontman who existed in the shadows. Along with Carter and his new so-called ride, two mercenary types were missing too, having signed on with him, no doubt, for money alone.

It sure as hell wasn't his sparkling wit.

"Carter's ship registered its maximum certified mass when it departed here, meaning it was likely fully fueled and armed, or else carrying some significant cargo," Netty reported.

"Did he file a flight plan? Any destination?"

"His flight plan gives his destination as Crossroads."

"Crossroads? What the hell is he going there for?" Torina asked.

"If I had to guess, I'd say it's probably just an intermediate destination. Crossroads is the lowest-energy twist available to a settled system, so it uses the least fuel," Netty replied.

"So he's probably twisted there, then twisted right away again to wherever he's going," Torina said.

I pressed my mouth into a frustrated grimace. By design or fluke, Carter had managed to stay a step ahead of us. We were grounded at Anvil Dark, giving him a few days of leeway to get up to all sorts of shenanigans, and there was nothing we could do about it.

As soon as the *Fafnir* was certified to fly, we departed Anvil Dark and set course for Halcyon. For obvious reasons, we didn't want to head directly to the Pathway sanctum world, so we decided Halcyon would be the next best thing. Without the facial-recognition scramblers we'd used last time, our reappearance as a Peacemaker and his retinue shouldn't set off any alarm bells.

We hoped.

Anyway, we'd do what we could here, and then—something. Whatever it was, it needed to be something that produced revenue. Between the two hundred and eighty thousand bonds for the repairs and another seventy thousand bonds for the new REAB armor wrap around the midships, we were suddenly down three hundred and fifty thousand bonds. And considering that a rail gun slug only cost a few hundred bonds, I'd say our attackers got their money's worth.

Our attackers. Presumably, they were the crew of the *Empty Space.* Once they'd disabled us, they'd simply left, their signal vanishing from any scanner data we could find. Either they'd managed to twist away on their own, or they'd stealthily rendezvoused with another ship and escaped that way. Either way, though, they'd escaped. But only for now, I told myself. Only for now.

We reached and docked at Halcyon without incident and set about a low-key sweep through the station looking for someone we could persuade to shill for us and get their hands—or claws, or tentacles, or pseudopods, I didn't much care which—on one of the Pathway's bug-tainted artifacts.

We didn't conceal our identity as Peacemakers but didn't make a big deal out of it, either. I wore my duster, Torina had started wearing a coat that broadcasted *danger*, and Icky stayed on the *Fafnir*, fiddling with the drive. Wu'tzur weren't exactly an uncommon sight in known space, but their intimidating bulk tended to attract attention we didn't necessarily want. Besides, Icky was convinced she could tweak the *Fafnir*'s drive to offset the added mass of the new REAB armor and bring her performance back up to full spec.

Perry was, well, Perry. We couldn't do much to disguise him, so he literally gave us top cover, flying and soaring around us from girder to kiosk roof to conduit and keeping watch from above.

See anything dangerous? I asked Perry through my earpiece.

Nothing other than Torina. And you, of course, but—

I know. She's got that menacing stroll going on. It's working.

Menacing is right. She looks pissed. She okay? Perry wondered.

Here's an idea—why don't you ask her?

No thanks. I'm not that dumb. There's some gear up ahead. You might want to check it out.

We stopped to investigate a kiosk selling various chips and electronic components. They were no doubt all knockoffs, probably full of enough flaws to drive the error-correction AIs built into most devices crazy. More than a few probably also came preloaded with malicious software, and a few were obviously broken.

I had another reason for stopping by, though.

"I'm looking for the most sophisticated AI substrate chip you've got," I told the vendor, keeping my duster coat closed.

The alien, which kind of resembled a taller, ganglier version of ET from the movie, made a syrupy sound of what was no doubt delight at a possible sale. "Yes, have chip you want," he rasped, reached under his counter, fiddled with something, then retrieved a chip big enough to cover my palm.

"This is top of the line? Really?"

"Very much. Best can buy."

"I have a friend named Perry who's an expert on this stuff. If I showed this to him, what would he say?"

Perry, sitting atop a structural beam above us, spoke up in my ear bug.

Actually, Van, he's probably right. That probably is as good as civilian chips get.

"He say very, very good," the merchant said.

"How much?" I asked.

"Special today. Ten thousand bonds."

Torina hissed in a breath. "My, that's expensive. Van, we can get the same chip on Spindrift from a friend of my father's for, oh, seventy-five hundred, tops."

I nodded and offered the chip back. "Thanks anyway—"

"No, not finish. Ten thousand bonds is normal, for you and lovely lady, seven thousand four hundred."

"I'll think about it, thanks," I said, and handed the chip back. The vendor looked at us, maybe impatiently, or angrily, or for that matter, happily, I really couldn't tell.

We moved on.

"Okay, so substrate chips seem to be readily available. That means there's some osmium out there, right?" I said, grabbing something gooey and sweet on a stick from a vendor. It was rated as human consumable, but I took a tentative taste anyway. It was pretty damned good, having a kinda sorta mango-coconut thing going on.

Perry answered from atop an awning. *There is, sure, and that was definitely an AI substrate chip, but two things. First, it was probably crap, a factory reject that should have been recycled, or a knock-off. Even ten grand is a little light for a top-flight civilian chip. Second, that chip was a lot bigger and clunkier than any we've seen our identity thieves using.*

I looked at Torina. "That's a good point, yeah. Put that together with the fact that Steve back on Anvil Dark has had trouble finding that specific chip architecture anywhere else, and—"

"They're making their own chips. They're not relying on what they can get legitimately, or from the black market," Torina finished.

I bit off more of the gooey, fruity confection and chewed for a moment, loving the taste. "Which means they not only have a source of osmium, but some sort of facility where they're making these chips *and* the expertise to do it. That's got to be a significant operation, right? Perry?"

Significant, yes. Large? Maybe, but probably not so big that it couldn't be operated out of a single freighter, so it could move around.

"So instead of looking for the operation, we come back to the osmium and wherever it's coming from—such as, for instance, Rigel."

It's a long way away, but yeah—you can't really move a mine operation around. It kind of is where it is.

"Sounds like we need to start planning a trip to Rigel—hello, what's this?" I said, cutting myself off when I saw a grubby little alien skulking near the small suite maintained by the Pathway

Unburdened. Something about the way the furtive little creature—and I mean little, as in four feet tall and impish—gave passersby a *psst, hey, buddy* stare tweaked me.

"Didn't we see him the last time we walked by here?" I asked.

Torina nodded. "And the time before that."

I tossed away the gooey remains of my snack, then set course for the suspicious alien. I'd planned to give the Pathway's suite a wide berth, but this was too interesting to pass up. We changed course, passing right by the alien. He must have found us suspicious because he looked anywhere but at us, in a way that practically shouted *I can't see you, so you can't see me either!*

"You're not very good at this, are you?" I said, stopping.

"I—what? Sorry, I don't—"

I held up a hand. "I only have one question. Do you have anything to do with them?" I asked, pointing at the nearby Pathway suite. "Because if you do, I might be interested in a deal."

That immediately and obviously caught his interest. He really *wasn't* very good at this low-key crime thing.

"What sort of deal?"

"I'm in the market for a religious artifact. Specifically, a religious artifact from those guys."

"Why?"

"Because I'm experiencing a yawning gulf of spiritual emptiness and need it to fulfill me. What do you care?"

The alien shrugged. "I don't. How much, what do you want me to do—and did I ask how much?"

"Two hundred bonds if you go in, listen to their pitch, and then come out with an artifact. I don't much care what it is."

The alien hesitated. "They're paying me three hundred to try and steer people through their door."

Business must be slow if they're hiring this *guy to be their face*, Perry put in.

I smiled. "Wow, you are new at this. I'd have gone to five hundred, but I'll offer you four."

"Uh, no, now I want five hundred—"

"Sorry, doesn't work that way," I said and turned away, Torina right behind me.

"Wait!"

I turned back. "Fine. Four hundred."

I handed over two hundred. "You get the rest when you hand over an artifact. Make sure you make a big deal out of wanting to think about whatever they pitch to you. That should be their cue to try and give you one."

The alien stared for a moment, then shrugged. "Whatever."

He turned and walked to the door. Torina and I moved behind some air ducting and discreetly watched.

The alien touched the door chime. The door opened, revealing Tosneek, the alien we'd dealt with before.

"You know, I've been thinking—" our shill said, then went on describing how he'd been thinking, had been looking for spiritual fulfillment himself, blah blah. He did a good enough job that Tosneek actually gave him an appraising look, then ushered him in.

"Now don't you feel good about yourself, having given a poor, lost soul a new spiritual path?" Torina asked, grinning.

"I do. Of course, that path leads right back to those waiting two hundred bonds, but hey, I do what I can to make the universe a better place."

14

THE ALIEN CAME THROUGH, having procured a tacky, abstract sculpture made of what amounted to colored glass and brassy wire. Before we met with him and did the handoff, though, we kept our distance and had Perry confirm what, exactly, the thing was transmitting back to the Pathway.

If you're worried that it's sending back images of what's going on around it, it's currently not. Right now, in fact, it seems to be dormant, Perry said.

"They probably won't activate it right away, and give it a day or two, instead. Wait until whoever they gave it to gets complacent," Torina noted.

I smiled at her. "Clever."

"I know."

We made the exchange with the alien and took the thing back to the *Fafnir.* There, we turned Icky and Netty loose on rewiring it, co-opting it into being *our* bug.

"The question now is, how do we get this back into the hands of the Pathway without rousing their suspicions?" I asked.

"You guys could put on your rich asshole personas again and drop by for another visit," Icky suggested, scanning the so-called relic with a data slate and studying the results.

I drummed my fingers on the *Fafnir*'s galley table, just watching for a moment as Icky picked up her tools and got to work, helped by Netty's scans. It wasn't enough to *just* co-opt the thing. We had to do it in such a way that the Pathway would continue thinking they had sole control over it, and that was where the wiring got tricky.

"We'd have to leave here, go back to The Quiet Room, borrow their yacht, come back here—" I shook my head. "Too time-consuming."

"You'd also have to explain how Mister and Missus Moneybags came into possession of a relic that was given to a skeezy little alien," Perry noted.

Torina sighed. "And here I was excited about getting back into character—*dahling*."

We finally settled on having the skeezy alien return it, coaching him to utter some mumbo jumbo about how it just didn't resonate with him, making him feel no particularly heightened interest in joining the Pathway, and so on and so on. It took all that remained of that day and most of the next to get the thing rewired and set up the exchange, but it worked. The next day, we had ourselves yet *another* of the ugly bits of statuary, and the Pathway had our rewired one.

"Receiving data quite nicely. In fact, for a group that makes extensive use of electronic eavesdropping, their own electronic security kinda sucks," Netty said.

While we just let that particular iron sit in the fire and warm up, we turned our attention to our other bug, which required us to contact Schegith. She'd somehow wired our ugly little duck statue into the Empty Space's twist comms system, hinting at her being a skilled engineer on top of everything else. I guess being what was apparently hundreds of years old gave you time to develop a wide variety of skills.

"Anything from our duck, Schegith, of particular note?" I asked, once Netty got her on twist comms.

"This one can confirm that the Empty Space is involved in covertly shipping osmium, among other things."

"How much osmium?"

"Enough that its removal from the regular market would be noticed. This one believes that it is being extracted from some location independently of normal production."

"They've definitely got their own mine," Torina said.

"A logical conclusion. Which suggests that this operation is large and sophisticated. Osmium is very, very valuable. Perhaps even more valuable than your Perry's alloy feathers,"

"I've never felt more beautiful. In fact, I'm blushing," Perry put in.

I looked at Torina. "I hear Rigel's nice this time of year."

"If we can get there—"

"Hate to interrupt, but I've just detected a signal I think is going to interest you," Netty said.

Perry perked up. "It's a chip. A stolen identity has just arrived here, at Halcyon."

I perked up, too. "Where?"

"A fast freighter named *Legs, All the Way Up*. It's docking at port eleven, off to our starboard."

"*Legs, All the Way Up?* Seriously? Is it crewed by a bunch of teenagers from the 1930s?"

"Hey, I just report the names, I don't make them up," Netty replied.

I nodded and stood. "Okay, well, let's hold that thought about Rigel or anything else. We've got an appointment with a ship bearing one of the stupidest names I've ever heard."

"It's only stupid if you don't appreciate great gams, Van," Perry said smugly.

Torina flexed a calf muscle, then twirled. "If you got 'em, flaunt 'em."

I lifted a brow, giving Perry a bland look. "We're using vaguely sexist slang from a century ago? I mean—it's not what I expected out here in the stars, but—"

Perry wolf whistled, then turned to me, laughing. "To the clip joint, and step on it."

I FLASHED my badge at the airlock assigned to the *Legs, All the Way Up*. "Peacemaker Van Tudor. I've got some questions."

A voice crackled back over the intercom. "Oh, for—we paid you guys already."

"I—uh, okay, we'll just let that admission of bribery slide. I'm not here for money."

"What do you want then?"

"Answers."

"To?"

"Questions? And the first one is, what's with the name of your ship?"

"That's your first question," Torina muttered at me.

I shrugged. "Inquiring minds want to know."

"You'd have to ask the owner. I just fly the damned thing. And for the record, no matter how stupid you think that name is, I think it's even stupider."

"Fair enough. Okay, now the real question. You have a stolen personality on board your ship, don't you?"

"What?"

"A stolen personality. An identity on a chip."

"Currently located in your aft section," Perry said.

"What the hell are you talking about?"

I sighed. "Look, playing dumb is just—"

The airlock unsealed, revealing a gruff human with a shaggy, iron-grey beard and wearing greasy coveralls.

He frowned at me, hard. "I have *no* idea what you're talking about. What's a stolen personality?"

WE TRACED the signal from the identity chip to a maintenance drone used for miscellaneous chores around the engineering bay. The man who'd greeted us, a grizzled old spacer named Dornan, shrugged when I challenged him with it.

"Look, all I know is that we needed a new drone when the old one crapped out. We got a pretty good deal on this, especially considering how many features it has. I mean, it's semi-autonomous. And since this ship's AI is about as smart as a toaster, having a drone that runs itself is a big deal." He frowned at it. "Are you telling me there's actually someone, an actual person, inside there?"

I nodded. "There is, yeah. Which means we are going to retrieve them and see if we can restore them to, well, some sort of normal life."

Dornan stepped back. "Hey, do what you have to. I sure as hell wouldn't want that done to me."

It took only a moment to retrieve the chip, while Dornan repeated several times that he knew nothing about this.

I held up a hand. "It's okay. I believe you. What you can tell me, though, is where you purchased this drone."

"Spindrift. Regular dealer. No idea where he got it."

I nodded. "Thanks. Tell you what, here's five hundred bonds to help you buy a replacement chip for your drone here."

Dornan gave me an impressed and appreciative nod. "Thanks. Heh. I'm not used to getting money *from* Peacemakers, only giving it *to* them for—you know, fees, surcharges—"

"Administrative cost, duty, yeah, I know the drill." I flashed a smile. "Well, there's a new sheriff in town now."

"You're a sheriff? I thought you were a Peacemaker."

"Oh, for—never mind."

"WAIT, he's from *Helso*? He's from my homeworld?" Torina asked, her eyes wide.

Perry bobbed his head. "His name is Selavon. Selavon Trianis."

Torina's eyes widened a bit more. "We know his family!"

"Well, fortunately he was only taken about six weeks ago, so his mind and personality are both pretty much intact. Needless to say, he's *pissed*."

Torina and I both grimaced at that. We'd brought the chip back to the *Fafnir*, connected it to a standalone reader we'd acquired for the purpose—to keep us from having to plug chips that might be booby trapped with malware into the ship's systems—and had Perry interface with it through a series of firewalls.

"You're not seeing viruses or anything?" I asked him.

"Nope. Even as sophisticated as these chips are, a single personality essentially fills it up. As it is, he'll no doubt have lost a bunch of memories, because there isn't room for them. We intelligent beings are a whole pile of data."

That gave me a bit of pause—*we intelligent beings*. It did raise an interesting point. Perry and Netty were both personalities on chips, too, weren't they? And that led to some grey moral and ethical places—

Which I wasn't prepared to visit right now, so I just inclined my head. "Can we give him a voice?"

Since the chip seemed to be clean, we plugged it into Waldo Two and activated it through his logic processor, with some additional computing horsepower added by Netty.

"Where the hell *am* I? What the hell *is* this?"

I glanced at Torina. "That's going to take some explaining, Selavon. What do you remember?"

SURPRISINGLY, Selavon, a human merchant banker in his fifties, took the news of his new state of being in stride. If anything, although he was understandably pissed, he was also intrigued.

"So I'm an AI now?"

"Well—no. The legal opinion of the Peacemaker Guild is that you're still a person," I replied.

"Huh. So are the people who did this to me guilty of murder?"

"Uh—yes, of course. Why?"

"Well, because I'm not dead."

I gave Torina a surprised look. "Sounds like you're taking their side."

"No, no, of course not. I'm just wondering what the exact legal status of this case would be. Kidnapping, maybe—?"

"Um, Selavon, I think we're drifting away from the point a bit. This was done to you, and we're going to try to undo it."

"So what happens to me?"

"You end up in a new organic body. It's the best we can do—"

"No, I mean what happens to *this* me?"

I paused, choosing my words with care. "It—well, that version of you would be restored to an organic brain," I finally offered.

"Ah, but you're dodging the question. What happens to the *me* on this chip? Do you just wipe it away?"

I exchanged a look with Torina, another with Perry, a third with Icky. I'd have done it with Netty, too, but I suspected she'd just return as blank a look as everyone else.

I sighed. "The honest answer is that I don't know. I don't think the legal, much less the ethical or moral ramifications of this have even begun to be explored." I turned to Perry. "Have they?"

"Nope. At least, not that I'm aware of. And I doubt the Masters have been discussing it, what with the scheming and politicking and stuff."

"Okay, let's hold that for now. Selavon, for the moment, we won't make any plans to erase that chip you currently call home. In the meantime, we'll bring you back to Helso while we sort this out—since questions like this are way beyond us sitting here and ruminating over them."

I saw Torina looking at me. I knew exactly what she was thinking. We'd never considered the implications of "transferring" someone from a chip to an organic body. Was it an actual transference, or was it a case of one entity being destroyed and an identical one being created? So what did that mean for all of the people we'd rescued and restored to organic bodies so far? We'd deliberately wiped broken minds off of chips. Had we inadvertently wiped perfectly good and intact ones, too?

Were we well-intentioned killers?

———

RETURNING to Helso was a damned good idea for other reasons, too. For one, we could check in on the Synergists, the Space Hippies, and see how they were progressing with cleaning up the nanoplague that had been released into the soil. More to the point though, we just needed a break.

I said so to Torina as we set course for Helso. "I was thinking this was only going to be a brief visit, just a stopover to drop off Selavon. But I'm thinking we should take a few days." I looked up at her from the *Fafnir*'s instruments. "I don't know about you, but this endless procession of scheming, violence, and overall misery is getting to me. I need some time to recharge my emotional batteries."

She nodded. "You won't get any argument from me."

"We could watch a sunset together."

"Make that two or three," she replied, smiling.

"I could use a break," Perry said.

I shot him a glance. "Really?"

"Nah, not really. I just like to be part of things."

Torina rubbed his head. "You can come and stretch your wings on Helso as much as you want, bird."

"I register and acknowledge the pressure of your hand on the sensors built into my cranial structure."

"Oh, you sweet-talking thing, you."

"What's so funny?" Icky asked, pushing into the cockpit.

"Perry and Torina are whispering sweet nothings to one another. I think it might be serious," I said.

Icky looked from Perry, to Torina, then shrugged. "Who am I to stand in the way of true love? Anyway, I've been back there working with Selavon, trying to figure out where he was captured. While he tried to remember, I monitored his chip to see what I could figure out about its basic architecture."

"And?"

"And, it's pretty amazing. Whoever designed it is a genius. I made notes about a half dozen things I want to steal and take back to my father to try out."

I gave her a patient smile. To her, the engineering stuff was the most interesting, by far. And it *was* interesting, sure, but not as inter-

esting as opening up another possible lead in our case. "Okay, sure
—but what about Selavon? Did he end up remembering from where
he was taken?" I asked.

"Oh. Yeah, he did. Some place called You Bet."

"You Bet."

"That's what he said."

"Netty?"

"Sorry, there's no reference to it in any cartographic database I
can access," she replied.

"That's because it isn't on any cartographic database," Torina
put in.

I stared. "Okay. That implies you know something about this
place."

"I've heard of it. It's a place that deals in junk investments,
buying outstanding debts and flipping them to collectors for a profit,
inflated or even bogus stocks—oh, and they're a shady tax haven,
too."

"Sounds like a glorified call center. So where is it?"

She shrugged. "No idea. I remember my father and uncle
ranting about it when a genuine investment turned out to be a scam.
It wasn't losing the money that pissed them off, it was—"

"Being scammed. It wounded their pride," I said, nodding.

"Exactly."

"Yeah, you don't spend as much time in cyberspace as I did back
on Earth without seeing it all, pretty much. And most of it ugly. In
fact, I suspect You Bet probably also plays host to online gambling,
and probably lots and lots of porn, too."

I turned to Perry. "How has a place like this managed to fly
under the Peacemakers' radar?"

"What makes you think it has?"

"Hasn't it?"

"Remember how, shortly after we first met, I told you there were some things I have stored in memory that are locked, so I can't reveal them? This is one of those things."

That made me frown. "Really? I mean, you're my combat AI. Can't I just order you to reveal it?"

"Hey, if I had my way, I'd broadcast it all over known space. But you just don't have command authority to override these locks, Van. Sorry."

While Netty spooled up the twist drive, I drummed my fingers in frustration. I believed Perry, but it didn't make it any less aggravating that he had information that I couldn't access.

I turned back to him. "What would it take to have all the locks inside you removed? Who would have that authority?"

"A majority of the Masters."

"Which means a majority of Yotov's lackeys, based on what's going on back at Anvil Dark."

"I'm sorry, Van—"

"Never mind," I said, calming myself with an effort. I was getting mighty tired of politics, and I was still a newer Peacemaker.

"I'll talk to my father and uncle. They might know more," Torina said.

I agreed. We flew most of the rest of the trip in slightly strained silence, which made me feel a little bad—I trusted Perry, and this wasn't his fault.

But.

But this little exchange reminded me that Perry was a machine, which meant he could be programmed to do things he might not otherwise do.

Like spying on us for someone else.

I sighed. That thinking was heading in the direction of para-noia, and I knew it. But when it felt like everyone really *was* out to get you, paranoia was just smart thinking.

15

Fortunately, Helso was just the balm I needed to soothe my tattered mood. We spent three days there, taking in the work of the Synergists and generally enjoying some time away from corruption and scheming and violent death. The Space Hippies had done stellar work, despite adding a trio of musicians who sang and played instruments that were like small harps. In true Synergist fashion, the trio of singers, known as Vocalutors, sang in their lilting voices, urging the engineers on in the field. In truth, I wanted to roll my eyes at the sheer silliness of it all, but then I heard them singing a chord as the sun set, and every note reached deep into my bones like the song of a forgotten love.

In that moment, I understood why they were there.

I did not, however, go so far as to excuse the Vocalutors hats, which were nearly a meter wide, hideously green, and smelled like decaying lily pads rubbed with raw garlic. When I met the singers up close and personal, they beamed with the positive energy of people who were utterly secure with their purpose in life. The lead singer, a willowy woman named Danci, asked if I wanted a hat of my own, and when I politely declined, she managed to look wounded *and* hopeful.

"It's a generous offer, Van," Torina said, shaking her head in mild reproof.

Perry, helpful as ever, chimed in. "Generous. Very."

Danci looked up from under the pungent brim of her own massive hat, freckled and smiling. "I would love to share this with you, Peacemaker Tudor."

I looked to the stars, if only for a second, then gave a small nod. "I, um… would be honored. What are these hats called, anyway?"

Danci looked injured. "Hat? Oh, this is no mere hat, Peacemaker."

"Yeah, Van," Perry added, again helpful to a fault. His tone managed to imply I was a thankless barbarian, all in two words.

"It's not?" I asked.

Danci beamed, and reached to her bag, from which she pulled an even *bigger* hat made from—whatever they picked out of a pond. Or a dumpster. Maybe both.

With great ceremony, Danci plopped the massive, damp construct on my head and tugged the brim down with a waft of intense stink. Stepping back, she smiled and brought her hands to her mouth, ecstatic. "Perfection. I've never seen a *zhigbrao* fit better."

"Zhigbrao," Torina said, one hand on her heart. "A noble name for something to protect one from the elements. He loves it, Danci. Don't you?" Torina's eyes glittered with mischief, but at least Perry was quiet.

I knew when to cut my losses. "I do." As I spoke, the brim

bobbed, and something dripped down my arm. The zhigbrao was, apparently, a fresh one.

Danci leaned up, kissed my cheek, and wheeled away, swinging her harp around as she strummed a cheery note. "Back to work, then."

In moments, she'd rejoined the other Vocalutors, and they made their way to a crew of nine Synergists who were coaxing life into the land.

Under my breath, I murmured, "Perry, I'm gonna run you through a—"

"Boss, I urge you to reconnect with the land and let your anger go," he interrupted.

I turned to Torina, who was nearly purple with laughter. Flicking the brim of my zhigbrao, I began the walk back to the main house. "If you'll excuse me, it's time for my mid-afternoon drink. Or two."

"After you, good sir," Torina managed.

Perry made the excellent choice of flying high enough that I couldn't throw anything at him, and the four of us—three beings and one giant, stinking hat—left the Synergists to their work.

Unfortunately, our case wasn't progressing anywhere near as well as the restoration of the land. No one in Torina's family knew the location of You Bet, or really anything else about it other than its existence. In fact, the only new piece of information we had about the place was something Netty had found while connected to the Anvil Dark archives. It was a canceled Peacemaker reward for information leading to the arrest and conviction of parties involved in piracy on behalf of You Bet. It hadn't been for much, just fifty thousand bonds. Not that I'd turn down fifty thousand bonds, given our recent outlays, but it wasn't the money itself that piqued my interest.

"Why is it canceled?" I asked. Torina and I had just stepped off the expansive veranda of her parents' house and started toward the fallow lands being restored by the Synergists, to get a close-up look.

"No idea. It was canceled just over a year ago," Netty replied over the comm.

"Huh. By whom?"

"Master Yotov."

"Well, shit." I looked at Torina. "So we again have Yotov implicated in something fishy but no way of chasing it."

"She's good at covering her tracks—and always in the most frustrating way possible. It's like you can see the tracks and follow them to a dead end, every time."

I nodded morosely. "It's almost like she's trolling everyone."

"Trolling?"

"Yeah. She could have just had that Peacemaker bounty deleted. Instead, she canceled it and just left it there for people like us to find." I narrowed my eyes as I spoke, as my own words kickstarted a new line of thinking. "Maybe she *is* trolling. If she's the arrogant control freak I think she is, this might be a bit of pathology on her part. She might have an obsessive need to not just be in control, but to constantly demonstrate it to everyone—maybe even herself."

Torina glanced at me with respect. "That's some elegant psychological insight for a guy who mostly worked with machines."

I shook my head. "The truth is that hacking and cyber ops are only partly about the tech. They're mostly about people. Those computers only do what they're told by their users. They're just tools. The real target of hacking is the *people* using those tools."

"You need to be a people person to do it well."

"Absolutely. Frankly, I've managed to access as many systems by social engineering people into revealing their log-in credentials and the like as I have by busting into them with actual hacking." I put my finger to my lips. "Don't tell anyone. We hackers need to preserve our aura of technological wizardry. We don't want people to know we often resort to manipulation or blackmail just to get people to give us their passwords."

We wandered for a while and ended up at the pond visible from the veranda of her parents' home, where we appreciated the green sprouts and shoots and spindly saplings sprouting from soil that, when we'd last seen it, had been dead, grey dust.

I sighed at the water. It, unfortunately, hadn't yet been cleaned up. Runoff from the dead land had choked it with silty sludge, leaving it a drab, milky grey.

Still, green speckled the land all around it, a sort of halo of hope surrounding the pond. I took comfort in that.

Torina stepped up beside me. "Not ready for swimming yet, I don't think."

"Not unless you like swimming in mud," I agreed.

"I wonder how they do it. The Synergists. My parents couldn't find any technological solution to this damned nanoplague. None."

I shrugged. "They have some sort of psionic potential, don't they? Mind over matter?" I sniffed. "Although, when I say it out loud, it sounds like magic."

"I don't know. I kind of like the idea of it being magic, even if it really is entirely explainable—they have psionic powers that can bypass technology."

I'd been about to try skipping a stone across the pond but stopped and looked at Torina. "Wait. Say that again."

"I like the idea of it being magic?"

"No, the other part."

"They… have psionic abilities that get around technology?"

"Yes, they do, don't they?" I threw the stone and got two bounces—my personal best was seven—but ignored it.

"Torina, can you arrange for the leader of the Space Hippies to meet us at your house as soon as possible? I have a little side gig for them."

"I REALLY SHOULDN'T LET you do this, Van," Perry said.

"Why not? Is it illegal?"

"No, but—"

"Immoral? Unethical?"

"Maybe? That would depend on your particular—"

"So that's not a yes, either."

"But it's a violation of Peacemaker protocols—"

"Which may be concealing wrongdoing. Now, wouldn't that be illegal, immoral, and unethical?"

"Well, sure, but—"

"And shouldn't we determine whether that's the case? Aren't we supposed to hunt down and put an end to wrongdoing and crime and stuff?" I asked.

"So you want me to accede to circumventing Peacemaker security protocols, to determine if those same protocols have been violated, by examining the very stuff those protocols are meant to protect?"

"Is this the part where you start going crazy and then explode?"

Perry stared at me. "What?"

I shrugged. "Happens on TV and in movies all the time. The advanced AI is trapped in some logical loop, so it spirals out of control, repeating things like *error* and *does not compute* over and over, until it finally blows up or turns murderous or something."

"I'm—no, I'm not going to explode," he replied.

"Or turn murderous?"

"We'll see."

"Excuse me, but there is too much disharmony in this place. Too much negative energy," the Synergist said, rings and bracelets and things softly chiming as she spoke.

We sat on Torina's veranda with the head Space Hippy, who had no title, apparently because *titles implied a hierarchy, and there are no hierarchies in a truly whole and enlightened universe.* She simply called herself the agent of the Synergists who happened to be dealing with this particular request.

Which was fine. I didn't care. I was just looking for her to help with finding out something Perry couldn't reveal, by doing exactly what Torina had noted they did with the nanoplague—using the power of their mind to circumvent technology.

Sure, it might be a long shot. But since we'd had ample, grim experience with human minds being replicated on chips, it stood to reason that there was some commonality in their architecture. I was hoping that the Synergist could, in fact, read Perry's mind, since there was no better way of putting it. The data was there, it was just locked away behind a wall of security we couldn't circumvent normally. Again, this was a Hail Mary, I realized—it might not be possible or, even if it were, the data was no doubt encrypted. The Synergist may only be able to access hints and shadows.

"I apologize," I said to her.

The Synergist nodded sagely. "I accept your contrition. The humility of your thoughts cleanses much of the negativity. Now, let us all observe the candle and use it as a focus for our thoughts. Look at nothing but the candle. Only the candle exists, all else is illusion."

Alrighty, then. I nodded and looked at the candle, which floated in a small vessel of water. It sat adjacent to a star map, which we hoped the Synergist could use to point out the location of You Bet. I was the only one present besides Perry and the Synergist, apparently since *including more minds within the circle of understanding will increase the negative energy.* The single reason I was present was because my contribution to the *circle of understanding* was exactly what we were looking for.

So I stared into the candle, which burned in a steady, yellow flame without smoke or flicker. It was more of—a glow, really, and less of a flame. It was kind of mesmerizing—

The Synergist began to chant softly. The chanting morphed into a lilting song, then back again, every note and word filled with the stories of a time and place that flickered at the edge of my understanding. Bracelets and trinkets rattled and chimed. The candle began to gutter, as though nudged from side to side by errant wafts of air I couldn't feel.

No, wait—it was moving in perfect harmony with the Synergist's soft, ceaseless chant. And now even the jingle of bracelets and trinkets fell into the same rhythm, as did a metronome tapping she did on the table with her hands. It was one song, one pattern, one story, all revealed in the ceaseless, gentle beat as inescapable as a rising tide.

I was captivated by the dancing flame, the steady beat and silvery noise of her bracelets, the rising and falling chant and surges of song. It all seemed so—so *perfect*, and in such a satisfying way, like the flawless harmony of a skilled acapella group, or the finished picture of a jigsaw puzzle—

"There."

I blinked, startled, and looked around, momentarily stunned. I felt like I'd just woken up but knew I hadn't actually been asleep.

"Wow," I said, then noticed the Synergist was pointing at the map, at a particular star system.

"That's... Halcyon," I said and sighed. We'd been to Halcyon enough to know that, unless it was heavily stealthed and without even a glimmer of signature, You Bet couldn't be there. Okay, so maybe it was somehow part of Halcyon itself and we'd just never noticed—

But the Synergist shook her head. "No, this place has no star. It is alone, in harmony with nothing but itself, and the universe as a whole."

I noticed her finger actually pointing quite close to Halcyon, but it was offset slightly. At the scale of the map, that slightly was still two or three light-years, though.

But what was actually there? Was You Bet some sort of station or facility literally floating in the void? That would be odd, because as I understood it, twist navigation to arbitrary points in space away from actual, fixed waypoints like stars was notoriously unreliable. That didn't rule it out, of course, but—

On a hunch, I touched my comm. "Netty, I'm going to read you off a set of nav coordinates. Can you tell me if there's anything at all near them, other than the Halcyon system?"

I gave her the coordinates, and she came right back.

"The closest object to that point, aside from the Halcyon system, is a rogue planet called UGPS 0722−05 on Earthly star charts. It is about the same size as Sol's Jupiter, but with about eight times Jupiter's mass."

A rogue planet? Now *that* was interesting.

"Do we know anything else about it?"

"Not really. It's been visited twice by stellar cartographic survey-ors, and that's it—there aren't any records of other close observa-tions. It's essentially a dense gas giant just a little shy of being called a brown dwarf, with absolutely no companions."

"So it's perfect."

"It is? For what?"

"For a hideout. For bad guys. Thanks, Netty."

"For the record, I want to make it clear I had no part in what just happened. I've just been sitting on this table, beside this candle and star chart, minding my own business," Perry said.

The Synergist clicked her tongue. "The negative energy has returned. I can do nothing more here," she said, then stood and simply walked away.

"Way to go, Perry. You disharmonized her."

Perry dropped his beak, then laughed. "In all my years, this is the first time I've ever been accused of killing a vibe."

"Wait, we now have a way of bypassing security protocols on information systems? That's huge," Icky enthused as we ran the *Fafnir* through her preflight checklist.

"Yeah, you'd think so, but the Synergists made it clear that it's not something they're likely to do again, aside from emergencies," I said.

"And for good reason. Can you imagine what would happen if word got around that Synergists can read the minds of AIs and tease out things meant to be secret?" Torina said.

"Yeah, they'd never be allowed anywhere near—huh, pretty much anything mechanical, ever," Icky replied.

"The only reason they agreed to do it this time is because they were as curious as we were if it was even possible. And it is, and that's the reason they won't do it again," I agreed.

"Which is unfortunate, because that could be a useful trick," Perry said.

We all looked at him.

"What happened to *this might not be illegal but it's still ethical and immoral?*

"You'll recall, I started to add a qualifier, *depending on your particular point of view* before you so casually cut me off. As it happens, I think it was quite clever. Moreover, if I'm completely honest, I'm glad we can get at these bad guys now." He held up a wing. "But, again, for the record—"

"Yeah, yeah, you had no part in it. Duly noted," I said, activating the flight controls and lifting the *Fafnir* off of Helso. Per the protocols we *didn't* want to violate, we'd already decontaminated ourselves, and entered and exited the *Fafnir* only by cycling through the airlock, which we'd also decontaminated. Until the nanoplague was declared over, that would be a requirement for all ships leaving Helso. So was the detour we had to take to within a prescribed distance of Helso's sun, exposing the entirety of the *Fafnir*'s exterior to its heat and radiation to scrub off any nanobots that might have hitched a ride. The risk of contamination of other worlds was simply too great.

On the way, we pondered the connection between Halcyon and You Bet. Selavon insisted he'd been taken on his way to Halcyon, but only gained awareness on You Bet, realizing he was installed on a chip. Everything in between was a blank, the memories gone, erased, or repressed by a mind that was fighting for survival.

"It sounds like they might be grabbing people on their way to Halcyon," Icky suggested.

"Piracy? Hmm. I wonder if they looked you and me over when we did our indolent rich act on the *Aetherswift*," Torina said.

"Now there's a scary thought," I replied, wondering if we had indeed been in the crosshairs of the identity thieves without even realizing it.

"Maybe we should do that again—borrow that yacht and have you guys take it to Halcyon. You know, use you as bait," Icky suggested.

But I shook my head. "For one, as much as I'd love to expose myself to pirates aboard an unarmed yacht, I don't think it's all that good an idea, or even necessary. We can just twist to You Bet itself and start there."

"For one? What's the other reason?"

"They had a chance to grab us—and passed. I don't think I could take such rejection a second time."

"Welcome to the middle of nowhere," Netty said.

The movement of the rogue planet was carefully mapped, so it hadn't been hard for her to twist us here. As soon as she had, I saw why this was such a great place to hide away bad behaviour. There was absolutely *nothing* here.

Except for the rogue planet itself, UGPS 0722−05. I had to use the tactical overlay to even find it. It didn't radiate at all in the visible light spectrum, only infrared. To the naked eye, it simply vanished into the blackness of the void.

But it wasn't all that was here. We'd powered down everything except the twist drive and a few critical systems like life support and inertial dampers. It by no means reduced our chances of detection to zero, but it was better than appearing powered up and hammering away with active scanners. So we just hung motionless where we'd twisted in, casting a wary eye on the station, a central hub surrounded by three toroidal rings stacked one above the other.

"Not as big an operation as I'd expected. That's, what, only a couple of hundred meters across, maybe?" I said, studying the enhanced image Netty projected on the *Fafnir*'s center console. She'd also added an infrared layer to view out the canopy, so we could now see the planet as a dim, ruddy disk.

"How much room do you need to run—what did you call it? A glorified calling center?" Torina asked.

I smiled. "Close enough. So what do you guys think? Just a straight-in run?"

Surprisingly, Netty spoke up. "Van, I have a suggestion. Right now, we're looking at the orbital plane of the station almost edge-on. If there's anything else that shares an orbit with it, it could be on the far side of the planet."

"Okay, so what are you suggesting?"

"That we position ourselves directly above one of the planet's poles and approach from there, so nothing can take us by surprise. I mean, the other side of that planet is literally the only place out here anything *could* hide."

"But they'll detect us once we start maneuvering, won't they?" Torina asked.

"Not if we just twist there. It's going to burn more fuel, but it's better than being ambushed, I think."

I nodded. "Netty, you are very wise. Make it so."

"Make it so?"

"Just something I'm trying out."

16

THERE WAS NO AMBUSH, as it turned out. In fact, there were only two other ships present besides ours, a yacht registered to a holding company and a class six workboat that had supposedly been scrapped three years ago. Both were docked at the station, and neither made any attempt to run once we lit the drive and started our approach. In fact, aside from some scanner pings, there was no reaction to our arrival.

"Not exactly the most prepared villains, are they?" Torina said.

"Maybe they were expecting someone else and we just happened to show up first," Icky suggested.

But I pointed at the comm panel, at the transponder controls. "We're broadcasting our Peacemaker identity and credentials. It's more like they just don't—I don't know, *care?*"

We cautiously approached until we were only a klick from the station. Still nothing. Not a call over the comm, no sudden barrage of active scanners, just silence."

"Oh. I just had a thought. What if they're all dead over there? An accident, or something?" Torina asked.

Perry answered. "I've been scrutinizing the incoming data. There's clearly power being generated, the station is heated and pressurized, there aren't any unusual amounts of radiation—if they are all dead over there, it's owing to nothing we can detect from out here."

I shrugged. "Okay, then. Netty, take us in to one of those empty UDAs. Let's just try the front door, shall we?"

We made it to the open universal docking adapter without incident, established a hard dock, and readied ourselves at the airlock. I had The Drop drawn and ready in my right hand, while I rested my left on the pommel of the Moonsword. Over my b-suit, I wore the shoulder pauldrons Linulla, the Starsmith, had made for me. Torina likewise wore her vambraces, and Icky her helmet. We were going to enter in full Peacemaker mode, credentials blazing.

Netty opened the *Fafnir*'s outer airlock door, revealing that of the station. I raised The Drop, Torina hefted her own sidearm, and Icky stood behind with her massive sledge poised. "Okay, Perry, see if you can get that door—"

It abruptly slid aside.

"—open. Uh—yeah, thanks."

"It wasn't even locked," Perry said.

I nodded and pushed into the station's airlock. Only its inner door stood in our way. Surely it was going to be locked. Still, I gave the control an experiment tap.

It opened.

Without hesitating, I entered the station, ready for a dire confrontation.

"Moist!"

———

I WAVED AWAY the elderly Fren-okun. "No, I do not need to be kept moist! Just—get away from me and—no, do *not* open your mouth in my direction!"

The old Fren hesitated, peering around with milky eyes. "Moist!"

"Oh, for—what's *she* doing here?" I snapped, again trying to wave her off.

Torina, her tone annoyingly amused, shook her head. "I don't think it's the same Fren as the one that was keeping your cousin—"

"Moist!"

"Yeah, that," Torina finished, smirking.

I pushed past the elderly Fren, but she kept shouting *Moist!* and threatening to regurgitate all over someone. Torina and Icky both laughed. I was about to turn around and assign them the job of looking after the old alien when a new voice spoke up.

"Mother, mother—we've been through this, you do not need to moisten anyone!"

Another Fren had just rounded a corner and hurried toward us.

I eyed him warily. "Who are—"

"Moist!"

"Mother, just come over here and wait, please," the younger Fren said, then turned to me. "I'm sorry about that. And you are?"

"Peacemaker Van Tudor. Now let me ask you the same thing. Who are you?"

"My name is Oly'ski'tr, but you can call me Olly. And you're a Peacemaker? Oh, that's not good."

"Not for you it isn't—I think," I said, suddenly realizing that we had no evidence whatsoever of any wrongdoing, just a rather bland and dumpy Fren and his mother aboard a space station in the very center of nowhere.

I holstered The Drop. "This place is called You Bet, isn't it?"

"It's a code name. A rather silly one, if you ask me," Olly replied.

"Okay, so—wait. Help me out, Olly. What are you doing here?"

"Well, until now, overseeing the operation of this station. I suppose it was too good to last, though."

"What do you mean?"

Olly expelled a breath I assumed was meant to be a sigh, but it was hard to tell with an anthropomorphic platypus. "We were assured that measures had been taken to ensure we were never found, so we didn't have to worry about law enforcement. That's obviously not true."

"Assured by whom?"

"The owners."

It was my turn to sigh. "Who are?"

"I honestly don't know. I was offered a rather obscene amount of money to oversee the operation of this place on their behalf, which I couldn't turn down because, well, taking care of mother is expensive. But two or three years of doing this, and I'd be able to afford the care she needs."

"What is it with your old people all wanting to make everything moist—"

"Moist!"

"—all the time, anyway?" Icky asked.

"That, I'm afraid, is how most of our elders end up. Our females, in particular, revert back to wanting to take care of infantile Fren," Olly replied.

"Which involves slathering them with regurgitated goop? Yeah, that's a yuck," Torina muttered.

"And how about your younger people? We've met some of those, too, and they're… well—" Icky hesitated. I was surprised. Was Icky developing a smidgen of diplomatic sense?

"Morons?" Olly offered.

We all kind of just stared back at that, and Olly shrugged, at least as much as an upright giant platypus can. "They are. We are. Our young are born as virtual imbeciles, then they work their way to morons and become more and more intelligent after that. It's just how our race works."

"More intelligent until—" Perry said, then bobbed his head a few times in the direction of Olly's mother.

"We become delusional, yes."

I had to admit, I was a little impressed by Olly's candor. We'd been talking as we walked, following him, and now we entered an expansive compartment. It must have occupied a good third of this toroid's circumference. I had to blink a few times to make sure I understood what I was seeing.

Back in my college days, I'd worked a job in a call center, dealing with people trying to claim rebates on stuff they'd bought. It was a grinding, monotonous job I did while hemmed into a cubicle competing with my dorm-room closet for *smallest space ever*. I was looking at that very same call center now.

Well, except for all the aliens, of course. Despite the variety of species working here, though, the place still managed to instantly convey that sense of dreary, stressful conformity I still associated with that damned call center. I even felt myself tensing up the way I did right before I started a shift.

I took a deep breath and scanned the bleak-scape of aliens jammed into cubicles, hunched over data pads and terminals. "So what, exactly, are they all doing?" I asked Olly.

He waved a hand in one direction. "Those are various types of scams tied to stocks. Over there are direct investments in fake corporations, or ones whose success has been dramatically inflated. That's the enforcement unit over there—"

"Enforcement unit? What the hell do they *enforce?*"

Olly shrugged again. "Various types of cons intended to scare people out of their money. You know, your passport has been flagged as possibly being involved in criminal activity, now you have to pay a fine to have it cleared, that sort of thing."

Torina was shaking her head. "And you're just coming out and admitting all of this."

Olly shrugged a third time. "I assume you wouldn't be here if you didn't already know what this is all about. I'm just a little surprised it's only the four of you, and only one ship."

I saw Icky open her mouth, but I cut her off. "We've got a backup Peacemaker flotilla on standby. We wanted to try this the easy way, first. And, I must admit, this has been... ah, *easy,* at least so far." I moved where I could loom a little over Olly. Icky, apparently getting it, moved slightly to make herself loom behind him, too.

I waved a hand at the call center generally. "However, as interesting—and by *interesting*, I mean *disgusting*—as all of this is, it's not what we're primarily interested in. We're chasing literal identity thieves, scumbags who murder people, but not before installing their minds onto chips as cheap surrogates for AIs and selling them into digital slavery."

"Oh, I think that all happens in the lower toroid," Olly replied mildly.

I wasn't sure if I should be horrified at his casual attitude toward crime, or just impressed he was this capable of it. He was a middle manager in a corporate structure based on evil.

Which led to an inane thought. How many Ollys did movie supervillains need to build and operate their secret lairs and city-killing death rays? For that matter, how many sleazy call centers back on Earth peddling fake lottery wins or bogus credit card deals were managed by quiet, efficient people like him?

I gave my head a disbelieving shake and just moved on. "Okay, take us to the lower toroid."

This time, though, Olly shook his head. "I'm afraid I can't."

"Why not?" Icky growled from immediately behind him, making Olly wince.

"Because I don't have access down there. My only involvement with the things going on down there is making sure systems maintenance gets done—you know, water, air and atmospheric integrity, heat, that sort of thing. Aside from that, I just see ships occasionally come and go, and that's all I know."

I crossed my arms. "I see. So… you're like a clerk working at a concentration camp. You don't do any of the dirty work yourself, you just make it possible for others to do it."

"I—" he started, then sagged a bit. "That's probably an accurate way of putting it. How much does that implicate me in those crimes? Because they sound serious."

"Hold that thought," I said and turned to the others. "Okay, let's round everyone here up and get them somewhere we can keep an eye on them. Same for any other employees in this place. In fact, let's just bring them all here."

I turned back to Olly. "I want you to make that happen. Every employee aboard is to report here now. Do you have a list of all of them?"

Olly looked mildly offended. "Of course. How could we manage them otherwise?"

"Fine. You're going to give that list to Perry here, and then he is going to confirm that every single person who works here is in this room and accounted for. Got it?"

Olly, still sagging, just nodded. "I understand."

"Torina, I'm going to leave you and your natural charm to keep an eye on things here. Oh, and your sidearm, rifle, and superior combat skills, too," I added, a little more loudly, to make sure it was overheard by everyone nearby.

I turned to Icky. "You and I, Icky, are going to pay a visit to the lower toroid."

She grinned and hefted her sledge, the head of which was as long as my forearm.

"Anytime you're ready, boss."

PERRY'S VOICE hummed in my helmet's headset. "Okay, Van, we can confirm that all the employees on Olly's list are here and accounted for. I've done a quick fly around both of these two upper toroids and haven't scanned any stragglers."

"Thanks, Perry." I turned to Icky. "Ready?"

"Never been more," she said, raising her sledge and crouching slightly. It was a hell of an intimidating sight, I had to admit—especially since she also wielded a boarding shotgun in her two *lower* arms.

Hope I never have to face a Wu'tzur in combat, I thought, then turned to the data pad I'd wired into the door per Netty's instructions. She would use it as a sort of conduit to hack the door's security system and open it when we gave her the order.

"Okay, Netty, whenever you're ready."

A moment passed. Then another.

"Is there a problem, Netty?"

"It depends on what you mean by problem. I've accessed the door's control module, so I can open it any time. Unfortunately, that will also trigger a containment failure in the station's fusion reactor and—well, you see where I'm going with this?"

"Vividly. Can you work around it?"

"Probably."

"Netty, *am I going to avoid being blown to bits* is not one of those questions that should be answered with a probably."

"And yet, here we are. I'm sorry, Van, but there's no way for me to predict this. Even if I can bypass the security locks, there's nothing to guarantee that opening the door won't trigger a hidden switch, or even if a change in air pressure caused by the door opening could do it."

JN. CHANEY & TERRY MAGGERT

I turned to Icky. "Can we cut through it?"

She'd relaxed her ready stance—a little. "Um, that's a blast door, which means it's probably made of what amounts to spaceship armor. So, sure, if you give me a day or two with a plasma torch." She frowned at the door. "Maybe three."

"Shit. How about accessing it through an external airlock?"

"Unfortunately, I think we'd have to assume it would present the same problem," Netty said.

I ground my teeth in frustration. I couldn't help thinking that the door's security lock, which we apparently could bypass, wasn't just a way of daring a would-be entrant to find another way. Worse, we couldn't even have Netty open the door and see what happened. There were only three ships present—the *Fafnir*, the yacht, and the illegal workboat. Even jammed shoulder to shoulder, we wouldn't get more than half of the people off this station.

Which meant that we were stymied.

For a moment, I was tempted to have Netty open the door anyway. But, who knew, it might *just* be a trap and there was nothing on the other side except for reactor containment failure. I doubted that, but I couldn't rule it out—which meant we couldn't take the chance.

"Sorry, boss," Icky said.

I glanced at her. "For what?"

"For not being able to get through this door. I can tell it's driving you crazy." She sighed and lowered her weapons. "If it helps, me too. If we had the actual, correct access code, this would be a whole different thing."

I glanced at her again. "Icky, come with me. We might not be able to get in there today, but we might in the near future."

"YOU'RE NOT ARRESTING US? Shutting this place down? You're just going to let us keep, ah, working?" Olly said, his tone one of disbelief.

"Yes and no. Perry is going to see to it that all of the security and scanner logs for this station are wiped and their time indexes reset, so there won't be any record of us even having been here." I nodded to where he'd jacked into Olly's master terminal, in his cramped little office. "You and I are then going to be partners. You're going to feed me information about what's going on here— ship movements, the identities or at least images of everyone who comes and goes, that sort of thing. Most of all, you are going to get your hands on the access codes to that lower toroid for me."

"I—but—my employers would never—"

I held up a finger. "You know, people use the phrase *failure is not an option* a lot. It's almost always bullshit because failure is always very *much* an option. A shitty one, but it's there. Not in this case, though. Failure isn't an option for you, Olly. You're going to figure it out, and you're not going to get caught because I can't imagine your employers would take you being a Peacemaker informant very well. In fact, that discovery will likely be fatal."

"For you," Perry added, cheery as ever.

Olly looked like he was about to continue objecting, but Icky leaned toward him with a hand cupped to one ear. "What's that? What are you about to say to Van in answer to his very reasonable offer?"

Olly finally slumped in defeat. "I'll do it. Somehow."

"You're at the peak of Fren intelligence, Olly. I have faith that you will."

Perry unplugged from the desk terminal. "Okay, it's all set. It's basically a virus set to trigger in four hours and wipe all of the security data and scanner logs back to half an hour before we twisted in."

"And reset the time indices, right?" I asked.

"Netty and I have done one better. Just resetting the time stamp risks having things that the bad guys know happened, like the arrival of a ship, not be logged. So we recreated logs from scratch, including events that we want the bad guys to see, with the rest filled in by extrapolated bits and pieces from older logs," Perry said.

"We reason that these criminals won't be checking the logs in such detail that they'll notice that worker X sat down at their workstation earlier today in exactly the same way they did two weeks ago," Netty put in.

"No, probably not. That's genius, guys." I looked around, resigned to that being it. "And with that, I guess, we might as well head—"

"Actually, Van, there's something else. About a week ago, a ship transmitted a twist message back here from the Halcyon system. They said they had a problem with their drive and needed another ship to come and spell them off *in the target location*, as they put it."

That stopped me short. "Really? Did they say where this target location was?"

"Nope. They were too careful for that."

"Oh, for—Perry, why are you—?"

"It's okay, Van. What they weren't too careful to do was remove the metadata from the twist message. It includes their exact location when they transmitted."

I smiled. So did Torina and Icky.

The bad guys, who forever seemed one step ahead of us, might have finally screwed up.

17

Low on fuel, we twisted to Spindrift, topped off, then twisted back to Halcyon. The so-called target location was one of the Lagrange points of the outermost planet, the point where the combined effects of gravitation from it and the sun were balanced. It made a terrific place to hide a ship, since you could power right down and not worry about slowly drifting out of position owing to unbalanced gravitational forces. Moreover, the outermost planet was close to the most direct twist trajectory from the most populated parts of known space, and would be for a long time—it took four hundred years to revolve around the star.

Sure enough, it took some doing, but by hanging motionless and silent, we could scrutinize the Lagrange point with passive scanners. We finally confirmed a ship parked there, mainly because of its faint thermal signature. Unless you were looking for it specifically, like we were, you'd never notice it.

We mused over the best approach and decided that we'd light

the drive and head toward Halcyon just as we usually did. Netty crunched all the numbers and determined the closest we could get on that trajectory before we had to burn hard to abruptly shunt the *Fafnir* onto an intercept course. It would give the bad guys about an hour to do something about it, but by planting themselves in a Lagrange point, which by definition was inside the planet's gravity well, they couldn't just twist away. Nor could they realistically run, because they'd have to accelerate from what amounted to a virtual dead stop relative to the *Fafnir*.

"So the only outstanding question is, what the hell are we facing?" I gestured at the telescoping picture captured by the *Fafnir*'s imager. At this distance, the other ship was little more than an elongated, slightly fuzzy blob.

"Whatever it is, it would be class eight or nine, so close to our size."

I pulled at my lip. Size *did* matter, but so did firepower. We'd discovered that, when we tried to rendezvous with the escape pod from the *Empty Space*, at the cost of a lot of money and very nearly our lives.

"To hell with it. We've come *this* close to what might be a major break in the case and walked away empty-handed. I'm not doing it again."

I WATCHED the tactical overlay closely. We were ten minutes away from the full-power burn that would shove the *Fafnir* onto an intercept course. The other ship hadn't moved, apparently content to let us pass by.

"They might have done that every time we've come here, and decided to let us just be on our way since we're Peacemakers," Torina said.

"I'm surprised they didn't hit you guys when you were aboard that bougie yacht. A couple of rich douchebags seems exactly like the sort of people they'd like to nab," Icky said.

"Bougie? Bougie? Icky, have you, by chance, been on human social media again?" I asked blandly.

She managed to look away and seem guilty all at once. "No."

"Uh-huh. And since you learned the word *bougie* out here, in deep space, I'm sure you didn't create social media profiles and link back to satellites in Earth orbit—which would be a stunning feat of engineering."

"She's got verified accounts," Perry said idly. "At least that's what I heard."

"Heard?" I asked.

"From me, maybe," Perry admitted.

"Verified accounts? Really?" I turned to face Icky, who loomed over me but had the energy of a kid caught in the middle of something forbidden. "What picture would you use, pray tell? Since, you know," I said, waving at her four-armed, fuzzy bulk.

Icky mumbled something.

"What's that?" I asked.

"I used your pic. But, like, not your *actual* picture. I, ah, had Netty switch your gender with this cool app, and—"

I held up a finger. "Netty?"

"Netty is unavailable due to a system reboot," Netty said.

"Of course. Well, we can chat about this later, after I—and I can't believe I'm saying this—ground you and take away the internet. The Earth internet, anyway," I said, which was officially the weirdest thing I'd uttered since leaving Iowa.

Icky slumped. "I was up to almost three thousand followers," she mourned.

"Three thou—you know what, never mind. And as to my picture, I want you to—"

"You're a hottie as a girl, Van. Great bone structure," Torina said.

"Et tu, Torina?" I snorted in mock disgust, then pointed to the screens. "Back to business, and yes, I'll need to see all those accounts at some point. I can't have us vulnerable due to Icky's connections."

"They're firewalled and interstellar. Ain't nobody getting in my house, Van," Netty said.

"Reboot complete?" I asked.

"Yes, thank you. You were saying, boss?" Netty prompted.

"I've been thinking about the fact that we might have been watched by the enemy, back there where they were lurking for targets. I suspect they didn't risk attracting the attention of a Peacemaker, because it would compromise their whole scummy operation."

"I thought these assholes had a Master covering for them, though."

"They do. But they can't be sure that any particular Peacemaker is in on the deal. And there are a few. Like Lunzy, or Alic, or K'losk. And us, of course."

Torina shifted in her seat. "You sure about that?"

I looked at her. "What do you mean?"

"Well, aren't you covering for those thieving jerks back at You

Bet? You're letting them continue operating their scams, after all. I know it's for a greater good, but still."

I opened my mouth to protest it wasn't the same but didn't. I didn't know that for sure, did I? As much as I suspected Master Yotov of being a corrupt and narcissistic villain, I couldn't prove it. Could she be covering for the operation of these identity thieves to preserve an even *greater* good?

"Pfft."

We all looked at Perry, who'd uttered the clearly dismissive sound.

"Using criminals to catch worse criminals is nothing new. Van, even your grandfather had an extensive network of, ah, let's call them *semi-willing helpers*."

"He used informants?"

"He had a few practically on retainer, yeah."

I stared. "How come you never told me this?"

Perry shrugged. "Your grandfather was very clear about that. He even made it an explicit order to Netty and me. We were not to tell you about him using informants and just let you come to discover it on your own."

"But—why?"

Surprisingly, it was Netty who replied. "Van, imagine if back when you first discovered a spaceship in your barn, we'd handed you a list of criminals your grandfather kept as paid—or, in a few cases, intimidated—informants."

"Well, I would have…"

But I trailed off. I was going to say something like, I'd have filed it away for future use, but that was now-me talking. Then-me would have been appalled that Gramps was in league with crooks, no matter how noble the apparent purpose."

"Your grandfather was very wise in letting you discover it on your own," Icky said, neatly encapsulating my thoughts.

I glanced back at her. She was right.

"See, Van, your grandfather knew that you'd figure it out eventually, about the first time you inevitably recruited your very own informant," Netty said.

"Huh. Okay, then. So what happened to Gramps' informants?"

"Well, most of them actually ended up dead. Only a couple of them bought it because they got found out, though. Let's just say that the sort of people who make the best informants aren't necessarily known for their good life choices or healthy living," Perry said.

"Are there any left alive?"

"A few. We've lost track of most of them, though. We only know of three for sure, but for all we know, at least two of *them* might be dead by now, too."

"What about the third one?"

"Oh, she's almost certainly still alive. Not very friendly, but alive," Netty said.

"If you can convince her to become your informant, she'd be pretty handy. And after your performance with Olly—backed up by Icky of the many arms and weapons, of course—I like your chances. Oh, and not only is she only two systems over, but you're also going to love what she used to do for a living," Perry said.

"Tell me it has something to do with chips."

"Even better. She ran a scrapyard for ships and was considered a master at armor and weapon upgrades."

I glanced at the tactical display. Our burn was only three minutes away.

"Well, we'll stop in to see her after we visit our pirate friends out there at the L-point. But I noticed you said *was*? What happened to her, this armorer?"

Netty answered. "Your grandfather. That's what."

———

"I'm beginning our course change now," Netty announced. Behind me, the fusion lit, making the *Fafnir* softly thrum. The drive's prodigious thrust was directed at an angle compared to our current trajectory so that, viewed from a fixed point in space, the *Fafnir* would be skidding almost sideways, like a car drifting around a corner.

"Let's go active with the scanners and hot with the weapons, folks," I said, watching the tactical display. If our alleged pirates were concerned about us, they'd probably do something other than just sit there. My money was on something to play for time—a message asking for help, or the exchange of data, or anything designed to reduce our vigilance and create an advantage.

But even then, they'd have to paint us with scanners prior to firing, and I've always believed that a good offense is a good offense. They'd attack sooner than later.

Sure enough, a minute into our course change, the comm chimed with an incoming message.

"This oughta be good," I said.

Icky stuck out her meaty hand, putting it between Torina and me in our seats. "Ten bonds says some scientific research thing mapping that planet."

Torina gave Icky a sideways high five. "I'll take that action. I'm betting archaeological survey."

"Make mine a mission of medical mercy," Perry added, brushing a wing across Icky's palm.

Torina looked askance at Perry. "You getting paid by the M?"

"Alliteration isn't always an affront," Perry said. "But on to more critical things. Van, are you in?"

"Eh, what the hell. Let's go—something related to traffic control," I said, tapping Icky's hand. "Netty?"

"Stellar cartographic survey. Icky, consider your hand slapped or shaken or whatever."

"Okay, Netty, put them on," I said.

"Approaching Peacemaker, this is the stellar cartographic survey ship *Observer*. Please don't approach us, as any noise from your ship, scanners, and such will affect our work."

I curled my lip. "Netty, I can't help but notice a bit of a delay between their first call and that audio. They hadn't already identified themselves before you made your bet, had they?"

"Van, are you implying I cheated?"

"Uh—actually explicitly stating it, I think."

"Oops. Sorry, Van, I just suffered a glitch and lost the last thirty seconds of elapsed time. What were you saying?"

"That you're not getting my ten bonds, you scalawag."

"What ten bonds?"

I grinned, but it faded as we got back to business. "Okay, Netty, assuming you haven't forgotten anything else in that huge memory of yours, is there a stellar cartographic survey ship named the *Observer?*"

"There are three survey ships with that name in service. One of them does generally match the configuration of this vessel, but it's based at a scientific institute in Tau Ceti."

"So she'd be a long way from home."

Perry cocked his head at me. "Van, do you really think that's a stellar cartography ship out there?"

"Oh, hell no. But if we shoot and it does, by a fluke, turn out to be some science vessel—that'd be a problem, wouldn't it?"

"Well, I suppose you could argue a misidentification, tragic accident, etc. But that would be unethical, I guess. Maybe as unethical as using Space Hippy, ah, *abilities* to bypass some poor AI bird's security protocols—just to throw out a random example."

"Perry, does it really bother you that I did that, and as a result found You Bet where we are about to confront what's almost certainly a pirate preying on unsuspecting people to kill and chip them? Really?"

"Well, when you put it that—"

"Peacemaker, we notice you're still deflecting toward us. Again, our instruments require nearly perfect electronic silence to operate properly. Please break off immediately," the voice on the comm cut in.

I looked at the tactical display. Four minutes from maximum missile range.

"You going to answer them?" Icky asked.

I nodded. "All in good time, Icky. All in good time."

The other ship tried twice more over the next minute or so to get us to break off, but it still didn't light us up with fire-control scanners or start maneuvering. Based on Netty's projections, no matter what direction or how hard the *Fafnir* and the other ship accelerated, there was no chance of them getting out of our effective weapons range in anything less than thirty minutes.

In other words, we were both committed.

Still, I really didn't want to fight a point-blank range battle. I waited a bit longer, then nodded to myself. "Okay, time to rattle their cage," I said, and activated the comm.

"Observer, have a question for you. During your cartographic surveys, did you ever happen to collect data on the rogue planet called—"

Netty helpfully painted the name onto the *Fafnir*'s canopy in big, flashing letters and numbers.

"—UGPS 0722−05? Because *You Bet* I'd like to learn more about it—"

The supposed stellar survey ship abruptly splashed its fire-control scanners all over us. An instant later, its main drive lit.

"Is it just me, or is that an awful lot of electronic noise?" Torina asked, her fingers poised over the weapons console beside her.

"I'd say so," I replied, tapping at my own weapons console. I fired two pairs of missiles while leaning the *Fafnir* even harder into her drift, until the g-meter almost touched red—the point at which we'd start feeling the ship's acceleration through its negators.

Two missiles flashed back around, and the other ship burned directly toward us. He'd apparently decided that one, close, high-speed pass was inevitable, after which the two ships would be rapidly separating. That would expose them to the minimum possible firing window, which also meant they weren't keen on fighting us.

That made me want to spit nails.

"Freakin' cowards. They're okay taking on a yacht or punky old workboat, but when it comes to something with teeth—"

"Protracted space battles aren't their thing, Van. Pirates really just want the other guy to give up without a fight," Perry said.

"I know. Just pisses me off, is all."

We passed the next couple of minutes in tense silence. The missiles flashed past one another on their way to their respective targets. With only two inbound, we weren't exactly saturated with targets. Torina slewed the rail gun to life and took out one of the missiles with her third shot. The other dodged our point-defense fire and detonated close to starboard. A series of dull thuds reverberated through the ship. Their sounds were a chorus of conflict that rattled in my bones.

"That's the REAB detonating, deflecting shrapnel," Icky said.

I scanned the instruments. No significant damage.

"Suddenly, the extra cost of that stuff seems like money well spent," I said, just as our missiles reached the so-called *Observer*.

She managed to take out two with her sole point-defense battery, but the other two bracketed her, one detonating to each flank. She didn't have REAB, or even much armor at all, judging from her prodigious acceleration curve. Like Perry said, she wasn't really meant to fight, and relied on stealth, subterfuge, and intimidation to prevail over ships that weren't something like the *Fafnir*.

The other ship's drive immediately died, and she just coasted on amid a growing cloud of shimmering vapor as her atmosphere bled into space. Her power emanations dropped to nearly zero.

"Aw, I never even got to shoot at them," Torina grouched.

"Actually, my dear, if you could stand by on the mass driver and laser, that'd be peachy. I just want to make sure these guys aren't playing possum by coasting dead silent."

"It means playing dead," Perry put in, as both Torina and Icky opened their mouths.

I flipped the *Fafnir* end over end and burned hard against our direction of travel, slowing down. We still flashed past the other ship before coming to a halt, and then starting after her again. During our pass, we were able to confirm she'd been badly hurt, myriad wounds gaping across her hull where shrapnel had slammed through her hull plating.

"Yeah, I can see why they didn't want to fight," I mused.

It took another four minutes, but we finally matched course and velocity with the ship that obviously wasn't the *Observer*. Still, I hung about a hundred klicks away, watching her warily. There was zero variation in their speed, and the course held true.

"At its current velocity, that ship is on course to reach the next star system in about sixty thousand years. Were you planning on accompanying her, Van?" Netty asked.

"*Et tu*, Netty? Isn't one snarky AI enough for this ship?" I said, studying the tactical display.

"Actually, Van, your grandfather always complained that Netty was the snarky one," Perry said.

"Really? Netty, is that true?"

"What a shocking thing to say. And after accusing me of cheating—"

"You were cheating."

"Well, yes, but it's the accusation that hurts."

Torina interrupted. "Van, is there a reason you *aren't* just taking us in to board that ship?"

I kept staring at the tactical display. "No. But—also yeah. I'm having trouble getting past what happened the *last* time we approached something we thought was disabled. Coasting or not, it might have some punch left in it."

"Okay."

I sighed. Unless we were going to just keep indefinitely coasting along in close company with this disabled ship, our only other choices were to finish it off or just leave it.

I tapped the thruster controls. "No time like the present. We board, and now—but remember, we're going to be cool, calm, and collected."

Icky gave a cartoonish nod and hefted her warhammer. "Got it, boss. I'll be a picture of restraint."

WE DID GET SHOT AT, but not until we boarded the other ship. Three crew opened up on us with a hail of slug fire as soon as we breached the airlock door.

In a smooth motion, I fired The Drop twice, Torina next to me, her own sidearm blasting away without any hesitation. The corridor and attached cabin descended into a charnel house as our rounds went home—the pirates had courage, but no armor, which was proving to be fatal. Rounds smacked into my b-suit and clacked off my helmet and pauldrons. I returned fire, again, targeting the middle pirate, but missed.

Torina didn't. Her dead-eyed shooting took the second and third pirates clean in the helmets, shattering faceplates and releasing an astonishing amount of blood. The crimson globules danced and wobbled in the no-g cabin, and then things got *interesting*.

Icky charged the remaining pirate with a bloodcurdling howl that, unfortunately, only we could hear over our headsets. Still, I imagined having a hulking Wu'tzur silent screaming behind a helmet visor, a massive sledgehammer raised. The pirate, wounded but alert, raised his weapon and shot, but he may as well have been firing in the dark. His jangled nerves pulled the shot wide, giving all of Icky's mass a chance to accelerate with the fury of a runaway train. The hammer blurred to life in her hand, connecting with the pirate in an explosive impact that crushed his midsection like a tin can under a tank. He dropped, and although I didn't think he would ever get up again, I popped him with an energy round from The Drop.

"That was very restrained, Icky," I said.

"Yeah, restrained. My swing was, ah, intensified by the lack of gravity."

"Let's go with that," I agreed.

We did a thorough search of the ship, and despite an attempt by the pirates to wipe their computer of any useful info, Perry was still able to extract some interesting tidbits. First, he found some fragments of nav data, which Netty examined and matched to possible candidate systems.

"The data's incomplete, but what has survived is a perfect fit for navigation, and in the vicinity of three places, including You Bet and Spindrift."

"Well, if there was any doubt about their connection to You Bet, that confirms it. And Spindrift isn't surprising. But you said three locations, right?"

"I did. And you're going to love this. The third data set fits the parameters for a supergiant star that exactly matches the gravitation of—"

"Rigel."

"Got it in one."

Icky frowned. "There is no *way* this little bucket made the twist to Rigel."

"Not unless it was carried as cargo aboard a larger ship, no," Netty replied.

Bingo. Rigel had just become a must-visit location. First, though, we had to figure out how to get there.

Perry's second find was also fragmented, but he was able to glean two sources for it. The first was, again, Spindrift. No surprise there.

The second was Anvil Dark.

"Well, shit. Any record of who they were talking to there?" I asked, anticipating the very answer I got.

"No, Van, sorry. I've only recovered a few scraps of metadata. I can't tell you anything about the contents or recipients of the messages. All I can say is that whatever they were, they were sent to or received from Anvil Dark," Perry replied.

We made one more discovery. A grim one.

It was a personality chip. We retrieved it from the ship's waste-reclamation system. However, it had been fried by an EMP generator apparently installed for that very purpose. Whoever had been enslaved on it no longer existed.

I gave a slow nod. "Fine. Perry, I have a question."

He gave me a wary look. "Okay."

"Have I got sufficient grounds here to implement Section 1, Article 6 of the Guild Protocols?"

"Extreme Field Sanction? Do you believe that it's necessary to use lethal force to prevent further loss of life?'

I stared at the cooked-off chip. "I do."

"You may be called to account for enacting it—"

"Good. I hope it's Master Yotov that calls me on the carpet," I said.

"Well, in that case—yeah, it's your call, if you're prepared to stand behind it."

I turned to face Netty and Torina. "How about you guys? Do you see any reason we shouldn't just leave and destroy this ship?"

Torina glanced at the pirate I'd stunned. Icky had broken his collarbone with her swing, but he wasn't dead.

She turned back and pointed at the incapacitated pirate. "I take it that's the Extreme Field Sanction part."

"It is. And just to be clear, I'm not suggesting this lightly. I won't murder someone out of hand, but it's clear we *are* going to have kill people if we're going to end this damned identity-theft ring. At least, I think so. But if even one of you objects, we'll just take him into custody and haul him back to Anvil Dark."

"Is this even a question?" was all Icky said.

I looked at Torina.

She touched my arm with a gloved hand. "I hate the idea of killing anyone. But if these assholes aren't the ones to die, then innocent people will be. No discussion or explanation needed here."

"Netty? You're part of the crew, so you get a vote, too."

"I won't lose any sleep over it.'

"You don't sleep."

"Well, if I did, I wouldn't lose any over it."

"Fine. Let's do one last pass through this thing to make sure we haven't missed anything, and then we'll be on our way."

I took the fried chip with me when we left and placed it on the top of the *Fafnir*'s instrument console like a dashboard ornament.

As we opened the range to a klick, I looked at it.

"I don't know who you were, and I'm sure you weren't perfect, but you deserved better than this. So you're going to stay right there until we've stopped the assholes who did this to you. We never knew you, but we won't allow you to be forgotten."

I turned to Torina. "I'll do the shooting if you want."

She shook her head. "Nope, I'm good. Just say when."

"Anytime. Netty, make sure you capture this, in as much detail as you can."

Torina tapped at the controls, targeting the mass driver and lasers both. When she had them locked, she fired.

The other ship vanished in a cloud of melting and vaporizing debris.

We stared in silence, that Perry finally broke.

"You know, I heard an Earth saying once, from Kentucky. It goes like this—he needed killin'."

I glanced at him. "Where'd you hear that?"

"From the seat you're sitting in, Van. It was your grandfather that said it."

I nodded. "Okay, before we go on to save the universe, let's visit that armorer. I have a feeling we'll need her skills."

18

"I'м curious. With a beautiful super-Earth here, why isn't this system buzzing with activity?"

I'd said it as we headed sunward from our twist point, falling toward the system's primary, Luyten's Star. Our destination was said super-Earth, a planet called Dustfall. On the imager, it looked every bit as green and hale as Earth, with terrain varying from tundra to prairies to thick rainforests. It looked like the perfect candidate for settlement by millions, not the paltry few thousand who apparently did live here.

Netty answered. "Because, about six hundred years ago, this was the homeworld of a pre-spaceflight race known as the Tskul."

"What happened to them six hundred years ago?"

"They obliterated themselves in a thermonuclear war."

"Ouch."

"And that's the reason it's called Dustfall. Atmospheric winds blow radioactive debris around the planet, making it unsuitable for habitation for at least another two hundred years."

"Which hasn't stopped some developers from buying options on it, counting on future investment," Perry said.

"Really? Developers are sitting on a world that's been nuked, waiting for the radiation to die down so they can subdivide and sell it off?'

"When you put it that way, it sounds sleazy.'

"When you put it *any* way, it sounds sleazy, Perry. Who the hell are the people living there now?"

"They would be the P'nosk."

I frowned in thought. The P'nosk. A race native to—Teegarden's Star, as I recalled, either from my implanted memories or the stuff I'd learned since, all of which was now blurring together into just memories.

"So what's the great attraction of an irradiated world to the P'nosk?" I asked.

"Well, for one, they are extremely resistant to radiation. P'nosk often find work in things like ship scrapping because exposure to irradiated engineering components doesn't bother them," Perry said.

Torina suddenly nodded. "Oh, right, I've heard of these P'nosk. I remember seeing a clip of one of them standing beside a working reactor core and waving at the imager. It was radioactive enough to kill a human in just over a minute, the voiceover said."

"So just because this planet is contaminated by fallout, they couldn't resist coming here?"

"Not exactly. A small group of them were settled here by the developers. See, without anyone living on it, Dustfall was fair game for anyone who might want to claim it. Now that the P'nosk are there, the developers have secured their ownership of the rights."

"Resettling part of a race to proclaim your ownership of a planet that's basically the tomb for *another* entire race so you can make money from it in a couple of hundred years?" I shook my head. "Ain't money grand?"

We made planetfall and started our descent toward the only space port, or at least the only one with an operating beacon. It was located on a long peninsula jutting out from an equatorial continent. Right after we began to deorbit, though, the threat alarm buzzed.

That snapped my attention back to the tactical overlay. "*Now* what?"

"Someone on the ground fired a missile at us," Netty announced.

As soon as she said it, the tracking data appeared. We had less than thirty seconds until it intercepted us.

"Oh, for—Netty, random evasive maneuvers and full counter-measures. Icky stand by—"

The missile vanished.

I stared, blinked, then noticed Torina had her fingers on the laser controls. She gave an apologetic shrug. "Sorry, Van, I didn't mean to cut off your commanding presence like that, but I figured you'd rather just blow it up."

I smiled. "If it's going to save our asses, don't worry about my commanding presence. Cut away."

I swung back to the overlay. "Netty, any evidence of another launch?"

"None so far."

"If you even get a hint of one, go ahead and hammer a few

missiles right back at them—and make them count." I hit the comm, broadcasting across the channel spectrum. I gave my credentials, followed by a warning that we'd respond to any further force in kind.

Silence followed. But there were no more launches, and we were able to touch down at the spaceport unmolested.

"THAT RADIATION THING is too bad. Looks like a beautiful day," Torina said.

I took in the ruddy sunshine and clear, purplish sky. I didn't think I was ever going to get used to basking in the light of different suns... especially under skies of hues not known to Earth. I knew that by Dustfall standards this was a nice day, maybe a little on the cool side for my taste, but still reasonably pleasant. It didn't change the fact it was utterly *alien* to my human senses.

Nice or not, the pervasive radioactive contamination forced Torina and I into our sealed b-suits. Icky stayed aboard the *Fafnir*, while we clambered out with Perry and waited to see what would happen next.

That turned out to be a boxy ground vehicle departing a squat, chunky building about a klick away. The—truck, or whatever, began rolling toward us on oversized balloon tires. Torina and I moved apart, me toward the *Fafnir*'s prow and her toward the stern. We both kept our hands by our weapons. Icky also had the point-defense battery under manual control, so she could give us supporting fire if things went pear shaped.

But the vehicle just rolled up to the *Fafnir* with a soft whir of bulbous tires and stopped. A pair of plump humanoid aliens dismounted, wearing formfitting outfits that—let's just say they weren't flattering. They had bright red ears that looked sunburned and bushy whiskers that only added to the sense I was speaking to a sapient walrus.

Excuse me, *two*.

I stepped forward. "I'm Peacemaker Van Tudor, here on business for the Guild. Mind explaining those shots at us?" I asked, a touch of heat in my words.

"Without warning, I might add," Torina put in.

One of the aliens stopped a few meters away from me and shrugged. "Sorry about that. Someone left the local defense grid in autonomous mode—and its AI is a bit of a maniac."

"Why are you here?" the other alien asked. "We get almost no traffic thanks to"—he gestured all around us—"ah, to the rads. So if you're looking for a criminal or something, they're probably not here."

I glanced at the rad meter in my heads-up. We weren't giving, say, Chernobyl a run for its money, but the number was still notably high. I grimaced at the thought of the alpha particles and gamma rays sleeting against my b-suit, trying hard not to remember that it had been made by the lowest bidder.

"Maybe we're here for one of you. I mean, you're P'nosk, right?"

The two aliens looked at one another. "For us? I can't remember the last time one of our people left the planet, and Peacemakers generally don't involve themselves in local law enforcement, so—"

"Okay, you got me. I am here on official business, but not to arrest anyone or anything like that. I'm looking for—"

I stopped. Shit. It just struck me that neither Perry nor Netty had actually mentioned the name of my grandfather's old P'nosk informant.

Perry came to my rescue. "We're looking for Zenophir."

The slightly chubbier and more rotund of the two P'nosk wrinkled his face up. "Zenophir? That old monster? Why?"

"Uh, monster?" I asked.

"Yes. Monster, as in miserable old—" The next word didn't translate, but from the tone I assumed it was roughly equivalent to *bastard*, maybe even *asshole*.

"That's okay. I don't care if she's a miserable old anything. I just want to meet with her," I said.

"Well, suit yourself. She lives like a hermit in those mountains way off to your right."

I looked that way and saw mountains, alright—a tiny, rugged line of them on the horizon. "Hmm. Looks a little too far to walk. Can we take our ship there?"

"Still won't get you closer than a few hours' walk. We've got a skimmer that can take you right to her doorstep, and do it a lot faster."

"Okay. We'll pay, of course. How much?"

The bigger P'nosk screwed up his face again. "We don't have much use for bonds. What have you got in terms of luxury goods?"

I stared a moment. "Sorry, luxury goods?"

"Yes. Off-world food and spices in particular. We have almost no off-planet trade, so anything we can get would be great."

"I—" I started, then looked at Torina and Perry, who both shrugged. Luxury goods? We didn't carry much in the way of luxury goods aboard the *Fafnir*. In fact, aside from—

I smiled. "You know what? I think I've got just the thing you're looking for."

———

I WINCED as the skimmer slewed around a spire of rock, then aimed itself for a narrow gorge slashed into the side of the mountain looming ahead of us. About as big as a mid-sized sedan, the skimmer used some sort of gravity-repulsion tech to get airborne, then flew along at what felt like a million miles per hour straight toward hills and forests—and rocky spires, like the one flashing past seemingly close enough to touch.

I gave the pilot, the smaller of the two P'nosk who'd greeted us, a nervous glance. "You know, I kind of meant for you guys to enjoy that stuff sometime when you weren't, ah, flying a rocket sled. And especially a rocket sled with me." I cringed as we raced directly toward a rock wall, only veering at the last second. "A rocket sled with me strapped into it!"

The P'nosk lifted the bottle I'd given him. "What did you call this? Moonshine?"

"Yeah, made by space hillbillies—and also *really* alcoholic, which raises the whole issue of drinking and driving."

The P'nosk shuddered in what I'd learned was their way of laughing. "Our biochemistry isn't affected by alcohol. I just enjoy the flavor," he said, taking a swig while throwing us into a blistering turn to avoid another cliff face. We shot over some jagged ruins, some of many scattered around the planet, remnants of the civilization that had destroyed itself. We even saw a few blast craters in the distance that were now filled with water.

"You like the *flavor?*"

"Oh, yes, it's delicious. I'd take more of this stuff for sure."

"Sounds like we have a commercial opportunity here, Van," Perry said.

"What, running moonshine between here and the space hillbillies?"

"Sure. In fact, we could expand from there—"

"Perry, let's talk about getting into the rum-running business some other—holy *shit!*"

The P'nosk had flung the skimmer into a screaming climb, followed by a wrenching turn that brought us into a narrow valley. Torina uttered an excited shriek worthy of a roller coaster as my stomach and teeth briefly reintroduced themselves. The pilot abruptly slammed on the brakes and neatly brought us to the softest of landings on a pad scraped out of the hillside.

He lifted the bottle again. "Hmm. I wonder if it's better hot or cold."

I took a shuddering breath. "Well, while you ponder that, we're going to go and see Zenophir—who I assume is that P'nosk over there."

I pointed at the P'nosk who'd just exited another chunky building—P'nosk architecture seemed to be universally *chunky*—and stood glaring in our direction, radiating all the charm of a yellowjacket.

Our pilot nodded. "That's her." He shook a bit. "Enjoy. I'll wait here."

We dismounted and sorted ourselves out. Torina still had a dumb grin splitting her face. "That was fun!"

"Fun. Yeah. *That's* the word I'd use for it."

We walked toward Zenophir, who spoke up while we were still about ten paces away.

"That's close enough. Now, you can turn your unwelcome—whatever you call your posteriors—around and get the hell out of here," she snapped, then turned and stiffly trudged back toward her house.

"I'm Mark Tudor's grandson," I called after her.

She stopped but only turned her head back toward us. "Good for you. All the more reason for you to piss off."

"Wow, she really is a miserable bitch," Perry said, keeping his voice confined to our headsets.

I sighed and followed her. "Look, I didn't come all this way just to be sent packing."

"Well, that's unfortunate, because that's exactly what's going to happen here."

"I want to employ you, the way my grandfather did."

This time she stopped and did turn back to face me. I could tell at once that she was old, her whiskers pale, skin wrinkled, and a humped posture well in advanced stages. But her eyes? They were lively and bright.

"Employ me. Is that what he told you he did? *Extorting me into his service* would be more correct."

"He didn't tell me anything about you. He died almost a year ago now and bequeathed his Peacemaker gig to me."

"He's dead?"

"He is."

I expected her to snap back something like *Good*, or maybe *I hope he rots in hell*, and prepared myself for it. Instead, she surprised me by looking—sad?

"That's too bad. He was a good person."

I blinked. "Okay, I'm confused. Just a second ago you accused him of extortion, but now he's a *good person?*"

She cocked her head at me. "Maybe both those things are true."

"Look, I just want to talk."

Zenophir eyed me a moment longer, then turned and gestured for us to follow her.

"Fine, I'll give you a few minutes. Not because I'm really interested in what you have to say, but because it'll give me something to do."

"Hey, whatever works," I said and started after her, Torina and Perry right behind me.

"So Mark Tudor is dead, eh?" Zenophir said as we settled into her sparse but still comfortable front room. It overlooked the valley, offering a terrific view.

"He is." I looked at her through my visor since her home was as irradiated as the rest of the planet. "Does that make you happy?"

"What? No, of course not. Mark Tudor probably saved my life. He broke up a nasty little civil war that erupted among my people, and arrested me in the process. If he hadn't, I'd likely be dead now, the way things were going."

I glanced at Torina. "You don't seem very sad about him dying —but you also do."

"I'm conflicted, let's put it that way. He saved my life, which was good, but he also sentenced me to what amounts to this house arrest for one hundred years."

I sat up. "What? A hundred *years?*"

"Well, the average lifespan of a P'nosk is about three hundred years, maxing out at about three hundred and fifty. He just scaled the sentence accordingly."

"So—you hate him for that? Or you don't?" I shook my head. "I'm confused."

Zenophir shook with brief laughter. "So am I. I don't know what else to tell you. I guess it's just possible to be grateful to someone, but also resent them."

"Okay, yeah, I get that—I guess. Anyway, he apparently kept you on a sort of—I don't know, a retainer?"

"He gave me an opportunity to work off my sentence and shorten it, in exchange for my help. I've only got another twenty-eight years to go."

"Oh."

"Yeah, tell me about it. Look around you. This is all nice, right? Well, try enjoying it for a hundred years, never being able to leave." She leaned toward me. "I am bored beyond belief. I'm sure that's what's ultimately going to do me in, not old age." She sighed, an entirely human gesture, and then waved at the view outside. "Pastoral senescence isn't how I saw my life ending. Or, at least draining away for all these years. I'm dying, just at a slower pace."

"Okay, I have to ask—why don't you just leave? I don't see any walls or anything keeping you here, and I find it hard to believe Van's grandfather would plant a bomb in your brain that detonates if you stray too far," Torina said.

"You don't know the P'nosk very well, do you?" Zenophir said to her.

"Not really, no."

"We have a concept called *Obligation*. It's more than just some idea or something abstract, though. We can enter into an Obligation with another person, whereupon we become irrevocably bound to whatever the Obligation is about."

"So it's… a strong sense of honor?"

"Way more than that. It's biochemical. If we break an Obligation, we get sick and can eventually die." She offered a slight, awkward shrug. "So, in a way, he did stick a bomb inside me. Or, actually, we both did since I had to agree to it."

"Does it make a difference that he's dead now?"

"Nope. My Obligation is to the agreement I made with him. House arrest for one hundred years, less the time I've worked off." She shrugged again. "The alternative was to be found guilty of sedition by my own people and executed."

I felt a pang of unease at this revelation about Gramps' creative sentencing decision, but then, the core truth of it settled in. For Zenophir, it had been a lifesaving event, if distastefully wrapped in a long, dull sentence on this quiet world.

For a century. An entire *century*.

I mulled that reality, looked at her expression of mute acceptance, and asked a question.

"Can you be freed of this Obligation?"

"Only if my sentence is commuted by someone with the authority to do it."

I turned to Perry. "Can I—?"

"Commute her sentence?"

"Yes, but only if she agrees to perform some service as reconciliation that's commensurate with her remaining sentence. So, no paying a one bond fine in lieu, that sort of thing."

I nodded and turned back to her. "Fine. I'm going to do that, commute your sentence. In exchange, I want you to help me with all that engineering know-how you've got stored in that head of yours."

She nodded. "Well, that's definitely better than being stuck here. So, to bind that as an Obligation—"

I held up my hand. "No need. I don't want you to do that. I want you to help me because you want to, not because you have to."

She stared for a moment. "You mean you're just freeing me?"

"Effective immediately. I believe the term is manumission, or something close to it. Been a while since freshman history. Perry, make a formal record of that."

"Done."

She blinked. "So, I can just… leave?"

"If you want."

"Without actually being required to help you?"

"Well, I think for this to work, you do have to help me, to offset your sentence, but I get to decide how much is enough, right, Perry?"

"You do," he replied.

"In that case, I'd like you to take a look at my ship and make what you believe is the single best upgrade you can manage. Do that, and your sentence is done." I shrugged. "I'd love to retain your services after that, but it won't be required."

She sat in silence for a moment. Finally, she nodded, and her face lost some of its hardness. "I'm… grateful. More than you know. Not just because you're commuting my sentence, but because you're trusting me."

"Gramps saw something in you worth saving. Me, I see something worth trusting."

"Alright. Bring your ship here, and I'll take a look."

I touched my comm. "Icky, you and Netty come and join us. Use our comm signal as your beacon."

"Good. Just sitting here is getting boring."

I glanced at Zenophir, who just shook with laughter.

WE DISMISSED our skimmer and waited for the *Fafnir* to arrive. Netty handled the landing, settling straight down nearly two klicks onto the landing pad, which was *just* big enough for her bulk. Even then, thanks to gusty winds whipping around the surrounding mountain peaks, she had to make three tries at it. I saw, now, why we'd come here in the skimmer.

Zenophir tottered her way to the *Fafnir* once her thrusters had been cut and slid a hand along her flank.

"Always loved this ship. We meet again, old girl."

Netty spoke through my comm. "Who are you calling old?"

Zenophir laughed. "Hello, Netty. It's been a while."

I looked at Perry. "Are you and Zenophir old friends, too?"

"Not really. Your grandfather had me off doing other business when all of this civil war and house arrest Obligation came into being."

The airlock slid open, and Icky stepped out, wearing her vac suit. "What I wouldn't give to feel that wind. It's not fun going from stuck inside a spaceship to stuck inside a vac suit."

"Okay, Zenophir, I'll give you some time to look the *Fafnir* over and—"

"Point-defense," she said, gesturing at the lower turret.

"What about it?"

"I've got something in mind that will give you at least a ten percent improvement in point-defense performance."

Icky scoffed. "Ten percent? You'd have to redesign the whole damned gun—"

Zenophir held up a hand. "I already have. When you've got nothing but time on your hands, you can put a lot of thought into a problem." She unholstered a data slate from her belt and began tapping at it. "Let's see. Right there—no, wait, that's not right. Where the hell is that—?"

We waited as she fiddled with the slate. Finally, she brightened. "Ah, there you are." She turned the slate toward us. "This is what I have in mind."

We all stepped closer to see what it was displaying. I saw a complex schematic. Torina looked as blank as I did.

Icky had a distinctly different reaction.

"By the sacred hammers, are you serious?" she asked Zenophir.

"Damned right I am. I've always wanted to try this out, but I don't happen to have a point-defense battery lying around."

I shook my head. "Can we get the *Point-defense Weapons for Dummies* version of this, please?"

"She wants to add a secondary magnetic accelerator to the end of the barrel and have it generate a progressively faster, higher-frequency EM pulse that will propagate—"

"Did you miss the *For Dummies* part, Icky?"

She gestured at the data slate. "She wants to make the rounds come out of the point-defense guns faster, without changing the ammo or even redesigning the weapon itself. It's literally just an add-on, and a damned clever one."

"How long would it take for you to get this together?" I asked, trying to project ahead so I could plan to come back here in—days? Weeks?

"Few hours, maybe?"

"A few *hours*?"

"Hey, I can only work so fast."

19

Icky studied the data on her engineering panel. "Oh, yeah. So much for a ten percent improvement in the point-defence effectiveness," she finally said.

I switched the weapon back into standby mode, ensuring it wouldn't be spooked by a false target, like the P'nosk missile tube. Before we launched again from Dustfall, Perry spoke to the AI in control of the area, ensuring we wouldn't get shot at again.

"Wow, that guy's an asshole," he'd said, closing the comm link.

"The AI?"

"Yeah. Maniacal is right. All he wants to do is shoot at stuff. That's the problem when you buy military-grade gear for civilian use. He complained about people he called *free flyers*, which I soon realized meant—"

"People he hadn't shot at yet?" I asked.

Perry paused, then leveled a gaze at me. "Impressive. Almost like you've met his kind before."

"Once or twice. Netty, if you please? Let's kick it."

We'd cleared the planet without incident, then taken a few minutes to test our upgraded point-defenses. That we hadn't hit the promised ten percent was a little disappointing, but also not that surprising. After all, Zenophir had really just based all of it on theory.

"How close did we get to ten percent?" I asked.

"Off by two and a half percent."

"Well, 7.5 is pretty good."

"Yeah, it is. But this was a *12.5* percent improvement. The PD rounds not only travel faster, they're also more accurate because they don't have to compute as much lead."

Torina smiled. "I'd say we got our money's worth."

"And then some," I agreed.

The best part was that Zenophir had declared herself obligated to me—though not Obligated, the P'nosk biochemical version. She simply stated that she would gladly help us out with upgrades to the *Fafnir* in gratitude for her release from bondage. In fact, she obtained system schematics from Netty and said she'd get to work on looking for other, worthwhile upgrades.

After she took a vacation from her home, that is, where she'd been stuck for nearly twenty years. She planned to head to the nearest P'nosk settlement and just spend time not being alone. I got it and told her we'd check back in a month or so.

"I should be sober by then," she said.

I frowned. "I thought you P'nosk couldn't get drunk."

"Not from alcohol, no. But we've got our ways," she replied, a twinkle in her eyes.

"Do you have a, um—a liver?" I asked.

"No. I have two, and I intend to beat the hell out of both of them."

"You're going to fit right in with us. We'll see you when the floor stops spinning, then," I said, and Zenophir shook with laughter.

"One final thing, Van? It's been on my mind."

"I'm listening."

"The identity theft… the stolen people. If they need osmium, maybe it would behoove you to look for where it *used* to be mined."

"Why would we do that?" Torina asked.

But I knew the answer to that and was already grinning. "Because they'll go back to played-out mines and process the spoils."

"Didn't know you were an expert in mining, Van," Perry said.

"I watched a lot of cable TV about gold mining. Reality shows, that sort of thing. They all say much the same thing. Why dig a new mine when you can work an old one?"

THERE WERE dozens of mining operations scattered across known space that produced osmium, always in small quantities as a byproduct, along with things like copper, nickel, and cobalt. Many were still in production, and all but a few were either on planets or in locations thoroughly regulated by some jurisdiction or other.

That made our job a lot easier, since we were only interested in operations that had been played out and shut down, and we were also in territory that was more lenient in terms of law enforcement. It only left us with seven candidates, four of them in the anarchic Wolf 424 system, the other three scattered among asteroid belts in otherwise empty systems. We visited each in turn—and, in turn, ruled each one out.

I stared glumly at the remains of a mining operation on a big asteroid called Paydirt, orbiting about five hundred million klicks from Wolf 424. Just under thirty klicks across, Paydirt had been riddled with pits, tunnels, and excavations, testament to the rich seams of copper and nickel it had once served up—along with a side of osmium.

"Nothing. Not even a hint of any activity," I said, parsing the tactical overlay. It depicted Paydirt as a cold, dead lump of rock with a few flickers of copper and nickel signals. That was it.

"The scans show us that there's no ore left," Netty said.

"None? Are you sure? I'm seeing a few hints of it here and there."

"But it's not ore. Ore is, by definition, rock you can mine at a profit. If you can't make money from it, then it's not ore. It doesn't matter what commodity you're talking about."

"Huh. I didn't know that."

"Doesn't change the fact that there's no mining going on down there now," Torina said.

I nodded. "No, it does not. So unless our bad guys have some sort of tap into a legitimate operation somewhere, they're getting their osmium some other way."

"There is still one obvious candidate, Van. It's a little far away, but as Schegith said, it fits perfectly with the bits and pieces of nav data we obtained," Perry said.

"Rigel."

"That's right."

Icky leaned into the conversation. "Van, I've been toying with different ways of fitting out the *Fafnir* so we have enough fuel for a return trip that long. It's not doable without completely repurposing most of her interior space for fuel. Even then, the twist drive is right on the very edge of being able to take us that far."

I sighed in mild annoyance. "I know. The *Fafnir*'s just not up to the job."

"And we've hit another dead end in this damned investigation, and it's back to square one," Torina muttered.

But I shook my head this time. "No we haven't."

"So what are we going to do? The *Fafnir*'s just not up to the trip."

I turned to the others, smiling. "You guys are forgetting that the *Fafnir* isn't the only ship we have."

As NETTY SNUGGLED the *Fafnir* against the looming bulk of the *Iowa*, our repurposed battlecruiser parked in the lonely outskirts of the Solar System, Icky made a hissing sound through her teeth.

"Van, I don't know about this. The twist drive aboard this thing has seen better days."

"But it's big enough to get the job done, right?"

"Oh yeah, if the drive was working at one hundred percent, it could probably twist us twice that far. But it's likely running at about —I don't know, sixty-five? Maybe pushing seventy? Good enough to get her here, anyway, and move her pretty much anywhere in known space. I hadn't counted on a nearly nine hundred light-year hop when I brought it back online," Icky said.

We connected with a thump, followed by several clunks as the docking clamps engaged. Netty confirmed a hard dock. As we unstrapped and clambered toward the airlock, I clapped Icky on the shoulder.

"I have faith in you, Icky. I know you'll get that drive working right."

"I'm glad someone thinks so," she muttered.

As soon as we stepped through into the *Iowa*, I caught a faint, acrid whiff of something decidedly unpleasant. Icky and Torina wrinkled their noses, too.

"Some of the pong from the previous owners is back. Did we miss something somewhere?"

Icky sniffed at the air. "Maybe something got behind a bulkhead. It's going to take a while to find, though." She glanced at me. "What's the priority, getting the drive working or getting the stink out?"

"Drive. The stink's going to have to wait."

Icky nodded and lumbered aft, followed by Torina, who was going to be her helper for the day. Perry and I headed for the bridge. Along the way, he suddenly spoke up.

"Uh, Van?"

"Yo."

"We need to talk."

I stopped and glanced at him. "Is this it? Are we breaking up? Are your next words going to be, *it's not you, it's me?*"

"What?"

"I thought you passed the time watching Earthly TV and media. How have you not come across that whole *it's not you, it's me* breakup thing?"

"I stick to quality programs, paid for by viewers like you."

"Ah, you're a media snob." I resumed walking. "Anyway, what did you want to talk about?"

"Time."

I nodded. "Yeah, I know, I can't help feeling we're on a clock here, too—"

"That's not what I mean. I'm talking about time and how it passes."

I slowed. This was starting to sound ominous. "Where are you going with this, Perry?"

"Van, twisting doesn't just involve moving in space, because space is only three parts of reality—up and down, left and right, back and forth. There's a fourth part: time."

I stopped again and looked down at him, a sense of foreboding growing in my gut. "Go on."

"Okay. From our frame of reference, inside the *Fafnir*, twisting is instantaneous. We literally experience no passage of time. But that's not the only frame of reference. If you had an external observer who could watch the *Fafnir* twist from departure to destination, they'd see her vanish, and then reappear in her new location a few seconds later."

"Wait. Are you telling me that twisting actually shifts us in time as *well* as space?"

"No, I'm saying it shifts us in space-time, which is a single thing. But even that's simplified, because inside each frame of reference, time passes just as it always does."

I looked at the bulkhead over Perry's head. "So every time we twist, no time passes for us, but seconds or minutes—or longer—do for everyone else?"

"For everyone not aboard the *Fafnir*, that's right."

"Perry, we've twisted a hundred times. How far out of sync am I with the rest of—" I stopped. "Hang on. Is this why, every time we go back to Earth, it seems like more time has passed there than I'd expected?"

"Yes."

I just kept staring at the bulkhead. It wasn't that I was trying to make sense of what Perry was saying, because I got that. I stared because my mind had suddenly dissolved into a swirl of implications. I finally had to shake myself out of it and focus on the most important questions, like—

"Perry, why the hell haven't you told me about this before now?"

"Your grandfather ordered Netty and I not to until the variation in time between you and the Earth exceeded a month."

"Why the hell not?"

"Because he wanted you to have some time to fully understand the implications—the importance, as he put it—of being a Peacemaker *before* you had to face a decision about the sacrifice it entails. For whatever reason, he decided that you giving up a month of your life relative to Earth was sufficient. Like he put it, it's really not much different from going on some wilderness retreat for a month."

"So how much time has passed on Earth that—that I didn't experience?"

"A little under three weeks."

"So I have lost three weeks of my *life?*"

"No, Van, you haven't. In fact, relative to Earth, you've gained three weeks. If you twisted enough, decades, even centuries could pass on Earth while you only aged a few years or whatever during that time. To borrow a word from your esteemed Albert Einstein, it's all relative."

"Yeah, but—I've still lost three weeks compared to Earth, right?"

"You can look at it that way. But let me ask you this—what have you missed during those three weeks on Earth?"

"Like, everything that's happened there?"

"Well, sure, but what did *you* miss, Van Tudor? You specifically? What would you have done for those three weeks on Earth that you weren't able to do?"

"I—"

Had no answer to that. The truth was, I lived a mostly solitary life anyway, which permanently moving into the farm in Iowa would only reinforce. I had few real-life friends, really only traveled for work, and definitely wasn't deeply involved in my community or church or whatever. Miryam was on retainer to look after my affairs, keep an eye on the farm, make sure taxes got paid, and so on. Which meant—

I sighed. "Okay. Fine. I get it, I guess. So why are you telling me this now, and not when the full month has elapsed?"

"Because you want to go to Rigel."

"So?"

"The greater the twist distance, the greater the time disparity."

"Oh. Shit. I don't think I'm going to want to hear this." I took a breath. "How much will I be out of whack with time after a trip to and from Rigel?"

"Well, the math is complicated, and there are a lot of variables, like the efficiency of the twist drive—"

"Ballpark it for me, Perry."

"Rough minimum? Five months or so."

"What's the rough maximum?" I asked, bracing myself.

"Call it closer to a year."

"Sorry, Van, I guess Icky and I just assumed you knew about time dilation. It's all part of how the universe works," Torina said, peering at me around part of the twist drive's casing.

Icky, who was poking around inside an open access hatch, pulled back and looked up at me. "You just kinda factor it in, you know? Like, I'm twisting to Tau Ceti and back, so I'll see you in a day, even though it's only going to be a few hours for you."

"To the extent anyone even thinks about it, it's sometimes called me-time and you-time. As in, I'll be gone for two days in you-time," Torina added.

"How have I not had even a clue about this so far?"

"Because it's like—well, packing for a trip. You automatically pack clean underwear, you don't really have to think about it very much."

"I don't, 'cause I don't wear underwear," Icky put in, her voice muffled from having her head stuck halfway into the access port. "I'm all natural like that."

"Too much information, Icky, thanks—wait, you don't wear underwear? Why?" I asked, feeling a bit bewildered.

"I don't like being constricted when I dance. It's a habit I got into when I was a lot more sociable."

"You... danced?" I asked. Even Perry rotated fully to face her for whatever she was about to explain.

"Torina knows. Sometimes a girl just wants to shake it all on the floor with her crew, and—right, Torina?" Icky asked, wiggling all four of her arms in what appeared to be a mild seizure.

"Um. . yes. That's. . . that's what a girl wants."

"Hey, crew? As much as I need—and yes, I *need* to see video of Icky breaking it down at the club, I'd like to revisit the idea that I'm about to outlive the few connections I have on Earth. Which means —Torina, this doesn't bother you? At all?" I asked.

She shrugged. "Why should it? It's just the way things are."

I marveled at her laconic attitude of being *shifted in time*. How could she be so casually dismissive of it? This was a *huge* deal—

Except, it wasn't. It was a massive issue for me. Her comment about packing clean underwear made me think about my own extensive traveling back on Earth. And if I thought about it, I completely took for granted things less experienced travelers found a big deal. Take airport security, for example. I no longer even spared a thought for how I packed my carry-on luggage or that I had to arrive at least two hours before my flight to ensure I wasn't stuck in a security line running late. But I'd seen more than a few people having to face enhanced screening because they'd packed scissors, or working themselves into a lather of frustration because their flight was leaving in twenty minutes and the line looked like it would take at *least* that long.

Still, inadvertently packing something sharp or underestimating the wait for security were a far cry from slipping in time—

But not really. "I'm being entirely too, ah… earthcentric." When Icky opened her mouth, I added, "I know, not a word, but it is now. And you know what I mean. Sorry, guys, I'm processing something here. This is more than just finding out there's a lot of life out here.

This is finding out that my life is—it's changed, fundamentally, by my occupation."

Icky extracted herself from examining the twist drive panel, her manner serious. "Van, time for a command decision. If we're going to Rigel, I need four or five days, maybe even a week, plus about a hundred grand in parts to get this drive ready. If not, and the *Iowa's* not leaving known space, then it's probably good as is. This isn't me being cautious, this is your lead engineer telling you the ugly truth about this power plant."

I stared at the drive, thinking hard.

The better part of two years. What would happen on Earth during that time? Or anywhere else, for that matter? Torina and Icky both seemed nonchalant about even that big a time distortion, but for me—

I imagined myself resigning my Peacemaker credentials and returning to Earth. The identity theft case would become someone else's problem. I could just putter around the farm, work remotely as a cyber-specialist—and, sure, maybe I'd try to get involved in the local community. Start going to church. Attending events. Making the occasional trip into Chicago to take in some big city life—

And looking up at the night sky and wondering how it *might* have been.

I blew out a ragged sigh because the universe was never going to stop singing to me, and I would not ignore the song. "Fix the drive. We're going to Rigel."

"AH, this is where you are, hard at work with your feet up on a console," Torina said, entering the *Iowa*'s bridge.

I'd been sitting and staring at the stars on the imager. "I wonder how old my grandfather was."

"From the way you've described him, in his seventies, I'm assuming? Maybe late seventies?"

"That's not what I mean."

I sat at one of the bridge stations not in use. In fact, the only live stations were the helm and the captain's, both rigged into Icky's automation and offering a single place from which to operate the *Iowa*, and a pair of tactical stations used to control her weapons. The remaining stations were all dark. Torina came and sat down in the one adjacent to me.

"I know it's not. But does it really matter?' she asked me.

"I… I think it does, or at least I can't help thinking it should. I mean, two years just in this one twist. If I did that often enough, I could visit Earth in the far future and arrive fresh-faced."

"It'd be awfully expensive, what with all the fuel."

I shot her a glance, but she just smiled back at me.

"How do you adjust to this reality?" I asked her.

She shrugged. "Honestly, Van, the vast majority of people across known space only travel a bit, and just spend their life in their home system. If they end up with any dilation it all, it might be minutes, maybe a few hours. It's only dedicated spacers who build up any appreciable amount—and even then, just flitting around known space doesn't change things by more than a few months to a few years."

She sat back. "On top of that, consider that many spacers either have no permanent home, or they move from system to system, and even those bits of time dilation don't really matter." She smiled again, sifting memories. "I've even heard stories of spacers racing one another to their next birthday, stuff like that."

I considered my own family history. "I get it, but it spawns questions, like when was my grandfather born? I always assumed it was sometime in the 1940s—by the Earth calendar, and boy, does it feel strange to be saying that—but, who knows? If he did some long twists like this, he might have been born long before that."

"Why don't you ask Netty or Perry? They must know."

I held up a finger. "Netty, tell me again what terrestrial year my grandfather was born, and what year he became a Peacemaker."

"Again, my answer is that I can't tell you because your grandfather explicitly forbade it."

I shrugged at Torina. "So there you go. He might have been born in the 1930s. Or the 1830s. Or, hell, sometime in the Middle Ages, for that matter."

"Van, to pile up a dilation of more than a few years takes a lot of twisting long distances, or a *whole* lot of shorter ones."

"Yeah, I know. I guess it just irritates me that Gramps is hiding his true past. From me."

"That's only if he was displaced relative to Earth by more than a few years. And even if it was more, even much more than that, he obviously had his reasons. Maybe he didn't want you to think of him any differently just because he happened to be a lot older than you thought."

"Why? Because he might have been born during the US Civil War? Or the English Civil War, for that matter? Why would that matter to me?"

"Really? If you found out your grandfather was five hundred years old, that wouldn't change the way you think of him?"

"I—um—"

She gave me an *and there you go* smile. "Anyway, you should be proud of me. I actually know what you're talking about with the US Civil War—1861 to 1865, incidentally. The other one, not so much," Torina said.

"The English one? Oh, a long time ago—Netty?"

"1642 to 1651," she said.

I gave her a wry smile. "I guess that as long as we're all twisting together, that's something."

"That sounds a touch lewd, all twisting together."

I laughed and lowered my feet to the deck. "It does, doesn't it?" I took a deep breath, then let it out slowly. "Okay. Netty says we need to remove the ventral point-defense turret to fit the *Fafnir* into this thing's cargo hold. Care to do a little spacewalking together, my dear?"

She batted her eyes at me, wearing a coquettish grin.. "Hand in hand in the freezing, airless, radiation-ravaged void?" She offered her arm. "You charmer."

20

"Welcome to Rigel," Netty said.

I blinked. It felt absolutely no different than any other twist.

And yet, here we were, bathed in the searing radiance of a blue-white glare that seemed to fill half of space.

I opened my mouth to quip, *well, there goes six months of my life*, but I bit it back. I had to remind myself that wasn't true. *I* hadn't lost anything, except in relation to almost everywhere else in the universe. Not that I particularly cared that some random star in the Andromeda galaxy just aged about half a year more than I had. On Earth, though, an entire winter had passed, and spring now bloomed across Iowa. The farmhouse would thrum with the distant buzz of trucks and tractors busily planting this year's crop of corn or sorghum or whatever. At least I'd been able to get a message to Miryam, telling her I'd be gone for an indefinite period, maybe as much as a year.

"Van?"

I glanced at Torina. "What? Oh… sorry. Bad time to be wool gathering, I guess."

I sat in the *Iowa*'s command station, with Torina at the helm. Icky had stayed in engineering to monitor the ship and twist-drive performance. My first move was to touch the comm.

"Are we in one piece? How'd the drive fly, Icky?"

"You can hear my voice, so that'd be a yes. As for the second question, let me see how close I got the drive to full efficiency."

"Icky, we're here, at Rigel. I think the drive worked well enough."

"Well enough? Hah. I can tell you're not an engineer, Van."

I smiled, then looked at the tactical display. Ironically, the *Iowa*'s scanners were currently inferior to the *Fafnir*'s, simply because we hadn't upgraded them yet. One of the downsides of having a second ship is that we now had to upgrade and maintain a second ship.

"Not seeing any other ships here," Torina said, studying her own display.

"Nope, neither am I. Just that big-assed star, four—no, make that five planets, a lot of rocks, and—huh, that's something. Rigel really is multiple stars, isn't it?"

The massive star had three companions—a binary pair orbiting one another, that in turn orbited Rigel itself, and a fourth, dim little companion star far off in the void. The main event here, Rigel Alpha, also had five planets. Two of them, closest to Rigel, were airless, rocky, radiation-scoured worlds. One was the size of Earth, the other closer to Mercury. The remaining three worlds were all gas giants, including one spectacularly big one that fell just shy of making this complex little system's *fifth* star.

"Van, Netty and I are ready to launch," Perry said over the comm.

"Go for it."

We'd loaded the *Fafnir* into the *Iowa's* hold, cheating our way around the implacable mathematics of twist mechanics by carrying her as cargo. Netty opened the cargo hold and played out the winches that had cabled her into place, letting her ease her way into space. The whole arrangement was makeshift, to the extent that we couldn't accelerate the Iowa above a certain low threshold to avoid damaging the *Fafnir*. If we wanted to fly her separately from the bigger ship, we had to manually unhook the cables. It was cumbersome and potentially dangerous, but an actual, full-blown docking adapter was still some way down the upgrade list.

"Necessity is—" Perry said, but I interrupted.

"—the mother of invention. I took that class in college, bird."

"Score one for the Renaissance, ah… space cop."

"Thanks, friend. Appreciate the nod. Steady as we go, everyone, and keep the *Fafnir's* scanner on stand by," I directed.

We didn't want to fly the *Fafnir* separately from the *Iowa*. We wanted to employ her superior scanners, and to do that, we only needed her to clear the battlecruiser's hold.

New data immediately sluiced into the tactical displays as the *Fafnir's* scanners came online. It confirmed our original observation of no other apparent ships or threats but added a lot more detail. For one, we quickly got returns from several asteroids, as well as the Earth-sized world, that could only come from alloys that didn't occur in nature.

I let out a sigh of relief. This hadn't been for nothing after all. "Are we lucky or just good?"

"Luck is the residue of preparation. I didn't take that class in college, because I didn't go to college on account of not having a, ah, body," Netty said.

"Not everyone in my first year classes was there in body, either, Netty. Where'd you hear that idiom?" I asked.

"Read it on a fortune cookie," Netty said.

"Netty, you don't eat cookies."

"I can read, though. Anyway, plot a course, boss?"

I gave it some thought. "Indeed you can. As to our luck, I was kind of hoping to find the *Empty Space* here, too."

Torina arched an eyebrow. "Really?"

I shrugged back. "I'm trying to feel prepared."

"Van, the closest signal is that asteroid labeled on the display as Target One. If we wind the *Fafnir* back into the hold, we could have the Iowa there in about eight hours. If we cut the *Fafnir* loose, she could do it in about two," Netty said.

I tapped a finger on the console. While I'd appreciate saving time, the idea of separating the *Iowa* and the *Fafnir* by two hours in this strange, uncharted star system didn't appeal to me at all. Maybe it was because I was keenly aware of that almost nine hundred light-year gap behind us, like an incessant, cold wind blowing on the back of my neck.

It also drove home an implacable point. Discovering that "known space" was a thing presented me with the dizzying reality that life was scattered over more than a hundred light years of space —that *happened* to include Earth. There were only the most fitful bits of evidence of life beyond that, suggesting that for whatever reason, that little pocket of galactic space was amenable to the formation of life. There may have been others, but even at a hundred light-years across, it paled in comparison to the almost one thousand we'd just traveled.

And the Milky Way galaxy was more than one hundred times larger than that. And the observable universe was how many times larger than *that*—

I shook my head to clear it, because eternity was a well you could fall down forever. "Bring the *Fafnir* back aboard, guys. We're taking the slow boat for this trip."

"WELL, IT *WAS* A MINING OPERATION," Torina said.

I nodded. The asteroid, two hundred klicks across, was pocked and riddled with excavations where mechanical diggers had pulverized rock and fed it into some sort of processing facility. There was evidence of slurry turned into a concentrate, and maybe even refined into raw metals. The low gravity precluded free-standing diggers, as they'd have just pushed themselves away from the surface before breaking any rock. The miners had come up with a clever solution—a system of monorails anchored into the asteroid's bedrock, along whose meandering tracks the excavators and ore carriers ran.

But it was all dark, silent, and cold with disuse. There had been mining going on here, but not for some time. From micrometeorite abrasion, Netty estimated it to be between two and ten standard years since any rock had been broken on the lonely little world.

"Van, there are six pieces of machinery parked on a siding near the asteroid's north pole. They may contain useful information," Netty said.

"Yeah, I see them. What's the likelihood anything survived, though, considering the radiation from that big ol' star? Based on these readings, it's pretty wild out there," I said.

"Shielded electronics should still be operable," she replied.

Torina stiffened. "Oh. What if there are *people* down there?"

Oh, shit. I knew exactly what she meant. If there were digital slaves installed in those machines, and they'd just been abandoned here—

Hell might be fire and brimstone, but being trapped and helpless on a radiation-scoured, frozen, airless rock impossibly far from home wasn't far behind.

I glanced at her. "Thanks, Torina. Now we *have* to check it out." I sighed, thinking people might be alone in the endless darkness out there, and I sure as hell wouldn't leave them behind.

"Kinda wish we had one of those P'nosk, with us. This radiation might as well be a gentle breeze, as far as they're concerned," Icky put in.

"Perry, how will our b-suits hold up out there?"

"If you limit your exposure to no more than thirty minutes in every eight-hour period, you should be fine," he replied.

"Alrighty, then. Torina, let's you and I go play in the radiation storm."

"I'll say this again. You're *brilliant* at planning dates."

WE LANDED THE *IOWA*.

Okay, not quite. We brought the battlecruiser to about two hundred meters away from the asteroid, then had Netty keep station there. Torina and I were able to make the trip using maneuvering units, taking about five minutes each way. That left us twenty minutes to do what we could on the surface. I made myself ignore the scary red rad warning in my helmet's heads-up and focused on the task at hand: retrieving chips.

It took us three excursions over the next day to finally decide we'd done everything we could. On the last trip, we brought back the remaining chips we'd scavenged from the mining machinery, then waited for Icky and Perry to analyze them.

"Well, the good news is that there are no personalities on any of those chips," Perry finally proclaimed as we all stood on the *Iowa's* bridge around a workstation Icky had reactivated for the chip analysis.

"Okay, what's the bad news?" I asked.

"What makes you think there's bad news?"

"Well, the *good news is*, is what you normally say ahead of bad news, right?"

"That's a fallacy, though, Van. Good news doesn't intrinsically imply the existence of bad—"

"Perry, focus?"

"Fine. If there is bad news, it's that most of these chips are just what they look like—devices for processing information related to the operation of those machines. Even then, most of them are fragmented all to hell by radiation. In fact, about half of them are blank."

"Okay, so that's the bad news. We didn't learn anything new," I said, sighing.

"See, there's that fallacy again. Did you not hear me say things like *most* and *half of?*"

Icky scowled at him. "What Pedantic Bird here is apparently not trying to tell you is that we did discover something interesting," she snapped.

"Pedantic Bird? Accuracy in communication isn't mere—"

"Perry, please!"

He turned to me. "Pluto."

I stared. "What about it? Or *him*, if you're referring to the Disney dog?"

"I—no, not the dog, even though he is one of my favorite Disney characters. The planet-not-planet."

Icky scowled again. "What the hell are you—?"

"Pluto, ninth planet in the Solar System. Or not. Depends on who you talk to."

I tried to restrain my mounting impatience. I was starting to think Perry and Icky working together was a bit of an exercise in one-upmanship. "What *about* Pluto?"

"One of those chips—that one, right there, in fact, by your right hand—came from an ore concentrator down there. It contains remnants of data related to the feedstock parameters for a refining facility somewhere. Remember how ore is just stuff you can mine at a profit? Well, the trick to doing that is minimizing the amount of waste, of junk rock, you let go into your concentrator so you don't dilute the grade of your actual ore. Let the dilution factor get too high and you stop making money—ore just becomes ordinary rock again."

"Okay, and?"

"And, that chip contains dilution factors for a number of mining operations involved in recovering osmium. And one of those operations is on Pluto."

"Well, I'll be damned. We've just flown an almost two thousand light-year round trip just to end up back where the *Iowa* here started, in the outer reaches of the solar system." I shook my head. "I guess I'm going home."

21

THE TWIST back to Sol was uneventful. Well, *uneventful* except in the sense that nearly eleven months had passed in what, to me, had felt like a few days. In fact, it was only the day before yesterday that I mused about how I'd missed an entire winter in Iowa, but that was okay because it was winter there again today.

I sighed. It made my brain hurt just trying to reconcile the fact that time, which had always studiously flowed one way at a steady, sedate pace, was actually as malleable as rubber.

In fact, Icky had done a few tweaks to the Iowa's twist drive, bringing it up to nearly ninety-two percent efficiency. She was still profoundly dissatisfied with that, even though it had shaved a relative two weeks from our journey and reduced our antimatter fuel expenditure by almost ten percent. It still meant we'd now just spent as much on fuel for this single round trip as we had for all of our twists over the past six months, which would have been a serious financial problem if not for Torina's family.

I listened to the recorded message Torina played for me. Her parents had offered to not only pay for our fuel for the trip, but also the recent upgrades we'd done to the *Fafnir*.

"Surprise!" she said brightly.

I just shook my head. "Torina, that comes to like, almost a million bonds. I can't accept that—"

"You don't have to. I'm accepting for you. I'm your second, remember?"

"Yes, but—"

"Van, you have saved my parents' lands, and maybe all of Helso, twice now. They want to do this. Hell, they *need* to do this. And you *need* to let them."

"I—well, okay. I guess I won't turn it down. Tell them I'll bake them a thank-you cake next time I'm on Helso."

"You can bake?"

"Um, not really. I was going to buy one. But don't tell them that."

We twisted in close to the planet's orbit away from the planet— I'd decided to keep calling Pluto a planet because I'd been a lot closer to it than any Earthly astronomer—and had to take some time to get our bearings. Increased uncertainty of the exact destination point was another reality of long twists. As known space slowly spread away from its immediate galactic neighbourhood and it became easier to gas up during a series of shorter ones, travel would become more feasible. But that expansion was slow. So slow, in fact, that at its present rate, it would be another four hundred years or so before the edge of known space reached Rigel.

As it turned out, though, our error had worked in our favor. When we got the *Fafnir* and her better scanners unloaded from the

Iowa and flying free again, we got a clear image of just what was happening at Pluto. Frankly, I'd expected to find out it had been mined out, too. But it wasn't.

"That is one hell of a big ship," I said, studying the data collected from the vicinity of Pluto and repeated from the *Fafnir* to the *Iowa*'s bridge. "Some sort of bulk carrier, I assume?"

"Actually, no. That large ship's signal matches that of a class thirteen heavy cruiser," Netty replied.

"A class thirteen—holy shit. That's almost as big as the *Iowa*," I said.

"Much more heavily armed, too," Netty added.

"How much more?"

"Well, since I make it out to be an Aurigae-class fast-attack cruiser, I'd reckon four petawatt twin laser mounts, two heavy missiles batteries, two close-range particle cannons, two mass-mass drivers, and six point-defense batteries."

"Is that all?"

"Isn't that enough?"

I glanced at Torina. "Enough for me. How about you?"

"More than enough, thanks."

"We gonna attack?" Icky asked eagerly.

Torina, Perry, and I all turned to look at her.

"Icky, have you heard *anything* we've said in the past ten seconds?" I asked her.

"Sorry, I was trying to damp out a harmonic in the Iowa's fuel feed. Let those things get out of hand and, well, you know." She made an exploding motion with her hands—all four of them, which made it that much more emphatic.

"Well, you just keep your priorities on not having us go—that, what you just did. Anyway—" I gestured at the tactical overlay, at the data for the Aurigae-class cruiser. She read it.

"Oh."

"Exactly."

"The question is, what the hell is that thing doing there? Whose is it?" Torina asked, frowning hard at the tactical data.

"Aurigae-class are made by the Algo Shipyards at HD4629, aka Nesit. They're available on the open market—if you can afford it, that is," Netty said.

"So this was built by the *Nesit?*" I remembered their homeworld as a place of serene, rugged beauty, soaring peaks, and waterfalls. I'd never gotten even a hint of arms merchantry from it.

"Actually, Algo is a joint venture between the Nesit, the Seven Stars League, and a private consortium. Nominally, the Aurigae is built for use by the Seven Stars fleet. However, the League has a habit of placing orders and then cancelling them over budget concerns. That leaves Algo with a nearly completed hull—"

"Which they then sell to recoup their costs, yeah, I get it. I'd even call it clever, if it weren't so appallingly obvious."

Perry spoke up. "It gets better, Van. When the suddenly surplus Aurigae hull is sold to a new buyer, its construction certificate is revised to officially reclassify it to fast freighter, with no weapons except a pair of point-defense batteries. After all, it's illegal under interstellar law to sell warships to the private sector."

"Let me guess—all of the weapons hardpoints are still in place."

Perry raised a wing. "Upgrade points, they're called, suitable for installing additional scanner suites, comms arrays, point-defense batteries, but definitely not military-grade boom-boom hardware."

"Boom-boom hardware?"

"Something I decided to try out."

I could only shake my head. "So these assholes are doing a blatantly obvious end-run around the laws intended to prevent crap like that from getting into the wrong hands."

"When you put it like that, you make it sound sleazy."

"Even so, a ship like that must cost millions, probably tens of millions of bonds," Torina put in.

"Plus millions more for all that boom-boom hardware," Icky added.

I glared at Perry. "This is your fault."

He shrugged.

I crossed my arms. "Okay. So whoever is operating that damned thing is rich."

"Rich and involved in mining osmium from Pluto. There's an actual freighter outbound, directly away from Sol. Since Pluto's gravitation isn't very strong, he'll be… gone, that's what he'll be. He just twisted away," Netty reported.

"So that suggests rich, mining osmium on Pluto, and probably also involved in our stolen identity ring," Torina said.

"I don't know about you guys, but I can think of only a very few candidates." I raised a hand and crooked one finger after another as I worked through the list. "The Salt Thieves, the Arc of Vengeance, the Stillness, mercenaries like our friend Pevensy, or an entirely new outfit. Have I missed anyone?"

"How about an actual government, like the Seven Stars League?" Torina asked.

I'd clenched all my fingers, so I raised my thumb and then closed it again. "And that."

"Well, the Salt Thieves are a large organization, but they've only ever used actual, repurposed civilian ships, so something like this is probably beyond them," Perry said.

"And the Arc of Vengeance has no history of operating outside of a couple of systems, and even then, they generally use small ships, up-gunned workboats and a few things up to corvette-sized," Netty added.

"And we've got no evidence at all of a new organization. Not even a hint of intelligence suggesting it. That's actually what makes this identity-theft ring so damned hard to run down. They just don't seem to have any sort of clear overarching structure," Perry went on.

"Not to mention that it's not enough to just buy a ship like that. You also have to operate it and maintain it," Icky put in. "That requires static facilities big enough to do it, since you're probably not just going to hire some private shipyard to work on your maybe-legal fast-attack cruiser."

I nodded along as they spoke. "Okay, so it hints at someone organized, with lots of resources, probably permanent bases somewhere, and also probably well-connected. A well-established merce-nary company like Pevensy's is a candidate for sure. But my thinking keeps going back to The Stillness."

"They have been awfully quiet since we tangled with them near the Pleiades in that void—oh, with the android station—" Torina bit her lip in frustration.

"Afterthought," Perry said.

Torina brightened and pointed at Perry. I nodded.

"Yeah. I'd honestly expected some blowback from them after that little incident, but they just seemed to go completely dormant. Could they realistically own and operate a ship like that?"

"Easily," Netty said.

"Your grandfather knew that only too well. He once said that confronting The Stillness wasn't a matter of law enforcement, it was a matter of war," Perry added.

"So a ruthless and powerful criminal syndicate, or a dedicated and professional mercenary company." I sighed and rubbed my eyes.

Netty spoke up. "Between a rock and a—"

"Hard place. I know. I got that fortune cookie too."

———

SINCE TAKING on that warship was currently out of our league, we turned our attention to things that we *could* influence. I didn't want to leave without keeping eyes on Pluto, to use the military phrase, so we put the *Iowa* into a parking orbit, completely powered down except for her passive scanners. If the bad guys hadn't detected us by now—and they gave no sign that they had—then their chances of spotting the *Iowa* at this distance were slim to none.

So now we sat in the *Fafnir*, in our accustomed places, ready to go… somewhere. I considered Anvil Dark but decided to check with Lunzy first. I'd told her our plans a few days—or, for her, almost a year ago—so she was plugged into our prolonged absence.

"I hear Rigel's lovely at this time of year," she said over the twist comm.

"And what time of year would that be? The one I think it is, or the one it actually is back on Earth?"

She shrugged. "It's how the universe works, Van. And for the record, I think your grandfather was right to give you the choice *after* you'd had a taste of Peacemaking. That way, you'd know full well what you were giving up, or not." Her image cocked its head. "And I assume it's *or not*, since you're talking to me."

"I don't like leaving things unfinished."

"Hear hear."

I asked her about Anvil Dark to get the lay of the political landscape that had taken shape while we'd been gone. Her news wasn't good.

"Yotov is now the undisputed Master—pun intended—of the Guild, at least insofar as its leadership is concerned. She and her cronies now firmly hold four of the seven chairs at the Masters' Table."

"Shit."

"Oh, it gets better. For reasons I can't fathom, she's made your cousin, Carter Yost, her official liaison. Technically, he and I are now coworkers."

My army background kicked in, my next dozen or so words consisting mainly of one, a versatile f-word that I spat out variously as noun, verb, and adjective. My old Sergeant would have been proud.

"I shouldn't have gone to Rigel," I finally snapped, shaking my head.

"Van, whatever's going on between your cousin and Yotov isn't likely something you could influence anyway. In fact, Yost came looking for you with a big shit-eating grin on his face. You should have seen how soon that turned to abject disappointment when you turned out to be *on assignment and unavailable for as long as a year.*"

I shrugged. "That's something, I guess."

"It's good you were gone in another way. The anti-Yotov faction hasn't given up, they've just dropped under the scanners. Since you've been away, though, no one associates you with either faction. You're one of the very few Peacemakers that's considered truly neutral. You also have a healthy amount of cred, given the things you've accomplished in only a year—well, two years now, I guess. That means that, when you do get back to Anvil Dark, you're probably going to find both factions courting you, hard."

"You should stay away from Anvil Dark for now," Torina immediately said.

Perry bobbed his head. "Absolutely agree. We go back to Anvil Dark and you'll get sucked into the quagmire of shitty politics. And so will we, by association."

I looked back at the comm image. "Which faction are you, Lunzy?"

"The one that's trying to actually investigate crimes and enforce the peace, while the rest of the Guild rips itself apart with political infighting. It's the same faction I'm hoping you'll join."

"Oh, happily. No question there." I sighed. "Thanks, Lunzy. We'll be in touch."

She signed off, and I settled back in my seat.

"So Anvil Dark is out, at least for now. I guess our choices are—"

"Van?" Netty cut in.

"What is it, Netty?"

"I've been monitoring radio-frequency comms emissions from Earth, just in case anything that might particularly interest you did happen while we were at Rigel."

That made me sit up. "And?"

"And, I've encapsulated it all for you in a summary you can read at your leisure. There is one item, though, I think you'll want to know about right away. It's just a brief item on a defense news site, not even something that made the big media—"

"Netty, I just found out my asshole cousin has been anointed into a cushy position he doesn't deserve—which is the story of his life, actually. Anyway, my patience is as thin as tissue paper—"

"It's about your father, Van."

"My—*father?*"

"Yes. An oceanographic survey located the wreckage of what is almost certainly his aircraft, resting on a seamount about five hundred klicks west of the southernmost tip of India."

I didn't hesitate.

"Earth, Netty. And step on it."

LIKE NETTY SAID, it had just been a blurb on a defense website, maybe two hundred words. *In a press release issued today, the Department of the Navy has confirmed that the wreckage of an F/A-18 Super Hornet from the carrier* USS Harry S. Truman—

It then went on to give a few scant details—the wreckage had been located during an oceanographic survey five hundred kilometers west of Kanyakumari on the southern tip of India, roughly midway between the Indian island of Minicoy and the northernmost of the Maldives Islands. It was near the summit of a seamount at a depth of just under three thousand feet. An image of the wrecked Super Hornet taken by an ROV had confirmed the tail number of the aircraft, noting it had been flown by Major Van Tudor II, and had crashed during a landing attempt in poor visibility. The cause of the accident was unknown, beyond my father reporting a flame out in one of his engines, followed by no further communications.

And that was it.

We put the *Fafnir* into a geosynchronous orbit directly over the apparent location of my father's plane, but even her formidable scanners couldn't resolve anything useful from thirty-odd thousand klicks away, through the full thickness of the Earth's atmosphere *and* through almost a mile of water.

"We're going to have to get closer," I said.

"Van, be aware that there is a US Navy battlegroup based around the carrier *USS Abraham Lincoln* currently operating less than one hundred kilometers from the wreck site," Perry said. As he spoke, the scanner imagery zoomed in, until we were looking straight down through patchy clouds at a group of ships trailing feathery white wakes through the deep blue water.

"Is that a problem? I mean, they can't detect us, right?"

"Generally, no. Some late-generation military radar could generate a weak return from the *Fafnir*, however, which might pique their interest."

"Is that what those videos released a couple of years ago were? The ones captured by those fighters and splashed all over the internet? And if so, how come they were so easy to detect?"

"Well, you know how sometimes people go drifting or doing donuts in their car just to show off?"

"Uh… yeah, what about——" I stopped, catching his meaning. "Wait, are you saying those ships caught on that video were doing it *deliberately*?"

Perry shrugged his wings. "Some people are just trolls, to use the Earthly term."

"Trolls? Wait, is that another species here? I thought the dominant one was humans. Did I get that wrong?" Icky asked.

I smiled and shook my head. "Trolls are what we call people who deliberately do stuff to attract attention to themselves, usually by annoying or outright offending everyone they can." I pursed my lips. "So maybe they are kind of another species, yeah. One composed entirely of assholes."

We mused for a while about what to do. According to Netty, if we remained stealthed, the *Abraham Lincoln* and her consorts had little chance of detecting us. At best, their powerful search radars might get a few flickering returns. So we could descend to the surface. Then what?

"Netty, since the *Fafnir* is airtight—" I began, but she cut me off.

"I knew you were going to go there eventually—can we use the *Fafnir* as a submarine, right?"

"Yeah."

"We can, and she should withstand the pressure."

"*Should* withstand it? Didn't you guys tell me when I took my very first flight that the ship is designed to move stuff out of the way, so she's always effectively flying in a vacuum?"

"That's true in low-pressure fluids like air. A few thousand feet underwater, not so much. But the bigger issue is going to be keeping ourselves hidden. In the air, the acoustic energy from the ship and her thrusters is fairly limited. Under water, though, it's going to be much more distinct."

"Ah. And if there's one group that's really, really good at detecting noise underwater, it's the US Navy."

"Indeed. We'd only have our thrusters to maneuver, and they're going to make quite a racket, at least in terms of how sensitive their equipment is."

I tapped a finger against my chin. If we took the *Fafnir* down to the wreck, then, we'd likely be detected. I remember my father telling me how much of a carrier battlegroup's resources are devoted to anti-submarine warfare, so if we spooked them, they might very well respond with lethal force—especially if they thought we might be some foreign power trying to poke around the wreckage of my father's plane. It was, after all, a military aircraft and might still contain classified tech. At the very least, they'd do some thorough investigating.

But I couldn't pass up the chance to see my father's wrecked plane for myself. I'd said goodbye to him almost three months before he actually died. Even then, I'd only seen him for a couple of weeks, when he'd taken leave. Somehow, just seeing the plane might give me—closure? Was that really a thing? The word got used a lot, but what did it actually mean?

Not what I was feeling right now, was the best I could do. What I was feeling right now was a keen sense of loss, heightened by the somber reality that we'd missed most of each other's lives.

Of course, the wreck wasn't going anywhere. On the other hand, the US Navy typically had a force on-station in the Indian Ocean. Moreover, there was a good chance they'd have placed a hydrophone not far from the downed Super Hornet. Even if they weren't interested in doing battle, they'd still likely want to get a sense of who might end up snooping around the wreck.

Screw it.

"Netty, we're going for a swim."

22

WE DEORBITED and swept through a majestic descent over China, Myanmar, the Bay of Bengal, and southern India. We located the remote but surprisingly well-developed and populated Indian island of Minicoy, then turned south, toward the Maldives. Flying less than a klick over the wavetops, we switched to active sensors and swept a path across the ocean floor. Even a mile of water didn't deter the scanners at this infinitesimal range, and we soon piled a bunch of contacts.

"There is a lot of stuff down there, isn't there?" I said, staring at several dozen returns. Assuming that when the press release said *midway between* Minicoy and the Maldives it literally meant halfway, there were still a dozen possible hits.

"Van, what's your father's airship made out of?" Icky asked.

"Air*plane*. An airship is a huge, lighter-than-air gasbag."

Torina smirked. "I think I know a few of those. My father does business with a couple, in fact."

I flashed her a quick grin, then turned back to Icky. "A Super Hornet? Mostly aluminum, actually, with some heat-resistant alloys in its engines and exhaust, some titanium—"

"Titanium, eh? Not too common in nature. Netty, can you layer on a scan channel for—"

"Titanium? Done."

Only three of the targets returned a decent titanium signal, and only one of those was even remotely close to that elusive midway point.

One of the others, though, was moving—currently, generally eastward, along a track that would pass about ten kilometers from our best candidate.

"Netty, can you zero in on that moving target?" I asked.

She did, focusing the active scanners onto it and amping up their power. Thanks to some complex quantum physics I didn't really understand, we were able to clearly resolve an elongated shape, bulbous at one end, sleekly tapered at the other. Stray, high-energy neutrons streamed away from it in all directions.

It was a nuclear submarine.

There was always at least one, I knew, accompanying an American carrier. And if there was any single vessel that could hear far-off things underwater, it was an American nuclear sub.

"Why don't we just wait? Maybe go spend a day or two at your farm, then come back?" Torina asked.

I sighed. "Yeah, you're probably right. Hopefully by then this carrier and her escorts will have moved on—"

"Van, I'm reading a signal from the wreck of your father's plane that doesn't—well, it's incongruous," Netty cut in.

"Incongruous how?"

"It's giving off ionizing radiation that wouldn't be explained by any system normally carried by an atmospheric craft of that type unless it was, say, carrying a nuclear weapon."

I stiffened. Had dad been flying with a nuke slung under his Super Hornet? A so-called "Broken Arrow" situation, meaning a lost nuclear weapon? Because if so, then the Navy wouldn't rest until they'd either retrieved it or satisfied themselves that it simply *couldn't* be retrieved.

"Shit. That means they'll be watching the crash site like hawks."

"Probably why that underwater thing—submarine, right? Anyway, that's probably why it's hanging around here," Icky said.

Perry spoke up. "Actually, Van, there's another possibility, one that might fit the characteristics of that radiation better than fissile material. See, when a particle beam hits something, it can induce secondary radiation in its target. And the data Netty's collecting looks more like that than a weapon."

But I shook my head. "That can't be right, though. No one on Earth has a useable particle—"

My voice trailed off. I looked up from the tactical overlay, at Perry and the others.

Torina nodded. "No one on Earth has one, but someone not from Earth could."

I slowly settled back in my seat as the horrifying realization sank in.

My father hadn't died in an accident. He'd been shot down with a weapon that, on Earth, was still just science fiction.

In other words, my father had been murdered.

IN THE VACUUM OF SPACE, the *Fafnir* had to be strong enough to maintain standard atmospheric pressure, about fifteen pounds of weight pressing on every square inch of her interior. If that's all she'd been designed to take, then she'd have been crushed like an empty pop can long before she reached three thousand feet depth in the ocean, where the pressure was about one hundred times that. Fortunately, the Dragonet class of ship was designed to accommodate many different species. After all, a Peacemaker could come from essentially any sentient race in known space—in that sense, it was a truly egalitarian organization.

"And that includes people from some pretty high pressure worlds," Netty said.

"I think the most extreme case would be the Slegnites," Perry added.

I gave him a blank look. I couldn't recall ever having heard anything about a species called Slegnites.

"And they are?"

"An aquatic race whose home planet is a water world. Well, actually, a *weird mixture of water and hydrocarbons and stuff*-world, but for our purposes, suffice it to say that their native pressure is pretty close to what's down below."

"So we can do this then?"

"We'll be at the limit of what the *Fafnir* can safely tolerate," Netty said.

I nodded and turned to Torina and Icky. "Okay, I'm going to take you guys back to Iowa and—"

"And what, exactly?" Torina cut in. "Keep us safe in case you end up getting yourself killed? And what do you propose we do then? Your friend Myriam is going to wonder why your Italian girl-friend is home, but you're never seen again."

Icky just leaned between the seats and waved. "Wait'll she gets a load of me!"

"Okay, fine, I'll take you back to the *Iowa*. That way, at least—"

"Van, would you just shut up and *dive?*" Torina asked, smiling to take the sting out of her words.

I knew I wasn't going to make any headway on this, so I finally just shrugged. "Okay, Netty. Take us down."

Netty eased the *Fafnir* into the water. We were briefly jostled by waves, their accelerations too small to trigger the dampers. Then daylight became wobbly twilight as the water closed over us.

The first part of the descent was easy—we just let the *Fafnir* sink. That brought her to about a hundred meters, at which point she became neutrally buoyant and came to a gentle stop.

"I guess this is the part where we'd flood some ballast tanks or something, to keep sinking—which would be great, if we had any," I said.

"Believe it or not, there isn't much call for ballast tanks aboard spacecraft," Netty said. "I'm going to start applying some downward thrust."

The ship rumbled slightly as the thrusters powered up, and we resumed sinking. As we did, I kept my eye on that nuclear sub, which was now about thirty klicks north of us. For several minutes, it just maintained its stately course and speed. As we passed through a thousand feet, though, it abruptly began to veer, at the same time accelerating slightly. Her new course was aimed directly toward us.

"I think we've been made," Torina said.

I nodded. I was no expert in submarine warfare, but I knew enough to realize that the approaching sub was probably as silent as a kitten padding across a carpeted floor. She had no idea that we could see her clearly, a darkly sleek and sinister shape slowly getting closer.

Netty, if that sub were to fire a torpedo, and it detonated close to us—"

"We'd probably die. The *Fafnir's* structure likely couldn't absorb the sudden increase in water pressure from a shockwave."

"Shit."

The last thing I wanted to do was risk destroying an American nuclear sub. Not only would it entail the loss of dozens of professional submariners just doing their job, but it could also very well trigger a serious international incident. So that wasn't even an option.

On the other hand, if we were wrong about the radiation coming from dad's plane, and this actually was a Broken Arrow, then the Navy might try to recover it—or just detonate something close enough to it to knock it into the abyss beneath the seamount, beyond even the *Fafnir's* ability to descend.

Besides, I needed to know. If my father had been murdered by someone or something that originated off Earth, then I had questions I needed—and, come hell or high water, would *get*—answered. *Who* and *why* would be a start. When my father died, spaceships and aliens and intergalactic crimes were, to me, just more of Gramps's wild stories. So it must have been a blow intended to strike at him in some way.

And the foremost suspect for doing something like that would be The Stillness.

But why? How would killing my father, an Earthly naval aviator, have any impact on events in other parts of known space?

"Two thousand feet," Netty said, and as if to accentuate it, something behind the cockpit creaked. It actually made me wince. I'd come to know virtually every sound the *Fafnir* made outside of battle, and that wasn't one of them.

"That's… unsettling," Torina muttered.

"Good term for it. I was going to go with terrifying. I like your gusto."

Torina sketched a small salute, and then our humor deflated as the ship popped again, this time with the metallic ring of a collapsing can. I tried not to wince, and almost succeeded.

"Me too, boss," Perry said.

I pushed my attention back to the overlay. The sub was closing on us at about a klick and a half every two minutes. It had leveled out at a depth of a little more than a thousand feet.

"That's probably as deep as she can go," Perry concluded.

Which meant she wasn't a problem right now, but she certainly could be on the way back up.

We continued sinking, pushed down by gradually increasing power to the thrusters. To us inside the *Fafnir*, we heard only a slight thrum. Whatever the sub actually heard, it was probably not just distinct, but completely unrecognized. I knew they had databases of sonar signatures aboard, but I doubted that *Dragonet-class spaceship* was listed in them.

Another creak, followed by a loud thump. Icky unstrapped and turned for the back of the cockpit. "Just going to make sure that wasn't anything vital."

Torina gave me a thin smile. "If it was, I suspect we'll soon know it."

"Twenty-five hundred feet. The wreck of your father's aircraft is about four hundred feet below us, and about six hundred to our west," Netty said, altering our course slightly.

I found myself gritting my teeth as we descended the last few hundred feet. Icky came back and opened her mouth—

Crack.

Ping.

She cursed and clambered back out of the cockpit.

"Van, the wreckage should be coming in sight now," Netty reported.

I peered out into the gloom. We were well below the point that sunlight reached, but Netty just overlaid the scanner returns, which themselves combined a variety of information, onto the canopy. It struck me that that canopy was five millimeters thick, which had always seemed flimsy in space and seemed *far* beyond flimsy now. Many times atmospheric pressure bore down on it from the water outside, but it didn't even creak. The material somehow became stronger the more stress was applied to it, a fact that seemed counterintuitive but, hey, who was I to argue? As long as it didn't fail and implode, it was all good.

Of course, if it did fail and implode, I wouldn't have time to be disappointed. I wouldn't have time to be *anything.*

So I made myself ignore the fact we were thousands of feet beneath the Indian Ocean and concentrate instead on the wreckage just coming into view.

There was no mistaking the twin tail fins of an F/A-18 Super Hornet, although the rest of the plane had been mostly reduced to scrap. The only recognizable parts were the nose cone, tilted against a rock about ten meters away, and a part of the left wing wedged into a crevasse. The nearest tail fin, painted black and yellow, bore the skull-and-crossbones insignia of VFA-103, the Jolly Rogers.

The Jollies, as they were called, were my father's strike fighter squadron at the time he'd been—

I was going to go with *lost*, but given the apparent emissions from the wrecked plane, lost might not be right. *Killed* or *murdered* might be.

"Is that your father's airship—sorry, air… plane, right? Anyway, is it your father's?" Icky asked, leaning forward between the seats to peer out the canopy.

I stared at the tail fin as Netty brought the *Fafnir* to a stop a few meters away. "It has all the right markings for his plane, yeah. And I don't see any other crashed Super Hornets around here, so I'd say it is."

We spent a few moments in somber silence, looking at the wreck and—and that was it. Just looking. There seemed to be an unspoken agreement among everyone present, even Perry and Netty, that we needed to spend this bit of time just sitting and being quiet.

I finally spoke up. "Netty, what's the verdict?"

"The emissions are actually coming from a location about five hundred meters to our right. From the shape of the debris, it appears to be a wing."

As she spoke, I found my eyes drawn to a place I'd been deliberately trying to avoid—the rough location of the Super Hornet's cockpit. Gramps and I were only ever told that he'd died when his plane crashed during its approach to land on the Truman, and that he simply had too little altitude to make a survivable ejection.

However, there was no cockpit. Everything forward of the tail and behind the nose cone was now indistinguishable shreds of debris. The closest I could get to even identifying a part of the cockpit was a twisted, roughly triangular sheet of aluminum sporting an inverted black triangle labeled *Danger—Ejection Seat*. I remembered that from my last visit to my dad's ship. It was stenciled on the fuselage immediately beneath the canopy. My father would have been sitting only centimeters away from this ragged piece of metal—

"Van, the wing is just ahead," Netty said.

"You know, the fact that this wing is so far from the rest of the wreck suggests it might have come free of the airplane while it was still in flight," Perry said.

I grunted my understanding. It was possible, but I'm not sure how likely it was. A flat airfoil like a wing might just have flown itself through the water when it broke free of the plane on impact.

Except.

"That wing did not just break off of this airplane," Netty said.

No, it hadn't. The break, where the wing had separated from the rest of the Super Hornet, was pocked, discolored, and fused smooth, as though it had been sliced off with a huge cutting torch.

"And that is our source of radiation—that damage to the wing. The metal skin and internal structure all along the break have been bombarded by high-energy particles, which has made them temporarily radioactive."

That was conclusive. That was it. My father's plane crash had been no accident.

He'd been shot down.

I cracked my knuckles, scowling as a black rage began to suffuse my bones.

23

"I WANT TO KNOW WHO," I finally said, breaking the strained silence in the *Fafnir*. I knew everyone had been waiting for me to speak, but it took me a moment to find the words amid the sudden agonizing rage that had come boiling up inside me.

"That might be hard to determine—" Perry started, but I wheeled on him.

"Then let's find a way. Whatever it takes. I want to know who did this."

Perry stared right back at me. "Okay. Let me think about it for a bit."

"It's too bad this—Super Hornet? Cool name," Icky said. "Anyway, if it had had something like Netty, who records everything—"

I sat up. "Icky, you're a genius. Netty, this airplane has a data recorder. If the Navy hasn't managed to retrieve it, we should—"

A flashing icon appeared on the canopy a few hundred meters away. "There's a distinct device containing digital memory components right there. It likely generated a signal for a time after the crash, but if it wasn't located by the time its power source failed, then it wouldn't be—and there it is."

"Can we retrieve it?"

"That's a problem. The *Fafnir* doesn't have any external manipulators dextrous enough to retrieve something that small."

I snapped a string of curses. If the *Fafnir* couldn't somehow retrieve it, we had no other options. Our b-suits were good, but they'd never withstand this sort of pressure. And Waldo, who could only walk, would inevitably get stuck in the silty mud liberally coating the seamount.

"Uh, Van? I can go get it if you want," Perry said.

I shook my head. "You'd never survive."

"What, a couple of hundred atmospheres of pressure? Child's play. Remember, Van, I may look gorgeous, but I'm an assemblage of solid components that can't be compressed. Venus might have been beyond me, but this is nothin'."

I gave him a wary look. "Are you sure?"

"Bah. I can do twice this much pressure before I'd even start worrying. The bigger problem is going to be that once I'm out there, I won't be able to come back inside. The water in the airlock will be under too much pressure to displace it with air."

Icky raised a finger. "But, if we just leave the outer door partly open, the pressure will equalize as we head back up." She clambered out of her seat. "Just give me about five minutes to bypass the safety meant to specifically prevent that from happening, and we'll be good to go."

I nodded at her, then turned back to Perry. "Thanks, bird. I really appreciate this."

"I'm really not just another pretty face, Van."

"No, you're not," I said, smiling.

He started to turn away, then glanced back. "Wait a minute— that was a compliment, right?"

"Let's go with that."

"THIS IS *LIVIN'*!"

Perry flashed by the canopy, corkscrewing through a barrel roll as he did. His thrusters were useless at this depth, producing less pressure than the water itself. But that didn't matter because he could fly.

And he was proving it by showing off. The amber glow of his eyes marked his location, the rest of him being lost in gloom.

"Glad you're having a good time out there, Perry, but we'd prefer not to spend any longer down here than necessary," I said. "On account of the threat of a crushing death and that boomer over there."

"Killjoy," he shot back, then wheeled around in a tight bank and descended toward the data recorder. "And why are you scared of some old dude boring the hell out of you about why music in the 1960s was so much better?"

"Different kind of boomer. I'll explain later, preferably while we're listening to early 2000s power pop."

"I accept your offer of cultural enrichment," Perry said, executing another flawless turn.

"He really does know how to fly, doesn't he?" Torina said.

"He does, and smoothly," I agreed.

Perry flapped his wings to stir up the sediment and uncover the data recorder. Gripping it in his talons, he flapped again, trying to lift it. Suction held it in place for a moment, but his wings kept churning up the silt, and it abruptly came free.

"Got it. On my way back now—"

Something dark flashed past, and Perry disappeared.

I blinked. Torina sat up. Icky muttered, "Wha—?"

"Netty, what happened to him?"

"I think Perry was just swallowed by a large fish, apparently of the species *Lophius piscatorius*, aka the anglerfish."

"I can confirm that. I am, indeed, inside a fish," Perry said, his voice muffled—which was bizarre, because he wasn't actually talking but transmitting via the comm. Then it struck me that whatever had swallowed him was carrying him further away from us, and the intervening water was degrading the comm signal.

"Oh, for—Netty, follow that fish!"

She powered up the thrusters and wheeled the *Fafnir* off in pursuit.

"That must be one hell of a big fish," Torina said.

Netty nodded. "The question is, what do we do about it? Shoot it with a point-defense gun?"

"You mean the ones we just got upgraded to make them even more deadly? Yeah, no thanks. Just leave this to me," Perry said.

He'd only just finished talking when another problem reared its most unwelcome head. A far more serious one. A warning sounded, and the tactical overlay lit up with a new and dangerous threat.

"Two projectiles inbound. From the high-frequency sonar pings and propeller sounds, I'd say they're torpedoes," Netty said.

I stared at the overlay. Torpedoes, launched by the nuclear sub still prowling above.

We'd just been fired on by the United States Navy.

"I guess they don't like us fooling around with their crashed airplane," Torina said, bringing the weapons online.

I grunted in assent but kept studying the overlay. On the face of it, the torpedoes, contemporary Earth tech, should be no match for the *Fafnir*. And if we were airborne and they were missiles, they wouldn't be. But this was their natural environment. It wasn't the *Fafnir*'s.

"Can the point-defense take them out?" I asked Netty.

"Possibly, but only at quite short range. Even upgraded, the projectiles are going to lose energy very fast."

"The lasers?"

"Same problem. Severe attenuation through water full of suspended sediments and other particles."

"*Damn* this water. Our own missiles?"

"Detonating one of our missiles' warheads down here is likely to damage or destroy both the *Fafnir* and the submarine."

"So, we've got no answer to this? None? A super-advanced spaceship, and—"

"Spaceship, Van. That's the operative word. If the *Fafnir* was designed to work as a submersible at these depths, we'd be having a very different conversation."

I examined the overlay again. We had three minutes. At that point, the detonation of a conventional warhead like those mounted on the torpedoes would fling out a pressure wave that could easily buckle the *Fafnir*'s hull.

Our only recourse was to maneuver away. But that wouldn't help Perry, who could very well be caught by the blasts and damaged, maybe even destroyed.

"I hate this part," I muttered.

Torina glanced at me. "What part?"

"The part where we have no options, and everything looks lost, and only some amazing, off-the-wall scheme can save us." I looked at her. "Don't suppose you have any amazing, off-the-wall schemes ready to go, do you?"

"Sorry, no."

"Yeah, neither do I. Icky?"

"What? Oh, sorry, I was just calculating how likely we are to survive those things exploding close to us, within a couple of hundred meters, say."

"And?"

"You don't want to know."

I sighed. "Perry—"

"You're going to have to leave me down here, I know. It's okay, Van. My fishy friend and I just had a conversation that consisted of me kind of forcing my way out of him. Believe it or not, he just swam off. I mean, eats me, then leaves. What an asshole—"

"Perry!"

"Van, I'll see if I can take cover, then you can come back for me."

I opened my mouth to object but closed it again because we were out of options—and time. I made the call. We would leave.

"Okay, listen—"

"Van, I have an amazing, off-the-wall scheme."

I glanced at the overlay. Two minutes, and counting down. "Make it quick, Netty."

"We have another way of defeating those torpedoes that doesn't rely on line of sight or even care much about the pressure down here. We've got the *Fafnir*'s fusion drive."

"Uh, Netty, that's the equivalent of detonating a small nuke, right? I don't think that's going to do us, or that sub, or anyone else for that matter, much good."

"No, but if we apply maximum power to the magnetic collimators, we could generate a sufficiently strong magnetic field that it would likely disrupt the torpedoes' guidance mechanisms."

"And a magnetic field wouldn't be affected by the water," Torina offered.

"Good. Fine. Do it!"

Icky muttered something, and I turned to her. "Problem?"

"The collimators are designed to operate hot, like a few-centimeters-from-drive-plasma hot. If we run them up to full power cold like this, they're not going to like it."

I shrugged. "They work for me. If they have complaints, they can take it up with HR."

I turned back and watched as Netty amped up the power to the collimators, essentially magnetic probes that guided the incandescent plasma from the *Fafnir*'s drive into tight, almost coherent beams that maximized their thrust. As Icky had predicted, they immediately began to complain, flashing yellow caution alerts that I grimly ignored. I kept my focus on the torpedoes, now just a minute out.

For agonizing seconds, nothing happened. Then, the two torpedoes began to veer away from one another. One eventually turned through ninety degrees and sped off southward. The other kept veering, but more slowly, in an unhurried way as it carved the frigid depths.

We watched, an unseen clock ticking away in my head until—

The torpedo detonated about six hundred meters away. An instant later, the shockwave thudded into the *Fafnir*, as though someone had smacked a massive hammer against the hull. I winced and closed my eyes. Again, if the hull failed, I'd never know it—

I opened my eyes again. "I guess we're still in one piece."

"More or less, though I hope you don't want to leave Earth anytime soon," Icky grouched, pointing at a now red warning on the panel. "The collimators packed it in a second or two before that thing went off."

"Which means we don't have that particular trick up our sleeve anymore. We need to get Perry back aboard, and fast, before they shoot again," Torina said.

Perry's voice hummed out of the comm. "I'll be there in about two minutes—as long as nothing else decides to eat me along the way, that is."

I LOOKED UP AT ICKY, who was standing on a stepladder and peering at the collimators enclosed within the *Fafnir*'s drive bells. The stark whiteness of the barn's stealth system glowed around us, uniformly bright without actually being bright at all.

"What's the verdict, Icky?"

"The verdict is that the collimators are now officially scrap." She looked down at me. "We'll make a few bonds from recycling them, though."

I nodded and turned to Torina. "Guess we're here until Icky's dad arrives with new parts."

She shrugged, then touched my hand. "I don't mind a couple of days off."

"You just had a couple of days off, back on Helso—"

She gave me a *look*.

I smiled. "Ah."

Perry appeared in the *Fafnir*'s open airlock. "Success. Netty and I have managed to access your father's data recorder."

Torina pulled her hand away and nodded. I stopped and made a point of sniffing the air.

"Wait. Do I smell fish?"

"Hah, and in case you didn't hear me the first time, hah. Van, you're an absolute riot. Tell me, are you ever going to get tired of making that joke?"

"Not for the foreseeable future, no," I said, leading the way back aboard the ship.

"Anyway, immersion in salt water at those pressures for that long didn't do the recorder any favors," Perry said, hopping onto the galley table. The recorder sat in the middle of it, cabled into a data port.

Netty spoke up. "We retrieved about twenty percent of the data it originally contained. Most of it deals with routine flight data, with video captured from the aircraft's gun camera. I think this is the part you'll be interested in, Van."

The display over the table lit up with a fuzzy, grey scale image superimposed with hash marks and numbers. It was the view through my father's heads-up display. The view slowly turned, the sea rotating to bring the *Harry S. Truman* into view in the far distance. The numbers and other indicators rotated and changed in unison as the Super Hornet rolled out of its bank.

A sudden burst of chatter in that clipped, almost harshly professional tone of pilots on radios.

Victory 113, confirm when you've captured the glideslope.

The next voice was one I hadn't heard in years.

Roger, confirm glideslope capture, Victory 113, my father said.

An instant after he said it, a dark shape appeared out of nowhere directly ahead, blotting out the view of the carrier. I caught the briefest reaction from my father, a surprised gasp, then the image shuddered, slewed into a blur, and ended.

I just stared.

"Netty, were you able to identify whatever that was?" Torina asked.

"I was able to extract a single still image. Even cleaning it up as much as I could, it doesn't give much detail."

The frozen terminal moment of the video vanished, replaced by a still image showing a sleek, dark, arrowhead-shaped craft only a few hundred meters directly ahead of the Super Hornet.

I narrowed my gaze at the sinister shape. "So what the hell is it?"

"The closest fit is to a Ravager-class atmospheric fighter. It's a standard military craft manufactured by a shipyard consortium in the Tau Ceti system. A little more than a thousand of them have been built to date, with about a third of those being lost in battle or to accidents."

"I'm willing to bet that one, right there, is one of those supposedly lost ones. Unfortunately, we can't discern any markings, so we can't prove that."

"How come we can see it, though?" Torina asked, looking at me. "Your father's aircraft wouldn't have the ability to detect it."

"Not unless it wanted to be detected," I said.

"What—oh. A message."

"Yeah. Whoever did this wanted it to be known."

But Perry shook his head. "Van, that doesn't make any sense. Even if the recorder had been recovered at the time, I can't imagine your government revealing its contents to anyone, your grandfather included."

I looked at him. "You're assuming that this is the only imagery of him being shot down."

Perry stared for a moment. "You think there were other recordings made of it."

I nodded and pointed at the ominous delta shape on the display. "They weren't thinking of the plane's gun camera. Hell, they didn't care one way or another. I'm sure they made sure to capture the whole thing, and I'm sure they also made sure to share a copy of it with my grandfather."

"If they did, he never told us, Van. I just want to be clear about that. Netty and I knew nothing about this."

"I believe you. In fact, I'm sure he kept it from everyone—especially me."

"But why?" Torina asked.

I sat back. "Same reason he didn't tell me about the time dilation thing. He wanted me to understand the whole picture first."

Torina stiffened. "Oh. Whoever they are, they weren't just trying to warn off your grandfather. They were eliminating his successor, too."

I nodded. "Yeah. Fighter pilot, accomplished military officer, well-versed in tactical and operational doctrine, demonstrated leadership skills. Of course, they assumed that if anyone would be taking over from Gramps, it would be my father—not the computer nerd who washed out of the army because of a screwed-up knee."

"Uh, Van, if that's true, and your father was assassinated—" Perry said.

"Way ahead of you, bird," I said, nodding at the image. "It means they're still out there. And by now, they'll realize that killing my father didn't finish the job. To do that, they're going to have to kill me, too."

24

"Van, are you really sure this is a good idea?" Torina asked me.

I looked up from the traffic pattern depicted on the *Fafnir*'s nav console. "That's a change of tune."

She shrugged. "Now that we're here, I'm having second thoughts, yeah."

I turned back to the traffic. Anvil Dark always bustled, but this seemed particularly busy, a lot of ships coming and going in a stately ballet of maneuvers intended to prevent them from running into one another. Actual collisions between spaceships were extraordinarily rare, but they did occasionally happen, usually in close proximity to spaceports while ships were traveling at a low speed. But we had no such risks, a volume of space around the *Fafnir* having been declared clear by Anvil Dark's traffic control AI. As long as we traveled at the specified course and speed, we'd be fine.

At least until we got to Anvil Dark. Then, *fine* became decidedly less certain. And that was where Torina's sudden doubts came in.

Back in Iowa, waiting for Icky's dad to bring us the new collimators, she'd agreed that we should finally return to Anvil Dark. That was partly to show that we weren't put off or intimidated by whatever shitty politics now permeated the place, following Master Yotov's effective takeover of the Guild. But it was also because Anvil Dark was the logical place to start looking for whoever had killed my father.

But if Torina was suddenly getting skittish, I had to pay attention. Icky didn't really care, and both Perry and Netty seemed unwilling to view Anvil Dark as a true threat, even if they did counsel caution. Perry summed it up in a single, dismissive sentence.

"Van, Netty and I have seen some unbelievable turns in the political winds blowing through Anvil Dark. The Peacemakers that get things done are the ones that mostly ignore them—like your grandfather."

Netty spoke up, adding a bit of embellishment. "As he used to say, *politics are like assholes, everyone's got 'em.*"

I looked back up at Torina. "Second thoughts about coming here?" I asked her.

She pursed her lips, then shook her head. "I… can't say. It's just a—I don't know, a feeling. If Yotov's as dirty as we think she is, and she's involved in the identity theft ring, then strolling right into the seat of her power might not be a good idea."

I returned a morose nod but shrugged. "Cutting ourselves off from Anvil Dark completely isn't going to help, though. We need access to Steve and his people, to Bester… hell, even to the barkeep in *The Black Hole.*"

"The heavy repair facilities as well, including easy access to spare Dragonet parts. The barn in Iowa is great, but it's only suited for basic maintenance and repairs. After all, it took us almost four days to replace the drive collimators, a job that would only have needed a few hours here," Netty added.

Torina sighed. "I know, and I agree with you, believe me. It's just that—"

She stopped and stared at Anvil Dark, now visible dead ahead.

"Approaching Spindrift or Halcyon, or Crossroads, or any of those places, I'm wary, ready for trouble. Coming here, I'd never felt that. It felt like somewhere we could step off the *Fafnir* and not have to worry, not have to keep looking over our shoulders." She turned from the forward view back to me. "It doesn't feel like that anymore."

Icky, who'd been slouched in her jump seat reading a data slate, looked up. "Besides, maybe it was this Master Yotov character that sent those assassins after your dad in the first place," she said, then resumed her reading.

"And Icky casually accuses a Peacemaker Guild Master not just of conspiracy to commit murder, but just to make it even more egregious, throws in a little intra-Guild treachery by making the target another Peacemaker," Perry said drily.

Icky glanced up again and shrugged. "I call 'em like I see 'em. Besides, Van's dad wasn't a Peacemaker."

"No, but your grandfather was still the target," Torina said.

I sighed. "Yeah, you've actually all got really good points. And believe me, if I could convince myself there was somewhere better to go, I'd wheel the *Fafnir* out of the pattern right now and go there." I glanced at the antimatter fuel level. "Although it would have to be somewhere we could gas up again."

I turned to the others. "Can anyone give me a reason, besides vague feelings of dread, why we shouldn't just carry on?"

I looked at Torina as I said it, and after a pause, she gave a reluctant nod.

Veering toward Anvil Dark, I said three words. "Neither can I."

I'D BRACED myself for some sort of reception—and an unpleasant one at that. My mind remorselessly conjured unpleasant little fantasies as we waited for the airlock to cycle open. Yotov, standing and waiting for me, murder on her mind. Or maybe an armed party, intent on arresting me, or even me and the others, on trumped-up charges. And that could lead to a firefight, us having to battle our way off the station in a desperate, headlong flight—

As the *Fafnir*'s outer door slid open, I found myself clenching my teeth, my fingers ready to twitch toward The Drop on one hip, the Moonsword on the other.

And—nothing, because of course there would be nothing. In the greater scheme of things, I was only one Peacemaker, chasing identity-stealing ghosts and making about as much progress as *molasses in an Iowa winter*, as Gramps used to say.

"Well, this is a letdown," I said, stepping into the corridor that led to the primary docking concourse.

"What were you expecting? Master Yotov to be standing here herself, ready to arrest you?" Perry asked.

"No. I mean, *pfft*, what a dumb idea. Who'd think something like that?"

Icky put up a hand. "I would. That's why I brought Mjolnir here along with me."

I glanced at the massive sledge she carried in her two bigger, more muscular arms. "Mjolnir?"

"Yeah. That's the hammer of Thor, God of—"

"I know who Thor is. The question is, how do you know who Thor is, and that he's got a hammer named Mjolnir?"

Icky answered by whipping out a data slate with one of her smaller, more dextrous arms and proudly turned it toward me.

"Comic books? Really?"

"Yeah. Netty introduced me to them. They're awesome!"

Despite the tension, I had to smile. "Icky's new hobby is reading Earthly comic books. Sure, that might as well happen."

"Well, it was either that, or have her endlessly tinkering with the ship," Netty said over the comm as we reached the concourse.

"Hey, tinkering is how you get stuff done," Icky countered.

"Increasing the efficiency of the galley food-waste reclamator is not going to affect the *Fafnir*'s overall—"

I held up a hand. "Whoah, there, folks. I sense that I've just pressed *play* on an argument that's been on *pause*. Let's just worry about the present, shall we?"

I looked around at the couple of dozen people in sight. Honestly, the one I dreaded the most was Carter Yost. He'd inevitably arrive borne on a tsunami of vindictive smugness, and if that happened, I might not be able to resist asking Icky to show me just how good Mjolnir was. Splitting his melon would be *deeply* satisfying, not to mention spectacular given Icky's strength.

But, aside from a couple of people I recognized but didn't really know, everyone else was strangers going about business of their own.

We set off, heading generally in the direction of Steve's shop. We'd asked him to keep poking away at the chips we'd retrieved and handed over to him, and he'd had nearly a year to do it. He might therefore have useful insights. More to the point, he was someone I trusted, a commodity in short supply right now.

Ordinarily, when we arrived at Anvil Dark, we'd split up and multitask our way through several things at once. This time, we stuck together. I did get Icky to sling her hammer on her back, so we didn't look quite so much like an armed and wary patrol entering hostile territory. About halfway to Steve's shop in Anvil Dark's lower decks, someone called my name.

I froze, fingers yearning in the general direction of my weapons. But it was Sil, one of the very first Peacemaker's I'd met so long ago. The lizard-ish alien was considered a loner, one of those few Peacemakers who genuinely eschewed the internecine politics of Anvil Dark and just roamed known space enforcing the peace. That was why I was a little surprised to find her here. I waved at her as she caught up to us.

"I hate this place," she hissed.

"And hello to you, too, Sil," I said, then cocked my head. "So, question one—if you hate this place, why are you here?"

"Haven't you heard the new Edict?"

She said it that way, *Edict*—I could actually hear the capital *E*. "Why do I not think I'm going to like this?"

"All Peacemakers are to report here monthly and present a summary of their cases to the Masters—accomplishments to date and next steps."

I glanced at Perry. "Did you know about this?"

"Just got the download when we arrived. Um—surprise?"

"Why didn't you tell me?"

"Because, it being an Edict, it's supposed to be delivered in-person, not via comm or through an AI."

"Why?"

Perry shrugged his wings. "Old tradition. It dates from the days when the Peacemakers were more like the Galactic Knights, all monastic and honorable and such."

"Monastic? Not sure I like the sound of that," Icky said.

We all looked at her. She stared back.

"What? That means you have to be poor, right?"

"That's often one of the vows, yes," Torina said.

"What are the others?"

Torina patted Icky's arm. "I'll tell you later."

I turned back to Sil. "So you just *happened* to be wandering by and saw us?" I said, practically giving her a wink and a nudge. She returned a look as blank as Icky's had been, though.

"Yes," she said, without even a hint of guile.

"Oh. Well, since you did, let me ask you a question, as you were the first one to point us in the direction of the Stillness and my grandfather's dealings with them." I went on to give her the thumb-nail version of my father's death, and our subsequent findings and suspicions about it. I did so in hushed tones because Anvil Dark was no longer my haven, and the air of suspicion permeating our surroundings left me vaguely on edge.

"—and that's what I know, not what I suspect. As to the owner of the attacking spacecraft, it's pure intuition."

"But damned if it doesn't *feel* like the Stillness," Torina growled.

Sil gave a hesitant nod. "That sounds like the Stillness. They take ruthless to a whole different level. As a matter of policy, they tend to strike at the friends and loved ones of whomever they've got in their sights. They only finish them off once they've inflicted as much pain and suffering as they can."

"Bastards." Now it was my turn to growl.

"Your grandfather had a different term for them. He called them mother—"

"That sounds like him," I said with a snort. Gramps was military, right down to his choice of nouns.

"Anyway, given your grandfather's profile, and the fact he made himself practically enemy number one to the Stillness, I'd guess they hired the Cabal to do the job. That would fit the M.O. of your father's death, too. The Cabal makes a point of ensuring everyone knows they've assassinated someone. No quiet, low-key kills for them."

"The Cabal?" I frowned. "Haven't heard of them before. Perry?"

"They probably exist."

"And?"

"And, that's about all we know. They remain one of the most inscrutable groups in known space. Rumor is that they're actually an offshoot of the Galactic Knights that split off because of some schism hundreds of years ago. Since then, they've devoted themselves to undermining the Guild."

"Okay, why haven't I heard of this before? It seems to me that it would have come up, you know, sometime before now," I snapped. Yes, I was annoyed. Sometimes, Perry and Netty let the information flow freely. Others, I felt like I had to pry it out of them like an encrypted drive that didn't want to give up its secrets.

"Because, Van, there was no reason to believe the Cabal was

involved. For that matter, there's really no reason to believe they still even exist. They're more Peacemaker urban legend than viable target. Even your grandfather gave up on them quickly, because there were simply no leads to follow. Like, none."

"There's a lead now," Sil said, yanking my attention back to her.

"What sort of lead?"

"About two months ago, I picked up a smuggler running guns out of Dregs. I made him a deal and seized his cargo and the contents of his ship's data stores, in exchange for not turning him into a cloud of ionized gas. I found one explicit reference to the Cabal buried in his files. Someone sold him the name of a cutout used by the Cabal on Dregs."

"A cutout?"

"An intermediary in a clandestine operation," Perry said.

"So this smuggler wanted to hire some assassins?"

Sil uttered a sibilant, rising and falling tone, her version of laughter. "Oh, no. I doubt this idiot could have spelled the word assassin. No, it was just mixed in with some stolen data that he bought, mainly to get his grubby claws on some juicy bank-transfer information. Of course, by the time he'd bought it, it had probably been bought and sold a dozen times and any valuable financial data either already used to steal money or else patched and no longer worth anything."

"Do you have a name on Dregs?" Torina asked.

"Just one word: Pygmalion."

"So, whoever they are, they're probably human and from Earth, using a name like that from old Earthly myth," Perry said. But I held up a hand.

"You mean like how naming her hammer Mjolnir means Icky's obviously from Earth?"

"Uh... good point."

"On top of that, I've met a slug who rides on a ball and would consider herself at home at the Folies Bergère, and a gross translucent guy who considers himself some sort of relation to the Romanov Dynasty. You'll forgive me if Earthly references don't immediately point me back at, ah, Earth—"

The comm chimed. I glanced at the others. It wasn't Netty, who had clearance to just go ahead and speak at will over an encrypted channel we left open for her.

I sighed and answered. "Tudor here."

"Hello, Van."

There was no mistaking that smarmy voice. It was Carter Yost.

"Kinda busy, Carter. What can I do for you?"

"No one's too busy to see me, Van. Not these days, and especially not you. And since you're finally back on Anvil Dark, I'd like to see you. Now. In my office."

I looked at Torina and mouthed *his office?* She just gave a doleful shrug.

I got ready to tell Carter to pound sand, but Torina abruptly raised a hand.

"Carter, this is Torina Milon, Van's second. You caught him right in the middle of an important conversation."

"Not more important than—"

"Solving a case involving the deaths of dozens, maybe hundreds of people? Okay, I'm just going to file that in our log—"

"Wait, what? No, of course—I mean—"

I laced my fingers together in a praying gesture and raised them at Torina, this time mouthing *thank you.*

"Look, him coming to see me isn't going to interfere with your case—"

"So noted. Van, sorry, we have to go. That lead you just got is going to have to wait."

"Hopefully, it'll still be good by the time we get there," Perry added. "But you know how these things go—"

"Just tell him to get here as soon as he can," Carter snapped, signing off.

"You, my dear, are a gem," I said.

She offered a small shrug. "If there's one thing I've learned from my parents, it's how to deal with nakedly ambitious assholes. Just make them think they're about to make a mistake."

I turned to Sil. "Thank you. I owe you one."

"And I will collect someday," she replied, then turned away with a wave.

"Okay, so let's get the hell back to the *Fafnir* and get out of here —" I started, but Torina again held up her hand.

"I think you should go see your cousin."

"What? *Why?*"

"Because you need to know the new lay of the land here, Van, whether you like it or not. You need to know what he's up to and, more importantly, what he knows."

"She's right, Van. And not only that, but if your cousin has been invested as a Masters' Liaison, then ignoring him is technically a violation of Guild protocol," Perry added.

"Yeah, I don't think you want to give them any ammunition here, boss," Icky said.

"I hate it when you guys make sense."

"Sorry. We'll try to be much more incompetent going forward," Torina replied.

"You do that. In the meantime—" I couldn't help another resigned sigh. "In the meantime, even though I'd rather have a tooth extracted with rusty pliers, let's go see my dear cousin."

"Van, would it help if the pliers weren't rusty?" Perry asked innocently as we changed course for the Keel.

"Bird?"

"Yes, boss?"

"Can pliers pull those spectacular tail feathers of yours?"

Perry flared his tail, then laughed. "Point taken. To the douchebag's lair, double time."

I tapped my fist to his outstretched wing. "Attabird."

"WELL WELL WELL, if it isn't my favorite cousin," Carter said as we entered his stupidly luxurious office.

I made a show of looking around. "It is? Where?"

Carter leaned insouciantly on his desk, a football field of some polished alien wood. "Kind of a turnaround, isn't it? Me being here, and you over there?"

"Yeah, it seems like you might actually be on the way to making something of yourself."

Carter's smile didn't waver, but it hardened along with the rest of his face.

"You know, I'd love to sit here and make small talk, but I'm a busy guy. I guess you are, too. Where have you been for the past year?"

"Here and there, chasing down a really complicated case."

"The identity theft thing, as you call it, right?"

"That, among others."

Carter scowled. "I see we're going to have to do this the hard way. Van, I want a full accounting of every day that's passed since the last time you were at Anvil Dark."

"A full accounting of every day? Okay, where would you like to start? With everything that's happened on Earth, or did you want to do Tau Ceti first, or——"

Carter slammed his hand down on his desk. "That's enough, Peace-maker Tudor. You will answer the question you know I was damned well asking. What have you been doing since you were last here?"

"Every day?"

"Every day."

I turned to Perry, who nodded.

"Starting with the last time Van was here, at time index 14156.1423, he left the *Fafnir*'s cockpit to use the lavatory. He was so occupied until time index 14156.1421, whereupon he moved to the *Fafnir*'s galley and began preparing a snack, a peanut butter sand-wich. He completed that by time index——"

"*Enough!*"

Carter stood and strode around the desk. "I will not be disre-spected——!"

"Then do something worthy of respect, Carter," I snapped.

"How *dare* you——"

"No, how dare *you!*" I hadn't forgotten Torina's wise words about learning what Carter knew and all that, but I had a shit ton of baggage when it came to his obsequious, oily stupidity.

"Want to get caught up, Carter? Fine, let's get caught up. Let's see, first, I rescued your sorry ass. And then, let's see—oh, right, I rescued your sorry ass for a second time—"

"Moist," Torina muttered, making Carter wince and Icky giggle.

"—and then you involved yourself in a ship called the *Empty Space*, which is heavily implicated in the really, *really* nasty case we're out there trying to run down—in between bouts of saving your worthless carcass, I might add—and then you suck-holed your way into this job. Does that about cover it?"

Despite the surging anger, I had noticed something interesting, a brief flicker of what I could swear was panic sweep across Carter when I mentioned the *Empty Space*. I was tempted to drive that wedge as deep as I could right now, but a more sober part of me realized that was worth keeping tucked away—a point of vulnerability I might be able to exploit in the future.

Carter made himself grin in a way I supposed was supposed to be fierce. "Fine, Van. Fine. I can just requisition your ship's logs anyway. In the meantime, I'll let Master Yotov know just how cooperative you've been."

"Is that it? Because if so, I've got actual Peacemaker work to do."

"No, it's not. There's one other item you should be aware of. And I've been dying to reveal it to you."

I tensed. "What's that?"

"The Masters have ordered a complete audit of all of the Guild's finances, including Peacemakers' annuities currently held in trust. So I'm afraid that, until your account is cleared, you won't have access to any of those funds."

I took a step toward him. So did Icky, which actually made Carter shrink back a little. I enjoyed it but waved her back. "You can't do that. It's my money."

"Hey, you're the one who handed it over to the Guild to manage, earn interest, all that stuff. And the Guild just wants to make sure your investment is protected. That's just good customer service, don't you think?"

"You—"

Torina touched my arm.

"—are going to have to tell me how long it will be before I can access that money again."

Carter smiled a poisonous smile. "We'll get back to you."

When the rage cleared from my vision, I was about to tell Icky to inform Carter we were closing our account, now, but the door to his office suddenly slid open, admitting a small, unassuming figure.

I'd only seen her a couple of times, and had never talked to her, but I recognized her immediately. It was Master Yotov.

YOTOV WAS A LIGURITE, a reclusive race native to Sunward, the innermost planet in the Procyon system. Ligurites rarely ventured outside their mostly closed society—they occupied a sprawling island archipelago with only one open spaceport, on an isolated atoll —but when they did, they tended to be overachievers. Ligurites had a reputation for quickly rising to the top of whatever career or vocation they chose to follow. More than a few executive officers of large corporations were Ligurites. So were a few prominent politicians, at least in societies that didn't insist on being governed by their own species.

I knew all of this because I felt I *had* to know all of this. I'd known I was going to cross paths with Yotov eventually. What I hadn't expected was to have it happen out of the blue, but I realized this was probably deliberate. She'd probably told Carter to bring me here specifically so she could arrive unannounced.

I shifted uncomfortably and looked at Torina. Her face was a study in warnings. She didn't have to tell me, though. Carter was irritating and, sure, potentially dangerous, simply because he could end up doing some actual harm as he flailed around, being Carter. Yotov, though—

Yotov was *danger* made flesh. The reason Ligurites rose so quickly to prominence wasn't just because they were smart—they were brilliant and *devious*. They also possessed no true sense of empathy or connection with other individuals, at least outside their own species. They were literally sociopaths, and often bordered on full-blown psychopathy. But they were worse than that because they were also eminently charming, often oozing charisma. They were what the likes of High Doctor Markov, or the mercenary, Pevensy, or even Carter aspired to be: indifferent, ruthless, and entirely charming.

"My apologies. Am I interrupting?" Yotov asked. Her voice was smooth, mild... practiced. She was part news anchor and part friend, a seamless mix that I knew to be an absolute lie.

Carter shook his head. "No, no... not at all, Master. You're welcome to come into my office anytime," he said, and in a rush, like he needed to say it fast and get it out there."It's an utter delight to have you as a, ah, welcome guest in my office. Excuse me, the office on your floor." Again, I glanced at Torina, and again, I got what her expression was telling me.

Carter was inferior in this room, despite his own ideas.

"This must be the esteemed Peacemaker Van Tudor," she said, favoring Carter with an offhanded nod. Her interest switched to me with a febrile intensity, veering away only briefly to take in Torina, Icky, and Perry. The latter two she barely glanced toward again, but I noticed she kept sparing brief flickers of attention toward Torina.

"I have wanted to meet you for some time, but the exigencies of service to the Guild have kept us apart," Yotov said, smiling as she walked toward me, extending her hand. Her smile was warm, too, the smile of an indulgent old aunt you only saw occasionally, on Christmas and the odd Thanksgiving, maybe, who pinched your cheek and gave greeting cards laden with crisp, clean—

I caught myself. Something felt… off. I wasn't usually given to such flowery, metaphorical thoughts. I cleared my throat and took her hand. It was warm and soft, in a way that reminded me of the fur of a kitten—

Shit. There was *definitely* something strange happening here.

"I—uh… yes. Yes, service. To the Guild."

"We're both obviously very busy," she said. "You in particular, it would seem. It's been, what, almost a standard year since your last visit here?"

"Something like that."

"Master Yotov, I just told Van that his annuities—"

"Are fine. I only just received the latest report on the audits we've undertaken, and Peacemaker Tudor's are all in order."

Carter closed his mouth with an effort, his face turning red.

"Isn't that good news?" she asked, turning to him.

I could see the frustrated anger draining from Carter's face. He finally let out a breath and managed a smile. "It is. I mean, I hated to have to give him that news, so this is a great relief."

Again, I glanced at Torina. I saw the consternation in her eyes. Something was happening here, something beyond just subtext and charismatic delivery.

Icky… looked bored.

"So, anyway, Van—may I call you Van?" Yotov asked.

"You—yes. Yes, by all means."

"So, anyway, Van, we were discussing your long absence from Anvil Dark. Can I assume it has something to do with this case you've been pursuing?"

As she spoke, she seemed to somehow diminish slightly. Her posture didn't change, but she gave the impression of an older woman, maybe even your grandmother, and you haven't seen her in a long time and you realize you haven't talked to her, either, not even a call—

"Van, we have a problem," Netty cut in, her voice efficiently clipped and mechanical, almost harshly so, in contrast to Yotov's.

"What sort of problem?"

"We just had a severe over-voltage in the starboard power bus. It started a small fire. Waldo has put it out, but—"

Icky exclaimed something and headed for the door.

"We're on our way," I said to Netty, then turned to Yotov. "Master, you'll have to excuse me—"

"By all means, attend to your ship," Yotov said, waving a hand. Damn, I felt bad just leaving her like this—

"Come on, Van. This could be serious," Perry said while leaping into the air and sailing between Yotov and I. And just like that, I didn't feel bad about leaving Yotov at all.

I nodded to her and hurried after Perry, Torina right behind me. I only glanced back once, to see Carter already turning to the Master, his face tight in an anxious, almost desperate way, like he was determined to please her.

She, on the other hand, just stared straight back at me.

Damn. I needed to arrange to meet with her again—

"Van, let's go!" Perry snapped. His voice pulled my attention back toward the door, so I rushed through it without looking back.

———

As WE BUSTLED out of the Keel and back into the main sprawl of Anvil Dark, on our way to the *Fafnir*, I heard Icky muttering.

"Power bus over-voltage, no way. I rigged in those new interrupters myself—"

I ignored her and turned to Torina. Before either of us could speak, Perry cut in.

"More hurry, please. There'll be time enough for talking once we've got the *Fafnir* sorted out."

He stared straight at me as he said it. I kept quiet, moving with brisk purpose. I still had no idea what was going on here, but it was clear that Perry wanted us to get back aboard the *Fafnir* before we said anything else.

We reached the ship and found the outer airlock door sealed. Netty opened it as we approached, and a gust of acrid stink wafted out. It was the smell of something hot, like an empty pot left on the stove.

I frowned as I stepped into the airlock. An empty pot left on the stove. The smell reminded me of that, having done it once or twice back in Atlanta, once setting the smoke detector off in my apartment. But that was it. It reminded me of that, and nothing more.

The airlock sealed behind us.

"Netty, what's going on—"

"Nothing's going on," Perry said, then he hopped onto the galley table with a metallic scrape and rattle of talons. "Or, at least, there's no power-bus fire."

Icky had grabbed a portable extinguisher in two hands and was digging around in her tool belt with the other two. She stopped. "I knew it! There's no way that bus could fail like that!"

"So what the hell do I smell?" I asked.

"I had Waldo short the bus with a torque spanner—after we switched all systems off of it and onto the other bus first, of course."

Of course. The bus was the crucial backbone of the *Fafnir's* power distribution system, carrying energy from the reactor and smoothly feeding it to the components that needed it. That's why there were two of them, one running the length of each side of the ship. Switching those components to feed only from the other bus protected them from—

A deliberate short.

"We wanted to get you away from Yotov," Perry said.

"And we wanted to make sure that if anyone was scanning the *Fafnir*, they'd detect a genuine power-bus failure," Netty put in.

I nodded. "Okay. I appreciate that. I'll appreciate it a lot more once you explain just what the *hell* was going on back there."

"Yotov obviously has some sort of psionic aura, one that makes you implicitly want to trust her, and see her in the best possible light.

344

The real question is, why didn't anyone mention that?" Torina said, shooting Perry a glare.

"Uh, because Netty and I didn't know about it? Believe it or not, we haven't interacted with every single member of the Peacemaker Guild. And even if we had, we're machines. We have some degree of limitations regarding the metaphysical."

"More to the point, your grandfather never interacted with Master Yotov, or any other Ligurites, for that matter," Netty added.

Icky hefted a torque spanner she'd retrieved from Waldo. It had been rendered into warped, iridescent colors by intense heat. "Well, here's three hundred bonds shot."

I gave Icky a quizzical look. "Did you notice it, Icky?"

She glanced up at me. "Huh? Notice what?"

"Yotov's weird ability to make you think nicely of her."

"Nope. She bored my pants off—if I wore pants, that is. Didn't really pay too much attention to her."

I gave Icky's—skirt-pants, for lack of a better term—a glance, then looked back at her. She was genuinely confused about our reaction and went back to mourning over the damaged tool.

Interesting. Torina and I had both been affected, but Icky hadn't. Something about her Wu'tzur physiology rendered her not only immune to Yotov's aura, but it might actually have worked against her. It was a fact I filed away for future reference. In the meantime, we had other problems.

I leaned against the bulkhead. "So talking to her is a perpetual struggle to not fall under her... ah, *spell.*"

"Only if you're strong-willed enough to do it in the first place," Torina noted.

"Which explains Carter slobbering all over her—not that he needs a mysterious psychic aura to do that," I said.

"It also explains how she's risen to the position she has. She's literally charmed everyone she's met on the way up." Torina glanced at Icky. "Well, except for you."

Icky shrugged. "Yay me?"

"So what about that whole *your funds are frozen to be audited, and now they aren't*, thing? What was that all about?" I asked the group at large.

"If I had to guess, I'd say that your cousin was the one who flexed his newfound muscle and tried to lock your funds down. That obviously didn't fit with Yotov's plans, though," Perry offered.

"Which are?"

"Again, if I had to guess, I'd say Yotov is going to scrutinize and trace every bond we—the Fafnir, I mean—spend. But you in particular. You're a bright point on her scanners, Van. No doubt about that."

Torina nodded. "It does make sense. Just freezing your funds risks leaving you dead in the water, which might suit your cousin, but obviously not her."

I sighed and rubbed the back of my neck. Yotov was a further complication I sure as hell didn't need. The idea that she'd be watching our expenditures bugged me. It might seem innocuous enough to buy fuel at, say, Spindrift—except that would show her that we were at Spindrift on a particular day.

"The worst part is that we don't even know her true motives. We don't know if she's involved in the identity theft thing, or if she's just more concerned about consolidating her own power."

"Or both," Perry put in.

"Yeah. Or both."

I sighed again. "I guess we're just going to have to accept Yotov looking over our shoulder and hope she doesn't use it to undermine us at a critical moment."

"Why? Why don't you just hit up some of the people you've helped for cash, then pay them back out of your money? All this Yotov character would see then is, like, lumps of bonds going to different people," Icky suggested.

Torina and I looked at her for a moment, then we both stiffened.

"So, money laundering," Torina said, smiling.

I snorted with laughter. "But money laundering for good? Hell, now *that's* a business model I can support."

Icky shrugged and tossed the heat-ravaged spanner onto the galley table, forcing Perry to hop out of the way with a squawk of protest.

"Fine. First thing we can do with our freshly cleaned money is buy me a new torque spanner, 'cause I ain't flying without one."

Perry flexed his tail, glaring at Icky. "And feather polish too. I won't allow this brute to ruin my natural magnificence."

I looked to the heavens. "One can of feather polish for the fancy boy, coming right up."

Perry dropped his jaw open in laughter. "I prefer the term *dandy*, thank you."

———

IT TURNED out that when people trust you, they'll give you money.

Between Torina's parents, Schegith, and the S'rall Princess So-Metz, we were able to obtain more than enough funds to keep going. And all that Yotov, Carter, or anyone else would see was lump-sum payments to each of them, with no details of expenditures. Only operating funds provided by the Guild had to be itemized in detail, but we could forgo those and just work off the funds I had in trust. It meant they'd slowly deplete, but I wasn't worried about that, at least not in the short term. My far bigger concern was keeping meddling eyes out of our investigation. Yotov was a serpent —that much I could sense with ease from our single meeting, and from that moment on, I would act in a defensive manner.

Gaining funds left us at something of a crossroads. On one hand, our best lead in our identity theft case was busily mining osmium from Pluto, albeit under the watchful gaze of a powerful warship. On the other, we had a lead from Sil, the opaque cutout for the mysterious Cabal on Dregs, who apparently went by the name Pygmalion.

I sat at the *Fafnir*'s galley table, toying with a cup of coffee. "I can't help thinking that we're going to go back to Pluto and find it mined out and the bad guys in the wind."

"Possibly. But do you really want to tangle with that big warship?" Torina asked.

"Not really. The *Fafnir* and the *Iowa* together wouldn't be a match for it."

"I talked to my dad. He's willing to bring the *Nemesis* in to help," Icky said.

"That would make things more even, emphasis on *more*. Just adding her firepower to ours probably leaves us at about eighty percent of the punishment that cruiser can dish out," Netty said.

I looked at Icky. "Tell your father thanks, and hold that thought.

Until we can manage to gain a distinct advantage, I don't want to risk taking that thing on."

"How about if we ask for some other Peacemakers to help? Like Lunzy, Alic, and K'losk? We've worked with all of them before," Torina suggested.

I leaned back and shrugged. "I hate to say it, but we can't be one hundred percent sure about any of them, can we?"

"What, you suddenly don't trust them? Why not?"

I shook my head. "It's not sudden, though, is it? It might only feel to us like a few weeks or months since we've worked with them, but it's actually that plus a whole year, isn't it?"

"And a year during which Yotov has gotten her hooks into who knows how many Peacemakers," Perry added.

"You really don't think we can trust *any* of them?"

"Not necessarily. What I'm not prepared to do is test that trust in the middle of a space battle against a warship bristling with weapons," I replied.

We sat for a moment in silence, then I sat back up. "Okay. Let's shelve Pluto for now and go to Dregs to find our mysterious Pygmalion. It might not be as direct a route, but I can't help thinking that it might be a back door into The Stillness, who I still think are heavily implicated in our case. Besides, I want to find whoever killed my father."

"Are you looking for justice, Van, or just vengeance?" Perry asked, and I shrugged.

"Whatever comes first, my friend. Whatever comes first."

25

WE DIDN'T LEAVE Anvil Dark right away because I didn't want to give the impression we were fleeing. Instead, I wanted to make sure that Carter, and Yotov, and anyone else that might be unduly interested in us saw that we weren't intimidated and would keep to our own schedule.

Of course, that risked us running afoul of them again, and while I was in no hurry to see Carter, I wasn't anxious to cross paths with Yotov under any circumstances. I scoured everything Netty and Perry could dig up on her, and on Ligurites generally, and it amounted to a whole lot of nothing.

"It's as though these Ligurites have gone out of their way to remain mysterious," I said, puffing out a breath and leaning back from the *Fafnir*'s galley display.

"I think that's exactly what they've done," Netty replied. "They're furtive by design."

"Quite a trick, keeping most of a whole race under wraps while not xenophobically walling yourselves off from the rest of known space, like the—oh, the ones who become judges and things like that, look like octopuses—"

"The Justicars."

"Uh... yeah, right. Those guys. Their world is pretty much off-limits to everyone." I leaned toward the screen again. "These Ligurites don't seem to care much who pays them a visit. But they still somehow manage to stay a question mark."

Torina had just wandered into the ship from an errand in the station, where she'd visited Steve and his Artificers for an update on any of the various technological bits and pieces we'd brought him. She stopped and leaned against the galley table.

"Sorry to eavesdrop—"

"No you're not."

She smiled. "You're right. I'm not. Anyway, can you imagine going to a planet full of Yotovs? Where every single person is radiating a psychic compulsion to like *them* the most, to think of *them* in the most favorable way possible?"

I tried, taking a moment to imagine being in a room full of beings just like Yotov. Every time one of them spoke, they'd seem to be saying the most reasonable thing possible, regardless of what any of the others said—which would also seem like the most reasonable things possible.

It didn't take me long to wince at the implications. "Yikes. That could drive someone insane—and I mean *actually* insane."

"Which explains why the Ligurites don't have much of a tourism industry," Netty said.

"No shit. They must be immune to their own effects?"

"I would think so, yes."

I frowned at the screen. "So what stops them from just, I don't know, taking over known space? I mean, if everyone they speak to thinks they're the best thing since sliced bread, what prevents them from setting themselves up as benevolent dictators all over the place?"

Torina gave me a puzzled look. "What's so great about sliced bread?"

"It's… something new you can learn about Earth," I replied. We were using cultural oddities as a method of learning about each other, our respective planets, and dumb jokes. It was going well.

Torina got the message and gave me a wry look. "Well, if Yotov's any indication of her people, they're capable of being just as personally ambitious and self-centered as any other race, so what happens when a rival Ligurite comes along and tries to take over? You've potentially got a whole population stuck in some weird limbo where they think both contenders are absolutely fantastic," she went on.

"Good point. I guess the ambitious ones just settle on influential positions, like Yotov has."

"Which might actually make them more dangerous. It keeps them behind the curtain, pulling the actual levers of power, not putting on a big show out in front of it," Torina said, then flashed me a triumphant look. "Yes, I went and read up on that Wizard of Oz thing you mentioned the other day—the same way I'm sure you immediately went and researched what a *Helso backstop* was when I mentioned *that*."

"Back*stop*? I thought you said back*rub*. That explains a lot, actually. I just wasn't getting the connection and thought maybe you were hinting at something you wanted to, you know, try sometime.

Oh, on an entirely unrelated note, don't do a search on *Helso backrub.*"

Torina rolled her eyes. "Anyway, I don't think our problem is the Ligurites generally. Like anyone else, most of them are probably decent, ordinary people with no particular desire to manipulate anyone. It's the greedy and power-hungry ones we have to watch out for—one in particular, sitting in the Keel right now with your cousin fawning all over her." She made a *yuck* face. "To sum up... gross."

"*Gross* sums up Carter quite well. Anyway, we've got one Ligurite to worry about that we know of." I went on to explain a vague suspicion that had sparked to life, albeit still just a glowing ember with no flame or smoke. Ligurites were the supreme manipulators, uniquely well-equipped to insinuate themselves into large organizations, like governments, corporations... or criminal enterprises. I wanted to dig a little more deeply into that and see if we could find any connection, no matter how tenuous, between the bad guys we knew about, such as The Stillness, and the Ligurites. For one, I wanted to know if we were up against any more of the schemy, Machiavellian aliens. More directly, I wanted to find out if any of those connections actually pointed back at Yotov herself.

Torina started to turn away when we were done, but she stopped and turned back. "Oh, by the way—remember that bizarre little statue we found aboard what's now the *Iowa?* Steve says that it briefly activated, generating a signal three days ago for about two minutes. Then it went silent again."

I sat up. "What sort of signal? Was it a message? What did it say?"

Torina held up a hand and shook her head. "He says it wasn't a message, just what seemed to be a carrier signal. He wasn't able to figure out why it happened, if something triggered it, or if it was just random."

"So something or someone here on Anvil Dark must have tripped it," I said.

"Or something or someone aboard a ship that was visiting here," Netty observed.

Torina tapped the data slate on her belt. "He looked into that but couldn't find anything conclusive. He did give me a list of all of the ships present at Anvil Dark when it happened, though."

She uploaded the list to Netty, who put it on the galley screen. There'd been twenty-eight twist-capable ships present, including several I recognized, like Lunzy's *Foregone Conclusion*. Sil and Alic, two of the Peacemakers on my very short trusted list, had also been here at the time. And all of them had been broadcasting signals of various types at the time index Steve noted for the sculpture's mysterious burst of activity. But that wasn't unusual. Between regular traffic-control chatter and routine interactions among crews and AIs and Anvil Dark, ships were almost always generating signals of one sort or another. The *Fafnir* probably was right now.

Still, it was another worrying little development. Unless it was entirely a fluke and something had accidentally triggered the sculpture to generate a spurious signal, it hinted that someone connected to the Pathway Unburdened and its wannabe-czar cult leader High Doctor Markov had been on Anvil Dark.

I blew out a sigh and rubbed my face. "Another puzzle piece to toss in the box. I tell you, it's going to be nice when we finally see how they all come together."

I sat back, stretched, and laced my fingers behind my head.

"You know what? I'm tired of Anvil Dark and the uncertainty of knowing who's our enemy. Let's go find some genuine bad guys." I stood. "Netty, call back Perry and Icky, pronto. We're heading to Dregs."

I HADN'T BEEN BACK to Dregs since my first visit here, the one in which Torina and I had been the targets of a shitty little murder plot orchestrated by an orbital shuttle pilot named Koba and his sidekick Balo. They'd both been on the payroll of the Salt Thieves, a fact that had become abundantly clear when they tried to suffocate us in vacuum to protect their erstwhile employers. In many ways, Dregs was the ground-based version of Spindrift, a sleazy, sprawling hive of crime and villainy. But Dregs has the potential to keep growing, while short of major and very expensive upgrades, Spindrift was kind of stuck inside itself, limited by its own hull.

As we descended toward the Dregs spaceport, it seemed to me that the place had grown noticeably in the time since I'd first been here. The pad from which we'd launched with Koba had been isolated on one side of the port, adjacent to nothing but open, arid scrubland. Now, tumbledown buildings surrounded it, and a new neighborhood sprung up around it and had already expanded into the nearby flatlands.

We landed the *Fafnir* on the pad we were assigned, one close to the most densely packed part of Dregs. Perry suggested this was deliberate so that as many people as possible would realize there was a Peacemaker present. There wasn't really anything to be done about it, so I just shrugged it away. Let them know it. Once we were among the throngs of people that packed the narrow streets, twisting alleys and crowded squares, no one was likely to know who we were anyway.

Which is why I wore my trusty duster coat over my b-suit, with the Moonsword and The Drop slung underneath. Torina had likewise dressed herself inconspicuously. Icky—was Icky. There really wasn't any way to make her less conspicuous.

When the *Fafnir*'s outer airlock door slid open, a wall of hot, dry air slammed into me, carrying the stink of a settlement jammed with people but obviously lacking enough waste reclamators to accommodate them.

"Ahh. Civilization," I said grandly.

Torina wrinkled her nose. "Yuck."

"You can say that again," I agreed as we stepped out of the ship. Perry waited until we'd walked across the landing pad, then slipped out of the *Fafnir* and took station over top of us, giving us a set of airborne eyes that could keep watch for any impending trouble we couldn't see on the ground.

We caught an AI-controlled taxi from the spaceport's terminal building, one of the few structures in Dregs that actually looked both complete and reasonably well-maintained. I recalled from the background briefing on Dregs that it had originally been intended as a whole new settlement, established by some big corporate consortium. But it had never progressed beyond building the port before the whole idea had been abandoned.

"The story was they intended to start up some mining and manufacturing operation here, but that kind of fell apart when the consortium did," Perry had explained.

"Fell apart, why?"

"The same reason all of these things tend to fall apart: greed. Someone decided they didn't like the terms of the agreement, tried to get them changed, then all those close friends suddenly became bitter rivals and the lawsuits and countersuits started to fly."

"A few bullets, too, I'm guessing," I said, nodding toward impact divots on a nearby wall.

"Words hurt, but small arms fire is forever," Icky said. When I raised a brow at her, she grinned. "What? Sometimes, I'm kinda romantic."

"Um. Right," I said, glancing at a plasma scar above a slumping doorway up ahead. "Romance. Hey, Perry, what happened during the lawsuits? And the fighting?"

"Someone else had then bought the abandoned port for a bargain-basement price, and Dregs was born. Before you ask me, I don't know—the buyer's identity was unclear, with speculation ranging from a criminal mega-enterprise to the original owners who wrote off their investment and decided to make their money the old-fashioned way—by stealing it," Perry added.

"Business is nothing if not predictable," Torina murmured, pointing out another weapon impact with her finger.

As we trundled along the dusty roads, though, I found myself less interested in what was going on outside, and more in our cab. Or, more specifically, in the AI running our cab.

"Hey, um… taxi."

"Yes?"

"Tell me a little about yourself."

"I am a standard Dynamic Enterprises model twenty-one-alpha synthetic intelligence, registry number XS-50—"

"That's—never mind."

I caught Torina's glance and shrugged. "You never know, right? These stolen identities pop up in the most mundane places."

She nodded. "Good point."

We rumbled on, weaving among other vehicles and throngs of pedestrians. I'd once tried to negotiate downtown traffic in New Delhi—one of the most nerve-racking experiences of my life, and I'm including fighting space battles in that—and this reminded me of it, vividly.

"Can I infer that you have a particular interest in synthetic intelligences?" the taxi suddenly asked.

I glanced at Torina. "Possibly. Why?"

"Because there are several non-standard instances currently operating here. Their behavior does not conform to established protocols."

I leaned forward. "Tell me more."

The taxi described three "non-standard" AIs operating in the Dregs settlement, notable because they didn't adhere to the standard procedures taxis and other smart vehicles used to communicate and coordinate with one another. Two of them were apparently offline, at least for the time being, but the taxi pointed us at one apparently working now, in the northeast quadrant of the sprawling settlement, well away from the spaceport.

"Perry, did you get all that?" I asked.

His voice hummed back through my ear bug. *I did. I'm heading that way now.*

I turned back to the cab. "Take us there."

"As you wish."

The taxi turned right at the next intersection, leaving the main thoroughfare we'd been following behind. Around us, the settlement became quieter, with less traffic and fewer people out and about. Normally, this would be a good thing—I was no fan of jammed-up traffic no matter *where* it occurred.

But the increasingly sedate character of the settlement actually put me *more* on edge. Dregs, Spindrift, Crossroads, and even Halcyon were all freewheeling places, busy, noisy and full of life and bustle, even if a lot of it revolved around bad people doing bad stuff. Here, it was... quiet. Too quiet.

Much too quiet, in fact. I pulled open my duster and checked to ensure The Drop and the Moonsword were in easy reach. I noticed Torina did the same with her sidearm, and even Icky, taking up most of the seat facing Torina and me, had shifted her sledgehammer slightly, making it easier to grab.

We reached the edge of a square maybe thirty meters across, with twisting roads converging on it from five directions. For no reason I really understood, I told the cab to stop immediately before we entered it.

"Perry, anything?"

I've located the other cab. It's definitely producing a signal characteristic of someone who's been chipped. It's across that little plaza in front of you and about fifty meters down that street that veers to the right.

I peered forward, around Icky. "Yeah, I see it."

But I hesitated to tell the cab to proceed.

Torina leaned forward as well. "Something wrong?"

"I... don't know. Maybe?"

I saw maybe a half-dozen people, sundry aliens, who all seemed to be moving with elusive purpose. Only a couple of them were in the square itself, the rest on the surrounding streets.

"Too quiet," I said.

"Perry, are you seeing anything up there?" Torina asked.

"I see lots of things."

"Not helpful, bird," she grumbled.

"Actually, I wish I could be more helpful. But I don't see anything that obviously poses any kind of threat. Your part of town just happens to be sleepy."

I sighed and sat back. "We can't start getting too jumpy, or we'll be seeing bad guys everywhere," I said. "Let's just—"

"Walk," Icky said.

Torina and I looked at her.

"What? Perry said that other cab isn't too far off that way, right?" she said. "Let's just walk the rest of the way. I'd rather be on foot than jammed inside this tin can."

Torina glanced at me. "She's got a point."

"Yeah, she does. Let's listen to the big girl."

"I prefer the term thick, thank you very much," Icky murmured, her eyes darting about with predatory intensity.

"Thick it is. Eyes up, friends."

I paid off the cab, and we dismounted. The cab dutifully wheeled itself away, leaving us standing in silence. We could *hear* the commotion of the busier parts of the settlement behind us, but only as a dull background rumble. Around us loomed a decidedly uncomfortable silence, stirred only by a fitful breeze that hissed around the rooftops.

I led the way, taking us around the right side of the little plaza. The buildings here were as ramshackle as the rest of Dregs, seemingly made from cast-off bits and more than a few repurposed spaceship components and cargo pods. None of it seemed open for business, though, suggesting it was mainly a residential area. Which,

I suppose, made sense. It was pretty much the daytime business peak in Dregs, so whoever lived here was probably back amid all that distant clamor. That didn't make the silence any less disquieting, though.

We picked our way to the other side of the square without incident and started along the street Perry had indicated. I glanced up and saw him wheeling overhead, a tiny speck against the sky glare. At least we had a combination of airborne early warning and top cover.

Okay, Van, the cab producing the signal is just around that next corner ahead of you, to the right. It'll be parked facing away from you, Perry said.

I glanced back. I led, with Torina right behind, and Icky taking up the rear. We kept about three meters between us, an instinctive distance that meant we wouldn't get in one another's way if we had to move fast.

"You guys ready?" I asked, my voice low.

Torina kept her eyes roving, paying particular attention to the upper floors and rooftops around us. "For what, exactly?"

"That's the thing. I don't know. Anything, I guess."

"Well, I'm definitely ready for anything."

I nodded and walked up to the next corner. Glancing around it, I saw the cab sitting just where Perry had said it would be, about ten meters away and pointing up the street. I could see as far as the next bend, maybe twenty meters past the cab. That was typical for Dregs, where the streets and alleys constantly zigged and zagged. I suspected that whatever passed for government in Dregs didn't put too much effort into municipal planning.

I stared at the cab, as though that might somehow reveal something about it to me. Somehow, this felt… off. Why was this taxi just sitting here? Was it waiting for someone? Was it broken down?

Was it meant to be found?

But that didn't make sense, either. No one knew we were coming to Dregs, at least not until we filed our flight plan at Anvil Dark—

Ah. *There* it was. My suspicion meter regarding Anvil Dark had been creeping steadily up the scale. It would be easy to know we were coming to Dregs if someone in a position of authority—say, a Master, or an officious scumbag minion like Carter—was able to access our flight plan and call ahead of us.

"I don't like this," I said, glancing back at Torina.

"Well, considering you've been standing there and peeking around that corner for at least a full minute, I got that, yeah."

Icky uttered a dramatic sigh. "Oh, for—" she said, then trudged forward, past Torina, then past me.

"Icky, what the hell are you—?"

"Doing? Well, *something*, other than standing around here and waiting for something *else* to happen on its own," she said, and plodded directly toward the cab.

"Icky, get your ass back here!"

She stopped at the cab and peered inside. "It's empty."

"Icky, for f—"

Was all I got out before, sure enough, the cab vanished in a searing flash and the world turned abruptly dark.

26

FOR A WHILE, I just lay where I was, quite comfortably ensconced in a warm, fuzzy cocoon of feeling not much at all. Every so often, I shuddered, though I wasn't really sure why. It was as though the whole world periodically shook.

Van.

Huh. Someone calling my name, but from a long way away. It reminded me of Gramps, calling me from the farmhouse when I was out in the barn, fiddling with some electronic gizmo or other. Maybe it was Gramps calling me. If it was, I had to tell him that, guess what, you've got a spaceship in your barn, did you know that—?

"Van!"

I blinked, and a face swam in front of me. It was—a woman. A beautiful one, too. Stunning, but her eyes were sad, like she was worried about—

"Van, can you hear me?"

Wait. I had met a woman like that. This one, in fact. And her name was—

"Torina?"

"Yeah. Just lie still. Icky's hurt," she said, then vanished.

I stared at the sky for a while, vaguely aware I should be doing something right now. Something… important. Yeah. Damn, what was I supposed to be—

Between one blink and the next, the fog cleared. I levered my head higher, then jammed my elbows under me and sat partway up. I could just see around the corner of the building I'd been using as shelter, to a street scattered with smoldering debris. The taxi we'd been investigating was gone, reduced to a chunk of its underframe, the rest flung around the street as shrapnel. And I could see Torina kneeling over Icky—

"Dammit, Icky!"

I dragged myself to my feet and staggered toward them. Along the way, it occurred to me to draw The Drop. The cab had exploded. Whoever was responsible might try to finish the job.

I stumbled to a stop and looked down at Torina and Icky, but I tried hard to stay focused and keep my attention roving up and down the street, and on the buildings, both lower and upper floors. An acrid stink of burning fumed the air.

"Torina—" I croaked, but I had to stop and clear my throat, trying to find my voice. "How is she?"

Torina glanced up at me. "Alive—unbelievably. She must have been right beside that cab when it blew—"

She cut herself off to apply what remained of her cylinder of first aid spray to a severe gash across Icky's upper right shoulder, then she tossed it aside and stuck out her hand. "Van, give me your spray."

I did and noticed a few people had appeared both up and down the street but were keeping their distance. A few peeked from behind cover. None of them seemed intent on doing anything more than gawking, which was fine. If anyone had approached us who wasn't clearly some sort of emergency response, it was even odds whether I'd shoot and then ask questions, or the other way around.

While Torina worked on Icky, I hit the comm. "Perry!"

Silence.

"Perry!"

Nothing.

I swore and switched to our designated backup channel. "Perry, where are you?"

"Netty here, Van. Perry seems to be off the comm net. Torina told me what's going on. I can bring the *Fafnir* to that square just to the north of you. It's a tight fit, but it should work."

"Do it. Declare whatever sort of emergency you have to."

"On the way."

A new voice suddenly shouted from further up the street. "Hey, you need a hand?"

I turned, The Drop ready. The speaker was a Yonnox in a grubby jumpsuit vaguely suggestive of a uniform. He had a hefty bag slung over his shoulder.

"Are you a first responder, medic, that sort of thing?"

"Yeah."

"Yes, we need help," I said, gesturing at Icky sprawled on the pavement. "She's hurt—"

"Got it. My base price is two hundred bonds, and—"

I raised The Drop and planted the sight right on his face. "You can go to hell—"

But Torina cut me off. "Van, we need whatever he's got in that bag," she snapped, then turned to the Yonnox, who'd flinched back and started to turn away. "Fine. Just get your ass over here and help."

I gritted my teeth and lowered The Drop, but I watched the Yonnox as he warily approached. I was ready for him to be another enemy, but he knelt beside Torina, opened his bag, and pulled out more canisters of first-aid foam. While Torina applied them, he unfolded bandages.

The next minutes were a blur. Even an explosion in Dregs wasn't apparently enough to trigger more than the most sporadic of responses—we never saw any sign of a fire service, while the only law enforcement who bothered to show up were a pair of magistrates, one of them a human who somehow managed to look both shocked and indifferent at the same time. Otherwise, the gawkers were it.

Our Yonnox medic, though, had pulled through for us in a way that made me feel genuinely bad that I'd come within a whisper of blowing him away. He actually seemed competent, and his manner with Icky was cool and professional, even caring. By the time Netty arrived with the *Fafnir*, he'd bandaged up her most critical wounds, foamed the rest, and even set and splinted a broken forearm. He helped us heave Icky back toward the square, where the *Fafnir* squatted, waiting. Netty dispatched Waldo Two to help us, which made it a lot easier to get her aboard. I tended to forget that the compact robotic drone was actually, in its own way, a powerful little machine, easily taking most of Icky's considerable weight.

While Torina saw to getting her aboard, I turned my attention back to the comm.

"Perry, where the hell are you?"

Nothing.

"Are you serious—" I started back toward the blast site. Perry must somehow have been caught in the explosion and damaged.

Van?

I stopped. "Perry?"

Yeah. Sorry about dropping offline like that, but I was following someone and trying to stay quiet about it.

"Following someone—who?"

The asshole who set off that bomb. I didn't want to transmit any signal until I was sure.

I practically leaned into my own comm. "Sure? About the bomber? Perry, what—?"

Van, that bomb was command-detonated. And I know who did it. In fact, I'm looking at him right now.

As MUCH AS I wanted to immediately go to wherever Perry was and start cracking heads, I made myself wait until we were sure Icky was stable. By the time I signed off with Perry and returned to the *Fafnir*, she wasn't just stable, she was actually awake.

She sprawled on the galley table, Waldo Two now in medical mode and tending to her wounds. I pushed in beside our Yonnox benefactor, who was packing up his stuff.

"I don't think you need me anymore, so I'll just—"

I stopped him. "Look. I'm sorry."

"For almost blowing my head to bits?"

"Yeah. I—"

"Had just been through an explosion that badly hurt your friend, yeah." He shrugged. "If it makes you feel any better, you're not even in my top ten when it comes to people threatening to kill me. But—Dregs, am I right?"

"Van?"

It was just a hoarse whisper, but it rang like a trumpet to me. "Icky?"

"That cab—it was a bomb," she said, even managing a weak smile.

"It was? Well, that explains all that noise and fire and shrapnel and stuff." I touched my head. "Also this ringing inside my brain."

"I—"

"Am going to rest now, is what you were just going to say, right?"

She stared back at me for a moment, winced, then nodded.

I turned back to the Yonnox. "Anyway, thank you. Look, whatever you'd normally charge, we'll pay you double."

He nodded toward Torina. "She said triple."

Torina, who was busy reapplying one of Icky's bandages, just shrugged.

The Yonnox held up a hand. "Look, double is more than generous and will definitely help pay the bills. Give the rest to charity or something."

"Who *are* you?"

"My name's Balik, and I'm that one Yonnox who tries not to be a greedy, money-grubbing fiend, thus being the exception to the rule."

Despite everything, I laughed. "Balik, my friend, you've earned triple, as far as I'm concerned," I said but stopped and cocked my head at him.

"Is this what you do? Wander around Dregs looking for people to help?" I asked him.

He shrugged. "No shortage of people who've been beaten up, stabbed, and shot, so yeah, it's a living."

"Huh. So you know Dregs pretty well."

"I doubt there's a piece of street or dead-end alley I don't, since I've probably treated someone in damned near every one of them."

I narrowed my eyes at him. Somewhere down my to-do list for Dregs was cultivating a contact here, someone I knew I could count on for useful information. Balik was the sort who could probably go almost anywhere, and do it in a way that didn't attract a lot of scrutiny. Of course, he was also someone who probably depended on being seen as neutral to carry out his chosen vocation, and I didn't want to risk compromising that.

"Balik, I will pay you triple, if you can answer me one question," I said.

He gave me a suspicious, sidelong look. "If you're asking me to become an informant, those sorts don't tend to have long lives around here."

"Nope, not an informant, just a friendly face who can give us the lowdown on goings-on in Dregs from time to time. Like, to grab a random example, does the name Pygmalion mean anything to you?"

"The guy who does disguises?"

I blinked. "I—yeah, sure. Him."

Balik shrugged. "If that's the guy, he has a hole-in-the-wall shop over in the Ditch—that's the far side of Dregs from the spaceport, where all the runoff from the place goes into that big swamp you've probably seen. It's kind of what passes for sewage treatment here."

"Naturally." I shook my head. "Anyway, this Pygmalion—"

"Yeah. Human, older than you. That's not the actual name of his shop, though. It doesn't really have one. He does prosthetics, but what he really does is make disguises for people, prosthetic ones, or even surgical ones." Balik's face fell a bit. "Don't tell me you're going to shut him down. He's one of the few places around here I can bring someone who's hurt and get them something resembling decent care."

"Community-minded, is he?"

"Very. He kind of operates a free clinic on the side, takes in pretty much anyone who shows up at his door, no questions asked. If you shut him down, it's going to leave an awful hole for a lot of people."

I just nodded, because I got it. Rather than trying to stay completely off the radar, Pygmalion—or whatever his name was—had chosen a different approach. He'd made himself popular, even indispensable to the community. It meant that said community would probably be fiercely protective of him, and *that* meant we had to approach him with care.

"I just have a couple of questions for him, part of an investigation we're doing here—or were, until this happened," I added, glancing at Icky.

I paid Balik and arranged to get his contact information in case we ever needed him again. He gave it, but with a firm caveat.

"What I do depends on having everybody trust me, good guys

and bad. Like I said, I won't compromise that to become your informant. Trust is way harder to come by around here than bonds, and way, *way* easier to lose."

I agreed with him as heartily as I could manage, then saw him off the *Fafnir* and returned to the galley.

"How is she?"

"Slee—"

A loud, wet snore ripped apart the air.

"—ping," Torina said, smiling. "Quite an, um, nasal cavity on her."

"More like a cave, but yeah, good to hear that. The sleeping part, not the—"

Another snore, loud enough to rattle window panes, tore through the air. I mimed wiping a tear. "She's just so damned adorable."

"I know. They're cute at that age. And weight," Torina said, smiling.

"Back to the fight." I switched to the comm. "Perry, where are you?"

In a holding pattern.

"What?"

I'm circling, Van, trying to keep an eye on our guy without being obvious about it. He's in a building over here in the part of Dregs called Ditch.

I stiffened, which also made me wince. The taxi bomb had definitely shaken my brain, but the rest of me, sheltered behind the corner of the building, seemed unscathed.

"Ditch? Look, is he anywhere near a place called Pygmalion's, or something like that?"

Just a sec.

I waited.

Yeah, I see it. Same side of the same street, four buildings away.

I looked at Torina. "Can we leave Icky under Netty's tender loving care?"

"She's more of a doctor than I am."

I nodded. "Netty, we're leaving Icky with you. Torina and I have an appointment with a doctor."

WE SAW Icky and the *Fafnir* safely returned to the spaceport, then Torina and I set out for the Ditch, on the far side of Dregs. This time, we decided to walk. My head still ached, and my ears rang, but I otherwise hadn't seemed to suffer any lasting harm from the blast that had injured Icky. Considering the amount of taxi shrapnel sent screaming through the air, the fact that I'd taken the concussive shockwave, and then only from the shoulders up, made me lucky. The fact Icky had had the thing detonate right in her face and could manage to still even be conscious was luckier still. Luckiest of all, no one else seemed to have been hurt by an explosion that clearly targeted us.

"Because there's no way it wasn't, especially if it was command-detonated. Someone was watching and waiting for us," I was saying as Torina and I wound our way through the crowds. This part of Dregs was always busy, and although we were hemmed in all around, I actually felt safer in the throng. Not only were we less conspicuous, but the command-detonation nature of the bomb also meant that whoever was targeting us wasn't doing so indiscriminately and heedless of collateral damage.

"It was a complicated plot, considering we'd only been here, what, half an hour maybe, from landing to bomb blast?" Torina said.

"Yeah. Too complicated. Someone got their grubby paws on our flight plan and called ahead."

"Someone who knew just what buttons to push to pique our interest," Torina added.

I nodded as we veered to bypass a wheeled contraption cobbled together from a haphazard combination of sleek alloy, grubby plastic and weather-beaten wood. It was piled with bales and boxes of—something, and to an alarming height at that. Torina and I gave it a wide berth in case it decided to tip over and bring its load crashing down on top of us. I wasn't about to survive a brutal assassination attempt only to die under a cascade of miscellaneous junk.

I nodded to Torina. "Exactly. Someone who knew we were leaving Anvil Dark to come here, and who knew just how to get us to a particular place at a particular time, and was able to do it all with enough time to get it all set up."

"So someone on Anvil Dark, then."

I gave a glum nod. "Yeah. And you'd think that would make it easy to narrow down the suspect list, but it doesn't. I mean, Yotov and Carter are obvious choices but, I don't know, Yotov seems too smart to get herself directly implicated in an assassination attempt on a Peacemaker, and Carter is—well, he's Carter. He might have done it, I suppose, but not on his own accord."

"So that leaves—well, everyone, doesn't it?"

I nodded again. "Yeah. Almost, anyway. Lunzy wasn't on Anvil Dark at the time, but Sil was, and I noticed that Alic and K'losk were there, too. And Steve, and Bester, and—" I shrugged. "It could have been any of them. Or it could have been someone else entirely."

"Well, that narrows it down."

We plodded in silence for a moment, then I stopped. Torina immediately turned, reaching into her coat toward her sidearm. I raised a hand and shook my head.

"No need to panic, my dear. I just had a thought."

She relaxed but kept a wary eye on the aliens, at least two dozen different species worth, streaming past us in both directions. I gestured for her to join me at the corner of a building, out of the main flow of traffic down the dusty street.

"We need to get less predictable," I said.

Torina pulled at her lip, pensive. "Unpredictable how?"

"We're playing by the rules. And that would be fine, if everyone else was playing by the same rules. But they aren't, and as long as *we* are, they'll have the advantage."

"I'm listening. Got a plan?"

"I'm… not sure yet. But when we get to this Pygmalion place, which should be just up around that bend, just play along with me, okay?"

"Of course, I'm with you all the way. And I hate to be so… detail-oriented, but what, exactly, are we going to do?"

"If I could tell you that, then it wouldn't be unpredictable, now would it?" I said, a smug grin pulling at my face. Torina poked my arm and sighed.

I activated the comm. "Perry, any change?"

Nope. He went into that building and never came out. That either means he's still in there—

"Or there's another way out you can't see."

Which is probably a pretty safe bet—safe, as in a safe house. And a good safe house has ways of getting out of it that aren't obvious.

"Well, we should be close by."

Yeah, if you guys walk up to that next bend in the street, it's the seventh building down on the right.

"And only a few doors down from our friend Pygmalion." I looked at Torina. "Coincidence?"

"I think not," she replied.

"Me neither."

We resumed our way, rounding the bend. I counted down the buildings on the right side of the crooked street, stopping at the seventh. It was utterly unremarkable, of exactly the same ramshackle character as the ones around it—of course. Pygmalion's place, closer by, was likewise blandly uninteresting.

"Okay, let's try our George Bernard Shaw aficionado first," I said, and got a smile from Torina.

"Hey, I know who that is—the Earthly writer who wrote the play Pygmalion, based on an old myth."

"You've been doing your homework."

We reached Pygmalion's storefront, although there was nothing to suggest it wasn't just another ordinary building. In my new spirit of unpredictability, I just opened the door and strolled inside.

A wizened little man looked up at us through a magnifier hanging in front of his face. He sat at a workbench, working on something—

Which I recognized. It was a cuff-like device that I'd last seen on the nasty assholes called Sorcerers.

So being unpredictable paid off, it seemed. I'd just established a hard link between this guy and the Sorcerers, which was an equally hard link back to the identity theft ring. And if he was connected to the Cabal who'd murdered my father—

I gave him a wide grin.

"Don't you love it when a plan comes together, Torina?"

27

"WHOEVER YOU ARE, you can't just come barging in—" the man, presumably Pygmalion began, but I cut him off.

"Actually, we *can*, as we just demonstrated by being, you know, here. I think what you mean to say is that we *shouldn't*, or *aren't allowed to*, or something like that."

"What?"

I smiled at him as he peered back through his magnifier, then I twitched open my coat, revealing my Peacemaker's b-suit. To his credit, he managed to show almost no reaction. But his eyes widened ever so slightly, and he stiffened just enough to show he understood.

Then, he gave a sigh of resignation and reached for what looked like a battered wallet.

"How much?"

I glanced at Torina. She just raised an eyebrow, but I got her meaning anyway. Pygmalion, or whatever his real name was, wanted to know how much of a bribe we wanted to leave him alone. Until a deliberately targeted bomb had detonated and almost killed Icky, I'd have brushed him off and told him I didn't want a bribe, I wanted information.

But that bomb had been the embodiment of my determination to play strictly by the rules, and, therefore, be drearily predictable. I'd learned to be *unpredictable* in how I approached my forays into cyberspace back on Earth, but I had to relearn the lesson the hard way when it came to dealings in the real world—or the real galaxy.

I smiled. "Right to business. I like that. Let's say a hundred thousand up front, and I'll defer my decision on regular payments for now."

Pygmalion blinked. His magnifier—well, magnified it, making him look like one of those big-eyed *chibi* figures so popular in anime—adorable, comical, and weird, all at once.

"Are you insane? A hundred *thousand* bonds?"

I turned to Torina. "That's what I said, wasn't it? A hundred thousand?" I turned back to Pygmalion. "Is my voice not working properly? Damnedest thing. I mean, I *feel* my lips moving—testing, testing, one two three—" I pointedly cleared my throat. "A hundred thousand bonds. There. Clearer that time?"

Pygmalion lifted the magnifier from his face. "You're either insane, an idiot, or you think you're clever. Whichever it is, I don't care. I've got more powerful people to worry about than some jacked-up, wannabe cop."

"He thinks I'm jacked," I told Torina, flexing my arm.

"Easy, killer." She gave me a patronizing squeeze on the bicep, made an impressed face, and turned to Pygmalion. "He's been doing interval training. Really getting beach ready this year."

"What?" Pygmalion asked in genuine bewilderment.

I waved his comment away and looked around the room, still smiling, until my attention went to a sophisticated piece of tech squatting on a table behind the counter. It had articulated arms and a variety of tools seemingly designed to do fine work on sophisticated electronics—like the device I identified as one of the cuffs used by the Sorcerers. I had one just like it back on the *Fafnir*, made for me by Linulla, the Starsmith. But it tended to malfunction, and Icky hadn't yet figured out why. I intended to take it back to Linulla for a tune-up but hadn't gotten around to it yet.

All of which was to say that they were finicky devices, in need of constant tinkering. And the machine behind Pygmalion's counter was probably crucial to keep them operating.

I gestured at the machine. "What is that?"

Pygmalion glanced that way, then back. "A fine-circuit manipulator. I use it to build and repair prosthetics. Why?"

I drew The Drop. "Because it looks expensive," I said, sighting along the big gun at the manipulator.

"Wait—!"

I fired, the throaty boom of The Drop seeming as loud as that bomb that hurt Icky. The round slammed into the manipulator, blasting a chunk out of it and sending debris clattering against the wall behind it.

Pygmalion stood, shoving his chair back and staring aghast at his ruined machine. "What the hell is the matter with you? Without that, I can't—"

I spun and stuck the still-warm muzzle of The Drop under his chin.

Van, was that a gunshot? Perry asked. I heard Torina answer him in hushed tones but kept my focus on Pygmalion.

"Without that, you can't do *what*, exactly? Fix any more of those Sorcerer's cuffs, like the one on this table?"

Pygmalion's eyes had gone almost comically wide again, this time without any help from the magnifier.

"What—who—?"

While he spun his mental wheels, I leaned in, until our faces were inches apart.

"So now my little visit has cost you the value of that manipulator *plus* a hundred thousand bonds."

"I don't have that kind of money!"

"Oh, but I'll bet you can get it, can't you? From your Sorcerer friends? Or maybe the Cabal?"

I'd watched Pygmalion's eyes as I said it.

Bingo. A flicker of recognition, followed by a quick flurry of emotions—surprise, fear, then calculation.

He licked his lips. "I'm more afraid of them than I am of you—"

"Are you sure about that?" I said, jamming the muzzle hard against the underside of his chin. "Because your Cabal killed my father, and although I can't do anything about that, I *can* prevent anyone else's father from being murdered by those bastards. And that prevention starts with stopping you and your shitty little operation here—"

A strange fluttering sensation rippled through me, followed by a sudden thump from somewhere in the back of the shabby little workshop. A couple of more clatters and thumps followed. Torina drew her sidearm and headed that way, poised like a cat about to pounce.

I kept my focus on Pygmalion. "Got friends back there?"

"No."

"Bullshit. You've been lying so long you don't even realize you're doing it anymore, do you? It's just a reflex now."

Van, you've got some magistrates heading your way. Three of them. They're about three doors down.

"Perry, can you slow them down for me?"

Sure. The novelty of flying in circles faded away about a century ago.

Torina reappeared. "There's no one there, but the back door to the place was open. There's some strange machine back there, too."

"You're not really here for the money, are you?" Pygmalion asked.

I shrugged. "Not really, although I'm not averse to profit. I really just want information. And how easy that information is to get out of you, and how complete it is—well, that'll determine what happens next."

I thought about my father, a professional at the peak of his career, an aloof and distant figure in my life, but a man I respected and admired. And then I thought about how he'd been gunned down by technology he couldn't even imagine existed, all to send a warning to my grandfather.

And then, the anger began to rise, a column of inescapable heat that seared me from within. I thought about how that must have made Gramps feel, knowing that his only son had been murdered to send him a message. How Gramps lived with that, I couldn't begin to fathom.

I gritted my teeth to gain control, and it worked—barely. "And what happens next is probably going to be me blowing your head off, because I am *that* pissed off. I'm sick of your flavor of psychopath, and your conspiracies, your casual disdain for life—and that goes doubly for you, *Doctor* Pygmalion. So I'm going to kill you, and plant a gun on you, and say I had to use lethal force in the performance of my duties, and I'm a goddamned *Peacemaker*, so who's going to say otherwise?"

I listened to myself say it with a bizarre sort of detached wonder. It was my voice, but it sounded like it was coming from someone else. And… it was.

It was coming from a boy who'd lost his dad.

Pygmalion didn't fall for it. There was nothing to fall for. Just as I was kind of amazed at the depth of passion and determination in that voice, so was he. We both knew that if he didn't give me what I wanted in the next few seconds, I was going to pull The Drop's trigger and end this.

"Look," he started, his voice a dry whisper. He licked his lips. "Look. I just set up the meetings. That's it. I set up the meetings, but the Cabal—they do the rest. They pay me. A lot. And I use that money to help people—"

"So that's what you tell yourself when you go to bed after a hard day of arranging a murder, huh? That the blood money it earns you goes to *help* people, so it's all *good*?"

Pygmalion stared at me. I stared right back with an intensity that made him begin to sweat.

"*Who* are you more afraid of, Pygmalion? Be honest, now. Right now, who are you more afraid of? Them, or me?"

"You won't kill me, you need me—"

"Wrong," I snapped. "I'll bet that if we dig around here enough, we'll find enough information to push on with our investigation. So I don't need you. In fact, the only reason I don't *want* to kill you is because I'm not the murderous type. But push a man far enough, attack his family and his friends, and all bets are off. So I don't need you—you need me. So you'd better prove your value to me right this instant, because I am *done* with keeping my face this close to yours, you miserable, amoral sonofabitch."

I saw the precise moment he crumbled.

He took a shuddering breath. "What do you want to know?"

"VAN, those magistrates are making a lot of noise about you surrendering this crime scene to them," Perry said.

I turned from the strange contraption squatting in the back of Pygmalion's shop. "Let them. Dregs adheres to the provisions of the Peacemakers' Charter, so quote them article four, section five, paragraph... uh, ten."

"All Peacemakers will submit receipts for any authorized expenditures no later than ten standard days after the expenditure is incurred, itemizing the full amount of actual expenditure?" Perry shrugged. "Okay, I'll—"

"You know, my killing mood might just come back real fast, Perry."

"So article *two*, section five, paragraph ten, regarding the jurisdiction of crime scenes related to a Peacemaker investigation."

"Bingo."

Torina came through the open back door. "It's just a grungy alley back—oh."

I glanced at her and tensed. "What?"

"There's something on my shoe, and now it's sticking to the floor."

"Oh. Yuck."

She stepped back outside, scraped her shoe on the ground a few times, and came back. "Anyway, it's just an alley, dead-ended to the left about twenty meters along, but to the right, it leads to that last main cross street."

I nodded and stared at the enigmatic device. Pygmalion had given up his contact information for the Cabal, a trio of comm channels between which encrypted traffic bounced in a complex pattern. The bouncing made the message appear to be random bursts of interference on each of the channels, but it only became a coherent whole when assembled properly at the other end. As a further layer of security, Pygmalion had no idea where the other transceiver was, other than somewhere on Dregs. It meant would-be clients of the Cabal had to first get connected to Pygmalion, then he'd use the cunning transceiver to arrange a meeting, and that was the extent of his job as cutout.

But he steadfastly refused to explain what this mysterious machine was—which I stood, contemplating in frustration. Even when we handed him over to the magistrates, he kept his secrets, and none of our implied threats made him talk.

"What do you think it is?" Torina asked.

I shrugged. "No idea."

It stood about two and a half meters tall, a pair of oval metallic hoops fastened at right angles to a base about a meter tall that obviously housed... something. But I had no idea how to access the mechanism inside, certainly didn't know how to do it safely, and even if I did, I'd have no idea what I was looking at. I'd normally have asked Icky to look at it, but she was in no shape to do anything but rest and heal.

Perry hopped back into the back room. "Okay, I put the magistrates off. They're good with letting us have the crime scene as long as we want it, as long as we hand unchallenged jurisdiction for Pygmalion over to them when we're done scouring the scene."

"So they can slap him with a fine or something similarly trivial," I muttered.

But Torina just shrugged. "By all accounts, he does help people here in Dregs a lot. Our medic, Balik, was pretty clear about that."

"Sure, if you overlook his role in setting up assassinations," I growled, but the heat faded.

"Okay, I'm done with my tantrum. You don't deserve that, apologies." I looked at Perry. "Tell the magistrates I'll agree to that as long as Pygmalion gives up what this thing is, and his connection to the Sorcerers and the identity-theft ring."

"Van, he doesn't have to. I hacked his comm log, which he never deleted—I guess you truly caught him flatfooted. Anyway, it records a transmission from Anvil Dark, with a time index about half an hour after we left there to come here," Perry replied.

"Are you telling me he set up that bomb on the say-so from someone on Anvil Dark? Because if he did, I'm going to drag him back there and blow apart this whole sordid little—"

"Actually, I don't think he did. He really is just a middleman—a cutout for the Cabal, and a place for the Sorcerers to get their tech fixed." Perry eyed the strange device. "I think this thing, whatever it is, is the key."

I let my eyes fall on the device again. "Fine. I'm going to go have a talk with our friend Pygmalion, then, and convince him to finish coughing up what he started."

"Now that he's in the custody of the magistrates, I don't think they're going to let you, um, interrogate him. I mean, if you want to fight a jurisdictional war, that's great, but if things are as murky in the Guild as we think they are, you might not find anyone back at Anvil Dark has your back."

"Shit." To have gotten *this* close and come up *just* short. I mean, we did have this end of the comm system Pygmalion used to contact the Cabal, but without Icky, we were stuck—

"Wait," I said as a thought suddenly slid neatly into place.

Torina started to ask me what I was thinking, but I put her off with a raised hand. "Netty, I want you to set up a twist-comm call with our friendly engineer Zenophir. Perry's going to transmit all the information and imagery he can about this strange device we've found, so she can give us her take on it."

"Will do," Netty replied.

It took a few minutes to set up the twist-comm link, and another few for Zenophir to look over the information, including the best scans Perry was able to make of the device's interior through its casing. I had to admit, this was probably a long shot, since Zenophir was trying to make a judgement call based on scant data transmitted across light-years, but when she replied, it was with a surprisingly emphatic enthusiasm.

"I know exactly what that is, Van. And you're going to be stunned," she said, her voice slightly distorted in that way of a twist-comm transmission.

"I'm a big fan of dramatic reveals, Zenophir, but now is not the time—"

"It's a teleporter, Van. It's a device that can move something from one place to another instantaneously. And it's probably the most compact, best-engineered one I've ever seen. In other words, it's a game changer."

I RECEIVED a rapid education in so-called teleportation, although twist porting was actually more correct. It was, in essence, a miniaturized twist drive that could cause two distant points in space to briefly merge, allowing something—or someone—to instantly move from one of those points to the other.

As soon as Zenophir explained it, the pieces fell into place.

Perry had tracked our bomber to the Cabal safe house just down the street from Pygmalion's shop. But Perry had never seen him leave, hinting at another way out. I'd assumed a tunnel or something, but it turned out to be a far more sophisticated operation than that. And, sure enough, when I sent Perry and Torina to check out the safe house, they found another twist porter. So the bomber had used it to move himself from the safe house to here, then simply fled out the back door.

"It explains that strange little flutter we felt right before we heard the noise," Torina said when she came back from the safe house. That was the twist effect working."

I put my hands on my hips. I had to admit, it was a pretty impressive little scheme. A scheme enacted in the service of evil, yes, but still pretty impressive.

Unfortunately, the twist porters were too cumbersome to lug back to the *Fafnir*, there was nowhere to land the ship close by, and they were too bulky to load into the little cargo space we had available even if we could. I had to settle for putting the two devices into the custody of the Dregs magistrates until we could dispatch a ship from Anvil Dark to retrieve them.

"And note that we've imaged the hell out of these two things, so if I find even a scuff mark on them, I swear I'll come back here with a flotilla of Peacemaker ships and we'll dissect Dregs one building at a time, looking for—" I smiled. "Well, I don't think it matters because I'll find more than enough criminality to go around, won't I?"

The head magistrate, a frumpy alien with a bulbous head and a vaguely serpentine body, just gave a glum nod. "Yeah, yeah, we'll keep them safe for you. But you release ultimate control of Pygmalion to us, right? No unannounced visit to reclaim the prisoner?"

Much as I hated to, I nodded. I had no doubt Pygmalion had tons more information we could have used, but it was pretty clear that Dregs was going to close ranks around one of their favorite sons, so it wasn't a hill I wanted to die on.

"Van, seven ships have departed the Dregs spaceport in the time window you gave me," Netty said over the comm.

I turned away from the magistrates and walked a few paces away, back into Pygmalion's shop. I'd estimated how long it would take someone on foot to escape through the back door of the place and make it to the spaceport, then asked Netty to track whatever ships left immediately after that. "Any likely candidates?"

"Well, three *un*likely ones. One was a diplomatic cutter from Tau Ceti, and two were robotic freighters with no internal life-support systems or crew modules. That leaves four realistic possibilities—two standard workboats registered to numbered holding companies, a class eight freighter carrying a load of salt from those flats that stretch off to the north of the Dregs settlement, and one yacht held under private ownership."

"Any flight plans?"

"The freighter loaded with salt was on its way to a mining operation at Wolf 424—not unusual, since they have no other access to salt and it's kind of required for most life as we know it. And one of the workboats filed a flight plan to Sunward at Procyon. The other workboat didn't file a flight plan, which is technically illegal, and the yacht, being privately owned, doesn't have to file one—although, if they're smart, they normally do."

I turned and looked back at the amazing, game-changing twist porter, frowning in thought. I finally made up my mind.

"I don't feel like trying to chase two ships around known space on the off chance one of them is our bomber. For all we know, he might still be right here on Dregs."

"What do you want to do?"

I took a deep breath and let it out slowly. We really only had one useful option, but it was one I was really, *really* reluctant to do.

"We're going back to Anvil Dark to find out who the leak is."

"That's probably the most unenthusiastic thing I've ever heard you say, Van," Netty came back.

"Yeah, I know. The trouble is, I don't know which is going to upset me more, that it'll be another deadend and we'll be left back at the beginning yet *again*—or that it won't, and we'll actually find out which Peacemaker we've come to trust has been stabbing us in the back this whole time."

28

I SIGHED as the docking status flicked to green, meaning the *Fafnir* was securely snuggled up to Anvil Dark. I remembered the very first time we'd come here, not long after my first job as a Peacemaker on behalf of The Quiet Room. I'd been overwhelmed with a sense of almost terrified wonder at the vast and somewhat sinister station. It had reminded me, appropriately enough, of medieval castles I'd happened to visit during my downtimes in Europe, piles of implacable grey stone brooding ominously over the countryside.

Since then, though, the sense of looming menace had faded, and Anvil Dark started to feel more like… home, or at least a home away from home. It was the one place in the universe that seemed safe from the vagaries and violence nibbling away at the social fabric of known space, protected by its dark reputation, not to mention its vast firepower. I could relax on Anvil Dark, let my guard down a little, secure in the knowledge that everyone around me was focused on the same job: stopping the bad guys.

Until today. Learning that a mole lurked somewhere aboard, leaking information expressly intended to harm me, Torina, and the others—

I sighed again and unstrapped. Bad enough that Carter had managed, against all odds, to insinuate himself into the place. And now, thanks to the ruthlessly ambitious Master Yotov, a cloying stink of corruption wafted through its corridors and compartments. No, this was the worst part of it by far. Someone supposedly on my side, someone I *trusted*, was betraying me.

"Look on the bright side, Van," Perry said, following me out of the *Fafnir*'s cockpit and toward her airlock.

I glanced back. "And just what would the *bright side* be, my metal-feathered friend?"

"Maybe it'll be your cousin who's the mole. Then you can be rid of him for good."

"That's my bird. You really know what my heart desires."

The trouble was, though, that I didn't really think it was Carter. Or, if it was, it wasn't him alone. For one, as nasty a piece of shit Carter was, my grim imaginings could never quite push him into the category of *murderer*. Carter was many things, but he wasn't a psychopath, and he didn't fancy getting his manicured hands dirty. Or bloody. The worst case I could really buy was him being coerced or cajoled into being part of a bigger plan—a cog in an evil machine that used him as a venal tool and nothing more.

Which made the next most obvious candidate Yotov, given Carter's pathetic desire to please her. But, as much as I distrusted the ambitious Ligurite, I again had trouble believing it was her. It was too… inelegant. Yotov was all about subtle manipulation. She'd spent many months, if not years, laying the groundwork for her soft takeover of the Guild. And while she might be corrupt as hell, she didn't need to resort to hiring assassins to stop me from uncovering that corruption. She had the clear authority to reassign any or all of my cases or, for that matter, just to have me ejected from the Guild entirely on some pretext or other.

Given her latent psionic talent, she'd have little trouble convincing others that it was the right thing to do. Not that for a minute I thought she would, because Yotov was smart enough to know that the best place to have someone who might be a threat was close at hand, where you could keep an eye on them.

So, if Carter and Yotov were out, then who?

"Ow-ow-ow-ow—"

I turned to the pained exclamation, which trailed off into a string of stunningly inventive vulgarity. Icky was clambering out of her temporary workspace in the galley, the cockpit jump seat being too small and awkward to work for her until she'd fully recovered from her injuries.

"Where are you going?" I asked her.

"Uh—coming with you?"

"Doctor Netty says you need to rest."

"Doctor Netty can kiss my—" Icky snapped, then caught herself.

It made me smile, seeing the actual burst of effort she'd needed to prevent herself from saying something nasty. *Our little Icky is growing up*, Torina had once said about her, and it was true. Original Icky, who'd grown up essentially in isolation with her father, wouldn't have bothered censoring herself. New Icky was, indeed, growing up.

Netty spoke up. "Actually, Van, I think Icky could do with some walking around. Her Wu'tzur physiology is taking care of the actual healing quite well, so she really needs to get her joints and muscles moving, her tendons and ligaments stretching—"

"You just don't want her hanging around the *Fafnir* bitching," I said.

"How dare you suggest such a thing. If she's not miserably hunkered down here in the ship, she can't endlessly moan, bitch, and complain about every... single... thing... can she? I've got to be honest here, the thought never occurred," Netty said, sounding more than a little dodgy.

Icky glared at the overhead, the default place to look when talking to Netty. "Yeah, well, you can take your moaning and bitching and stuff it up your drive bell, you cranky old—"

"Okay, kids—you two definitely need a break from one another. Icky, you hobble along with us the best you can. Netty, stop antagonizing our girl. That's an order, sort of."

"Fine, boss," Netty groused, sounding more like an aggrieved teen than I'd thought an AI could manage.

We disembarked, stepping into Anvil Dark proper. That weighty pall of looming dread hit me hard as we did. Even with her injuries, I was glad to have Icky trudging along behind Torina and Perry and me. Her granite presence made me feel at least a little safer, in a place that no longer felt safe at all.

Still, my hand rested on The Drop.

Just in case.

BREAKING into the Anvil Dark comm-log system was no easy matter. For one, it was heavily protected and encrypted. Another concern was that people with high levels of access were rigorously restricted. Sure, using my own skills, supplemented by help from Perry and Netty, I could probably work around all of that. But it would take time, and would likely be detected as an intrusion attempt. I was a wiz with Earthly computer systems and how to compromise them, but extraterrestrial computers used a slightly different architecture—as in, wildly different and based on tech that was still science fiction on Earth.

I was telling Torina this, muttering it to her sidelong as we walked along the main concourse and passed the Wall of Remembrance, pondering our next move.

"So, if we had days to do this, I might be willing to give it a try. But we don't."

"What's the rush?" she asked me.

I glanced at her. "Because we're actively targeted for murder?"

"So find someone to do it for you," Icky boomed.

I winced. I hadn't realized Torina and I had been talking loudly enough for Icky to overhear us, but the wince was more of a response to her booming it out like an announcement.

"Icky, first—a little more discreet, please. Second, yeah, I think you may be onto something. Perry, who on Anvil Dark would have the level of access to the comm logs that we need?"

"The Masters, of course. Technical types who operate and maintain the comm system as well. Otherwise, just a few, specific individuals who might need that level of access to perform their duties."

"Such as?"

He rattled off a list of a dozen or so people, including Bester, the enigmatic librarian who, for unfathomable reasons demanded items of personal value in return for access to certain parts of his archives, and Steve, the insectoid alien who oversaw technical and scientific aspect of investigations—basically, the guy who ran the lab. I recognized a few of the other names but didn't really know any of them.

"Let's try Steve first. Bester would probably want my very first love poem to my sweetheart or something like that to grant us access."

"Do you have one of those?" Torina asked.

"Oh, sure. *There was a young lady named Bright, whose speed was much faster than light. She travelled one day, in a relative way, and returned the previous night.*"

Torina smirked and gave me a look. "That's your idea of a love poem?"

"Excuse me, my *idea*? I'll have you know that's *art*."

"It's not even factually correct. Superluminal travel doesn't reverse time," Perry muttered.

I sighed as I changed course to go meet with Steve.

"Everyone's a critic."

"STEVE, have I got some nifty tech coming for you to check out," I said, walking into his lab.

He glanced up—sort of. Steve had compound eyes and could probably see almost three hundred and sixty degrees without moving his head.

"Is that those twist-porter things I read about in your summary report?"

"You bet."

He unfolded himself from his crouching posture and lifted himself to his full seven feet or so of height. "I've done some preliminary calculations—very rough until I can see the actual tech. First, as cool and clever as it is, its range is going to be pretty short, probably no more than a few hundred meters inside a gravity well. A device that small simply couldn't safely generate enough power for more than that. And that's only if it has twist porters at both ends, working in very, very close sync. Any more than a miniscule fraction of a seconds of delay in sharing data from one to the other would be a deal breaker."

"So it's not going to move people between stars anytime soon."

"No, not even a little bit. Still, it's pretty innovative, and the tech might have other applications. I'm really looking forward to getting a look at one in the flesh. You didn't bring one back here with you, did you?"

"No, sorry, we just didn't have any way of transporting it aboard the *Fafnir*. That's part of my reason for coming to see you. You're going to want to send a recovery team to Dregs to get them. Just have them contract the magistrates and tell them it's about the Pygmalion affair. They'll know what it means."

"Will do. So that's part of why you came here today. What's the other part?"

The way he said it made my neck hairs stand up. What was he expecting me to say? Had he realized that we must have recovered some intel from Pygmalion?

I glanced around. There were other techs busily beavering away at benches and workstations, presumably on evidence involved in other cases. "Is there somewhere we can speak privately?"

Steve motioned for us to follow him into a smaller, cluttered compartment with a desk but no chair, since his anatomy didn't accommodate sitting in one. I assumed it was his office. He closed the door and activated a privacy seal.

"What's up?" he asked.

"Steve, I need a favor. A big one. I need access to the Anvil Dark comm logs. Specifically, I need them for the day that we last left here, heading for Dregs," I said.

"Oh."

"Is that a yes, you can do that for us?"

Steve didn't answer immediately. I couldn't read anything even resembling an expression on his insectoid face, but I nonetheless got the impression he was struggling with something. Did he suspect something, too?"

"Actually, Van, I don't have to do that, because I know what you're looking for."

"I—uh, okay. So—" I got that far and stopped.

"So you know who's been sending messages to the Cabal from here?" Torina asked.

Steve did his best approximation of a nod.

"I do. In fact, I know for certain who's responsible."

I stared. "Okay, well, don't keep us in suspense."

He didn't. He went straight to the point.

"It was me."

I JUST KEPT STARING. So did Torina and Perry. Icky muttered something and started to crowd forward, but Torina held out a hand and stopped her.

One of the many thoughts skidding through my mind finally got traction.

"What? You?"

"Me, yes."

"But—*why?*"

I braced myself for crushing disappointment, for Steve to say he was paid well for it, or something equally vile and corrupt. But that wasn't his answer at all.

"It's my family, Van. They said that if I didn't cooperate, they'd kill them. No matter where I tried to send them or hide them, they'd find them and kill them."

Even Icky went still.

I stared as creeping anger made another appearance, this time in the form of a wintry chill going right up my spine. "The Cabal?"

"Yes. The only way to protect them was to do what they said. If I didn't, they'd—"

He stopped. I wasn't sure if his species could physically even get choked up, but that was sure how he came across.

I looked at Torina. "Holy shit."

She nodded. "Indeed."

Icky leaned in, glowering even while wincing with pain. "So this is the scumbag that almost got me blown to bits?"

I raised a hand to her. "Icky, just… back off, okay?"

I turned back to Steve. "Who else knows about this?"

"No one."

"You're sure about that?"

"I… am very, very good at covering my tracks, Van. Having the access to things like data archives and comm logs that I do makes it a lot easier."

I frowned at him. "You're not that good, Steve, sorry. We found the record of your comm message to Pygmalion on Dregs."

"I know."

"You *know?*"

"I do."

"So it was deliberate? You wanted to get caught?" Torina asked.

"I… don't know. I could have accessed Pygmalion's system remotely and wiped away any traces, but—" He paused. "But, I don't know. It just didn't seem worth the effort."

I took a breath. "Okay, Steve, I need to ask you a really difficult question." Again, I braced myself, because I had no idea how I'd react to whatever he answered.

"Were you involved in the death of my father?"

"No. That was… before I was compromised. Your grandfather even came to me to ask me what I knew, to help him out. That was actually what started it all. The Cabal found out I was snooping around, and—well, they turned the tables on me."

He might have been staring into space while he talked, and he might have then turned his attention back to me, but I wasn't sure. Compound eyes meant he was always effectively looking almost everywhere at once.

"What it comes down to, Van, is that I can't do this anymore. I can't live with it. When you came along, your grandfather's grandson, and proved to be such a damned good and devoted Peacemaker —well, it's been like working with Mark again. So, yes, maybe I did leave that comm log on Pygmalion's system intentionally. I guess if someone was going to finally root out the truth, I wanted it to be you."

I rubbed the back of my head. "Holy shit, Steve. I mean, *holy shit*. How many investigations have you meddled in? How many hits have you helped those bastards set up?"

"More than a few. Definitely long enough for me to end up on the Guild's prison barge, The Hole, for the rest of my life. Or maybe even face execution for high treason. But… I'm at peace with that. I only have one request, Van. You need to help my family. You need to find some way to keep them out of the hands of the Cabal. Please. What happens to me doesn't matter. But what happens to them—"

"Just… give me a second here, Steve. I need a moment to process."

"I'll step outside. When you need me, I'll come back."

Steve left, closing and sealing the door behind him.

"You're just going to let him walk away?" Icky asked, incredulous.

I shook my head. "No."

"But you just did that very thing, Van! He's probably on his way to a ship right now to bug the hell out!" She turned to the door, but again, Torina stopped her.

"He's not going to run, Icky," I said. And I was able to say it with certainty. But it just trailed into a mournful sigh because the betrayal wasn't just personal… it was a legal issue, too. It was a shit-show in every sense of the word.

"The question is, what do we do about this?" I asked.

"What can we do? We have no choice, Van. We have to turn him in," Torina said.

I nodded glumly but looked at Perry. "I notice that you've been awfully silent."

"That's because I'm facing one of *those* moments, Van."

"*Those* moments?"

"Yeah. *Those* moments. You know, a moment when I might be forced to choose between my loyalty to you and to the Guild."

"How so?"

"I know you, Van. You're probably trying to work out some way of letting Steve redeem himself so that you don't have to report him for what he's done."

Torina gave him a curious look. "You mean you'd have a choice in that sort of situation?"

"I don't know. That's the thing. You and your grandfather have both kind of skirted the edge of pushing us into one of those moments. I've never actually been faced with making that choice. I might find out I can make it, and then I'll *have* to."

"But you might find out you can't actually make a choice at all, and you're compelled to reveal this to the Guild," Torina said.

Perry bobbed his head in a nod. "Yeah. I mean, I know I've got certain protocols locked into me, like the ones that prevent me from sharing certain historical information. But this seems—" He stopped. "I don't know. It sounds dumb."

Despite the tense complexity of the situation, I was intrigued. "Perry, it doesn't sound dumb at all. Speak what's on your remarkable little mind."

"Knowing that I can't reveal certain things that are locked down is one thing. I know they're locked down and can tell you that. This time, though, it… it's different."

"How?"

"Because, Van, if you force me to make this decision, and I can't and have some protocol kick in, what does that say about my ability to make any choices? What does that mean about the free will of AIs like Netty and me? Honestly, the security locks on information are hard enough to deal with. A decision like this, though—" He paused. "I'd rather not face it. I'd rather be… free. Whole and autonomous. And I'm not, which means I'm not really a person, am I?"

I stood, silent, as the enormity of Perry's revelation sank in. He'd just opened up about aspects of himself that I'd never really considered much. To me, he was just Perry, one of my crew and—yeah, damn it, he was my friend, too. But to the Guild, he was likely just a machine, a combat AI assigned to me like any other piece of equipment. To the Guild, Perry was a weapon. A tool.

A convenience.

In all my dealings with the world of computation, I'd never actually encountered something like this before—what did the *machine* think of all this?

I would speak to Perry as a friend and help him work through his search for the truth. But not right at this moment, because Perry deserved my undivided attention, as well as a conversation that unfolded on his schedule. Organically. Authentically, and from a place of respect.

"Perry, I'm not going to just let Steve walk away from this. I can't. He's lied to the Guild, and he's lied to us. Yes, his family might have been threatened, but that doesn't change the fact of his betrayal—"

Icky pointedly cleared her throat. "He caused a bomb to explode in my face. Let's not forget that little tidbit, huh?"

"Oh, I haven't. He put all of us into a position where we could have been hurt or killed. Again, yeah, his family. And that should factor into what actually happens to him, how he has to atone for this. But he had other options, and he chose this one."

"So you're going to report him," Perry said.

"Yes and no."

"Van—"

"Yes, he's going to be reported. No, I'm not going to be the one doing it."

I got puzzled looks from the other three, and even Netty piped up. "What?"

I crossed my arms. "Steve's going to pay for what he's done, but he's going to get a chance to at least earn some redemption first."

CARTER STARED AT ME, dumbstruck, across the *Fafnir*'s galley table.

"You want my help? *You*? Want *mine*?"

"I do."

A look of sly wariness crossed his face. "You're up to something."

"You figured that out, huh?" I said, about to roll my eyes. But I caught myself. I actually did need Carter's help, and I wanted him malleable and relaxed—or as relaxed as the preening asshole could be, anyway.

"Carter, I need a Peacemaker ship that isn't mine, for one operation. It'll take a day or so. There is some risk, yes, but the payoff is going to be worth it for you."

Carter, sensing that I wasn't just trying to lay a trap for him, leaned back and laced his fingers behind his head. "Well well. The mighty Van Tudor has to come crawling—"

"Can I bust his head?" Icky asked. "Please tell me I can bust his head."

Carter tensed, but I held up a hand. "No, Icky, you can't. At least, not *yet*." I turned back to my cousin. "You know, Carter, I'm trying really hard to not have an adversarial relationship with you for a change. I'm hoping we can work together, as professionals, to try to help solve a case that's killing some people and making countless more suffer." I leaned forward.

"Now, is that Peacemaker uniform you're wearing just a costume, to make you feel better about yourself in the stupid, unending competition we've had going since we were kids, or is it a real uniform? One that shows you're actually dedicated to your job?"

As I'd talked, Carter's smug smirk—the one that I wanted to punch right off his face—faded. He sat up, eyes alert and keen.

"Okay, fine. A truce. So you want me to fly you somewhere. Why? And, gotta be honest here, Van—I really do need to know what's in it for me. You might not care about the bullshit politics around here, but I'm buried neck deep in them. Helping you is going to send a signal to some... uh, parties around here that I'm not sure I want to send it to."

I nodded. "As for the why, I'll get to that in a moment. As for the what's in it for you—well, Carter, I'm going to give you a ton of credibility with the Guild as a whole."

He blinked. "You are? How?"

"By making you a hero."

29

"Okay, Torina—last minute check," I said, shifting myself in the unfamiliar copilot's seat of Carter's ship, which he'd named *The Beast*. It was, in fact, a standard Dragon-class ship, not even as upgraded as the *Fafnir*. I was hoping that didn't matter, though, because if this came down to space combat, it meant things had gone terribly wrong.

"Everything's good here. We're ready to twist in to your meeting spot in two hours—or sooner, if you call us."

"Good. Okay, we'll be departing any moment here. See you on the other side."

I glanced at Carter. "Any time is good. Now is better."

"Okay, Beast, get ready to do your thing," he said.

A voice identical to Netty's replied. "At your command."

Beast. I allowed myself a little sigh. The AI that operated a Dragon was a standard model when installed, that then developed their own personalities in response to their Peacemakers' actions and decisions. They were, in theory, wiped and reinstalled fresh every time a Dragonet or Dragon changed hands, but in practice, a lot of Peacemakers didn't allow that to happen. Netty had started fresh with Gramps, but I was glad to have her insight and experience available.

She and Perry also made me feel I had a bit of Gramps with me, helping me out. He had been instrumental in shaping both of them into who and what they were, after all.

But Beast, Carter's AI, was clipped, efficient, and businesslike. I had yet to hear her offer a unique or original thought. It was a bit jarring, like hearing some alternate-reality version of Netty—a somewhat sinister version, at that, devoid of personality or warmth.

I wondered if this version of Netty was neutral—or would take an active hand in Carter's defense. Given Carter's lack of quality, I suspected the AI was an unknown quantity at best.

I turned back to Steve, who was folded into the rear of the cockpit. "Okay, Steve, remember—once we get to the meeting place, you're on. You need to convince your contact that this has to be a face-to-face meeting. I want to either get them aboard this ship, or us aboard theirs. We'll take it from there."

A gruff voice rose from the camped crew hab behind the cockpit. "And by take it from there, you mean crack some heads, right?"

"If necessary, Icky, yes—you can crack some heads."

"Good. Someone's gonna answer for that bomb in the face. It might have damaged my moneymaker."

Carter's mouth began to open, and Icky *growled*. "One word about my face, and your head gets cracked just for fun. Got it, fancy boy?"

"Um… yes. Understood."

Icky grunted, and the tension dropped... a bit.

After a pause long enough so there could be no doubt Icky was done speaking, Carter rolled the dice again, his ego driving his mouth. "And when this is all done, I get the credit, right?"

I sighed. "Yes, Carter. Per our agreement, you will be the one to turn Steve in, thereby uncovering an egregious security issue for the Guild. All the credit is yours."

He nodded. "As long as we understand one another."

I turned back to Steve. "You know, I wish there was a way——"

"Van, it's fine. Like I said before, I'm at peace with what's going to happen to me. Just make sure my family is cared for," he answered, and his tone was so earnest. I knew he was in fact, at peace.

"Already on that. Like I told you, my good friend Schegith is doing me a couple of favors. One of them is arranging for your family to be transported to her home planet, Null World, where they'll be treated as honored guests. Trust me, they'll be safer there than anywhere else in the galaxy. No one lands on Null World without Schegith knowing, and *no* one gets into her sanctum without her say-so."

I glanced at Carter. "My cousin here, in the meantime, is going to use some of his newfound credibility to arrange for them to be subsequently relocated somewhere safe for the long term. Right, Carter?"

I resigned myself to some smartassed answer, but he surprised me.

"I'll do everything I can for them, yeah."

I gave him an impressed face, then nodded.

"Okay, Carter—next stop, the Oort Cloud of Wolf 424, and step on it."

THE INSTANT we twisted into the cold and lonely space on the edge of Wolf 424, I studied the tactical display. We detected only one other ship, a workboat that matched the one Netty had observed leaving Dregs.

Winner, winner.

"Okay, Steve, you're on."

Steve got on the comm and started up a terse conversation with his contact, who went by the name—or title—Prime. He or she was, as far as Steve knew, one of three principle members of the Cabal. Prime had been his only contact, so we had to hope that if we could snag them, we could crack open their organization. And that, I hoped, would lead us in turn back to The Stillness and our identity thieves.

First, though, Steve had to convince Prime to actually meet face-to-face. He'd used the excuse of a big prize, a new encryption protocol that was about to be implemented across the Peacemaker Guild. By providing the Cabal with details of it, they could gain surreptitious access to all Peacemaker comms. I was hoping it was just too good an opportunity for the Cabal to pass up.

And, sure enough, it turned out it was. The workboat wanted to meet us in one hour, the time it would take the two ships to match speed and course. We needed to make it longer than that. I wanted to start the meeting before Torina arrived, but not so soon that we were left without backup for too long. But Steve came through, and with flying colors.

"I stole this ship because it was the only one I could access without raising suspicions. The reason for that is that it was in the shop with a balky drive, so we're going to have to make it about an hour-and-a-half," he said.

I tensed, as the silence at the other end dragged on. These people lived and died by their instincts, and if they felt something might be off—

"Fine. Ninety minutes," was the snappy reply.

"Alright, let's go say hello to our new friends," I said. Carter had Beast apply power, but in surges, as though the drive really was wonky. I raised a brow, impressed with his tactical instincts.

"Smart," I said.

He shrugged. "You said the drive was off, so it should look like it's off, right?" He shot me a scowl. "I'm really not the moron you seem to think I am, Van."

"I'm starting to see that, Carter—emphasis on *starting to*, mind you."

WE MANAGED to be about fifteen minutes late, ostensibly because the drive cut out completely and Steve had to restart it. It meant that, in about fifteen minutes, the cavalry—Torina—would arrive.

We closed in on the workboat. At one hundred meters, they told us to halt.

"Close enough. You can dump the encryption module out your airlock, back off, and we'll retrieve it. Then you get your ass back to

Anvil Dark before anyone gets suspicious." A pause, then the voice, presumably Prime, turned smug.

"We plan for you to have a *long* career working with us, Steve."

I cursed. Sure, there were always things that could go wrong, things you couldn't foresee, and all you could do was roll with them—or run. Unfortunately, I couldn't think of any way to make this work if we were just supposed to toss our ace in the hole, the supposed encryption module, out of the airlock.

I leaned back. "Paranoid bastards, aren't they?"

"It's how they stay in business," Steve said, then activated the comm.

"I can't do that. The device is designed to erase itself if it's ever lost. And being tossed out an airlock would count for that. We've got no choice here. If you want it, I have to bring it to you personally, or you have to personally come and get it."

I gave Steve a thumbs-up.

Another brooding pause, then Prime replied. "Fine. We'll dock. You'll be waiting in your airlock with that thing in-hand, ready to go. You'll hand it over, no questions, no discussion, then we'll disconnect. Oh, and if this is a trick, or you fail to deliver—well, you know what happens then, don't you, Steve?"

"I do."

I nodded to Carter, and he had Beast start nudging our ship toward the workboat. Icky and I clambered as far into the back of the Dragon as we could. We were both armored up, including the pieces made for us by Linulla. I checked The Drop and the Moonsword, while she readied a short-barrelled boarding shotgun that fired high-velocity flechettes and, of course, her trusted sledge-hammer. I raised my eyebrows at the latter. There was no way she'd have enough room to swing it. But it looked as intimidating as hell slung on her back, so I didn't have her ditch it.

We waited.

Just shy of docking, Steve clambered back into the airlock. He held a sleek little device, something he'd scrounged from among his many spare parts back on Anvil Dark. I asked him what it really was, and he gave an off-handed reply.

"No idea. I took it out of the box of bits and pieces that seem to regularly turn up. A lot of them are power cables, but this—well, it looks kind of impressive, doesn't it?"

A box of random power cables. Huh. Yet another universal truth—extra cables will pop into existence out of nowhere, maybe to balance out the mass of odd socks that keep going missing and keep the universe thermodynamically happy.

A heavy thump, and The Beast shuddered. I heard the brief, rhythmic thud of the docking adapter seating itself and locking, then the *hard dock* light turned green.

I hefted The Drop.

Showtime.

THE PLAN HAD BEEN for Steve to get us access to the other ship, and he had. Icky and I were going to take it from there, with Carter as backup. We just had to hold out long enough for Torina to arrive.

Of course, no plan survives its first brush with the enemy, and this was no exception.

As soon as the airlock opened, revealing a Nesit, Steve didn't step aside to let us take charge. Instead, he did something I hadn't even realized he *could* do. He reached out with his forelimbs like a—well, what he was, a giant praying mantis—and neatly decapitated the other alien. Blood fountained, but Steve shoved through, into the workboat, his mass taking up most of the open space.

I exchanged a wide-eyed look with Icky, then shouted, "Come on!" and charged for the airlock. I had no idea why Steve had decided to freelance this all of a sudden—he was going to get himself killed.

Ah. Of course he was. That had been his plan all along.

I'd almost reached the airlock when Carter shouted from the cockpit.

"Van, we've got trouble!"

I slammed to a halt, then spun to Icky. "Go, follow Steve! And try not to kill everyone!"

"No promises," she growled, and lunged through the airlock. I turned to *The Beast*'s cockpit, wincing as her boarding shotgun boomed.

"What is it—oh, *shit!*"

A massive ship, class twelve or thirteen, had twisted in almost on top of us. It bristled with firepower, lasers and rail guns, and I even saw the four-barrel array of a maser.

And every weapon was pointed directly at us.

———

OKAY, I'd expected something like this. Well, not an actual warship, but I'd expected the Cabal would have backup of their own. But as soon as I saw the big ship and its formidable array of firepower, I experienced a moment of clarity that left me chilled to the bone. We might have outmaneuvered the Cabal so far, but now they'd outmaneuvered us. I suspected that Prime, whoever they were, wasn't aboard the workboat, and that both it and *The Beast* were now about to be shredded.

"Starting to hate these pricks," I mumbled, sorting my options in a series of harried thoughts.

I was stuck, poised on the very sharp horns of a complex dilemma. Docked to the workboat, we couldn't maneuver. If we blew the dock and tried to run, Icky and Steve would be trapped over there. And even then, we'd barely be able to get underway before that big ship pummeled us to scrap.

I… honestly wasn't sure what to do next, but when in doubt, I prefer The Drop. I hefted my weapon with the intent to raise a little hell.

And then Carter Yost chose to save the day.

He snapped on the comm. "Unknown ship, this is Peacemaker Carter Yost. As you've probably guessed, this was a trap. Well, I'm not going to die out here, so I'm offering you someone I think you really want to get your hands on—Van Tudor. He's right here beside me."

I spun on Carter. I swear that I had The Drop raised and my finger touching the trigger, ready to blow his scummy, treacherous head off, but Carter did something I did not expect.

He raised a finger to me in a *wait* gesture. At the same time, he gave me an earnest look that begged me to trust him.

"You're lying to save your own skin," Prime said.

"No, I'm telling the truth to save my own skin. He's my cousin, and I hate his guts, and honestly I'm ready to step right into

Steve's... um, shoes, if he wore any. You guys want a contact on Anvil Dark? Well, I work for the Masters."

I found myself clenching my toes inside my boots. Any second, I expected those lasers and rail guns—and there sure seemed to be a lot of them—to flash, and then that would be it.

But they didn't.

"Prove it," the voice said.

Carter pointed at The Drop and stuck out his hand.

I stared for a second. Carter Yost wanted me to hand him a loaded gun, while he pretended to turn on me.

Was he pretending, though?

I finally decided it didn't matter. It was either this, or be reduced to glowing vapor and cooling bits of debris. I sighed and handed him The Drop. He reversed it, pointed it right into my face and activated the comm's video feed.

"Here he is. And he's all yours. Do we have a deal?"

I HEARD MORE shots from Icky's gun echo out of the workboat. I desperately wanted to help her and Steve, but I was stuck being Carter's prisoner—either pretend or real. I still wasn't entirely sure which.

"That *is* Tudor," Prime said, sounding genuinely surprised.

"Yeah. This was all his plan. But I'm not dying because of his goodie two shoes ways."

I glanced at Carter. *Goodie two shoes?* Really?

But I realized that Carter was in his element here. When it came to being obsequious and sleazy, he was an expert. He was either actually *being* obsequious and sleazy, or he was putting on one hell of a show. Either way, he nailed it.

"Okay. Right," Prime said, then paused again. Carter had clearly caught him flatfooted. He'd expected he'd either get the encryption device from Steve, or he'd just destroy both ships and call it a day. But Carter had just dangled a very tempting piece of fruit in front of them. Actually, two tempting pieces of fruit—a direct pipeline into the Guild Masters, and me.

"Alright, here's what's going to happen," Prime finally said. "You're going to undock from that workboat, then heave to. We'll be boarding you, and this is either exactly as you say, or you won't live long enough to regret trying to screw us."

"What about my people on that workboat?" I asked.

"Oh, you can forget about them. They're already dead."

I sank back. There was nothing more I could do. I turned to Carter to ask him if he was really turning me over—but he just pointed to the tactical overlay.

"I think I stalled them pretty well, didn't I?" he said.

I blinked.

We were no longer alone. A small flotilla of ships had twisted into existence, one after another.

The cavalry had arrived.

IN SECONDS, the cabal ship was flanked to its left by Schegith's cousin in his big battlecruiser. To its right loomed Icky's dad aboard his repurposed battleship, the *Nemesis*. Between them, the two ships *doubled* the firepower of the Cabal's ship. But we weren't done. Elliptically above the assassins' vessel the bulky shape of the *Iowa* had popped into existence, flown by Torina. And nearby, already getting underway in a flare of fusion exhaust was the *Fafnir*, piloted by none other than Perry.

Before I could even open my mouth, all three of the big ships opened fire on the Cabal ship, concentrating on its drive and weapon mounts. Laser pulses, rail gun slugs, and missiles pummeled it, smashing chunks of debris from its sleek hull. I could only stare at the orgy of violence, whistling low as bolt after bolt chewed the enemy craft into slag. It took me a moment to realize why all of our ships had opened fire without any warning at all. It was because the Cabal ship would have just twisted away, and we would have lost it.

Instead, it staggered under the impacts of the barrage. The *Iowa* lacked the raw firepower of Schegith's cousin or Icky's dad, but Torina made up for it by sniping off weapons mounts and scanner arrays, hammering shot after shot into the Cabal hull with little time in between rounds. She finished with a catastrophic blast of the point-defense systems, which shredded an entire quadrant of the enemy hull like paper in a storm.

Perry likewise focused on targeted hits, aiming at weapons with a lethal—and machinelike—accuracy. The others were less restrained and seemed happy to slam fire into the Cabal's cruiser, nominally attempting to avoid a reactor hit that would turn local space into a plasma barbecue.

We weren't unscathed, despite the savagery of our collected attack. One rail gun shot skimmed the top of Carter's ship, the depleted rod flickering across the combat space at a speed too fast for the human eye to follow. With a shuddering impact, one of *The Beast's* point-defense gun and comms array whirled into the darkness, trailing plasma and cables. Seconds later, a second shot gouged a chunk out of our stern, decompressing the aft end of the ship. Sirens howled, adding to the chaos, but Carter, showing savvy beyond what I expected, quickly silenced the braying klaxons as the fight came to a close.

And then, it was over. The Cabal ship had gone dark and silent, silvery clouds of vapor spilling from its battered hull into space. I didn't wait, just turned back to the airlock and drew the Moonsword to go and help out Icky and Steve.

"Van, don't you want your gun?" Carter asked, offering The Drop back to me.

I shook my head. "Nah. You hang onto it for now."

Carter's eyes widened, then he actually smiled. For an instant, he looked honest.

For an instant.

EPILOGUE

"Van? Are you sure you're up to this?" Torina asked.

I nodded. "I am. Let's, shall we?"

I turned to the server, a young guy named Corbitt. "We're going to start off with a bottle of the local Riesling. And then? Then, we're going to order a *lot* of food."

"All my favorite customers do," Corbitt said, laughing as he turned to the kitchen. I'd always liked the original Rathskeller, being a big fan of German food. We sat in the second version—reclaimed, reopened by a local family, and bustling with people who rediscovered the hidden gem in Elkader, on the banks of the Turkey River. I'd already recommended Torina try the potato pancakes, which were spiced perfectly—a real treat on a cold Iowa night, but then most winter nights in Iowa were cold, which meant we were in the right place. The restaurant was an actual cellar, boxed in with glass doors and windows under a century-old building now used as a furniture store.

"Bread?" Torina asked.

"Thanks." I tore at the pumpernickel, chewing meditatively as I watched Torina. Despite being on a different planet, she was at home here. I didn't know how much of that was the food, or the people—or me.

We sat for a moment. Despite my best efforts, my thoughts kept turning back to the battle against the Cabal. We'd been damned lucky. Aside from the damage to Carter's ship, and a few minor hits on the *Nemesis* and the *Iowa*, we'd come through almost entirely unscathed.

Except for Steve. Steve was dead.

I'd found Icky, chest heaving and sledgehammer in hand, splattered with gore and ready for more foes to appear. At her feet was Steve's body.

"*Try harder*, you miserable assholes," she'd said to the beaten bodies around her.

Between them, they'd taken down five, including the Nesit he'd decapitated in the airlock. The fact that the workboat had been crewed with armed mercs just demonstrated that the Cabal was prepared to betray us in every way possible.

We'd managed to betray them better, and sooner. We won. We were faster on the draw, and now I was looking back in that curious way where you can see death was a lot closer than you imagined—while you were in the fight.

I took a moment in the aftermath to think of my dad and my grandfather both, the former dead at the Cabal's evil hands, the latter having to live with that knowledge. I hoped this brought both of them, wherever they were, at least a little peace, and maybe even a bit of satisfaction.

I'd thanked Schegith's cousin and Icky's dad for their help, then we'd taken the workboat and the battered Cabal cruiser into custody and rounded up the survivors. They hadn't, unfortunately, included Prime. The surviving crew—a couple of humans, another Nesit, a trio of Yonnox, and a couple of other aliens—insisted he'd been effectively vaporized by a laser hit that had chewed almost completely through the hull from port to starboard. Whether that was true or not, or if he'd ever actually been physically present at all, we couldn't be sure. He probably wasn't one of those survivors, but we'd taken all of them into custody to see if we could dig out the truth.

Carter, in the meantime, had announced that the operation he'd masterminded had not only uncovered Steve as a turncoat, but also seized a vessel belonging to a powerful criminal syndicate and might even have one of the key members of the Cabal in custody. He'd made all of it abundantly clear in a summary report he'd transmitted back to Anvil Dark.

To be fair to him, Carter had also emphasized that Steve's sacrifice had been instrumental in "his" plan succeeding, and that he'd only been compromised because of the threat to his family. And upon receiving personal thanks from Master Yotov, he beamed with undeserved pride—typical for Carter.

I hadn't been able to resist. As we mopped up after the nasty little fight, I congratulated him.

"Thanks, Van," he'd said, returning The Drop to me. "And, yeah, I know that it was really all your doing, but what the hell—you don't want the credit, I'll certainly take it."

"Yeah, and it moves you into the big leagues. Hope you're ready for that."

He frowned. "What do you mean?"

I clapped him on the shoulder. "You're a Peacemaker. And a *hero*. You gave the Cabal, one of the most secretive and dangerous criminal organizations in known space, a bloody nose. Welcome to the wonderful world of having *really* bad bad guys out for your head."

He swallowed hard. "I—what?"

The memory still made me smile, and that surprisingly made me feel a little bad. Carter had actually come through when I needed him.

I felt bad… but only a little.

Corbett arrived with our wine, and we placed our orders. When he'd gone again, I poured wine and sipped it. Torina gave me an appraising look.

"That's really bothering you, isn't it? Steve's death?"

I sighed. "That's the problem. I'm not sure. Maybe it was the best outcome for everyone."

"Except his family."

"Yeah, except his family. But they're in good hands, with Schegith. And, not to put too fine a point on it—"

"With Steve dead, they're no longer targets."

I nodded. "It sounds harsh, I know. But groups like that tend to be pretty pragmatic. There's nothing to be gained by harming Steve's family anymore, so he probably did end up saving them."

"Which means he died… redeemed. Not stained. I guess that's the best any of us can hope for."

I looked at my wine. "Bit grim, but yes."

"So let's talk about something happier. Like, how we're going to go back to that farmhouse of yours and just spend a few days not being Peacemakers or flying around space."

I shrugged. "Yeah, I guess. There's not much to do there in the winter, though—"

She touched my hand, lips curled playfully. "You sure about that?"

"I—oh." I cleared my throat, grinning. "I take it back. I'm sure we can find quite a bit to do here in scenic Elkader."

"Indeed. I've got a couple suggestions, in fact."

I leaned in. "Oh, really? Tell me more—?"

Van?

I winced. "Perry. Your timing. It is, as the kids say, the worst."

I'm sorry. Were you and Torina about to engage in some—?

"Perry, there are some things a bird was never meant to know. Anyway, what do you want?" I kept my voice low, and Torina nodded along, as though I was talking to her. I glanced around at the nearby tables, but no one was paying any attention, and the Rathskeler was designed to be cozy and private.

I just thought you'd like to know that Icky and her father, helped by Schegith's cousin, have finished scouring that Cabal ship for information. And they hit a jackpot.

I looked at Torina. She'd been hearing what I was through her ear bug, and we both tensed.

"Go on."

We've got a name that we lifted from a data module they just didn't have time to wipe before, you know, they were blown to bits. It's Ewanaxamun.

"What the hell—lotta letters there. Who is—"

Ewanaxamun. She's a senior member of the Salt Thieves. She's only ever been known by the nickname No-No, but just getting her real name is a major score.

"So what's her involvement in all this?"

She's hired the Cabal on a few occasions, to help her protect her most treasured undertaking.

Which is?

Illegally mining osmium.

"Well, shit."

I thought you'd like that. We've managed to tie her to the operation on Rigel and a few others. We can't immediately tie her to what's happening on Pluto, but I'd be surprised if she wasn't involved in that, too.

"Okay, Perry. Let's bring it all to the farm tomorrow, and we'll—"

I'm not done, Van. First, she apparently owns the Empty Space.

"Okay, that makes sense—"

And she has a business partner, someone she served time with on the Guild's prison barge, The Hole, almost thirty years ago. His name is Markov.

"Holy shit, our High-Doctor-slash-Czar?"

None other.

I sat back. "Wow. That's… a lot to take in."

You guys enjoy… your dinner.

Torina grinned. "You know, I've never heard the word *dinner* uttered in such a suggestive way before."

I grinned back at her, then laughed. For once, the universe hadn't conspired to leave us facing another dead end. This had been a major break in our case, and I actually found myself chomping at the bit, wanting to get going and run down No-No, and talk to High Doctor Markov, and—

Torina reached over and took my hands in hers. "All in good time."

"What?"

"I can see it on your face. You want to get right back to it, chasing down these leads. But it can wait."

I smiled and made myself relax. "You're right. First, let's have... *dinner.*"

"Very soon, Van. Very soon."

I winked. "Wasn't talking about the food."

Torina shook her head, then winked back.

"Neither was I."

Amazon won't always tell you about the next release. To stay updated on this series, be sure to sign up for our spam-free email list at jnchaney.com.

Van will return in BLUE SHIFT, available now on Amazon.

GLOSSARY

Anvil Dark: The beating heart of the Peacemaker organization, Anvil Dark is a large orbital platform located in the Gamma Crucis system, some ninety lightyears from Earth. Anvil Dark, some nine hundred seventy years old, remains in a Lagrange point around Mesaribe, remaining in permanent darkness. Anvil Dark has legal, military, medical, and supply resources for Peacemakers, their assistants, and guests.

Cloaks: Local organized criminal element, the Cloaks hold sway in only one place: Spindrift. A loose guild of thugs, extortionists, and muscle, the Cloaks fill a need for some legal control on Spindrift, though they do so only because Peacemakers and other authorities see them as a necessary evil. When confronted away from Spindrift, Cloaks are given no rights, quarter, or considerations for their position. (See: Spindrift)

Dragonet: A Base Four Combat ship, the Dragonet is a modified platform intended for the prosecution of Peacemaker policy. This includes but is not limited to ship-to-ship combat, surveillance, and planetary operations as well. The Dragonet is fast, lightly armored, and carries both point defense and ranged weapons, and features a frame that can be upgraded to the status of a small corvette (Class Nine).

Moonsword: Although the weapon is in the shape of a medium sword, the material is anything but simple metal. The Moonsword is a generational armament, capable of upgrades that augment its ability to interrupt communications, scan for data, and act as a blunt-force weapon that can split all but the toughest of ship's hulls. See: Starsmith

Peacemaker: Also known as a Galactic Knight, Peacemakers are an elite force of law enforcement who have existed for more than three centuries. Both hereditary and open to recruitment, the guild is a meritocracy, but subject to political machinations and corruption, albeit not on the scale of other galactic military forces. Peacemakers have a legal code, proscribed methods, a reward and bounty scale, and a well-earned reputation as fierce, competent fighters. Any race may be a Peacemaker, but the candidates must pass rigorous testing and training.

Perry: An artificial intelligence, bound to Van (after service to his grandfather), Perry is a fully-sapient combat operative in the shape of a large, black avian. With the ability to hack computer systems and engage in physical combat, Perry is also a living repository of galactic knowledge in topics from law to battle strategies. He is also a wiseass.

Salt Thieves: Originally actual thieves who stole salt, this is a three-hundred-year-old guild of assassins known for their ruthless behavior, piracy, and tendency to kill. Members are identified by a complex, distinct system of braids in their hair. These braids are often cut and taken as prizes, especially by Peacemakers.

Spindrift: At nine hundred thirty years old, Spindrift is one of the most venerable space stations in the galactic arm. It is also the least reputable, having served as a place of criminal enterprise for nearly all of its existence due to a troublesome location. Orbiting Sirius, Spindrift was nearly depopulated by stellar radiation in the third year as a spaceborne habitat. When order collapsed, criminals moved in, cycling in and out every twelve point four years as coronal ejections rom Sirius made the station uninhabitable. Spindrift is known for medical treatments and technology that are quasi-legal at best, as well as weapons, stolen goods, and a strange array of archaeological items, all illegally looted. Spindrift has a population of thirty thousand beings at any time.

Starsmith: A place, a guild, and a single being, the Starsmith is primarily a weapons expert of unsurpassed skill. The current Starsmith is a Conoku (named Linulla), a crablike race known for their dexterity, skill in metallurgy and combat enhancements, and sense of humor.

CONNECT WITH J.N. CHANEY

Don't miss out on these exclusive perks:

- Instant access to free short stories from series like *The Messenger*, *Starcaster*, and more.
- Receive email updates for new releases and other news.
- Get notified when we run special deals on books and audiobooks.

So, what are you waiting for? Enter your email address at the link below to stay in the loop.

https://www.jnchaney.com/backyard-starship-subscribe

CONNECT WITH TERRY MAGGERT

Check out his website
http://terrymaggert.com/

Connect on Facebook
https://www.facebook.com/terrymaggertbooks/

Follow him on Amazon
https://www.amazon.com/Terry-Maggert/e/B00EKN8RHG/

ABOUT THE AUTHORS

J. N. Chaney is a USA Today Bestselling author and has a Master's of Fine Arts in Creative Writing. He fancies himself quite the Super Mario Bros. fan. When he isn't writing or gaming, you can find him online at **www.jnchaney.com**.

He migrates often, but was last seen in Las Vegas, NV. Any sightings should be reported, as they are rare.

Terry Maggert is left-handed, likes dragons, coffee, waffles, running, and giraffes; order unimportant. He's also half of author Daniel Pierce, and half of the humor team at Cledus du Drizzle.

With thirty-one titles, he has something to thrill, entertain, or make you cringe in horror. Guaranteed.

Note: He doesn't sleep. But you sort of guessed that already.

Made in United States
North Haven, CT
10 June 2022

20102121R00251